HOLDEN
11

BREAK
THE
ICE

A
LAKESHORE U
STORY

BREAK THE ICE

LAKESHORE U

L A COTTON

Published by Delesty Books

Edited by Kate Newman
Proofread by Sisters Get Lit.erary Author Services
Cover designed by Lianne Cotton

LAKESHORE U

Bite the Ice
A Lakeshore U Prequel Story

Ice Burn
A Lakeshore U Story

Break the Ice
A Lakeshore U Story

On Thin Ice
A Lakeshore U Story

AUTHOR'S NOTE

This book contains content may be triggering to some readers. It deals with topics such as disordered eating and (historical) physical abuse.

We are all fools in love.

JANE AUSTEN

CHAPTER 1

AURORA

"You can do this, Aurora Vivienne Hart. You will freaking do this."

You have good sense and a sweet temper, and I am sure you have a grateful heart that could never receive kindness without hoping to return it.

Inhaling a deep, calming breath, I repeated the quote over and over as I hitched the bag up my shoulder and climbed the three steps up to my brother's house.

It was a warm August day, the streets of Lakeshore—a small coastal town in Ohio—bustling with students returning from their summer break. I'd only been here once before when I visited my brother Austin last year. He'd had a rare weekend off hockey and taken some time out from his busy, important life to show me the sights of the place he now called home. It was the perfect blend of college campus and seaside resort, the stunning views of

Lake Erie one of its definite selling points. But I never visited again.

Until now.

A shuddering breath rolled through me as I gave myself one final pep talk and rang the doorbell. Austin was expecting me, but butterflies still swarmed my stomach as I tugged restlessly at my favorite oversized *plot twist* t-shirt.

I paused, caught like a deer in the headlights at the sound of heavy footsteps beyond the door, the rattle of the lock. It swung open, revealing my big brother in all his six-foot-two bulked-up hockey player glory.

"Rory, you made it." He pulled me into his arms, hugging the crap out of me.

"Hey, Austin," I chuckled, melting into his familiar embrace. Things might have been weird between us over the last few years, but he was still my big brother. That bond never truly died.

At least, I hoped it didn't.

"God, it's good to see you." He held me at arm's length. "Let me get a good look at you."

"Austin," I groaned, rolling my eyes as he studied me the way he'd used to when we were kids.

Don't look too closely. Please, for the love of God, don't look too closely.

"You look tired."

"I'm fine." The well-rehearsed lie rolled off my tongue. "Are you going to invite me in, or will we stand on the porch all day?"

"Come on. The guys aren't home yet, so we have the place to ourselves."

Relief flooded me.

Much like my brother, Austin's hockey friends were a lot

to handle. At least from the one time I'd met some of them, I'd concluded they were.

But I guess it came with the territory.

Lakeshore U was a hockey college, and the Lakers were treated like celebrities around campus. Girls and guys alike all wanted a piece of the five-time Frozen Four finalists.

"Let me give you the tour," he said, taking my bag. "Okay, we've got the living room." He pointed to the first door, and I poked my head inside.

"I love what you've done with the place." Humor laced my words as I scanned the hockey paraphernalia hanging off every available expanse of wall space. I was hardly surprised at the cyan and indigo Lakers jersey hanging in the center with a pair of sticks, gloves, and they even had—

"Puck coasters, really?"

"What?" He shrugged. "Con found them at the dollar store."

"Of course he did." I suppressed a laugh. "So long as I don't have to sleep in a shrine to the Lakers, I'm good."

No way did I want to spend my nights burrowed underneath a gaudy Lakers blanket.

"You won't. We keep that bedroom empty for... uh..."

"I swear to God, Austin, if you say hookups, I'm going to turn around and walk right out."

The girl living in the apartment above the one I was supposed to be moving into right about now, might have flooded the place with her overzealous bath-time routine, causing enough water damage to deem it inhabitable, but I could figure something out.

"Relax, Sis. I was going to say storage. We don't tend to party here. We have Lakers House for that." He grinned, and I found myself smiling back.

I'd missed this.

Him.

Even if part of me still resented him.

"It's really good to see you, Rory. I know things have been weird, but the last couple of years have been intense, and you were—"

"It's fine." I smiled. It felt all wrong, but Austin didn't seem to notice.

As much as it hurt to admit, he never had.

"I'm just grateful to you and the guys for letting me stay here. The woman at student housing said it shouldn't take too long to fix the water damage."

"There's no rush. Between practice and classes, we won't be around all that much, and you have the entire third floor to yourself, so you'll have plenty of space."

"I'll stay out of your way, I promise. I wouldn't want to cramp anyone's style."

"Rory, come on, it isn't even like that. You're my sister. And some of the guys have girlfriends, so you shouldn't feel like a spare part."

A sinking feeling went through me. "Gee, thanks."

"You know what I mean." Austin laughed. "We're not the sex-crazed, party animals you think we are." I raised a brow at that, and his laughter intensified. "Fine. We're mostly not like that. Holden can be a bit of a handful. But Connor is in deep with Ella."

Ah, yes, Noah Holden. Lakeshore U's resident playboy and star right-winger. He was the definite downside to moving in with my brother for a little bit. But it was either here or one of the girls' dorms on campus, and that really was a last resort.

As in, never going to happen.

I liked my space and needed it after everything that had gone down senior year.

"You'll love Ella. She's good people. Pretty sure Connor is going to pop the question soon," Austin went on as he gave me the tour. "Dude waited like two years for his shot with her. Two fucking years, I don't get it personally." he shrugged. "But they seem happy enough."

"Still relationship-phobic?" I asked. He'd always been a player in high school, going through girls like the world was ending.

"Have you seen me?" He flashed me a cocky grin, sweeping a hand down his body. "I'm far too pretty to settle down."

"Too pretty and vain, apparently."

"You call it vain. I call it confident."

"I see some things never change," I murmured as I ducked past him to check out the kitchen.

It was impressive—a big open-plan space that had bi-fold doors leading to a deck only dreams were made of.

"Pretty neat, right?"

"It's gorgeous." I moved closer to the doors, taking in the huge sectional sheltered under a wooden gazebo complete with fairy lights and a fire pit.

I could imagine snuggling up out there with a cup of hot milk and one of my favorite books.

"Feel free to use it whenever you want. The guys and I want you to feel at home here."

"Thanks, but I plan to lay low. I know it must suck having your little sister come to stay."

It was a joke. I was joking. Except, the second the words landed between us, Austin's hazel eyes turned cloudy with regret.

"Rory—"

"I'm joking." I smiled.

Forced. Fake. Awkward.

God, it wasn't supposed to be this hard. But things weren't the same between us anymore. Austin had left Syracuse three years ago and never looked back. Too much had happened since to just forget.

"Have you spoken to Mom lately?" I asked him, deflecting the conversation.

"No, why?"

"She landed a new deal with a local jewelry store. Anyone would think it was a deal with Gucci or Chanel."

"She still doing the Botox?"

The Botox... I snorted.

"Yep. And eating clean and working out like a hamster on crack."

Austin frowned. "Whatever happened to aging gracefully?"

"It's a foreign concept to Mom." I shrugged.

Susannah Hart put more work into her appearance than she'd ever put into raising Austin and me. But I'd stopped dwelling on it a long time ago.

She was everything I wasn't. Tall, slim, with delicate curves most women envied—a perfect complexion with a pearly white smile that brought out the flecks of emerald in her sparkling eyes.

She barely looked a day over thirty despite being in her late forties and the concoction of drugs she pumped into her body to stay young, beautiful, and functioning. But I didn't bring that up.

I was all hips and ass and boobs. Much to my mother's never-ending disappointment.

"Rory?" Austin nudged me with his shoulder. "Where'd you go just now?"

"Nowhere." I smiled up at him. "The journey tired me out. Mind if I go rest for a bit?"

"You don't need to ask. You live here now." He grinned again, but there was a shadow in his eyes. "Now, there's a sentence I never thought I'd say."

"Aus—"

"Relax, I'm only messing with you. Head on up. There's only one bedroom on the third floor; you can't miss it. There are clean sheets on the bed, and we got you some girly shit for the bathroom."

"Thanks. And Austin," I hesitated, overcome with warring emotions, "I really appreciate you letting me stay here."

"You don't need to thank me, Rory. I'm glad you're here. Perhaps later, I can give you the grand tour and introduce you to everyone."

Panic tightened my chest, but I managed to force out, "Uh, sure. Sounds good."

But it didn't sound good at all.

It sounded like my worst nightmare come true.

The third-floor bedroom spanned the entire length of the house. With its own bathroom and walk-in closet, it was the perfect space to retreat. But my absolute favorite feature had to be the curved window seat overlooking the yard, a stunning view of Lake Erie far off in the distance.

After leaving Austin downstairs, I headed up here and

unpacked a few essentials. Since my stay was only temporary, I didn't see any point in filling the closet and dresser with all my clothes. I'd only have to repack them again when the call came through to say my apartment was ready.

Then I climbed into the freshly made bed and slept.

For three freaking hours.

But moving to Lakeshore was a big deal for me. Bigger than Austin would ever know.

It was my fresh start. A chance to leave the past behind. To find myself again.

The rumble of male laughter drifted into the room, and a trickle of unease went through me. But I forced myself to take a deep breath. They were Austin's friends. His teammates. Even if my track record with hockey players wasn't good, I could handle the likes of Noah Holden and Connor Morgan.

What other choice did I have?

Slipping into the bathroom, I cleaned up the best I could before changing into a clean t-shirt; this one had *get lit* printed across my chest with a stack of books underneath. Then I pulled my hair into a messy high ponytail and checked my reflection. My gaze instantly went to my chest, following the exaggerated curves of my body. But I didn't linger, I couldn't, or I'd never muster up the courage to go downstairs and meet them.

Blood roared in my ears as I left the guest room, my heart pounding inside my chest like a drum. I could hear them distinctly now. The deep timbre of one of Austin's friends and the gravelly laughter of another.

Breathe, Aurora. Just. Breathe.

They were Austin's friends—his *best* friends. His teammates *and* housemates. And Austin was my family.

Everything was going to be fine.

Except when I hit the bottom step of the first floor, their conversation stopped, and three pairs of eyes all landed on me.

"Hi." I lifted my hand in a small, awkward wave. "I'm Aurora."

"Connor," the taller of the two said with a genuine smile. "We met when you visited last year. And this asshole is Noah." He thumbed to the other guy.

"Hey." Noah gave me a cursory glance that made me bristle.

So much for not having to worry.

"It's nice to meet you," I added, trying to lighten the sudden tension.

"Did they give you a date for your apartment yet?"

Wow, okay.

My cheeks flamed. I'd known coming to stay with Austin was pretty last minute, but he'd said the guys were good with it.

"Holden, dude. Not cool." Austin shot him a scathing look.

"Shit, I didn't mean... Sorry, Aurora, that sounded worse than it was. I just meant—"

"Seriously, bro, quit while you're ahead," Connor chuckled, laughing off the awkwardness of the situation. "Don't pay Holden here any attention, Aurora. He's a sure thing on the ice but seriously lacking in the brains department."

"Fuck you, man. I aced freshman year."

"You barely scraped by."

Noah flipped him off, and Connor grabbed him in a headlock, the two of them falling onto the couch as they fought.

"Are they always like this?" I asked, chewing the end of my thumb.

"Don't mind them," Austin said. "Hey, you hungry? We could head to The Penalty Box. They do the best chili dogs in town."

"Did somebody say chili dogs?" Connor released Noah, giving him a playful shove.

"Figured we could introduce Aurora to the rest of the team, and it beats ordering in."

"I could cook," I offered.

"You'd actually have to have food in the house to do that. We tend to live on more of a liquid and takeout diet."

"Don't you have to follow a strict meal plan during the season?" I frowned.

"Try telling Connor that." Austin nodded toward his friend.

"Hey, I burn it all off on the ice." He ran a hand down his stomach.

"You mean you burn it all off between the sheets with Ella." Noah smirked.

"Seriously, you went there, motherfucker? Because the last time you—"

"Relax, man. I'm joking."

"Seriously, guys. Can we not do this now? I'm starving, and Aurora is wondering what the hell she's gotten herself into with you two going at it like an old married couple."

"Sorry, Aurora." Connor smiled. "Holden, you coming with? Or has Sam finally convinced you to take her out?"

"Fuck off, asshole. There's nothing going on between Sam and me."

"Try telling her that. I told you not to stick it in her—"

"Dude, sister present." Austin ran a hand over his jaw, casting me an apologetic glance.

Did he already regret agreeing to let me stay? Because part of me already regretted saying yes.

"Sorry, Aurora. But Holden here has a little puck bunny issue."

"Don't sweat it," I murmured. "I'm going to grab my purse before we leave."

I didn't want to go, not really. But I needed to do this. I needed Austin to think everything was okay.

I needed to believe everything was okay.

Leaving the guys to their puck bunny discussion, I went to find my purse. But Austin wasn't far behind me.

"Sorry about that," he said. "They're not always so... oh, who the fuck am I kidding. They're always assholes. But they're both good guys, I swear. Noah puts his foot in it a lot, but he's—"

"Austin," I stopped him, "it's fine. I'm fine. Are we heading out then?"

"Yep. I can't wait for you to meet the rest of the team. Officially, I mean." Something flashed in his eyes. A hint of regret. Sadness even.

It was his senior year, his final season with the Lakers, and I'd never even watched one of his games live.

How sad was that?

But he wasn't solely to blame for the distance between us. When he left three years ago, I'd been angry. And I'd doubled down on my feelings, refusing to talk to him. Weeks turned into months, and months turned into years.

Until last fall, when I'd finally shoved down the bitterness and resentment festering inside me and came out to visit him.

We kept in touch a little more after that: texting one another, making the odd phone call, and emailing here and there. But I never told him the truth. I never owned up to why I'd shown up that weekend after two and a half years of barely any communication.

Austin had a life in Lakeshore; he had friends and hockey, and a line of girls all vying for his attention. He had everything he'd ever wanted. I didn't want to ruin that.

This was our fresh start. A chance to patch up our relationship and get back to being the Austin and Aurora we were before our lives went to shit.

And to leave lying, cheating ex-boyfriends and piece-of-shit ex-best friends where they belonged.

Behind me.

CHAPTER 2

NOAH

"There you are." Sam wrapped her arms around me, gazing up at me like I was her every dream come true.

"You're here," I said, my brows furrowing.

"Well, yeah. You said—"

"I said I was going out with the guys to eat. It wasn't an invitation."

"Noah, come on," she purred, trying—and failing—to be sexy. "Don't be like that. I've missed you."

Correction.

She missed fucking me.

I fought the urge to call her out on her bullshit, but a couple of the guys were watching us, and I didn't want to embarrass her in front of the team. I wasn't *that* heartless. Besides, Sam and I were friends. At least, we used to be before I made the fatal error of sleeping with her.

I should have known crossing that line was a mistake,

but I had a habit of making bad fucking decisions when I was drunk and horny.

Way to go, Holden. Always thinking with your dick.

"Sam, you're reading into stuff that isn't there," I said, keeping my smile relaxed. Easy... *Friendly*. "We had fun together, and I like you... as a friend." I quickly tacked on.

Jesus. This was awkward as hell.

Austin caught my eye over her shoulder and mouthed, 'Abort mission.'

Fucker.

"Friend, I see." She stepped back, the lust melting off her face replaced with irritation and a hint of dejection.

There was no denying Samantha Flores was hot. Tall and slim with curves in all the right places, she had long glossy blonde hair and legs for days. And she had big fuck-me eyes that were so easy to fall into when I'd had a drink or two.

But friends and sex didn't mix.

I'd learned that the hard way.

What started out as a friends-with-benefits arrangement at the beginning of summer had quickly snowballed into a stage-five-clinger situation. I'd been trying to let her down gently—keeping my distance and not feeding into her fantasies of her, me, and romantic days around campus —but she clearly wasn't getting the memo.

"Sam, come on. You know you're a good friend. Let's not—"

"Whatever, Noah." She twirled a strand of hair around her finger, trying to play it cool. "If you don't want me, I'm sure one of the other guys will."

"Seriously? You're going to hook up with one of my teammates?" Irritation rippled through me.

"You don't want me, right?" She shrugged. "So, I'm a free agent."

"Yeah. Whatever."

She walked away from me without so much as a second glance, but maybe it was better this way. I'd prefer it if she didn't hook up with one of my teammates, but perhaps it would get her off my case.

I flagged down the bartender Stu, who delivered my usual, an ice-cold bottle of Heineken.

"Thanks," I said, flicking him ten dollars.

"I've got two hundred bucks on you guys bringing home the trophy this season. So do me a favor, and score big."

"That's the plan." With a small nod, I headed for the collection of tables the team regularly hung out at.

"Trouble in paradise?" Austin asked, casting his gaze toward where Sam was chatting with a couple of the rookie players.

"I think she got the hint."

"I told you, Holden"—Connor slung his arm around my neck and smirked—"girls like Sam are trouble with a capital T. She's probably already picked out the name of your kids. I'm picturing two boys and a girl. Something like Brayden and Benson, and Brianne for the girl."

"Who the fuck are you right now?" I gawked at him.

"What?" He shrugged. "They're pretty good names."

"Did you hit your head when you finally got Ella to agree to give you a second chance?" Austin snorted at that, and I went on, "Because I swear to God you've turned into the BPOC since you two got together last Halloween."

"BPOC?"

"Biggest pussy on campus."

"Do I even want to know?" A familiar voice said from behind us, and Connor jumped up out of his seat.

"Babe, you made it." He pulled Ella in for a kiss. "Asshole over there was just telling us all about his budding romance with Sam."

"I thought you were trying to figure out how to let her down gently?" Ella frowned at me.

"I am. I mean, I was. She got the memo anyway, so we're all good."

"You know, Noah, there's a whole campus of girls dying to get their shot with the Lakers star right-winger. Did you really have to go and sleep with Sam? I thought you two were friends."

"Thank you," Connor drawled. "This is what I've been saying all along. Don't shit where you eat."

"Why are we even still talking about this? It's a moot point. Sam knows I'm not looking for anything serious." Or anything for that matter.

"Maybe you should try abstaining for a while," Ella suggested.

"What?" I balked, certain I must have misheard her because I was a twenty-year-old hot-blooded male. I had needs. "Why the fuck would I want to do that?"

"To focus on hockey. To avoid any more unnecessary girl drama. To make sure you don't end up with your very own hockey team full of baby Holdens—"

"Whoa." Panic sent a shudder through me. "I always wrap it. Every single time."

"Except that time with—"

"Whose side are you on, asshole?" I glowered at Connor.

"Sorry, bro, but she owns my balls now." He hugged Ella

into his side, gazing down at her like she was his whole world. "Tell him, babe. Tell him my balls are yours."

"Uh, maybe I should go," a meek voice said from behind me.

"Shit, Aurora. I didn't—" Ella elbowed Connor in the ribs before stepping forward.

"Aurora? Austin's sister? It's so nice to meet you finally."

"Hey." Aurora looked stunned. Big green eyes were wide and dazed as she looked to her big brother as if to say, 'help.'

"You'll have to excuse Connor and Noah. They're twenty going on twelve."

"Twenty-one," Connor corrected. "And that's not what you say when I—"

"Okay, why don't you and I go and get a drink, and you can spill all of Austin's secrets." Ella laced her arm through Aurora's and led her away from us.

"Seriously, can you two tone it down a bit?" Austin grumbled. "She'll be traumatized before the weekend's over."

"Relax, she's your sister. How naïve and innocent can she be?"

"I don't know." He ran a hand down his face, exhaling a long sigh. "She seems different."

"What's the deal with the two of you, anyway?" I asked.

"It's a long story, but we went through some shit as kids with our parents, and as soon as graduation rolled around, I got the hell out of there. I guess Rory thought I'd abandoned her or something."

"She a hockey fan?" Connor asked, and Austin nodded.

"At least, she used to be. Dated the captain of our high school hockey team for two years."

"Dated, past tense?"

"Yeah, decided to go their separate ways during their senior year because he got a full ride to Fitton U."

"No shit," I said. "He's going to be a Falcon?"

"Yeah." Austin sucked in a harsh breath, pinning me with a hard look. "I know you weren't too happy about her moving in, but you'd be doing me a big favor if you could make her feel welcomed. Maybe show her around a bit and keep her company when I'm in class. My schedule is slammed this semester. Between practice and my course load, it's not going to leave much time for me to look out for her."

"You're not seriously asking me to babysit her?"

"I'm just saying can you keep an eye out? She's my little sister, Holden."

"Ella will take her under her wing," Connor offered; thank fuck. Because I, sure as shit, wasn't the right guy for the job.

I'd probably do something stupid like get drunk and try to bang her.

Not that she was my type.

I preferred blondes—girls who made an effort. The oversized weird assed t-shirt and pair of leggings weren't exactly doing it for me, even if her shapely ass had my full attention.

Fuck don't think about her like that. She's Austin's sister. His little SISTER, asshole.

The Lakers had a handful of rules when it came to girls, but at the top of said list was the one all teammates silently promised to abide by.

Don't fuck your teammate's sister.

It was right up there with don't fuck around with any

female relation of one of your teammates or opponents. Although, I'd heard that Lincoln Parsons had scored big hooking up with one of the Broncos' player's moms a couple of years back. He was known as the MILF Fucker after that, but he'd graduated last year, and Aiden, our captain this season, had already warned us to keep our eye on the prize. And not on the petty rivalry we had with a couple of teams in our conference.

Not that I wanted to fuck Aurora. I didn't. Like I'd said before, she wasn't my type.

And even if she was, in Connor's words of wisdom— you never shit where you ate.

It was damn good being back together with the team. In between training camps, most of the guys had gone home during summer break except for Aiden, who had been exiled to Dupont Beach to stay with Assistant Coach Walsh. He'd gotten into some trouble back home and needed to lay low. No one had expected him—our fucking captain of all people—to go and meet some girl and fall ass-over-elbow in love with her. I only hoped it wasn't catching because we couldn't afford to lose more of the guys to new relationships. We had an important season ahead.

After crashing out of the Frozen Four last season, everyone was ready to sharpen our skates and get back on the ice to show everyone why we were still the team to beat.

I'd stayed behind in Lakeshore, keeping myself busy, helping out at Coach Tucker's summer camp for local kids.

It beat going home to Buffalo. Seeing *him*. Spending the summer listening to what an utter failure I was.

"Yo, Holden," Connor boomed across the bar. "You're up." He waved a pool cue in the air, and I got up to join him. Right as Aurora appeared.

"Crap, I'm sorry." She darted out of my way.

"You're good. Maybe watch where you're going next time."

Her eyes flashed to mine, full of sass and fire. "Excuse me? You almost mowed me down."

"Whatever, shortstack," I murmured before moving around her.

Shortstack?

I don't know where the fuck that had come from, but it suited her. She couldn't have been over a little five-foot-four, which, compared to my six-foot-one, made her short. And even under her baggy t-shirt, you could see her curves, her more than ample rack. It was the first thing I'd noticed about her earlier.

What could I say? I was a boob guy.

Jesus, Holden. Get your head out of the damn gutter.

"What the fuck are you smiling at?" Connor asked as I reached the pool table.

"Nothing."

His eyes narrowed, scrutinizing me as I lined up to break. "What do you make of Aurora?"

"What?" My hand slipped, sending the white ball crashing into the side cushion. "Fuck," I muttered.

"Sam really messed with your flow, huh? Or maybe it's our new houseguest that's got you all—"

"Fuck off, asshole. She's Austin's sister and not my type."

Folding his arms over his chest, he regarded me with a

knowing glint in his eye. "I thought your type was legs for days, a great rack, and big come fuck me eyes."

"Exactly. Hence not Aurora." She was short, curvy, and had that geeky bookworm thing going on. "I prefer my women a little more—"

"Dude," he shook his head.

"What? You asked, and I'm just saying, curvy, geeky types have never really been my type."

"Good to know," a small voice said.

Fuck.

I turned slowly, guilt plunking in my chest like a brick. "Shit, Aurora, I wasn't... We were just talking shit."

"So it would seem. But don't worry," she said, a trace of hurt in her voice. "You're not my type either."

"Baby, I'm everyone's type." I grinned, earning myself a few snickers from the guys milling around to watch me and Connor play pool.

It was my attempt at thawing some of the ice between us. A cocky retort to get her to smile. But Aurora wasn't smiling.

Not even a little bit.

"Well, I wouldn't touch a hockey player again even if he was the last man on earth," she seethed, but it wasn't the warning in her voice; it was the flash of devastation in her eyes that caught my attention.

Austin had said that she and her boyfriend—ex-boyfriend as the case now was—had parted ways because of college. But there was something in her expression, something—

"What's going on?" Austin asked, coming up behind his sister.

"Nothing." She flashed him a bright smile. But I'd seen

enough people paste on a smile, hoping to hide the cracks to know there was nothing genuine about it.

"I think I'm going to head back. I'm beat."

"I'll walk you," Austin said. "I need to be up early anyway."

"Let us finish this game, and me and Ella will come too," Connor added, looking at me expectantly.

"I think I'm going to stick around for a bit."

"Just don't get too wasted and make any bad decisions. Specifically, ones that start with an S and end with AM."

"I do have the ability to keep my dick in my pants, you know."

He and Austin both snorted, and I flipped them off, murmuring something about the sacred code of bros before hos.

"Finish your game," Aurora said, cutting me with a withering look. "I'll wait with Ella."

Jesus, the girl had claws.

It was a joke.

I was joking.

Even if my execution missed the mark.

She walked off, and Austin wasted no time addressing the elephant in the room. "What the fuck did you say to her?" he gritted out.

"Honestly, it's probably better you don't know." Connor wore a shit-eating grin, clearly loving watching me squirm under Austin's thunderous glare.

"Well, whatever you said, fix it," he said. "I want her to stick around, not run scared because she fell victim to the Noah Holden curse."

"Dude, she's your sister," I pointed out. "I would never go there."

"Then we won't have a problem, will we? You can smooth things out with Rory and reassure her we all want her here."

"Fine, fine, I'll apologize."

"Good. And while you're at it, offer to show her around."

"Austin, man, cut me—" His expression hardened, and I conceded. "Okay. Consider me her new best friend."

He slapped me on the shoulder and smiled. "I knew I could count on you, Holden. Now let Connor finish kicking your ass so we can head out."

Tour guide. Right. I could do that for a couple of days. Show her around. Help her get her bearings.

Then everything could go back to normal.

CHAPTER 3

AURORA

SHORTSTACK.

Noah had called me shortstack.

And a geek.

And not his type.

It wasn't anything I hadn't heard before. But still, it had caught me off guard hearing *him* say it.

Of course I wasn't his type. If the woman who had been hanging off him like a cheap throw was any indication, he liked tall, slender females with seductive smiles and confidence by the bucket load.

Not that I wanted him to like me.

I didn't.

He was Austin's teammate and one of his best friends. But nobody liked having their flaws highlighted. Least of all, in the middle of a bar surrounded by gorgeous hockey players and their adoring fangirls.

I couldn't change my appearance. God knows I'd tried

enough over the years. Mom had encouraged all the fad diets and exercise routines when I was younger, trying to mold me into her version of perfection. But I didn't have the height. I didn't have the eyes or the smile, or the right complexion. And I definitely didn't have the right body shape.

Spending your entire childhood having your flaws inspected, scrutinized, and analyzed over and over was enough to shatter the self-esteem of even the most confident supermodel, let alone a perfectly average girl from Syracuse.

I couldn't remember a time when I hadn't hated my awkward, disproportionate girl body. I hated that my hips were too wide and my boobs were too big. I hated that whenever I walked into a room, guys looked at my chest and not my face, as if my figure somehow defined me. I hated that even though I despised modeling, Mom still forced me to attend shoots until I was deemed plus size by the industry, and she finally lost the ability to use her name and connections to cast me for jobs.

It had taken me a long time to learn to accept myself. And then Ben—the one person who had always made me feel beautiful—had shattered my heart, breaking the fragile pieces he'd managed to heal, and I'd fallen back into old habits. Hiding under baggy, shapeless clothes, avoiding the mirror, and restricting what I ate.

Ella said something, and I blinked across at her. "Sorry, what?"

"I was just saying it's really nice having another girl around." She smiled. A genuine, warm smile that thawed some of the ice around my heart. "My best friend Mila got a boyfriend over the summer, and I've barely spoken to her.

Which I totally get. But as much as I love the guys, I need to talk about more than just hockey stats, dick size, and Noah's latest lay."

I bristled at the mention of him, and Ella frowned. "Oh no, what did he do?"

"Nothing."

"You can't take anything he says too seriously. He's a good guy underneath all that cocky playboy exterior."

"I'm sure he is," I murmured, barely meeting her gaze.

I didn't want him to be a good guy. I wanted him to be the villain. Because if he were the bad guy, it would soften the blow of his thoughtless words.

"He's probably feeling the pressure of having a beautiful girl move into the house."

"I highly doubt that."

"It's true," she chuckled. "Noah isn't exactly known for his ability to keep his hands off a pretty girl."

It was on the tip of my tongue to tell her that wasn't going to be a problem. Even if I wasn't Austin's sister, I wasn't his type. He'd made that crystal clear.

"So I was thinking," Ella went on, "do you want to come over tomorrow night? We could get takeout, watch a movie? Drink copious amounts of wine. Aiden's girlfriend, Dayna, is coming up from Dupont Beach. It'll be fun."

"I..." I hesitated.

Ella was nice. Kind and friendly, she'd been keen to get to know me tonight but hadn't pushed for more than I was willing to give. I appreciated that and got the vibe she was the kind of girl who uplifted others, not dragged them down.

Or stabbed you in the back the second you turned around.

"Yeah, okay," I said. "I'd like that."

"Great. Give me your phone, and I'll tap in my number. Then you can call me, and I'll have yours."

We'd just finished exchanging numbers when the guys reappeared with pizza.

"Sustenance has arrived," Connor said, sliding a box toward us. "Veggies for the girls. Meat for the guys. Although you can have my meat later." He winked at Ella, and she rolled her eyes, suppressing a smile.

"Here, grab a plate," Austin said, ignoring Connor's sexual quip as if it happened all the time.

I figured it probably did.

"Oh, I'm not hungry, but thanks."

"Not hungry?" Connor looked mortified. "But pizza after a night out is like the holy grail."

"It's a good job you work out two hours a day," Austin said. "Or you'd be rockin' one big muffin top."

Connor patted his stomach and yanked up his sweater a fraction. "Nothing here to see except washboard abs for days. What says you, Aurora?"

"Con!" Ella flashed me an apologetic smile. "You'll have to excuse my boyfriend; too many years of being worshiped by puck bunnies has gone to his head."

I shifted uncomfortably, my gaze darting anywhere but Connor's rock-hard stomach, which was still on display.

"Seriously, Morgan, put the goods away." Ella threw a bottle cap at his head, but he caught it, smirking at her. "Is there anything you can't do?" she murmured.

"What can I say? I'm an overachiever, kitten."

"You're an asshole," Austin muttered. "You sure you don't want any pizza, Sis?"

"I'm good, thanks."

"Suit yourself. More for us."

"Damn right." Connor winked at me, snagging another slice and scarfing it down in three bites flat.

"So, Rory... Is it okay if I call you Rory?"

"Sure," I said.

"What did you think of The Penalty Box?"

"It was okay."

"Okay? I think you just broke the hearts of every Laker in a two-mile radius." He clutched his chest dramatically. "TPB is like our nest, our domain, the heart of our team."

"Except Darillo's. I love that place," Ella added.

"Darillo's?"

"It's a cute little Italian restaurant overlooking the lake. So dreamy and romantic, and they do the best fettuccine Alfredo. I get excited just thinking about it."

"Babe"—Connor frowned—"we've talked about this. The only thing allowed to excite you is me."

"And Chris Hemsworth, Snow White and the Huntsman era, not Thor." Austin snorted, and Ella pinned him with a dark look. "Don't diss the Chris."

"I wouldn't dare. Care to weigh in on this?" He glanced my way.

"He's very easy on the eyes."

"He's a freaking god. Have you seen his—"

"Okay, you"—Connor manhandled her into his arms —"time to take you upstairs and remind you why I'm the only man you need to worship."

"Connor, put me down," Ella protested, banging on his chest like a drum.

"We'll see you two in the morning. Rory, word of advice, you might want to wear earplugs. I intend on making my woman scream tonight."

"Connor, I swear to God, put me—" Their voices became low rumbles as they disappeared out of the kitchen.

Austin's exasperated laughter vibrated through me. It was such a familiar sound, one I'd grown up with. But it came laced with bitterness and regret now.

"They're cute together," I said, needing to break the tension crackling between us.

I was here.

I wanted to be here.

But I didn't want to revisit old wounds, not yet.

"Yeah, they're the real deal. Same with Aiden and Dayna. You know, I always thought you and Ben would go the distance."

Surprise crashed over me, and I did my best to school my expression, the devastation I had no doubt was infiltrating every inch of my features.

"Rory?" Austin asked with concern.

"I thought so, too," I admitted, forcing down the pain that came with the words. "But then senior year happened, and we both realized that the long-distance thing wasn't going to work."

"You never know; you might get to reconnect at a game."

God, I hoped not.

I never wanted to see Ben Sudeikis again.

"Fitton U are in our conference."

Don't remind me, the words teetered on the tip of my tongue. But I forced them down.

I had no intention of sharing my deepest, darkest secrets with Austin.

Even if he was my brother.

Because he was.

"You sure you're okay?"

"Just tired. In fact, I think I'm going to call it a night."

"Yeah, I probably need to hit the sack. I promised Aiden and a few of the guys I'd hit the ice with them in the morning. But I'll be around later if you want to hang out."

"Ella said something about going over to her place tomorrow night."

"Check you out already making friends." He grinned, but his expression quickly sobered. "I'm really glad you're here, Rory."

A beat passed. Loaded with expectation.

"Yeah," I replied, and this time, I meant it. "Me too."

The next morning, I slept in. Maybe it was the move, or hanging out at the bar, or just the emotional turmoil I'd felt watching Connor and Ella all night, but when I finally woke, I felt like I'd been hit by a truck.

It was a little past ten, and Austin had texted to say he tried to wake me and say goodbye, but I was out cold. He also said Connor and Ella had left to meet Aiden and Dayna for breakfast. So I had the house to myself as Noah had yet to return from wherever he'd spent the night.

Probably in the blonde's bed.

My lips twisted with mild amusement. She had been so obvious, batting her eyelashes and running her fingers up and down his chest. Ella said he slept with lots of girls, and blondie had been obviously up for it.

I shoved all thoughts of Noah and his sexual proclivities out of my head and focused on getting ready for the day.

It felt strange to wake up in their house, go into the bathroom, and take a shower. Creeping out of the guest room and slipping downstairs to the kitchen like a thief in the night. Like I didn't belong here.

But I guess this was home now—at least, for the immediate future.

It was temporary though. And deep down, I was glad Austin had offered me somewhere to stay—for free, I might add—instead of having to stay at a hotel or accepting the student housing emergency accommodation.

I'd never heard a good story about that, and I really needed my first few weeks at Lakeshore U to go well.

The coffee machine whirred to life, the rich scent settling deep inside me as I hummed a quiet tune and waited. It was almost done when the front door rattled, and a voice called, "It's me."

Crap.

Noah swanned into the kitchen with messy bedhead and his t-shirt on backward.

"Did you dress in the dark this morning?" I fought a smile, although it was super annoying that he still managed to look so good, given his unkempt state.

He frowned. "What are you talking about, woman?"

"Your t-shirt." I pointed toward his chest. "It's on backward."

"It's not—shit." He threw down his keys, pulled his arms out the sleeves, hiking the material up around his neck to switch it around. "There, all better." A lazy grin tugged at his mouth as he shoved his arms through the sleeves.

"You really are—" I stopped myself. I didn't want to start a silly rivalry between the two of us.

So he'd said a few things about me? He hadn't been overly mean. He had a physical preference, and I wasn't it.

Big deal.

He was a hockey player, and that one hundred percent wasn't my type. I'd been there, done that, and gotten the heartbreak to end all heartbreaks.

"Go on, shortstack." Noah leaned against the counter, arms folded over his ridiculously broad chest, and smirked. "Tell me what you really think of me."

Irritation bubbled up inside of me, like hot lava flowing out of a volcano. "Please don't call me that," I said calmly, forcing myself not to pick up the spatula lying on the counter and throw it at his head.

"What, shortstack? Seems pretty fitting if you ask me." His smirk morphed into a cheeky grin.

God, he was too much for this time in the morning. Even in his messy, just-rolled-out-of-bed state, he still looked good enough to walk onto a GQ photoshoot and give it his all. His dark hair, curled slightly on top, fell into his eyes a little. Rich brown eyes that danced with bad intentions and a strong, chiseled jaw and cheekbones most women only dreamed of.

He wasn't quite as tall as Connor and my brother, but he carried more muscle, his biceps practically bulging out of his black fitted t-shirt. Swirls of ink peeked out from underneath the material and ran down his forearm.

Noah Holden was the kind of guy who would break your heart and skate right over it with a smile and a wink.

A mistake I'd made one too many times already.

A mistake I would *never* make again.

"Yes, well," I cleared my throat, uncomfortable with the way he looked at me. The intensity in his gaze. "It's early, and I'm not a morning person. So feel free to go take a shower or go back to bed."

"Are you trying to get rid of me... In my own house?" Disbelief coated his voice. "Because we might need to lay down some ground rules, short—"

"I swear to God, Noah." I inhaled a thin breath, pinning him with a seething look. "If you call me that one more time, I won't be held responsible for my actions."

"Relax." His hands went up in defense. "I'm joking with you. Listen, Austin asked me to show you around town; give you the Holden lowdown. What do you say, meet down here in an hour? Once the coffee"—he dropped his eyes to the mug in my hand—"has done its thing, and you're in a better mood?"

"I am not..."

Breathe. Just breathe. Don't let him bait you.

"Thanks, but I think I'm good." I started to move past him, but he snagged my wrist. Our eyes collided, and he grinned again.

Jesus, it was too damn early for this.

"What, no thank you? I'm offering to do a nice thing, and you're acting—"

"I'm sure you have far better things to be doing on a Sunday than babysitting your friend's geeky sister." My brow went up, and realization dawned on his face.

"Shit, Aurora. About last night, I didn't—"

"You did, and it's fine. But we can leave it at that."

"What do you mean?" His brows furrowed.

I looked right at him and said, "We clearly rub each

other all wrong, so let's agree to just stay out of each other's way."

Confusion glittered in his pretty eyes, but I didn't stick around to expand. Grabbing a banana from the fruit bowl, I walked out of there with my head held high.

And a smile of satisfaction on my face.

CHAPTER 4

NOAH

"So, who was the lucky girl?" Mason asked me as we jogged along Greek Row.

He was a junior, and split his time between Lakers House and his home in Pittsburgh, a ninety-minute drive from Lakeshore.

We'd bunked together last year, and as a freshman, he'd taken me under his wing and showed me the ropes. Between him, Austin, and Connor, I had the best damn friends a guy could ask for. But Mason wasn't like Austin and Connor. He was different.

I'd never truly gotten to the bottom of what his deal was —as far as I knew, nobody on the team had—but he was a good guy. Solid. Dependable. And a fucking beast on the ice.

"Some blonde from Beta Pi." I shrugged. "But we only fooled around. I wasn't feeling it. Went back to Lakers House to crash."

"The fuck?" He grabbed my t-shirt and yanked me to a stop. "You, the infamous Noah Holden, wasn't feeling it? Are you feeling okay?" He pressed a hand to my forehead. "Do I need to call 9-1-1? You do feel a little warm."

"Because we've been running for forty minutes, asshole," I grumbled, swatting his hand away.

He chuckled, and we fell into a gentle jog, cutting across the perfectly tended lawns outside the three sorority houses on campus.

"You could always knock and see if she wants round two."

"Nah, man. You know I never go for seconds." It was simpler that way. "Sam was the only exception, and look how that turned out."

"We all saw that coming a mile off," he chuckled again, grabbing the bottom of his tank and pulling it up to wipe his face.

Sweat rolled down my forehead, too, down my back and abs, but I liked the feel of it. The reminder that I was working hard and pushing my body to the brink.

I fucking loved working out. I loved a hard day on the ice with Coach Tucker and the assistant coaches yelling from the side of the rink, demanding more. My body craved the physical exertion, and my mind—thanks to years of childhood trauma at the hands of my piece of shit father— felt a strange sort of satisfaction.

My father was nothing short of an asshole, but at least I'd gained some redeeming qualities thanks to my shitty upbringing. I was dedicated, focused, and one hundred and ten percent all fucking in. It wasn't only my dream to go pro; it was my plan.

My *only* plan.

Anything less was simply not an option.

"Well, yeah, we're done. Pretty sure Sam left TPB with Ward."

"You're joking, right?" Mason scowled at the mention of Ward Cutler, one of our new right-wingers. He'd arrived early, and since I was around, I'd taken it upon myself to show him the ropes. "I hope you gave him shit for that."

"Nah." I shrugged. "He's welcome to her. The sex wasn't even that good."

Mason snorted. "You're a fucking dog."

"Takes one to know one." I winked.

He was as bad as me when it came to sex. But when the season started up, hockey players had intense practice and game schedules, classes to keep up with, and all the other shit college students had to deal with. Getting freaky between the sheets was a surefire way to burn off some steam and keep tensions on the ice low. Sex without any of the other bullshit that came with dating? Even better.

"How're things with your new houseguest?" he changed the subject. To one I'd rather not talk about.

"It is what it is."

"What the fuck does that mean?"

"Aurora's fine," I said, running a hand through my damp hair as we kept a steady pace, the balmy air filling my lungs.

"You're acting weird."

"No, I'm not."

"Yeah, Holden, you are." He arched a brow, and I knew I wasn't escaping this conversation without giving him something.

"Fine." I let out a heavy sigh. "Last night, she overheard a conversation she wasn't supposed to hear and got all snarky with me. Austin told me to apologize, so I tried to fix it this morning, offered to give her a tour around town, and she iced me out."

"Hold up." He drew up short again, and I slowed my pace. "You're telling me there's a girl in Lakeshore who is immune to the Noah Holden charm?" Laughter pealed out of him. "First, the Beta Pi chick, now Austin's sister. This is too much."

"The Beta Pi chick"—Melissa or maybe it was Melanie —"wanted my dick. My dick was just undecided about her."

Mason's brow lifted. "And Aurora? What did you say?"

"Something about her not being my type."

"So, big deal?" He frowned. "She's Austin's sister. It's not like you'd hit on that—yeah, you totally would. She a DUFF or something?"

"Dude!"

"What?" He shrugged. "It happens."

"She's not a DUFF, but she's got that geeky band camp thing going on."

"Yeah, but is she Michelle Flaherty geeky or Willow Rosenberg geeky? Because that's an important distinction to make."

"You're not helping." Now all I could imagine was Aurora doing very dirty things with a flute.

"You're thinking about it, aren't you?" His mouth twitched. "This one time, at band camp—"

"Stop." *Please fucking stop.* "Even if I did want to hit that"—and I didn't—"she's Austin's sister, and she has this whole 'I don't date hockey players' mantra."

Which, the more I thought about it, suggested Austin didn't have the entire story straight about Aurora and her ex. But it was none of my business.

"The ones you have to work for a little bit are the best kind." Mason smirked.

"Like you ever work for pussy."

Mason Steele had that brooding, mysterious angle girls couldn't resist. He rarely spoke to anyone outside the team, yet girls lined up for their turn with the Lakers' left-winger.

"We done?" I asked, checking the distance on my wristwatch.

"Yeah. I promised Scottie I'd stop by later."

"How's he doing?"

"He has good days and bad days."

Mason's younger brother, Scottie, was autistic, and thanks to puberty, he was going through a pretty rough time. Mase said it was all the new and unfamiliar hormones wreaking havoc with his well-structured life.

"You should bring him to the rink. Let him watch us practice." One of Scottie's special interests was hockey. More specifically, the Lakeshore U Lakers. He knew more about the team than me and the guys put together. I'd even go out on a limb and say he knew more than Coach Tucker. He could recite game stats like he was recalling the days of the week or the months of the year.

It was fascinating. But we all knew how hard it was on Mrs. Steele and Mase.

"Maybe, yeah."

In typical fashion, he ended the line of conversation. And I didn't push. I never did. Mase knew where I was if he ever wanted to talk.

"You ready for this season?" he asked as we walked back to Lakers House. I didn't have a room there anymore, but I still came over all the time.

Freshman year had been a blast. The constant parties

and pranks and general mayhem, but when Austin and Connor asked me if I wanted the empty room in their house just off campus, I had jumped at the chance.

I needed to maintain a 3.5 GPA if I was going to remain eligible for my scholarship. Lakers House was a distraction I didn't need. So now, I had the best of both worlds—a place to party on the weekend and a quiet room to retreat to when I needed to get my head down and study.

"As I'll ever be. You?"

"Fuck yeah. This is our season. I can feel it."

"I hope you're right." Because I came to Lakeshore U to win. To chase dreams of winning the Frozen Four and being drafted to a pro team.

I'd turned my back on the only family I had for this chance, and I needed it to pay off.

More than ever.

But it all hinged on maintaining my fucking GPA.

"You ready to hit the ice Monday? Dumfries is going to run a tight ship this season."

"Aiden can go fuck himself." I grinned, joking.

"Still sore over the fact he went and fell ass-over-elbow for Dayna?" Mase asked, and I nodded.

"You telling me you're not?"

His shoulders lifted in a half-shrug. "It is what it is. So long as she doesn't affect his performance on the ice and his decisions as captain, it's all good. Besides, I like her. She's good for him."

"Yeah." He had a point, but still, it didn't stop me from feeling a sense of betrayal.

Last year, Aiden was my idol. His focus and dedication to the game; the way he didn't let life interfere on the ice.

Sure, he had a temper that got the better of him sometimes, but hockey was his life. It was in his fucking DNA.

Until this summer, apparently, and a certain brown-eyed beauty from Dupont Beach.

So I was still a little sore about it. Losing Connor to Ella at the beginning of last season was bad enough but losing our captain to love... Well, it fucking sucked.

"What are you thinking?" Mase shoulder-checked me as Lakers House came into view.

"That we can't afford any more surprises this season."

"Love isn't catching, you know," he chuckled. "It's not going to sweep through the team like that time we all had food poisoning from that food truck in Kalamazoo."

"I know that," I murmured, unease sliding down my spine.

Because although I knew he was right, something about this season already felt different.

And that put me on edge.

I hung out at Lakers House a few hours before heading home. If I was being honest with myself—and I really didn't want to be—I was avoiding going back. After my verbal spar with Aurora this morning and how she'd iced me out without so much as a second thought, I really didn't want to be around her.

I preferred to lick my wounds in privacy.

But of course, the universe fucking hated me, and the second I entered the house and headed into the kitchen for a snack—because I was a growing boy—she was there. Summoned out of thin air to make my life miserable.

"It's you," she practically spat the words.

"I do live here, you know." I cocked a brow, watching as she cleaned off the counter. "What smells good?"

"I made cookies."

"You made cookies," I murmured.

"Is that a problem?"

"Why would it be a problem? I fucking love cookies."

"For a bunch of hockey players, you sure do all seem to eat a lot."

"We're growing boys, ba—" I stopped myself, confused at how easy it was to fall into this back and forth with her.

"Fine. Here. But only one." She pushed a cooling rack toward me, and I helped myself to a chocolate chip.

"This is good," I said through a mouth of gooey, chocolatey goodness. "Aren't you having one?"

A strange expression passed over her. "I'm okay. I'll have one later."

"Well, get in there quickly because you live with three hockey players now. If you leave that rack out, those cookies are going to be gone quicker than you can say, 'Noah Holden is the best I've ever had.'"

"Best, what exactly? Pain in my ass?" Aurora grinned, clearly pleased with herself.

And surprisingly, I found myself grinning right back.

"You know what, baby Hart? You're not all that bad. I know we had a rocky start, but you and me? I think we can be friends. What do you say?"

"So long as you don't try and sleep with me, then I suppose it doesn't sound too awful."

"Yeah?" I asked.

"Yeah."

"Well, then, Rory, you just got yourself a new best friend. Get ready, and I'll take you out in Connor's truck and give you the grand tour."

"Actually, I have plans tonight."

"Plans, with who?" Dejection swarmed in my chest for the second time at the hands of Austin's little sister.

It shouldn't have mattered. I had a contact list full of people who would love to hang out with me. I was mother-fucking Noah Holden, but Aurora had made my easy-go-lucky persona falter. And I had been a dick to her —*about* her.

"If you must know, Ella invited me over for girls' night."

"She did, huh? Well, I think you're making the wrong decision. I happen to know for a fact that I'm better company than Ella Henshaw."

"She invited Dayna too."

"And what does girls' night entail exactly? Painting each other's nails, pillow fights, and gossiping about boys?"

"Pillow fights?" She gawked at me. "You're not serious?"

"You mean girls' night doesn't entail half-naked girls jumping up and down on the bed, pillows in hand, feathers flying everywhere... because if it doesn't, you just destroyed my favorite teenage fantasy."

"You're an idiot." Aurora tried to suppress a smile but failed miserably.

"Made you smile though, didn't I?"

"Fine, I'll give you that. Now go away, you're annoying, and I need to get ready."

"So you're really going to pick a night of pillow fights over a night on the town with a Laker?"

"Don't talk about yourself in the third person. It's

weird." She brushed past me, shooting me a bemused look. "Why are you looking at me like that?"

"I…" I shook my head, trying to focus. "You have some flour, right"—I lifted my hand, gently cupping her face and brushing the pad of my thumb over the spot—"there."

"Thanks." Aurora's cheeks turned the cutest shade of pink. She looked fucking adorable all wide-eyed and flushed.

The fuck?

Where the hell had that thought come from?

"I… uh, yeah." I snatched my hand away and shoved it in my sweats pocket.

"Right, well, I need to get a shower ready for all the pillow fights. I guess I'll see you around." Her lips twisted with amusement as she ducked around me and hurried out of the kitchen.

And all I could do was watch her go, reminding myself that Aurora Hart was definitely not my type.

CHAPTER 5

AURORA

"Oh my God, he didn't," I said, smiling so hard that my jaw hurt.

Dayna grinned back, taking a sip of wine before she nodded. "He just smacked one right on me as if he went around kissing random girls all the time."

"I hate to break it to you, sweetie," Ella said. "But he did go around kiss—"

"Oh hush, you." Dayna grabbed a cushion and threw it at Ella's head. "He doesn't do it now; that's what counts."

"It must be hard, the distance thing."

Her expression sobered. "I won't lie. I've been feeling pretty insecure. Especially after what happened with my ex, Josh. We'd barely been apart a week when he cheated on me."

"Asshole," Ella murmured.

"Here, here." Dayna leaned over and clinked her glass against Ella's. "But what I have with Aiden is different, and I have to trust in that. In us. We're in a good place, and Dupont Beach is only forty minutes away."

"I don't think I could do it," I mused, and they both frowned.

"What do you mean?" Ella asked.

"Be with a college athlete. Not like it would ever happen."

"What are you talking about?" Her gaze slid to Dayna's in question, and embarrassment enveloped me.

"I... um, you know. Look at you two and look at me. I'm a mess." I tugged awkwardly at my *I party with Mr. Darcy* t-shirt and forced a smile. But they didn't smile back, and I got it.

Ella had invited me to girls' night, and I was being weird. I hadn't meant for it to slip out, but it had. And now I couldn't take it back.

"Aurora? Is there something—"

"I'm fine." I smiled. "It sounds like you and Aiden are the real deal."

My stomach knotted, my heart aching in my chest.

I'd had that once.

But it had all been a lie.

"God, I hope so. It's crazy, right? A few months ago, I was worrying about moving back home. At figuring out my relationship with Josh, and now I'm dreaming of a future with Aiden."

"I'm so happy for you guys," Ella said. "I've been waiting for one of the guys to get a girlfriend. Being the only WAG sucks. At least now, with two of us, we might stand a chance at keeping the puck bunnies at bay."

"We could always make Aiden and Connor get tattoos

on their foreheads saying, 'off the market,'" Dayna chuckled.

"Surely, they're not that bad," I said, relieved they'd moved the conversation onto a new topic.

"They can get pretty obsessive. Connor told me that when he was a freshman, one of the senior players came home and found a girl handcuffed naked to his bed. They had to call the maintenance guy to come and cut her free because she had conveniently lost the key. Another time, Linc, who graduated last spring, got invited to a bunny hop at one of the sorority houses."

"A what?"

"A group of sisters basically took turns, you know..." Ella waggled her brows, a strange mix of disgust and amusement etched into her expression.

"So, like a puck bunny orgy?" I clarified.

"Exactly! Turned out one of the girls had a boyfriend back home, though, and when he found out, he and a couple of his friends turned up at Lakers House looking for Linc."

"Oh my God," Dayna gasped. "What happened?"

"What do you think happened? The guys were ready to throw down until they realized Linc had the whole team behind him."

"I hope the girl apologized."

"They don't care. Bagging a Laker is like a rite of passage for some girls. But I swear to God if anyone so much as looks twice in Aiden's direction..." Dayna inhaled a sharp breath, her brows pinched with anger, and Ella chuckled.

"Ahh, young love. You have so much to learn, babe."

She winked, and the two of them burst into another fit of laughter.

When it subsided, and they had refilled their wine-glasses, they both turned their attention to me. "So, Aurora, tell us about you," Dayna said.

Oh no.

This was it. The part where I had to weave half-truths and lies together without tangling myself up so tightly that I couldn't find a way out. I'd gotten good at it with my brother. He was family, he'd had to learn his own coping mechanisms over the years too. But he'd failed to notice mine.

Ella and Dayna were my friends. At least, they had the potential to be. I didn't want to deceive them. I also didn't want to reveal too much and scare them away.

It had been a long time since I'd made new friends, since I'd trusted myself to open my fragile heart and let someone in.

The last time I did, it ended in heartache and tears, but I didn't come to Lakeshore to dwell on the past. I came for a fresh start.

A chance to put what happened behind me.

I was wary, though. Of getting too close. Of giving too much of myself away.

I'd given Ben everything, and he'd shattered my heart without so much as an ounce of care. So it was strange sitting here listening to Dayna and Ella talk about the men in their lives, hearing the adoration in their voices, the contentment. They were in love—anyone could see that. Yet, part of me wanted to warn them. To remind them that you never truly knew someone or their motivations. That 'I love you' meant everything... Until it didn't.

"Aurora?"

"Sorry." I snapped myself out of the melancholy I'd found myself in. "I'm just your average girl from Syracuse."

"Oh, come on. There must be some skeletons in your closet. A cheating ex or tragic tale of unrequited love. We've all got a story to tell."

"Dayna." Ella shook her head, offering me a strained smile.

Did she know? Or at least, did she sense something about me?

"Oh, shit. I put my foot in it, didn't I?" Regret flickered in her gaze. "Which is it? Cheating ex or tragic tale? Because I've got both, so I know all about heartache."

My brows furrowed as I tried to figure a way out of this.

"You know about Josh, the cheating asshole," Ella said. "But Dayna also lost her brother a few years ago to cancer."

"I had no idea. I'm so sorry."

A tidal wave of guilt rose inside me. Here I was, drowning in my past. And Dayna had been through so much.

"Thanks. It's taken me a long time to come to terms with it. After Dalton died, I was so lost. I moved to Boston and switched off from dealing with everything. So yeah, I know all about grief and loss and all that good stuff nobody wants to talk about."

"Hey, bitch," Ella pouted. "I want to talk about it."

"Ignore El." Dayna grinned. "Her life is far too perfect to off-load all my trauma onto."

"You know, Aurora, we're not always this bad. It's the wine, I promise."

"It's okay. I'm just relieved to be out of the house."

"Oh no, trouble in paradise already? You and Austin get

along, don't you?" Dayna asked, and Ella suppressed a smile.

"I don't think it's Austin she's worried about."

"Well, it's not Connor, which means... Oh no, what did Noah do?"

"Can we please not talk about Noah," I said, hoping my face didn't betray me.

There had been a moment between us earlier in the kitchen. A split second where I imagined what it might be like to catch someone like Noah Holden's attention.

But I'd quickly shoved it down. He was only being nice to me because he felt guilty. Because I was Austin's sister.

That's all it was.

I had more sense than to mistake his charm for anything else.

"He's not the kind of guy you want to get tangled up with," Dayna said. "I've heard some of the stories. Aiden got drunk once and confessed his magic number. And then proceeded to tell me all the locker room secrets."

"If he told you Connor's number, I don't want to know." Ella shook her head. "I mean it. That is one piece of information I can live without ever knowing."

"You really think it would be that bad?" I asked, and she nodded.

"These hockey players are worse than dogs, Aurora. They all have a strict rule about wrapping up, and they get tested every few months, thank God. But whatever number you're thinking, multiply it by five, and you're probably closer to the mark."

"But it's just sex."

Sex with Ben hadn't been anything life-changing. It had been nice, sure. But it was clumsy and awkward, and I was always too worried about being naked with him to really enjoy it.

It turned out I had every right to be.

"Just sex?" Dayna blinked at me as if I'd grown a second head. "If you say it like that, it means you haven't been doing it right. Oh crap, you're not a virgin, are you? Because if you are, I'm so sorry. Me and my big mouth—"

"No, I'm not a virgin. But I have only been with one guy. My ex."

There, I'd said it.

"Okay, now we're getting to the good stuff." They both leaned forward, wearing expectant expressions.

"We are?" I gawped at them.

"Yep." They shared a conspiratorial look. "We need to get you back on the horse."

"Back on the... Oh no. No." Absolutely not.

They both chuckled. "Aurora, you're eighteen, and you basically just admitted to never having experienced good sex," Ella said. "You're in college now. There are plenty of guys who would love to help you out with that."

"I want to focus on my studies."

"Says no freshman ever." Ella rolled her eyes.

"El's right; it's freshman orientation week. The perfect opportunity to find a gorgeous guy to give you the ride of your life." Dayna snickered into her now empty wineglass. "Oops, it's almost gone. Fill her up, babe."

"Aurora?" Ella asked.

"I'm good, thanks."

"You're still on your first glass."

"I don't drink a lot. I'm a bit of a lightweight."

And I couldn't handle the hangover cravings.

"All the more for me," Dayna sang, gulping down her wine like it was going out of fashion.

I glanced at Ella, wondering if this was normal Dayna behavior, but she was too focused on her friend to notice me.

"Dayna, honey, is everything okay?"

"Why wouldn't everything be fine? I mean, I'm fine. Are you fine? It's fine, right? Everything is fiiiine."

"Sweetie," Ella got up and scooched next to her. "Talk to us. What's going on?"

"Maybe I should go," I suggested, feeling like a spectator to their friendship. But the second I said the words, Dayna blurted, "AidensuggestedwethinkaboutgettingaplacetogetherandI'mtotallyfreakingout."

"Oh my God, he didn't?"

She nodded. "We stayed at the house last weekend, but he got pissed at Ward for interrupting us constantly. Then the next morning, we were lying in bed, and he just came out with it. But it's too soon. I mean, it's barely been three months."

"Holy shit, this is amazing. I mean, I knew you were getting serious, but I didn't *know*... Wait a minute, I'm over here all excited, picking out your moving-in present, and you seem like you're freaking out."

"Because I am freaking out. Tell her, Aurora. Three months is too soon, right?"

"I... uh, I mean, it is quick, but I don't think there's a hard and fast rule with these things."

"Exactly," Ella agreed. "You love each other, and being apart most of the week has got to suck. And I know what a drag it is staying over at your boyfriend's place when his friends are home. Present company excluded." She flashed me a bright smile.

I felt like an intruder in their conversation. I didn't know them yet, not really. Not in the ways that mattered. But I couldn't deny there was something about these two girls that made me want to be a part of their inner circle.

Still, I found myself on the periphery, listening to them hash out the pros and cons of Aiden's moving-in proposal. But the more wine they drank, the more Ella talked Dayna around. Until she finally stood up and declared, "I think I'm going to do it. I think I'm going to move in with my boyfriend."

"Oh my God, babe, this is so freaking exciting." The two of them hugged, squealing with excitement as I sat there, feeling like a third wheel. "You need to call him right now," Ella said.

"Oh my God, I do. This is crazy. It's not crazy, is it?"

"Just call him." Ella gave her a little shove and came and joined me on the love seat. "Sorry if we got a little carried away, but I'm so excited for them and maybe a teeny tiny little bit jealous."

"You and Connor haven't talked about it?"

"Not yet. He loves living with Austin and Noah, and I know he won't want to leave them in a bind." She got up again. "I'm going to grab a bag of crackers to soak up some of this wine, or I'll pay for it in the morning. You want anything?"

"I'm good, thanks."

"I have other snacks. Donuts, Reese's pieces, I think there's some B and J's too if you prefer ice cream."

"Honestly, I'm fine. I ate before I left." I thought back to the batch of cookies I made... and didn't eat. The ones Noah couldn't get enough of.

God, I really needed to stop thinking about him.

Ella went to the kitchen and armed herself with enough snacks to feed the entire building. When she returned, she dumped them all down on the coffee table and turned her attention to me again.

"Sorry about earlier if we overstepped about the whole get back on the horse thing. We would never push you into doing something you're not comfortable with, but Dayna did have a point. Every woman deserves to experience good sex in her lifetime."

"I'll keep that in mind." Nervous laughter bubbled out of me, my stomach tumbling.

"Are you excited about starting classes? English major, right?" I nodded and she went on. "That's cool. I'm a senior and work at the library, so if you need any help, just holler."

"Thanks."

"What are we talking about?" Dayna rejoined us.

Ella snagged her hand as she passed us to get to the other couch and yanked her down. "So... What did he say?"

"After he asked me like eight times if I was serious... He said, and I quote, 'I'm coming to get you. I need to be inside you, freckles, right fucking now.'" She got a dreamy look on her face as she let out a soft, contented sigh.

"So romantic," Ella said. "And slightly caveman, but we'll let it slide because, oh my God, you're moving in together."

Another round of shrieking ensued while I sat there, watching these two strong, confident girls celebrate, wondering if I'd ever find that. The negative little voice in my head whispering that I probably wouldn't.

I'd grown up in the shadow of my slimmer, prettier friends. Watched as they all got boyfriends, dates, and first kisses. I'd stood on the sideline more times than I could count, watching them chosen for school dances and events.

Until Ben.

He saw me—he *chose* me.

But it had all been a lie.

Because love was a lie.

One I wouldn't let myself believe in again.

Girls like me didn't get the guy.

They got nothing but a heap of disappointment and regret.

And bittersweet heartache.

CHAPTER 6

NOAH

"What the fuck was that, Holden?" Aiden bellowed across the ice as I lost the puck, watching Leon and Ward skate down the rink toward the goal.

"I fucked up, Cap," I called.

"Damn right, you did." He skated over to me. "If you're going to score this season, you might want to try keeping hold of the puck."

"Very funny." I flipped him off. "I'm a little rusty, is all."

Truth was, I'd spent plenty of time on the ice over the summer, keeping myself in shape. It was a bad morning, nothing more.

Mase scored, shooting me a cocky glance. "And that's how you do it."

"It's not even official practice yet. I'll be skating circles around you in a few weeks."

"You hope." He winked, doing a couple of victory laps. Asshole.

"If something's on your mind..." Aiden said, leaving the unspoken words hanging between us.

"It's not. You can count on me this season."

"Good." He nodded. "Because I intend on lifting that cup before I graduate. Let's run it again," he ordered, and like good little lap dogs, we moved into position.

Official practices didn't start for another three weeks, but that didn't mean we wouldn't be in the gym daily before we hit the ice. Aiden wanted us to gel before Coach Tucker got his hands on us. A lot of us had played together for at least a year, but we'd lost some great players after last season, leaving some big shoes to fill. Leon Banks was our new left D-man, a hot recruit from Boston, and Ward was tipped to be our next big star. I'd been that kid this time last year. New to the team and eager to make my mark.

Desperate not to fuck things up.

This time when Connor passed me the puck, I didn't fuck it up. My skates glided across the ice as I controlled my stick, moving it from side to side with deadly precision. Nothing felt more natural in the world than the ice under my feet and a stick in my hands.

Hockey was my constant.

My passion and obsession all rolled into one.

For as long as I could remember—and I could remember right back to being a little kid watching Tampa Bay Lightning with Grandpa Holden—I'd wanted to be a hockey player. But watching Martin St. Louis win the Art Ross Trophy for a second time cemented my dreams of going pro.

I'd spent winters out on the lake, teaching myself to skate, watching the older kids when they played during the holidays, imagining that one day, it would be me. Only I'd be playing for an NHL team—chasing fame and fortune. Proving to everyone who ever doubted me that they were wrong. That Noah Holden was worth something more than the shitty hand he was dealt.

I deked around one defender, lined up the shot, and sent the puck flying into the net right past Austin's glove.

"Yes," I breathed, relief trickling through me. I was the Lakers' star right-winger, on course to beat every record set by Dalton Benson, one of the best right-wingers the NCAA had ever seen.

Dayna's brother might have been gone, but his legacy would live on at Lakeshore U. Even when I beat his record for most goals in a season—and I would—he would still be one of the greats. If only his life hadn't been cut short.

That was the thing about life—about hockey—though, none of us knew what was around the corner. You could only play every game like it was your last. Live every day like you might not get another.

It was a motto that had worked out well for me so far.

"Better," Aiden swooped in behind me, clapping me on the shoulder.

"Ye of little faith," I chuckled.

Because that's what I did, laughed everything off with a smile or a joke.

It was better than the alternative.

"What now, Cap?" I asked, and he smirked.

"Now, we run it again."

So we did.

Over and over until my calves ached, my lungs burned, and my stick felt like lead in my hands.

And I loved every damn second.

After finishing practice, I hit Joe's on the way home, the coffee shop right around the corner from the hockey facility. The guys had invited me over to Lakers House to play video games, but I needed to get a head start on my reading for my Sports Marketing class. I'd heard rumors the professor was a mean old stick who harbored a serious grudge against athletes—especially football players and hockey players.

Just my luck.

Getting my order to go, I shouldered the door open right as Aurora appeared.

"You," she said, peering up at me, bringing a hand to her forehead to block out the midday sun.

"Me." I grinned.

"What are you doing here?"

"Getting coffee. What are you doing here?"

"I thought I'd explore."

"You didn't make it very far," I said. Joe's was the center point between the facility, Lakers House, and our place.

"I got lost. I've been walking past the same tree for almost an hour."

"Wow, your sense of direction must be terrible." Laughter rumbled in my chest. "You know, there's this thing called Google Maps—"

"Ha-ha, very funny. For as much as I enjoy... whatever this is, I'm in desperate need of coffee." She stared at me expectantly. When I didn't budge, she added, "Please move."

Shit.

"Yeah, sure." I stepped aside. "You know you could have taken me up on my offer to show you around."

"I told you I had plans."

"And how did the sleepover go? Any naked pillow fights?" The corners of my mouth tipped, and Aurora rolled her eyes.

"What do you think?"

"I think it's a pretty damn awesome fantasy."

"Noah." She blushed, her eyes dipping a little.

"Relax, shortstack. I'm just messing with you." Her expression dropped, and I realized my error. "Shit, Aurora, I didn't—"

"I'm sure you have things to do, so I'll just..." She nodded toward the door and went to take off.

"Wait, let me—"

"Noah," a voice called, and I glanced over to find a group of puck bunnies headed my way.

Talk about bad fucking timing.

"Looks like your fan club just arrived." Aurora gave me a weak smile. "I'll see you around, hotshot." She ducked into the coffee shop and left me at the mercy of Fallon and her Beta Pi friends.

"Noah, I was hoping we'd run into you." She beamed, flicking long platinum blonde hair off her shoulder. "We've organized a Pledge Party for the new pledges, and we were hoping you and some of the guys would attend."

"I'll have to run it by Dumfries. He's the captain now."

She stepped closer, lowering her lashes and gazing up at me the way girls did whenever they wanted something. Reaching for my t-shirt, she trailed her hand up my chest, smiling seductively. "I'll make it worth your while."

"I'm sure you will." I smirked because Fallon was a pretty girl, and I already knew she was good for it. Had discovered that little tidbit during freshman year at another one of the sorority's parties.

But she knew my rule. And I had no intention of breaking it. Not even for someone as hot as Fallon Bridger.

"Really?" She noticed my hesitation. "It's been almost a year." Her brow went up.

I tucked my free hand into my sweats and shrugged. "You know how it is, babe."

"Don't worry, Noah, it's not like I'm going to fall madly in love with you. We can fool around and have some fun without putting a label on it." Fallon batted her eyelashes, and I suppressed a groan.

It was too early for this shit. Not to mention, Aurora was probably watching from inside Joe's, judging me.

Without thinking, I glanced back, disappointment plunking in my chest when I realized she wasn't.

Damn, that girl was a tough nut to crack.

Except you don't want to crack her, asshole. She's Austin's sister. Not to mention your new housemate.

It had disaster written all over it.

But I'd never encountered a girl who had brushed me off so easily. Or at all, really. I was Noah fucking Holden. That meant something to ninety-nine percent of the female population at LU.

Although there was something about Aurora, something that had me all twisted up inside.

I didn't like it.

Anything that was a distraction—notably girls and relationships—was a big no-no for me.

"Sorry to disappoint you, babe." I turned on my charm.

"But it's not going to happen. I'll talk to Aiden about the party, though."

Some of the team were members of Sigma Delta Pi, and they had a long-standing partnership with Beta Pi.

"Do that." Her expression soured a little. "And if you change your mind about my offer, you know where to find me."

Of course, Aurora chose that moment to exit the coffee shop, coffee cup in hand.

"Friend of yours?" she asked.

"Who, Fallon? I wouldn't say friend." I shrugged, raking a hand through my hair as I watched them walk away.

"I see. It's like that."

"Like what?" I didn't like her tone, the knowing glint in her eye.

"Nothing, Noah." She let out a soft sigh and went to move around me, but I blocked her escape.

"No, come on, shortstack. If you've got something to say, say it."

"I'd really like it if you didn't call me that."

"And I'd really like it if you didn't judge me when you don't really know me," I shot back.

"Trust me. I know guys like you, Noah." Her gaze lingered, waiting for me to argue, but I was so fucking dumbstruck that I stood there gawking.

Aurora slipped past me and took off down the oak tree-lined street.

"Hold up there, shor—Hart," I yelled, taking off after her.

"Go away, Noah."

"Yeah, not going to happen." Falling into step beside her, she glanced up at me, frowning.

"You're very annoying."

"I want to know what you meant just now. That you know guys like me. What the fuck does that mean?"

"Look, I've heard the stories, okay?"

"The stories?" I frowned. "What the fuck—Ella and Dayna. They've been talking about me."

"Not just them. Your reputation as one of the Lakers' biggest players precedes you."

"I..."

I didn't really have a valid defense for that. Aurora was right. I liked sex. And I made sure never to sleep with the same girl twice. But I didn't like hearing the truth come out of *her* pouty mouth.

"If you can't deny it, Noah, it's usually the truth."

"So? I like sex." I shrugged. "That isn't a crime."

"I agree. You're entitled to as much dirty, hot, sweaty sex as you like. I'd just prefer not to know about it."

Fuck me. Hearing those words come from her mouth was downright sinful.

Aurora blushed, and I smirked. "Jealous, shortstack?"

I waited, anticipating the flicker of irritation in her eyes. But it didn't come. Instead, a sad kind of expression washed over her.

She inhaled a thin breath. "Do you know the first time someone called me that? I was eleven. My body was changing. I was already bigger than all my friends, and it was like overnight I woke up and grew two cup sizes. As if I needed any more excuses for guys to leer at me or boys in my class to tease me."

"What the hell are you talking about?" A strange sensation curdled in my gut.

"That nickname. Shortstack." She flinched as if it physically pained her. "It might be a harmless quip to you, but it means something else to me."

Fuck. Guilt slammed into me.

"Aurora, I didn't—"

"Look, Noah, I didn't tell you for sympathy or anything. I just really don't like remembering that time of my life, so I'd appreciate it if you could not call me that again. And you're right. I was judging you before with the girl. It was wrong of me, so I apologize. You're an adult. It has nothing to do with me what you do or don't do with your body."

My expression crinkled. I had questions, so many questions. Like, who the fuck had leered at her when she was just a kid or teased her for having boobs? But I was so stunned by her little outburst that I didn't have a clue what to say.

"I'm sorry," I said, feeling like the asshole I was. "I didn't know."

"Strange because I vividly remember repeatedly asking you not to call me that," she pointed out.

"Yeah. I know, but I thought... It doesn't matter." I rubbed my jaw, seriously regretting my decision to come to Joe's today. "I'm sorry. Me calling you shor... that word has no meaning for me besides the fact you are kind of short, and it sounded cute." I smiled weakly, feeling all kinds of awkward.

"Apology accepted. Now, can I leave?"

"Still so eager to get away from me, shorty?"

"No."

"Half-pint?" My mouth twitched.

"Absolutely not."

"Shortcake?"

A faint smile tugged at her mouth. "Please, God no."

"You sure about that? Because you're smiling."

"Am not."

"Oh, you definitely smiled, shortcake."

She wasn't smiling now, but I'd seen it.

"Noah."

"Aurora."

"You can call me Aurora or Rory." She sounded exasperated, but I kind of liked pushing her buttons. "Or Vivienne if you must."

"Vivienne?" I asked, intrigued.

"Vivienne Westwood. Mom's doing. Don't ask." A flash of disdain passed over her face.

"She was a model, right? I think Austin mentioned it once." But he didn't talk about her much.

Come to think of it, he didn't talk about any of his family much, including Aurora.

"Something like that," she murmured. "Unless you have any more burning questions, I really do need to go."

"I'm not stopping you." The conversation had been weird enough without prolonging it.

"In that case, I'll see you around, Noah." I watched her take off down the street like she couldn't get away quickly enough.

But I couldn't resist calling, "See you back at the house, shortcake."

Aurora scowled over her shoulder at me, almost tripping up the sidewalk as she crossed the street. For a second, I contemplated swooping in to check that she was okay. But something told me she wouldn't appreciate my attempt at chivalry.

And I wasn't sure I could take another dent to my ego.

CHAPTER 7

AURORA

GRUFF LAUGHTER GREETED me when I finally got back to the house. After yet another strange run-in with Noah, all I wanted was to retreat to my room and shut away the world.

But Connor and Austin had other ideas.

"Rory, get in here," my brother called.

"What's up?" I peered around the door, hoping it wouldn't take too long.

"Settle an argument for us," Connor said as if this was a regular occurrence. "Pineapple on pizza. Hot or not?"

"Not."

"Thank you." Austin slapped his hand down on the table. "This asshole is determined to get me to try his Hawaiian, but like I tell him. Every. Damn. Time. The only place pineapple belongs is decorating my piña colada at TPB's Happy Hour."

"Don't even get me started on the fact you drink that shit." I smothered a laugh, and Connor jabbed his finger in my direction. "See, even little Hart thinks her brother is a pussy for drinking that girly shit."

"Fuck off, both of you," Austin grumbled. "And you"—he pinned Connor with a hard look—"keep the pineapple off my pizza."

"Okay, if we're all done here, I'm going to head up to my room."

"You don't need to leave. You just got here. Stay. Hang." Austin smiled, pulling out a chair.

"Rain check?" I said.

Disappointment flashed in his eyes, but he quickly recovered. "Sure. We might head over to Lakers House later if you want to come? They're having a thing."

"A party thing?"

"It'll be nothing wild. Dumfries is in full captain mode," Connor said. "Ella and Dayna will be there. I think a couple of Ella's friends are going too. Maybe a few of the regular bunnies."

"Regular bunnies?" My brow lifted. "I didn't realize there were different categories."

"Oh yeah, there's a sliding scale."

"A sliding scale, wow."

"Yep." He leaned back in his chair and kicked his feet up, a playful grin plastered on his face.

I liked Connor. I liked how easy he made it. No pressure. No expectation. Just easy acceptance. He treated me like I'd always been here, and for that, I was grateful.

Unlike Noah, who—

Who I absolutely refused to think about.

"At the top of the scale, we have your Playboy Bunny. She's down to get dirty and doesn't require any maintenance."

"That is… disgusting," I murmured, not unsurprised. They were guys. Athletes.

Hockey players.

"But so much fun." Austin waggled his brows.

"You're a pig."

"Welcome to college, Sis." He winked.

"Next up is the Easter Bunny."

"Oh God, I have got to hear this…" I perched against the counter.

"I think you'll like this one, Rory." Connor smirked. "A total tease, too much work for little reward, and only comes once a year."

I choked on the breath I inhaled. "That is… wow."

"Good one, right?"

"Next is my personal favorite," Austin added with a shameless grin. "The Energizer Bunny. She can go alllll night long. Although Jessica Rabbit is also a firm favorite."

"Let me guess." I fought the urge to roll my eyes. "Seductive, sultry, and stacked."

"Bingo!" Connor clapped. "Then we have Bugs Bunny. Always chomping on"—he coughed into his hand, looking more than a little uncomfortable—"dick."

"Lovely." My lips pursed with disapproval.

"And at the bottom of the pile, we have the bunny boiler. The bunny that, at all costs, you want to avoid. Because if you cross a bunny boiler, you can bet your ass that you're headed for a whole heap of trouble."

"Don't forget the chubby bunny," Austin snorted.

I went still, a trickle of unease going through me. "I'm sorry, what?"

"The chubby bunny. You know, the girl who—"

"Yes"—my lips pressed into a thin line—"I think I get it.

Well, this has been enlightening and all, but now I'm going to go and clean my ears out and pretend I didn't just learn that my brother and his friends are a bunch of misogynistic a-holes."

"Oh, come on, Rory. Like girls don't do exactly the same to guys. We judge. It's human nature." Austin shrugged. "It doesn't mean anything, not really. It's just silly locker room talk."

It didn't mean anything to them, no. But what about the girl who got called the bunny boiler because, God forbid, she actually went and fell for a guy and then got upset when she realized he didn't feel the same. Or the chubby bunny when she realized the guy wasn't really interested in her but was using her as the brunt of a college guy prank.

God, men could be so denigrating and judgmental.

Austin had a point though; women weren't an innocent party either. But most girls didn't sit around making up labels and sliding scales to rate guys. Yes, we were all guilty of judging members of the opposite sex, each other, but men had such a gross way of going about it sometimes.

"I guess that makes it okay, then," I murmured, walking out of there without so much as a backward glance. Austin called after me, but I needed to be alone.

It had been a weird day between getting lost on campus, running into Noah and his little fan club, and listening to Connor and Austin's breakdown of the bunnies of Lakeshore U.

At least they would all be out at the party tonight, and I could have the house to myself.

I played my music loudly enough to ignore Austin's attempts at apologizing. He didn't get it; I knew that. Because he never had. Not in all the years he'd lived with Mom and me.

It wasn't like I'd tried to explain it, though. But things between us were different now. We grew up, and we grew apart—moved in different directions. His direction literally took him three-hundred miles away from me without so much as a backward glance.

Part of me got why he had to leave. To chase his own dreams instead of living in the shadow of our mother's. But part of me would never forgive him for leaving me there with her.

The guys left to go to Lakers House about an hour ago. Noah was with them. I heard him joking around with Connor, probably discussing his latest session with an Energizer Bunny or Jessica Rabbit.

The thought alone had me glancing up, looking at myself in the dresser mirror. I looked nothing like the girls he was with earlier. The ringleader, Fallon, I think I heard him call her, was a younger-looking version of Margot Robbie. Long wavy blonde hair, big bright smile, defined cheekbones, and perfect eyebrows. It was hardly any surprise Noah had been with her.

He had a type. Tall, blonde, and slim with curves in all the right places. So beautiful you had to wonder whether it was good genes or something else entirely. After hanging out with Ella and Dayna, I was beginning to wonder if being pretty and in good shape was a prerequisite for getting accepted into Lakeshore U.

If it was, I was screwed.

My cell phone blared away, pulling me from my thoughts. I groaned quietly at the word *Mom* flashing on the screen. "Hey," I said.

"Aurora, sweetheart. Thank God. I've been worried."

Really? I wanted to ask but swallowed the words.

Susannah Hart didn't worry about anyone but herself and her waistline.

"I've been busy settling in, Mom," I said.

"Yes, how is Lakeshore? Although, I supposed I'd know if your brother ever picked up the phone."

I suppressed a sigh. "You know Austin is busy with the team."

"You should never be too busy for family, Aurora."

That was the joke of the century coming from her.

"Did you need something, Mom? Because I have a ton of unpacking to do still." The lie rolled off my tongue with ease, despite the guilt slithering around inside me.

It was strange, really, to hate a person and yet still crave their approval. But I guess that's what years of childhood trauma did to a person. It messed with their internal sense of worth. The lens with which they viewed the world and themselves.

"I just wanted to check in and see how you're doing?"

"I'm fine. Everyone has been very welcoming."

"Good, sweetheart. That's good. Did you see my latest shoot? The photos made it to their national campaign. Can you believe it? After all this time, I'm on a double spread feature again."

Of course, that's why she had really called, to preen

about her new campaign. Not because she cared or had any interest in my life. It was all about her.

It always had been, and it always would be.

"No, I didn't see it yet, Mom."

She tsked. "You can check it out online, sweetheart. I'd love to hear what you think. You never know; you might feel inspired." She chuckled, but the sound only made something inside me wither and die. "They had some plus-size models on the shoot. A little smaller than you but so pretty. It's amazing what a little airbrushing can do here and there, and you know, Aurora, I think if we gave you a makeover and put you on a juice diet for a few weeks, you could—"

"Mom, we've been over this." And over it and over it. "I'm not doing that again."

"I know, I know, sweetheart." Disappointment lingered in her voice, and I hated that it still affected me. I hated that, even now, I let her words sink into me and take hold. "But you're at college now. Before you know it, you'll have gained the freshman fifteen, and there will be no undoing that damage." She scoffed as if the idea of gaining weight was utterly unacceptable.

Damage.

The word rattled through me like jagged shards of glass. Cutting me open and making old wounds bleed.

She had no idea how much her words hurt sometimes, how deep the scars ran. Even when I'd tried to tell her— and I'd tried a lot over the years—she didn't realize.

Or just didn't care.

Because to Susannah Hart, how you looked on the outside was *all* that mattered.

"I said no, Mom." I forced the words out, hating how,

even now, after all the therapy, they still sounded so unfamiliar and wrong on my lips.

She let out a disappointed sigh. "It was only a suggestion, Aurora. You don't need to take that tone with me."

But I did.

Time and time again, I had to set healthy boundaries between my mother and me. It was exhausting—she was exhausting. But, unlike Austin, I'd never been able to truly cut her off. Because, unlike him, part of me understood her. And because unlike him, the emotional damage I'd suffered at her hands had changed me.

"I'll never model again. You know that. So please don't bring it up again."

"Fine." She tsked. "Well, I suppose I'd better leave you to your unpacking. Call me soon."

"Sure, Mom. Bye."

She hung up. Just like that. But it was nothing I wasn't used to. When a conversation didn't go her way, she shut down. It was years of living in her mother's shadow, always trying to be perfect. To please Grandma Iris. To be seen and not heard.

It was a heavy burden to shoulder.

I knew.

I was her daughter, after all.

But today's brief conversation—if you could even call it that—was a painful reminder that I would never amount to more than a disappointment in her eyes.

I would never be pretty enough. Thin enough. *Worthy* enough.

Tears pricked the corners of my eyes as memories slammed into me, one after the other. Mom dragging me to get another photoshoot determined to mold me into her protégé. *Stand taller. Suck in your stomach. Angle your shoulder down.* Over and over, I was told to be something I wasn't until I looked in the mirror and no longer saw myself anymore.

That kind of damage stayed with you. Lived inside you. Festered and spread like a poison until it was impossible to see anything except the imperfect, flawed person they made you out to be.

"Dammit." I slammed my hand down on the desk, annoyed that she still had this kind of effect on me.

I'd spent years in therapy trying to undo all the hurt and pain she'd caused. I sat opposite numerous therapists and doctors, trying to learn how to love myself again. How to accept myself.

I still wasn't there—especially not after the setback I'd had in senior year—but I wasn't the little girl I was back then either.

They're only words. They mean nothing.

But they didn't mean nothing. No matter how much I tried to ignore them, the truth was words hurt. And the more you heard them, the more they stuck.

The more they scratched themselves on your soul—the very fiber of your being.

Until they were an intrinsic part of you.

I awoke to muffled moans. A bed creaking. Skin slapping.

Somebody was home, and they were having sex, rather loud, boisterous sex if the noises were any indicator.

Sliding my hands under my pillow, I pushed it around

my ears, trying to block out the sounds. It wasn't Connor and Ella. I'd had the misfortune of overhearing them the other night, and the moans were all wrong. And Austin had promised me he didn't bring girls back to the house, which only left Noah.

My heart sank.

After everything he'd said earlier, acting so offended that I'd had the gall to judge him when I knew so little about him. And I'd fallen for it. For a second, I'd felt guilty for chastising him when he was right—I didn't know him or his story.

Yet, here he was, fucking some puck bunny into the stratosphere if her muffled, breathy cries were any sign.

I couldn't help but wonder what kind of bunny she was. Energizer Bunny or a Jessica Rabbit, most likely. I'd caught Noah looking at my boobs more than once. He seemed like the kind of guy who would be a boob guy.

Ugh.

Irritation rippled through me. I didn't want to be thinking about their stupid bunny scale. It was a disgusting display of misogyny upholding the stereotype that college guys were nothing more than shallow, sex-obsessed dumb-asses who thought more with their dicks than their brains. That the girls who lusted after them were nothing more than sexual objects put on the earth purely for their enter-tainment.

Part of me had a good mind to go down there and applaud him for proving himself every bit the player I'd heard he was. But I didn't want to embarrass myself or the girl he was currently *entertaining*.

So I lay there, trying my best not to listen. While one

hundred and ten percent absolutely not wondering what it must be like to be one of them.

The pretty popular girls.

The cheerleaders and the puck bunnies.

The girls who always got the guy.

I thought I'd been that girl once. That my luck was finally changing. That for the first time in my life, a guy saw past my body hang-ups, my imperfections and my flaws and only saw me. But it was all a lie. He'd only been settling until something better came along.

He'd been my forever boy, and I'd been his good-enough-for-now girl.

And the kicker was, I always knew.

Deep down, I knew I wasn't good enough for him. I'd wanted so much to believe it, though.

I'd wanted it to be real.

I'd wanted—

"Fuck, Fallon, yes. Yes, baby."

Oh. My. God.

Noah was with her—the girl from earlier.

I don't know what disappointed me more. That Noah was exactly like I'd assumed him to be.

Or that I even cared.

CHAPTER 8

NOAH

"Yes, yes... fuck, yes."

"That's how you do it, baby!" I leaned over and high-fived Mase while Leon and Ward cried into their controllers.

"There's no way you just pulled that off," Leon complained. "We were five points ahead."

"The scoreboard says otherwise." I grinned, flipping him off.

I'd been hanging at Lakers House all day. Connor had taken Ella to the beach, and Austin had a thing, and I didn't want to be home alone with Aurora. Not after the other day outside Joe's.

We'd been avoiding each other—or more so, she was avoiding me, which suited me fine. Aurora Hart got under my skin in a way most girls didn't. And I didn't like it.

Sure about that, Holden?

I silenced the little voice of doubt. The only thing I

needed to remember was that she was Austin's sister. She couldn't be more off-limits if she tried. Besides, she took serious issue with hockey players and their sexual habits. I'd heard her and Austin arguing over the guys' puck bunny scale. Schooling him on what a bunch of misogynistic horseshit it was.

It didn't surprise me Connor had told her. He couldn't keep his mouth shut about anything since he convinced Ella to give him a second chance. It was probably all part of her plan to overhaul the team's approach to women, sex, and dating.

"How are things at casa de la Hart?" Ward asked. "You fucked the sister yet?"

"The fuck, asshole? Why the fuck would you say that?" I pinned him with a dark look.

"Holden's right, Cutler. Don't let Austin hear you talk about Aurora like that, or he'll kick your ass."

"He could try," he snorted.

Little fucker needed his ego and attitude brought down a peg or two. And if he talked shit about Aurora again, I had no problem being the one to do it.

"Rule number one: never hit on a player's sister or mom. It's the oldest rule in the book."

"Seems kind of stupid if you ask me." He shrugged, grabbed his controller, and set up another game.

Mase glanced at me and frowned. "You good?" he mouthed.

I nodded, shoving the hair out of my eyes. It had grown longer over the summer, and instead of having it all cut, I'd opted to keep it longer on the top.

"Who was the hottie at the party last night?" Leon changed the subject. "Holden looked all up in her business." His laugh grated on me.

Jesus, was I this annoying when I was a freshman? Like an excited little puppy?

"Fallon?" I asked. She and some of the Beta Pi girls had shown up at the house after Aiden had declined their invite to the Pledge Party.

"Blonde. Big tits. Tiny waist. Looked like she'd be down for a good time."

Mase shook his head, and I smirked. "Fallon would eat you alive, Banks."

"I'd show her a good time."

"Have at it," I said. Because fuck knows, I wouldn't be going there again.

My cell phone started vibrating, and I dug in my pocket to get it, groaning when I spotted the name.

"Noah?" Sam's breathless voice filled the line.

"Yeah?"

"C-can you come over? I think someone tried to break into my apartment."

"The fuck?" I sat up. "Have you called the police?"

"Not yet. I kind of panicked and called you."

"Okay, stay there. I'm coming straight over."

"Thank you. I didn't know who else to call."

"Stay put. I'll be as quick as I can."

"Problem?" Mase asked the second I hung up.

"Sam thinks someone tried to get into her apartment. I'm going over there to check it out."

"Shit, you want some backup?"

"Nah, I can handle it."

"Okay, keep me updated. She needs to report it to campus security."

I nodded, grabbing my keys. "I'll catch you, assholes,

later."

Leon and Ward both lifted their hands in a silent good-bye, too engrossed in their game.

With a little shake of my head, I left Lakers House and headed to Sam's place.

"Sam? It's me," I called, slipping into her apartment.

"Noah, thank God." She ran into my arms, trembling as she wrapped herself around me like a koala. "I was so scared."

"Come on, let's sit, and you can tell me what happened?"

We got comfortable on her couch, and I waited.

"I got home from my shift at the bar, and the front door was ajar. I thought maybe I'd left it unlocked or something, but when I came inside, I got this feeling... I checked the whole apartment, and the only thing missing was my favorite scarf. You know the one you got me for my birthday? The black one with the daisies on it."

My brows pinched. "You think someone broke into your place and stole a scarf?"

"I'm just telling you what I found. What if it was some creep who's seen me at the bar and followed me home?"

"Like a stalker?"

"Noah, this is serious." She inhaled a shuddering breath. "Someone was in my apartment."

"You're right, sorry." I pulled out my cell phone.

"What are you doing?"

"Calling the police."

"I already called campus security. They're going to review the security footage and send someone to get a statement. They'll decide if we need to report it to the police. God, I'm just so relieved you're here, Noah."

She burrowed into my side, sliding her arm over my stomach. Shit. This felt all kinds of uncomfortable. But what could I do? Sam didn't have many friends, and she'd escaped a shitty life too.

It's one of the reasons we hit it off. We'd bonded one night over drinks and stories from our miserable childhoods. It was an alcoholic father with a mean temper for her. Timothy Holden wasn't a drunk, but he did have a mean temper and a clear-cut view of how my life should go.

"You sure we shouldn't call the police? What if he comes back?" I asked, unease sliding down my spine. I wasn't interested in starting something with Sam, but she was the closest thing I had to a female friend.

"Campus security will handle it. I'm okay, Noah." She smiled up at me. "I promise. I just freaked out for a second."

"I know things have been weird between us lately," I said. "But I'll always have your back, Sam, you know that."

"I know. And I'm sorry for making things weird. You've always been upfront about where we stand. I shouldn't have cornered you like that. Forgive me?"

"There's nothing to forgive."

She nodded. "Will you stay a little? We could watch a movie? And I think I have a pizza in the refrigerator."

"Sure, whatever you need."

"Great." Sam leaped up and threw me the remote. "You pick a movie. I'll sort the pizza."

"Uh, sure."

I watched her go, unable to shake the feeling that I was missing something.

"Where the fuck have you been?" Connor asked when I finally got home.

It was past eleven. But Sam had freaked out when I'd tried to leave. So, I stayed. I'd waited until she'd fallen asleep, and then locked up behind me and slid her key under the door.

"Don't ask."

"Mase said something about a break-in over at Sam's place. She good?"

"Yeah. She thinks someone broke in and stole her favorite scarf."

"That doesn't sound like your typical break-in. It sounds like some crazy stalker-level shit."

"Yeah, it seemed... off."

"How do you mean?"

"I don't know." I ran a hand over my face. "It's been a long day, and I'm dog-tired. I'm not thinking straight."

"You think she set you up?"

"Asshole, right?"

"I'd say if you got a gut feeling, then it's worth listening to."

"Nah, I'm probably overreacting." I pulled out a chair and sat. "She wouldn't make something up like that."

"Yeah, it's a stretch. And she seemed pretty shaken up, right?"

"Yeah."

"You know she'll want you to be her knight-in-shining-armor now." His mouth kicked up, clearly amused by the whole thing.

"That's what I'm worried about," I murmured.

"Just stick to your guns, and don't let her little scared girl routine dent all that armor you wear."

"Fuck off, Morgan. I don't—"

He silenced me with a single look. One that radiated, 'I know all your dirty little secrets.'

He didn't.

He couldn't.

Because I'd barely spoken two words about my family since moving to Lakeshore. I wasn't looking for sympathy or pity. Everyone had shit in their past, baggage that they dragged around with them. I just chose to ignore mine.

"Who else is home?" I asked.

"Austin's out. Caught him sneaking out earlier for a little nighttime exercise, if you catch my drift. And little Hart is up in her room reading." He watched me intently as he talked about her.

"What?" I snapped.

"Nothing, bro. Nothing at all." A faint smirk traced his lips as he got up and clapped me on the back. "I'm calling it a night. See you tomorrow."

"Night."

Connor left, and I sat there, a hundred and one thoughts rolling around my head. It was always like this when I didn't have the pressure of the season hanging over my head—the intensity of back-to-back games and non-stop practice.

I'd never been good at standing still or taking time for

myself. When things were quiet, my demons roared the loudest. So I didn't give them space to surface.

But I could always feel them, circling, pushing against my defenses.

I shoved the dark thoughts away. I wasn't in Buffalo anymore with him. I was free. And I had my whole life ahead of me. One that included a shit ton of hockey and silverware if things went to plan.

Getting up, I helped myself to a glass of water, wishing it was something stronger. I rinsed the glass and added it to the drainer before hitting the light and heading upstairs. But as I hit the top step, a bare leg bit the bottom step of the stairs leading to the third floor.

"It's you," I said, parroting Aurora's words from the other day.

"I do live here too, you know."

"Oh, I know, shortcake. But I think you've been avoiding me."

"I'm not avoiding anyone." She lifted her chin a little. "You're barely even here."

My blood heated at the glint of defiance in her eyes. Aurora Hart was a feisty little thing when she wanted to be, but the fire in her eyes didn't completely diminish the shadows there.

I had to fight the urge to ask her what was wrong, to find out what—or *who*—had upset her. But I bit my tongue. We weren't friends. And despite my best efforts to get to know her a little, Aurora continued to reject my olive branches at every turn.

"Wait until classes start next week," I said. "Things really get crazy then."

"I'm sure they do." She pursed her lips, that flicker of judgment there again.

"Have I done something to upset you?" I blurted out like a fucking idiot.

Smooth, Holden. Real fucking smooth.

What was it about this girl that knocked me off my game? I barely knew her, and she turned me into a bumbling, stuttering idiot.

"Nope," she deadpanned. "Anyway, this has been fun and all, but I'm sure you have better things to do than hanging out on the stairs with me. Night, Noah." Aurora gave me a weak smile and slipped around me to go downstairs.

Huh.

It was like she couldn't get away fast enough.

As I headed for my room, I ran a hand down my face. Girls were hard fucking work. If you tried to do the right thing, they avoided you. And if you did the wrong thing, they hated you.

A guy couldn't win.

It wasn't worth the headache.

The sooner Aurora moved out into her own place, the better because she was a serious distraction.

One I didn't need.

Or want.

The next morning, I woke to the sound of raised voices. For a second, I was a little kid, back in Buffalo, listening to my mom and dad go at it. He'd call her an ungrateful whore, and she'd throw something at his head. It went on like that for years. Until she finally snapped and left.

Only, she didn't take me with her. She left me there with him.

I hated her for it.

And he hated us both.

Climbing out of bed, I ran a hand through my hair, then scratched my junk before pulling on sweatpants to see what all the commotion was about.

"If you're so interested in her life all of a sudden, why don't you call her?" Aurora yelled.

"I'm just saying she called me three times. Out of the blue. That isn't standard behavior."

"Of course, it isn't," she snapped. "You left, Austin. You left, and I was stuck there with her. And now I'm gone too, and she's alone and doesn't know how to..." Her voice trailed off to an inaudible muffle.

"What's going on?" Connor poked his head out of his room. "I heard shouting."

"Austin and Rory are fighting."

"Should we go down there?"

"Don't ask me. How the fuck should I know."

"Well, do they sound like they're about to get physical?"

"There's been no crashing, smashing, or cracking, so I think we're safe."

He nodded. "In that case, I'm going back to bed. I stayed up way too late sexting Ella."

"Seriously?" I glared at him.

"What?" He shrugged. "You could be up all night sexting your girl if you bothered to keep one around long enough."

"Asshole." I flipped him off right as he closed the door in my face.

The shouting had stopped, so I took my chances and headed downstairs.

"Morning." I breezed into the kitchen, stopping dead in my tracks at the sight of Aurora crying.

She glanced up and sniffled, frantically trying to dry her eyes with the back of her hands. "Sorry, we didn't wake you, did we?"

"What happened, and how hard do I need to kick Austin's ass?"

She laughed weakly, but it was a laugh, and I felt fucking ten feet fall that I'd made it happen.

"It was just a silly argument. I'll be fine." She turned away from me, inhaling a shuddering breath.

"Shortcake," I said, going to her. "You don't have to hide from me. We're roomies, remember. Roomies tell each other things."

"I swear to God, Noah. If you ask me to have a naked pillow fight with you, I'm packing my bag and leaving." She glanced back, flashing me a weary smile.

"There she is," I said, falling into her big green eyes.

"Noah?"

Aurora turned, and I was so aware of her proximity, so fucking stunned by how beautiful *and* sad she looked all at that same time, that I couldn't breathe. The pain in her expression knocked the air clean from my lungs, and at that moment, all I wanted to do was fix it.

"Yeah, shortcake?"

"You're looking at me weird."

"I... uh, I'm tired," I stuttered out. "I'm really fucking tired."

"Right." Her mouth twitched. "Do you want breakfast? I was about to make Austin pancakes before he took off like a coward."

"Asshole." I smirked, forcing myself to move away from her and to one of the stools at the breakfast counter. "Do you want to talk about it?" I asked.

"Oh, it's just boring family stuff." She didn't meet my eyes, and that told me all I needed to know.

"Aurora, look at me." Slowly, she lifted her gaze to mine and graced me with another weak smile. But I still couldn't get over how beautiful she looked. How raw and vulnerable and real.

"I know we're mortal enemies," I said, "but you can talk to me. I know a thing or two about boring family stuff."

Sucking in her bottom lip between her teeth, she contemplated my words. My offer.

Maybe I was a fool to keep putting myself out there when it was obvious she'd already made up her mind about me.

But there was something about Aurora Hart that made me want to keep trying.

CHAPTER 9

AURORA

Noah watched me intently.

I didn't like it. The way he saw past my defenses.

I couldn't tell him about the argument. He was Austin's friend, not mine. And yet, I found myself wanting to spill the tea.

"You know, my offer will expire eventually." He smiled, and that one simple gesture broke right through my defenses.

I was weak when it came to this guy.

"What has Austin told you about our mom?"

"Not much. He doesn't really talk about his family all that much."

My heart sank.

But I couldn't resent Austin too much because neither did I.

"Our mom can be... a lot. She's always had a lot of opinions on how we should live our lives. It's why Austin left and never looked back." I plated up the pancakes and slid a stack toward him with a bottle of syrup.

"Thanks," he said. "These look great."

"I'm not sure they're Coach Tucker approved, but if you don't tell, I won't."

"Aren't you having any?"

"Oh no, I already had some fruit."

"Don't tell me you're one of those girls who doesn't eat sugar or carbs before lunchtime?"

"Do I look like the kind of girl who doesn't eat sugar and carbs?" I rolled my eyes.

"What do you mean?" His brows crinkled as he studied me.

"It's okay, Noah. You don't have to do that." The words tumbled out because self-deprecation was my armor. "I know what I am."

"You lost me there, shortcake. What are you talking about?"

"I think the term you and your friends would use is chubby bunny." I flinched.

"What the fuck?" Anger flared in his eyes. "No one would ever call you that, Aurora."

"You're just saying that because I'm Austin's sister."

"Actually, I probably shouldn't say that *because* you're his sister."

"What—"

"You know, I think if you gave me a chance, you and I could be great friends."

I rolled my eyes, disguising the sinking disappointment I felt.

Friends.

Was I destined for a life on the sidelines?

Ben had chosen me over my best friend. At least, that's what I'd always believed. He'd been so good at it, making me feel special. But it was all a lie. He hadn't chosen me; he'd pitied me. Just like every photographer my mom had dragged me to and shoved me in front of, between the ages of five and twelve. They didn't humor her because they saw something in me and wanted to help unleash my inner fashion model; they humored her because they felt sorry for me. And because, more often than that, she didn't give them a choice.

"I don't need your charity, Noah," I said quietly, keeping myself distracted with the dishes.

"Whoever hurt you did a good job. I can see that." He hesitated, the tension pulling taut between us. "But I'm determined to crack your resolve, shortcake."

Noah's words made my stomach flutter.

I hated the nickname shortstack and the painful memories it conjured, but there was something endearing about shortcake.

Until I remembered his track record with women, the glaring fact he was one of Austin's best friends *and* his teammate. Noah Holden was lots of things, and maybe I'd underestimated the right-winger from Buffalo, but it didn't change the fact he was so completely and utterly out of my league.

Still, it didn't stop a little part of me from imagining what it must be like to be the center of his attention.

The heart was a fickle thing. She knew what it felt like to be broken and betrayed; she still felt the pain of it all these months later. But she still let herself fall into the fantasy. The one where the guy picked me, where I found my prince.

Or maybe it was the hopeless romantic in me. The girl who spent most of her teen years lost in fantasy, reading about wealthy dukes and fae princes, and the popular athletes who all chose love in the end.

It was already happening. Every time Noah tried to wear me down, I felt the fantasy dig in and take root. He made it so easy.

It was dangerous to spend time with him because the truth was, I liked him. I did. He infuriated me, sure. But he also made me smile and laugh, and, despite the warning bells whenever I was around him, I looked forward to my next interaction with him.

"Aurora?" he said with hesitation.

I turned slowly and smiled at him. No way was I about to fess up about Ben and what happened. But I did manage, "You know, Noah Holden, maybe I should give you a chance."

"Damn right, you should." He grinned, sending my heart into overdrive. "I'll be the best friend you ever had."

There was that pesky word again.

Friend.

"I think—"

The back door opened, and Austin dragged himself inside, damp hair plastered to his head, sweat glistening on his skin.

"Hey," he said sheepishly, glancing between the two of us. "What's going on?"

"Aurora agreed to give me a shot at proving I'm not the asshole she thinks I am."

He snorted. "Good luck with that." Austin grabbed a bottle of water from the refrigerator and leaned against the counter. "Sorry about earlier."

I nodded, not daring myself to speak. When I looked away, Noah caught my eye and smiled reassuringly.

"Heard from Sam?" Austin asked, and it was my turn to frown.

"Why would I hear from—oh, you're not talking to me."

I slid my eyes to Noah in question, and a guarded expression fell over his face. "My friend Sam had her apartment broken into."

His friend Sam. Something told me she was a different kind of friend than the one I'd ever be.

"Noah here ran over there like Superman to console her."

"It wasn't even like that." He cupped the back of his neck, looking all kinds of awkward. "She was scared and—"

"Wanted you to make it all better." Austin laughed, oblivious to the tension zipping between his best friend and me. "I bet you calmed her down real good."

Noah hissed, "Asshole," under his breath, flashing me an apologetic smile.

But he didn't owe me anything.

He could be friends with whoever he wanted.

It didn't stop the stab of jealousy I felt though. Was this Noah's real MO? To collect female friends that he had no interest in dating. Like his very own platonic harem. Maybe he had a savior complex and wanted to fix the world, one damsel in distress at a time.

Whatever it was, I wanted no part of it.

Because my broken, fragile heart wouldn't survive it.

"Hello, it's Aurora Hart again. If somebody could get back to me about the apartment, that would be great. My number is on file." I hung up and let out a weary sigh.

The student housing office was supposed to be open seven days a week, but I'd already called twice and gotten their voicemail both times.

Living with my brother and his friends was proving to be more difficult than I expected. Scrap that. Living with Noah was proving to be more difficult than I thought. Connor and Austin weren't around enough to get in my way. But Noah was making a bad habit of it.

On Friday, I plucked up the courage to walk the short distance to Lakeshore U campus and find the library.

It was a gorgeous federal-style building with a dome and elliptical fanlight windows above the main doors. It reminded me of a smaller version of the US Capitol Building.

I scanned my student card to gain access and slipped inside. They operated an automated checkout system during off hours, but I was only here to browse.

Growing up, books had been like a friend to me, letting me escape between the pages of a young adult fantasy or a larger-than-life romance. Reading gave me great comfort. It let me put my life on hold and step into someone else's shoes for a little while.

We all needed that sometimes.

A break from reality. From responsibility and burden and heartache.

I bypassed the non-fiction sections and made my way to the fiction section. It was tucked right at the far end of the room, but I didn't let that bother me.

Scanning the shelves, I chose a popular fantasy novel and found a seat. The library was practically empty, but I'd gotten used to being alone. My own company didn't bother me.

But no sooner had I read the first page, did my cell phone start vibrating. I dug it out of my purse, frowning at the group chat I'd been added to.

Austin: House meeting has commenced.

Unknown 1: Can you really call it a meeting if we're texting?

Unknown 1: Did you add Aurora? She should be here for this.

Austin: I added her. Aurora, you there?

I stared at the screen, wondering what the hell I was about to be pulled into.

Aurora: I'm here. I don't understand what's happening though.

Unknown 1: No one ever does. Holden, you there?

I realized that 'Unknown 1' was Connor and saved his number.

> Unknown 2: I'm here.

That was Noah then.

> Connor: Any idea what Austin wants? Because I'm kind of in the middle of something.

> Noah: You mean you're IN something.

> Austin: Correction. Someone!!!

> Aurora: Has anyone ever told you how disgusting you all are?

> Connor: Just spreading the love, little Hart. Ella says hi.

> Aurora: Hi Ella—your boyfriend is disgusting.

> Connor: She says welcome to her world. She wants to know if you want to go for drinks one night?

Aurora: Yeah. Maybe. Now was there a point to this group chat, or can I get back to my book?

Connor: You're reading?

Aurora: I came to check out the library. You know, the building that houses all the books.

Connor: Funny.

Aurora: I thought so.

I smiled to myself. These guys were something else. I couldn't help but notice Noah's lack of participation, though.

Austin: Okay, okay. I didn't add you all to shoot the shit. We need to figure out our costume for the Lakers' annual orientation party.

Connor: Hell yes!!!

Aurora: I don't understand…

Unless he'd added me by mistake.

Austin: Every year the Lakers host a big welcome back party. It's always a costume party and everyone goes ALL OUT. We need to pick our theme.

Aurora: I know what a costume party is Austin, I just don't understand why you're including me in this.

Connor: Rules are rules, little Hart.

Aurora: I'm not sure I want to go to a party at Lakers House.

Connor: What, why not? Ella will be there. Dayna too. You have to come. It's the rules, baby!

Aurora: Please, stop saying that.

My mouth twitched. I liked Connor a lot.

Austin: Holden, you there? You're awfully quiet.

Noah: Connor talks enough for both of us.

Connor: Asshole!

Aurora: I'm going to bow out of this conversation now.

Connor: What, you can't! We need you if
we're going to win.

Aurora: I don't really do costume parties.

With the hockey team at their house and what I could only imagine would be a flock of scantily-clad puck bunnies.

Austin: First time for everything, sis.

Noah: You know they're right, shortcake.

Austin: Shortcake? Something you want to tell me Holden?

My heart fluttered. Had he really just said that? In the thread with my brother?

Another message came up, but it wasn't in the group chat.

Noah: Shit, I'm sorry.

Aurora: I don't think it's me you have to apologize to.

Noah: Do you think he knows?

Aurora: Knows what? That you call me shortcake? I think you might have given it away.

Noah: Haha! You'll come though, right, to the party? It'll be fun.

Aurora: It doesn't sound like my idea of fun.

The group chat flashed up.

Austin: Holden?

Noah: Jealous I don't have a nickname for you? Because we can rectify that.

Austin: Fuck, no! Anyway, back to the point. We need a theme.

Connor: Teenage Mutant Ninja Turtles. We can be the turtles, Aurora can be April.

Aurora: No, she can't.

There was no way in hell I would be caught dead in a bright yellow jumpsuit.

Connor: Hush, woman. We have a
costume cup to win.

> Aurora: Now I know you're making this shit
> up. There is no such thing as the Lakers'
> Costume Cup.

Austin: There is. Winner gets $200 and
bragging rights. Last year, Linc won. He
dressed up as Dorothy from Wizard of Oz.

Connor: Pfft. We all know the only reason
he won was because he stole his
grandma's dog and carried it around in a
basket all night.

My eyes almost bugged.

> Aurora: I hope you're joking

Noah's name flashed up in our separate chat. The whole
thing was giving me whiplash.

Noah: He's not. He had the dress and red
slippers and everything.

> Aurora: I don't even know what to say to
> that.

I smiled. I'm pretty sure there was a rule about texting your brother's best friend whilst texting your brother as part of a group chat they were both in, but it was harmless. He was just being friendly.

I switched to the group chat.

> Aurora: You don't need to include me, I'm not sure I'm coming to the party anyway.

> Connor: Little Hart!!!

> Austin: You've got to come. What about Scooby Doo, Shaggy, Fred, and Velma.

Because, of course, I would be Velma in this situation. My brows pinched with annoyance.

> Aurora: No.

> Connor: I've got it. We can be Goldilocks and the three bears.

> Aurora: I'm muting this chat. Goodbye.

But it was Noah's private message that made my heart flutter.

> Noah: You're coming, shortcake. I won't take no for an answer.

When I finally got back to the house, my costume party nightmare had come true because hanging on the door were four garment bags with suspicious furry contents.

"You're here." Connor grinned. "Did you have a good day, little Hart?"

"You know, you can stop calling me that." I leveled him with a stern look.

"And why would I do that?"

My expression melted. Connor was like a big goofy puppy I just couldn't resist.

"Aus, Holden, get in here. Rory's home."

Home.

The word clanged through me.

This wasn't my home, but by God, it felt good to hear him say those words. To know that he'd accepted my presence without question.

I'd needed that.

More than I ever could have imagined.

"Thank you," I whispered, and Connor stared at me with confusion.

"Umm, okay."

I chuckled. "You're a good guy, Con."

"I like to think so." He winked and bellowed for Austin and Noah again. They came bounding into the kitchen, grinning when they saw me.

"We got lucky. Fantasy and Sparkles had what we needed."

"There had better not be four costumes in there," I said.

"Rory, baby," Connor came over to me and slung his arm around my shoulder. It was oddly comforting.

Austin frowned, his eyes lingering on where Connor touched me, and a sad, wistful moment passed between us.

We still had a lot to talk about. But we'd tried that the other morning, and it had ended with Austin walking out on me. So I wasn't in any hurry to do it again anytime soon.

I knew he harbored a lot of guilt at what went down. But guilt didn't change anything, and it didn't *fix* things. Eventually, we'd need to air all the tension between us.

"Here," Noah said, thrusting a bag at me. "We got you something."

"Do I even want to know?" My brow lifted, and a faint smirk traced his mouth.

God, his smile was dangerous, luring me in and making my insides turn to mush.

Opening the bag, I stuck my hand inside and pulled out the packet. "What is—"

"I've heard blondes have more fun," he chuckled, the smooth sound rolling through me like a warm breeze.

Bad. This was really, really bad.

Connor squeezed my shoulder. "May the odds be ever in our favor, Goldilocks."

"I'm not sure—"

"Like I already told you," Noah added, holding my gaze, drawing me in, and making me wish for things that would never come true.

"You're coming, shortcake," he said with a secretive smile. "We won't take no for an answer."

CHAPTER 10

NOAH

"You're not dressed," I said when Aurora entered the kitchen later that night.

"Because I'm not going." She barely made eye contact as she moved around me to get to the refrigerator. But I stepped back, cutting her off.

"Whoa, whoa, what do you mean, you're not coming? We need you."

"No, you don't," she said.

"Yes. We do. If you don't come, we're just the three bears and that's fucking lame."

"I'm sure you'll survive. Or you could ask Fallon or Sam to stand in for you. They wouldn't even need to wear the wig."

Tension bracketed my mouth because, what the fuck?

"Where did that come from?"

"Nowhere." She shrugged, managing to give me the slip this time. "It was just a suggestion."

"Austin and Connor are going to be pissed if you don't come, shortcake. Con has been talking about our costumes all week."

"I told you all I wasn't coming."

"And I distinctly remember telling you we weren't taking no for an answer." I stepped up to her and her breath caught, the sexiest little sound coming from her throat.

Shit.

I needed to abort.

I needed to back the fuck up and put some safe distance between us.

But Aurora got under my skin like no other girl ever had.

It was disconcerting, to say the least. But also kind of hot.

Scrap that. It was fucking hot, and all week I'd found myself craving these moments. Her smiles and snark. The way she let out a small, exasperated sigh whenever I pushed her buttons.

"Noah," she breathed.

"What, shortcake?" Electricity zapped between us.

"You shouldn't be—"

"What's up, lovers?" Connor breezed into the room, and my head shot up. But he drew up short when he saw Aurora and me. "What did I miss?" His brow lifted with accusation.

"Nothing, man. I was just helping Rory reach for something."

"Right." He rubbed his jaw. "Rory, baby, why aren't you dressed?"

I backed up, putting some distance between us, and

Aurora turned to meet Connor's gaze. Her eyes slid past him to me, and I mouthed, 'Please,' adding a little pout for effect.

We all wanted her to come. It was obvious she was trying to avoid integrating into our lives, but that shit wasn't going to fly with Austin or Connor.

Or me, for that matter.

"Ugh, fine. Just for a little while. But do I have to wear the wig?" she asked, and Connor and I both answered with a resounding, "Yes."

"You'd better not all abandon me for your horde of puck bunnies when we get there."

"Don't let Ella hear you call her that. She'll never forgive you," Connor chuckled. "Can't say Holden will manage to fly solo, though."

He winked at me, but the joke was lost on me.

I wasn't *that* fucking bad.

I could go a night without hooking up with anyone. Besides, Aurora would need someone to look out for her, and I didn't want to give her more ammunition for her 'Noah Holden is a douchebag' file.

"Who's been eating my porridge?" Austin growled as he entered the kitchen.

"Oh wow, that is… wow." Aurora snickered, fighting a grin.

She wasn't wrong. The bear onesie wasn't exactly a good look, but I'd left the hood part down, unlike Austin, who was rocking the full bear aesthetic.

"The puck bunnies won't be able to resist," she added.

"Nah, girls love a guy in costume."

"Yeah, something hot like a pilot or a cop, maybe. But this"—she wagged a finger at him—"isn't exactly sexy."

"Watch and learn, Sis. Watch and learn." Austin grinned, going to the refrigerator and grabbing a beer. He cracked it open and looked at Connor. "You better go get dressed. We need to leave in fifteen."

"Fifteen minutes," Aurora balked.

"Better hurry, shortcake," I said. "We have a costume cup to win."

"What's taking her so long?" Austin said, pacing the kitchen like a restless bear, pun intended. "We were supposed to leave ten minutes ago."

"She's a chick. It's a whole process."

"Since when did you become the oracle on all things female?" Austin pinned Connor with a bemused look.

"You really want me to answer that question?"

"You know, I think I liked you more when you weren't wifed up." Austin walked to the door and bellowed, "C'mon, Rory, we need to go."

"I'll go check on her," I offered. "I want to grab something from my room anyway."

"Extra condoms?" Connor laughed, and I flipped him off.

"Asshole."

"Nothing wrong with playing it safe, Holden."

I ignored him, leaving the kitchen and making my way down the hall to the staircase. "Shortcake?" I called, jogging up the stairs, taking two at a time.

"Just a minute," she replied, but I heard the crack in her voice. The uncertainty.

"What's up?"

"Nothing. I'll be right out."

"Seriously, Aurora, if there's a problem with the costume, we can—"

The door swung open to reveal her standing there in the yellow and white dress Connor had managed to rent.

"What—holy shit."

My jaw dropped as I took in the full effect. It hugged her body like a glove, cinching at the waist and flaring out at her hips. But the pièce de resistance was the corset top. It scooped low on her chest and left *nothing* to the imagination.

It was quite possible I'd died and gone to cleavage heaven.

"It's too small, I know." She turned around and walked to the mirror, tugging and pulling at the material. "I can't go like this. I look—"

"Hot. You look... Hot. As. Fuck, shortcake."

"Noah," she sighed. "You don't have to do that."

"What is it you think I'm doing? Because I'm telling you now, if we let you leave the house looking like that, we're going to spend the entire night fighting guys off."

Shit. Why did that make my chest squeeze? The idea of my teammates seeing her like this. Leering at her body. Filling their dirty little minds with all kinds of fantasies.

"You really think it looks okay?" Her gaze snagged on mine in the mirror.

I closed the distance between us until I stood right behind her. "I don't want to tempt fate, shortcake, but you could seriously improve our chances of winning the cup. You look..."

Amazing.

She looked fucking amazing.

Aurora blushed, lowering her eyes a little bit as she held my stare. The air turned thick, the stupid fucking costume I was in growing at least two sizes smaller until I was sure the damn thing would suffocate me half to death.

"I don't. Noah, I'm not sure I can leave the house looking like... like this." Her voice was a shaky whisper.

I grabbed the long blonde wig off her bed and stood behind her. "You don't have to be yourself tonight. Costume parties are about dressing up and being someone else for the night."

"Hiding, you mean," she scoffed as if the idea offended her.

"You call it hiding, but I call it"—I gathered her ponytail up and slid the wig over her head, straightening it out until the blonde locks spilled over her shoulders like a golden waterfall—"living out a fantasy. You're not Aurora Hart tonight," I said. "You're Goldilocks. A powerful, confident woman who manages to wrestle and defeat three bears. I'd say that makes you pretty badass."

"Hmm, Noah, I'm not sure what fairy tale you read growing up, but I'm pretty sure there's no bear wrestling involved."

"There's not?" I smirked. "Huh."

Aurora rolled her eyes, but some of the uncertainty clouding her expression had lifted.

"You look amazing, shortcake. I wouldn't say it if it weren't true."

She studied me. Two pools of green reeled me in, silently asking me things I couldn't answer.

"I don't know..."

"How about I make you a deal."

"I'm listening."

"We all go to the party, but after an hour, if you're not having fun, I'll bring you home."

Shit. Why did that sound like it was loaded with promises I had no right to make?

"I don't need a babysitter, Noah."

"I know. I'm not trying to baby you. I'm trying to be a good friend. If you don't like it, we'll leave. Simple."

"Why do you care?"

Good question. I swallowed over the lump in my throat. Was it hot in here? Because I felt fucking hot.

"I... uh..."

"C'mon," Austin yelled up the stairs. "Let's roll."

"He's right," Aurora rushed out, smoothing down her fake hair as she slipped around me. "We should go."

"Yeah." I rubbed the back of my neck, watching her hurry out of the room, with that sunshine-yellow dress— her perfect ass in that dress—taunting me.

Fuck.

I was in serious fucking trouble.

I'd been dead set on persuading Aurora to come with us to the party, but maybe she was right.

Maybe it was a bad idea.

Only not for the reasons she thought.

The party was already in full swing by the time we got there.

Ward greeted us at the door with Jell-O shots. Austin,

the greedy fucker, took two; and a third when Aurora declined.

"Goldy, you're killing me here," Connor drawled, slinging his arm around her shoulder.

A streak of jealousy went through me. But I shoved it down. *Aurora isn't yours, asshole. She'll never be yours.* Besides, Connor was good people. He wasn't hitting on her. He was being friendly. Brotherly.

He was being everything I was supposed to be.

But nothing about my thoughts and Aurora in that little yellow dress were brotherly.

I was so fucking screwed.

Thankfully, the stupid fucking bear onesie the guys had insisted I wear had enough room in the crotch department to disguise the fact I'd been walking around at half-mast ever since I'd barged into her room.

"I'll stick to water, thanks." She shot him a sardonic smile and slipped past Ward.

"She's a tough little thing, huh?" he said, glancing after her.

"Watch it, Cutler, that's my sister you're talking about."

He chuckled. "You just let her loose in a frat house full of drunken hockey players. I'd say she's fair game."

"Watch it," I snapped, anger rippling through me like an electric current.

"Holden's right," Connor nudged himself between us, flashing me a 'stand the fuck down' smile. "Aurora is as good as family to the team. That makes her off-limits."

The word ricocheted through me.

His message couldn't be any more obvious. I needed a strong fucking drink and a distraction or two.

Because Aurora Hart was bad news.

And a problem I didn't need.

"I'm going to get a drink," I said to no one in particular, ducking into the house.

But Connor caught up with me. "We need to talk."

"No, we don't."

"Holden, man, wait"—he grabbed my arm—"you like her, don't you?"

"Who?"

"Come on, this is me you're talking to. I can see it a mile away."

"Just because you've got a girl doesn't make you some kind of attraction-o-meter."

He grinned, his eyes creasing with laughter. "You like her."

"You need to stop with that shit. She's Austin's sister. Our housemate. I would never—"

"Never?" His brow arched.

"*Never*," I said emphatically.

"Good man. Because I don't want to spend my senior year in the middle of you and Austin. I love you, Holden, but I was Austin's friend first." He winked.

"Oh, it's like that, huh?" I said, and he threw his head back, roaring with laughter.

When he was done, he settled his hard gaze back on mine and smirked. "It's exactly like that."

"Where is Austin?" I asked as we made our way into the big open-plan kitchen. Aurora had already found the girls, tucking herself away in the corner of the room.

"She has no idea how hot she looks, does she?" Connor said.

"Don't let Ella hear you say that."

"We have something called trust, asshole. Ella knows

she holds my balls in the palm of her hand, and I quite happen to like them there."

"Nice visual... that I never need to imagine."

"Drink?"

I nodded. "Make mine a double." I eyed the bottles of hard liquor.

He glanced at me and then across the room at Aurora and back again, shaking his head a little. "Jesus, you are so fucking screwed."

"I have no idea what you're talking about."

Gripping my shoulder, he squeezed. "Keep telling yourself that enough, and one day, it might come true."

"What might come true?" Austin appeared out of nowhere, making my heart crash against my chest.

"Noah's dream of a three-way with Sam and Fallon."

"Fallon?" His brows furrowed. "I thought you told her you weren't looking for a repeat."

"I did, but—"

An arm slung over my shoulder, and I looked up to find Mase grinning at me. "And what the fuck are you three idiots supposed to be?"

"The three bears, obviously." Connor rolled his eyes.

"If you're the three bears, where's Gold—" Mase scanned the room, his gaze falling on Aurora talking to Dayna and Ella, "Shit, is that little sis?"

"Don't even think about it," Austin warned, standing two feet taller.

Jesus.

Mase held up his hands. "I wouldn't dream of it."

"Fuck this. I need a drink. Con?"

"Yeah. Line 'em up." Connor followed Austin to the counter, and they started pouring our drinks.

"She looks different." Mason stepped up beside me.

"It's the wig."

"Hmm, I don't know. But it's something alright. I should probably warn you; Sam showed up about ten minutes ago."

"Fuck," I muttered under my breath. Just what I didn't need.

All week, she'd been texting me. Asking me to come over and keep her company in the aftermath of the break-in. Campus security had taken her statement and replaced the lock on her door. But beyond that, there was no sign of forced entry and no useful footage on the security tapes.

I wanted to believe she wouldn't fabricate something like that, but I couldn't shake the feeling that something was off.

So I'd kept my distance.

I wouldn't be able to avoid her if she was here.

"Holden, get the fuck over here." I joined the guys and accepted a Solo cup from Connor. "To costume cup victory."

"Hmm, Con, I hate to break it to you, man, but I'm not sure our costumes are going to cut it. Tipper is dressed up as a giant inflatable dick."

"Little Hart, get over here," he beckoned her over.

Ella and Dayna nudged her in our direction despite the reluctance in her eyes. "What are you doing all the way over there, Rory, baby?" he asked her. "We're a team, remember."

"Is he always like this?" Aurora asked Ella.

"When he commits to an idea, he goes all in." She shrugged. "I've always appreciated a man who knows what he wants."

"Somebody pass me the bucket," Mason gagged.

"Jealous, Steele?"

"Jealous that your dick only gets to experience one pussy for the rest of its life. Yeah, no. Sorry, El." He flashed her an insincere smile, but Ella being Ella, laughed.

"One day Mason. One day, you'll get it."

"I'm hoping I'll get it in Wonder Woman in about two hours' time."

"I'm so glad I'm not single and don't have to endure this anymore," Dayna murmured. "Don't suppose anyone has seen my boyfriend lurking around anyway?"

"He had to put one of the rookies to bed. He got a little excited with the Jell-O shots. Fucking lightweight." Mason snorted.

"Hey, we've all been there," Connor said, wrapping his arm around Ella's waist. "If I remember correctly, you almost pissed yourself freshman year after one too many drinks at TPB."

Everyone exploded with laughter except Mason, who scowled. If looks could kill, Connor would have been six feet under.

"I hope you know what kind of guy you're with, El," he added. "One who can't keep a fucking secret."

"Mase, baby, I'm joking. It's a joke."

Except, it wasn't, and that did happen. I'd heard the story last year straight from the horse's mouth.

"Okay, children," Austin said, "are we going to drink or stand around bitchin' all night."

My eyes clashed with Aurora's as she watched everyone raise their cups in the air. She had a bottle of water in her hand, but her eyes went to the vodka on the counter.

"Want something a little stronger, shortcake?"

Everyone looked at her, and her cheeks flushed that adorable shade of pink. "Fine," she said. "One drink won't hurt."

We all cheered as Connor made her a vodka orange and handed her the cup. "Welcome to Lakeshore U, little Hart. May your days be educational. Your nights be full of excitement. And your weekends, all about hockey."

"I'll drink to that," Austin said. "Rory?"

She stepped forward and brought the cup to her lips, sniffing the contents. Her nose crinkled adorably as she shrugged. "What the hell, to Lakeshore U."

CHAPTER 11

AURORA

It was a bad idea.

Drinking.

Letting the guys talk me into shots.

But the truth was, I'd needed something to take the edge of the nerves jittering inside me as I stood wedged between Dayna and Ella, trying my best to hide in the shadows.

The Goldilocks costume was outrageous. It clung to every dip and curve and roll. Despite how uncomfortable I felt in the damn thing, I couldn't deny it did make my boobs look great. As for the rest of me, it was... a lot.

I wasn't used to wearing something so form-fitting. I didn't feel liberated. Not one bit. I felt on display. And not in a good way. It was like walking around with a neon sign above my head flashing, 'look at me, *judge* me.'

At least Noah had a point; in the blonde wig, I didn't

feel like myself. But it hadn't quite given me the burst of confidence I'd hoped for. All I could think about was how the flared skirt highlighted my wide hips and how the corset top creased at the back of my arms. I didn't dress up like this for a reason. Because drawing attention to my figure made me obsess about it. Made me fixate on trying to deconstruct what other people saw when they looked at me. Did they notice my hips? My ass? The way my thighs rubbed together under the dress? Or did they only see my boobs, which were far too disproportionate for my frame?

The vodka helped, though, making everything a little hazy.

"I'm so happy you're here," Ella called over the music.

We'd moved into the living room, if you could call it that. It was a huge space littered with couches and a big television mounted onto the wall. The furniture had been pushed aside to create a dancefloor full of girls dressed in sexy costumes vying for the guys' attention.

The team's stupid puck bunny scale kept popping into my head. I could easily pick out the Jessica Rabbits, but there wasn't a chubby bunny in sight. *Except me*. Everyone was beautiful. So beautiful that the longer I stood there, the more I was convinced I stood out like a sore thumb.

"Aurora?" Ella touched my arm.

"Sorry, what?"

"I asked if you wanted to dance."

"Oh, no, thank you." I tugged at the hem of the dress, trying to add a couple of inches to the skirt. "You two should go, though."

Her friend Mila and some girls they knew had turned up. Right around the time I slipped into the background, watching the party go on around me.

"You're sure? You should come. It'll be fun."

"I'm like Bambi on ice." Strained laughter bubbled up inside me. "But go, have fun."

She gave a little shrug and joined Dayna and her friends.

I decided to sit down on the couch tucked away in the corner of the room. Really, I wanted nothing more than to go back to the house, change into my pajamas, and get into bed with a good book. But they hadn't announced the winners of the costume contest yet, and Connor really wanted to win that stupid cup.

He joined the girls on the dancefloor, wrapping his arms around Ella and kissing her deeply. The two of them melted into each other, oblivious to everyone else around them. Aiden made a beeline for Dayna, and a couple of the other guys each grabbed a girl and then started dancing and laughing.

There was no sign of Noah.

He'd pretty much disappeared the second after we all had a drink together. I tried not to think about where he was—*who* he was with. It was a party full of beautiful girls; I knew the answer to that question.

Jealousy slithered around inside me. Earlier, in my room, there had been another moment. His eyes had lingered a little too long. Darkened with desire.

Oh, who was I kidding? Of course, his eyes had lingered. The costume was practically porn-show obscene.

The couch dipped as a guy I didn't recognize, thanks to his very authentic pirate costume, sat beside me. I looked up at him, and he flashed me a goofy smile.

"Hey, I'm Leon, but you can call me Captain Blackbeard. Let me guess, you must be a Disney princess. Cinderella?"

"Goldilocks."

"Close." He shrugged, taking a long pull on his beer. "Not enjoying the party."

"I'm here under duress." His eyes narrowed, and I chuckled. "I live with Austin, Connor, and Noah. It's a temporary thing, but they talked me into this." I swept a hand down my body, immediately regretting it because his gaze followed, lingering on my boobs.

"Ah you're the sister. Aurora, right?" I nodded and he added, "Nice, I should probably go thank them."

"Wow, that's... kind of gross." Shuffling away from him, I put some space between us.

"Shit, I didn't mean... that sounded all wrong. I just meant you look great."

"I look like I'm the star in some bad fairytale porno." My eyes rolled.

"Would that be such a bad thing?"

"I..." The words caught in my throat because, surely, he wasn't serious.

"Banks take a hike. Aurora isn't interested." Noah loomed over us, glaring at his teammate with enough ice to freeze the couch.

"I was just—"

"Leaving." He stepped aside, making room for Leon to get up.

"Guess I'll see you around, Goldy." He had the audacity to wink, but I was too busy watching Noah out of the corner of my eye to react.

"Well, that was rude." My brow quirked up.

"Just protecting your honor, shortcake." Noah dropped

down beside me, and his knee brushed mine, sending a streak of heat through me. "I'm fucking sweating in this thing."

I glanced away from him, smothering a chuckle.

"Are you... laughing at me, shortcake? I'm offended."

Our eyes met again, and my heart fluttered. "You do look a bit silly."

"Oh, really." His brow cocked, but he had a playful smile on his lips. "You didn't think to tell me that before we left the house."

"I mean, it's pretty obvious. I'm sure the puck bunnies love it though. You're literally a big cuddly teddy bear." I poked his fur-covered arm.

"I'll be a dehydrated bear taking its last breaths soon if I don't get out of this fucking thing." He yanked at the collar as if it might alleviate some of his issues. "Having fun?"

"It's... loud."

"It's a party, shortcake." He grinned, and those pesky butterflies took flight again. "It's supposed to be loud."

"I'm just not used to it, is all."

"I'm guessing you didn't party much back in high school."

"Correct. It wasn't really my scene."

"What is your scene, Aurora Hart?" His eyes drilled into mine.

He always did that—looked too closely, as if he was trying to unravel me. Unpick all my broken, jagged pieces and figure out how they slotted back together.

"I like to read. Watch movies. I like rainy days when you can hear it beating off the windows. I like—" I stopped myself.

What the hell was I doing?

"Sorry, I guess the vodka went to my head."

"Hey, I asked. I want to get to know you, shortcake. I want us to be... friends." He glanced away for a second, running a hand over his jaw.

That second was all I needed for the cracks to splinter —for the seed of doubt to spread.

"Friends," I repeated, the word leaving a dirty taste on my tongue.

I wasn't sure what I wanted us to be, but friends didn't sound right. Friends weren't supposed to make my heart flutter and my blood run hot.

Friends didn't—

Stop, Aurora. He's not like you. He's popular and gorgeous, and he's a Laker, for Christ's sake.

Besides, *friends* were all we could ever be. So to wish— to hope—for anything more was pointless. Noah was kind to me because he had to be the way Connor was. The way Dayna and Ella were.

I was Austin Hart's little sister. The new girl on campus. They'd taken pity on me. That was all.

"Noah, there you are." The leggy blonde from The Penalty Box towered over us. "I've been looking everywhere for you."

"Sam, sorry." Noah shifted awkwardly. "I was just chatting with Aurora."

"Aurora." She fixed her cool, assessing gaze on me. "I don't think I know you."

"She's Austin's sister."

"So, what, you're babysitting her?" She scoffed, flicking her glossy waves over one shoulder in a well-rehearsed move.

"Sam, come on. Play nice," Noah groaned. "Aurora is staying with us for a while. She's good people."

"It's okay," I said, getting up and smoothing down my dress because dear God, it was short. "I'll leave you two to it. Nice to meet you."

Sam pressed her lips into a barely-there smile, her judgment brushing up against me like shards of glass.

"Shortcake, come on—"

But I was already gone, weaving through the sea of bodies until a hand shot out and grabbed me. "Rory, baby, there you are." Connor grinned. "Dance with us."

"Oh no, I don't—"

"Yes, Rory. Dance with us." Ella wrapped her arms around me, a goofy smile on her face.

"You're drunk," I said.

"Don't tell anyone." She winked, grabbing my hand and moving it to the heavy beat. Billie Eilish's haunting voice rose above the bass, pulsing through me like a second heartbeat.

"I love this song," Ella shouted, weaving our hands together.

"I need water," I said, pulling away.

"What, no. Stay." She pouted.

"I'll be back."

I wouldn't. But I didn't have the heart to tell her that.

I managed to make it into the kitchen unscathed. A couple of guys leered in my direction. I didn't recognize them, but their zombie schoolboy costumes were pretty convincing.

"Excuse me," I said, slipping past them to get to the faucet.

They went back to their conversation, and I helped myself to a glass of water. Hopefully, they would pick the winner of the damn costume contest soon because I wanted to leave.

Digging my cell phone out of the little purse attached to my dress, I checked the time.

I was about to go in search of my brother when I overheard the guys talking.

"Hey, Adams, what about her?" I heard one of them say.

"Who?"

"Goldilocks."

"More like a chubby bunny. Have you seen her ass? It should come with its own warning label." He exploded with laughter.

"Oh, I don't know. She's kind of cute. And did you see the rack on her? If Mila turns me down again, and I sink some more shots, maybe I'll hit that. I bet she's a dirty girl with tits like that."

Spinning around, I glowered at them. "Well, *she* isn't interested in either of you."

I stormed past them, their laughter tearing into me like shrapnel, slicing old wounds open, and letting me bleed out on the floor.

Why the hell had I let the guys talk me into wearing this stupid dress?

Tears pricked the corners of my eyes, but I swallowed them down as I headed for the front door. Outside, I booked an Uber and quickly sent the group chat a quick message.

Aurora: I'm leaving, not feeling so good.
Sorry, Connor. I know you wanted to win.

Nobody replied, but then, I didn't expect them to. Austin had barely been around. Connor was dancing with Ella. And Noah... well, he had his hands full with Sam.

The car pulled up two minutes later, and I climbed inside, glancing back at Lakers House.

I didn't belong there.

I never would.

I was just about to get to the good part in my book, the third-act breakup where the hero realized he loved the heroine and needed to employ some epic grovel to win her back when I heard footsteps out in the hall.

"Austin?" I called, earmarking my page and placing the book down on the window seat. "Is that you?"

They'd been pissed when they finally realized I'd left. But I figured the fact it took them forty minutes to realize I was missing and check their messages made us even.

Gripping the door handle, I pulled it open. "Austin, what—you're not Austin."

"Surprise."

"What do you want, Noah?" An exasperated sigh slipped out.

"I came to check that you were okay. Feeling better?

Because I gotta say, shortcake, I expected to find you wrapped up in bed with a hot water bottle."

"A hot... Sorry, what?"

"You know, the thing you fill with boiling water to—"

"Noah."

"Yes, shortcake?" He smirked.

"I know what a hot water bottle is. But why did you think I'd have one?"

"Because I figured you got your period or something."

"I didn't, but thanks for the concern."

"Why'd you leave then?"

"Because..." I shrugged, dropping my gaze.

"Oh no, you don't, shortcake. I'm going to need a little more than that. Did something happen?"

"Nothing happened. I just wasn't feeling it. I did try to tell you all repeatedly that parties aren't really my thing."

"Funny because Mase told me he saw you bail after you gave Abel Adams and his friend a piece of your mind. What did they say?"

"Nothing, it doesn't matter. Good night, Noah." I went to push the door closed, but he kicked his foot out, giving himself enough leverage to push it back open.

"What did they say, shortcake?"

"Why?" I threw up my hands. "Why does it possibly matter to you?"

"Because I'll kick their asses if they upset you."

I rolled my eyes, frowning when Noah slipped into my room and closed the door behind him. Suddenly, the air felt too thick. Too heavy and suffocating, crushing my chest until it I couldn't breathe.

"Nice sleep shirt," he said, letting his gaze rake down my

body. Slow, slow, slowly, until he dragged it back up, lingering on my boobs.

"Eyes up here, Holden." I clicked my fingers, part outraged, part amused.

"Shit, sorry. I... you have an amazing rack."

"Seriously, does that line *ever* work?"

"You tell me." Noah shrugged, taking a step forward.

"What are you doing?"

"I don't know." He kept coming, his eyes dark with lust.

"Are you drunk?"

His pupils were blown but not glassy like they would be if he was drunk. But he seemed... different.

"You shouldn't be in here," I said, my voice a little shaky, the air unbearably thick. "I'm—"

"I'm not drunk, shortcake. I'm perfectly in control of myself right now."

I'm glad one of us was because I was a mess. He was too close. Too gorgeous. Too everything.

Ever since I'd arrived in Lakeshore, Noah had made it his mission to push himself into my life. I'd hated it at first. Resented it even. But bit by bit, he'd started to crack my resolve. It was a dangerous game, though. He was a Laker. Their resident playboy. I'd heard the rumors. Seen the proof with my own two eyes. A guy like Noah would break my heart in two without so much as realizing it.

But I couldn't seem to stop myself from falling for his charm.

"I can't stop thinking about you in that dress." His voice was a low gravelly whisper that made my stomach clench as he reached out to toy with the ends of my hair. "What did they say to you, Aurora?"

It was a soft demand. One that hit me straight in the chest.

"Nothing I'm not already used to hearing. I should never have let you all talk me into wearing that stupid costume."

His jaw clenched, anger radiating from him as he stared down at me. "You're beautiful, shortcake. Don't ever let anyone ever make you feel any less."

"Noah, I..."

He kissed me. Noah pressed his lips to my forehead and let them linger there. A bolt of lightning went through me, so deep and profound that I thought I might melt into a puddle.

His hand slipped around the back of my neck, holding me there, his thumb brushing my skin with a gentle possessiveness that rocked me to my core.

"I won't be that girl, Noah," I said quietly, breaking the spell.

"What girl?"

"Whatever girl you're hoping I'll be." I gave him a sad smile. "Friends with benefits isn't my style, and I can't be with somebody who is sleeping with other people."

"Whoa there, shortcake. Talk about jumping the gun."

"Oh, I thought... forget it." I pulled out of his hold, sheer mortification washing over me.

"Aurora. Shit, I—"

"No, it's fine. I drank too much, and it's late. Sleep, I need to sleep, and you probably have stuff to do."

Girls to do. Pretty, perfect puck bunnies.

"We should talk about this." He gave me a stern look.

"Talk about what? Nothing happened. You did a nice

thing coming to check on me, Noah. But I'm fine." I smiled. Too brightly. Too widely.

Too fake.

"You can go now, and everything can go back to how it was."

The lie sounded convincing enough.

Because there was no going back.

But there was no future for us either.

CHAPTER 12

NOAH

I NEEDED to turn around and walk out of Aurora's room before I did something I couldn't undo.

When I found out she'd left the party, all I could think about was going after her. Sam was like a bad smell I couldn't escape. She'd followed me around like a lost fucking puppy, complaining how on edge she felt since the break-in. How she wanted me to come around more often and keep her company.

Like that was ever going to happen.

I'd gotten rid of her eventually, but it was late, and I wasn't expecting Aurora to be awake. My plan had been to check that she was okay and then head to bed myself. A plan quickly thwarted once I realized she was still up.

Now I was standing here, two seconds away from kissing her, and she was telling me to get out.

"Noah!"

"Uh, sorry, what?" I blinked, trying to focus, trying to

look anywhere but at her delicious curves. Her soft pink lips. All that hair piled on top of her head in a messy bun that was so effortlessly her.

What the fuck was it about this girl that affected me so much?

"I said you can go."

"Go, right. Okay." I stalled.

"The door's that way." She flicked her gaze behind me, a flash of irritation there.

"Yep, got it."

I was an idiot. A bumbling idiot. But she had me all twisted up inside. It was the dress.

I blamed the dress.

And her curves.

And her smile.

Fuck me, her smile.

When she aimed that thing in my direction, it was like she was sharing a private joke just with me. And I'd happily lap up any scraps she gave me.

"Good night, Noah." Annoyance coated her voice.

"Good night, shortcake."

Her brows creased, and my mouth twitched. I loved getting a reaction from her—purposefully found new ways to elicit a smile or frown or smirk or look of sheer surprise.

I didn't want to admit it, but I had a teeny little thing for Aurora Hart.

Of course, the first girl to ever spark that side of me was off-limits. But it didn't mean I couldn't have some fun with it. Flirt a little. Spend time with her. Make her squirm the same way she constantly got under my skin.

Nothing was ever going to come of it.

She was Austin's sister, and I had an important season ahead of me. One I couldn't afford to screw up.

I left Aurora's room with a strange knot in my stomach. She was lying. Adams had upset her. I'd put money on it.

Not that it surprised me.

Abel Adams was an idiot, always saying the first thing that came into his head, no matter how fucking stupid it was.

The door closed behind me, and I hesitated. I'd seen the uncertainty glistening in her eyes tonight, the cogs working overtime in her mind as she'd stood in front of me in the mirror, uncomfortable in the sexy little dress wrapped around her body, accentuating her curves.

It didn't take a genius to see that Aurora had self-esteem issues. She hadn't wanted to wear the dress tonight, but we'd talked her into it. Then the first sign of someone criticizing her—because I could imagine exactly the kind of thing Adams had said—she ran out of there and back to the sanctuary of her room.

Shit.

Before I could stop myself, I turned around and knocked on her door.

"Noah, what are you—"

"I need to tell you something," I said.

"It's late. I really don't have time—"

"Whatever was going on in that head of yours tonight, shortcake, you're wrong."

"I don't know what you're talking about." Her gaze darted away from me.

"I think you do. You're under some illusion that you couldn't pull off that dress—"

"Because I couldn't, Noah. I looked ridiculous."

"Bullshit."

"You would say that." She let out a weary sigh. "You're gorgeous and popular and athletic. You're exactly what society tells us a young man is supposed to look like. But it's different for women. For girls like me."

"Come here." I walked into her room, grabbed her hand, tugging her toward the dresser.

Stepping up behind her, I met her wild gaze in the mirror. "What do you see when you look in the mirror?"

"Noah," she let out a soft, shuddering sigh. "I'm not doing this."

"Tough shit, shortcake. If you won't do it, then I will." I wrapped my arm around her waist, anchoring her body to my chest. "Look at you. You're beautiful, Aurora. Your eyes, your smile... fuck, I love your smile. And your tits." My hand glided higher, grazing the underside of her breast. "I fucking love these."

She sucked in a thin, shaky breath, her entire body trembling. "Noah," she choked out. "This is ridiculous."

Aurora rolled her gaze away from me. "I don't need self-esteem lessons from a guy like you," she whispered quietly.

"Because my life is fucking perfect, right?" I scoffed, turning her in my arms. Forcing her to look at me. "I thought we were past the judgmental, bitch routine."

"Glad to know what you really think of me." Aurora went to walk away, but I grabbed her wrist and pulled her back to me. "Noah, what are you—"

My mouth crashed down on hers as I buried my fingers into her hair, stealing her doubts, stealing every insecurity she had in that pretty little head of hers.

Jesus, she tasted good.

Like strawberries and silk. My tongue licked into her

mouth, sliding against her own. Aurora whimpered, and I pulled her closer, aware of every inch of her that touched every inch of me.

She was perfect.

Soft and curvy under my hands as they mapped her body. The girls I typically hooked up with weighed next to nothing, so there wasn't much to hold onto. But I fucking loved the feel of Aurora's ass in my hands.

"Noah..."

Her fingers twisted into the stupid bear onesie I was still wearing. But I didn't care one bit. Because Aurora was kissing me back, and it was every-fucking-thing.

My dick was rock hard between us, desperate for her. But somewhere in the back of my lust-addled brain, I knew I'd already crossed a line. Any more, and there would be no turning back.

"Noah—"

My name on her lips made the world come crashing down around me. She stared up at me with that glassy love-struck expression girls get when they catch feelings.

Fuck.

What had I done?

"Shit, Aurora, I didn't... I don't know what came over me." I stepped back, running a hand through my hair and down the back of my neck, barely meeting her gaze.

"Oh." Disappointment flashed over her face, and I felt every bit the asshole I was.

"I shouldn't have done that."

"It's a little bit late for regrets."

"I don't regret it," I blurted. Because how could I? She was perfect. "But I crossed a line. I'm sorry."

"Your mood swings are giving me whiplash." She

laughed, but it sounded hollow. "If you're worried about me telling anyone, I won't. Like you said, it was a mistake. I'm Austin's sister. He's your teammate. You have all your weird bro code rules. Besides, girls like me don't get the guy, Noah." Her smile turned sad. Empty.

And guilt slithered through me.

"This has nothing to do with you, shortcake. You're beautiful and funny, and I like hanging out with you. But hockey is—"

"The end goal." Her expression turned as cold as the air around us. "Got it."

"It's a big year for me. I can't afford any distractions."

And she was proving to be the worst kind.

"But I meant what I said earlier. I want us to be friends."

"Friends, sure. I can do that."

"Yeah?" My eyes lit up. I didn't want things to be weird between us, and I didn't want her to retreat into herself again. Not when she was finally starting to step out of her comfort zone.

"Yep. But now I really need to get my beauty sleep, *friend*." Her lips quirked, but the smile didn't reach her eyes.

"I can take a hint." Slowly, I backed up. "And Aurora?"

"Yeah?"

"I'd appreciate it if we never talk about this again."

Her expression guttered, but she recovered quickly, nodding once. "Of course. I have a rep to protect." Her expression was cold. Aloof. But I didn't know what to say—how to fix things.

So I walked out of there.

And this time, I didn't look back.

"Look what the cat dragged in," Austin said over his gigantic bowl of cereal. "Where'd you get to last night?"

"I... uh..." I scratched my chest, and he smirked.

"Oh, it's like that, huh? Say no more, man."

"Say no more about what?" Aurora said, padding into the kitchen in a baggy t-shirt with *blessed be the fruit* scrawled across the front and some kind of tight gym pants.

Jesus, her ass looked good enough to eat... and I was thinking about eating her ass while sitting opposite of her brother.

Fuck my life.

I ran a hand down my face, having a silent word with myself.

"So," she went on. "What were you talking about before I walked in?"

"Oh, nothing of interest. Just Noah's latest conquest."

"Oh." She stiffened, a ripple of hostility rolling off her.

"He's keeping his cards close to his chest, so I'm guessing it's either Sam or one of Ella's friends."

"Actually," I said, clearing my throat, "it wasn't."

"No? Well, shit, that's twenty dollars out of my pocket, then. I had a bet with Connor that you'd end up back at Sam's."

"Trust me, it wasn't for her lack of trying," I murmured, and Aurora caught my eye, narrowing hers slightly.

"What about you? Did you make it home?" I flipped the tables on him.

Austin got up and took his bowl to the sink. "I never kiss

and tell, Holden. You should know that by now." He chuckled.

"Okay, if you two are quite done," Aurora said, "I'm going to do some yoga in the yard."

"Enjoy. I'm going to grab a shower, then meet some of the guys at The Penalty Box. Holden, you in?"

"Uh, yeah." I tore my eyes off Aurora's legs and glanced up at him. "I'll be there."

"See you down here in a bit then." Austin left the kitchen, and I let out a small breath.

"Are you trying to kill me, shortcake?"

"Sorry, am I supposed to know what you're talking about?"

"Your outfit." My eyes dropped to her ass again.

"You mean my yoga pants."

"They should be illegal."

A faint blush streaked along her neck and into her cheeks. "Noah…" She glanced back to the door Austin had just disappeared through and slowly slid her gaze to mine. "Friends, remember."

I held up my hands. "Sorry. You just caught me off guard."

"Well, me and my yoga pants apologize. Now, don't you have somewhere else to be?"

"What? No. I'm going to be right here." *Watching you bend and stretch in those skintight pants.*

"This isn't going to work, you know." She cocked a brow, fisting her hips and glaring at me like I was a thorn in her side.

And maybe I was.

But she made it too damn easy.

"Sorry, what was that? I'm a little distracted over here, shortcake."

Her lips pressed into a thin smile, but I saw the flash of amusement in her eyes. Aurora enjoyed this easy banter between us. The harmless flirtation.

Even if my thoughts were anything but harmless.

"Whatever, Noah. I'm heading out." She grabbed her bottle of water and headed for the back door.

"Enjoy your yoga, shortcake," I called after her, almost certain I saw her shoulders shake with silent laughter.

Because I sure as hell was going to enjoy the view.

To my endless disappointment, I didn't get to watch Aurora do any yoga. Austin returned quicker than I anticipated, ready to head to The Penalty Box, and I couldn't exactly ask him to give me ten minutes to ogle his sister in the downward dog position.

"I can't believe classes start Monday," Leon said. "My schedule is a killer."

"Seriously, rookie? Wait until you're a senior," Austin grumbled. "I'm not looking forward to balancing everything."

"All work and no play makes Austin a dull boy," Connor squeezed his shoulder, grinning. "You should consider getting some regular pussy. One less thing to worry about."

"Seriously, if you don't stop with this shit, I'm banning you from guys' time."

"What? I'm serious. It has its perks, you know. Regular sex." He counted off his fingers. "Somebody to kiss all your boo-boos better." Another finger went up. "Someone wearing your jersey in the stands." And another. "If you ask me, you're all missing out."

"Okay, Romeo," Austin leaned over and snagged his glass. "No more happy juice for you."

"I'm just say—"

"I'll be back," I said, noticing Adams entering the bar. He had a girl in tow, who quickly put some space between them when she noticed me approaching.

"Hey, Noah," she purred as if she hadn't just walked into the place with my teammate.

I fought the urge to roll my eyes.

"Hey." I gave her a perfunctory glance. "Do me a favor and give Adams and me a minute."

"Uh, sure." Her gaze bounced between us. "I'll be at the bar." She smiled.

At me. Not him.

"She's—"

"So fucking hot, right?" He smirked. "What's up?"

"Austin's sister. What did you say to her last night?"

"Who?" He gawked at me.

"Goldilocks, the girl who came to the party with Austin, and Con—"

"Oh, shit." Realization dawned in his eyes. "The chubby bunny was Hart's sis—fuck!" He staggered backward, clutching his face. "What the fuck is your problem, Holden?"

"Talk about Aurora like that again, and it won't just be me you're dealing with."

"Coach will—"

I grabbed him by the collar and smashed him up against the wall. "Coach won't hear a word of this, got it?"

"Or what, Holden? What the fuck are you going to do about it?"

"Hey, we good here?" Connor came up behind me.

"Yeah, just teaching this asshole some respect." I glowered at him, a silent warning that he should back the fuck down and keep his fucking mouth shut.

"I think he got the memo, bro." Connor laid his hand on my shoulder.

"Yeah." Shoving Abel hard, I walked away, inhaling a ragged breath.

Fuck. I hadn't meant to let it get that far, but I fucking knew he'd run his mouth to Aurora. No wonder she'd hightailed it out of there before anyone could intervene.

"What?" I barked at Connor as we made our way back to our table.

"I have one question." He studied me. "Did he deserve it?"

"What do you think?" I shot back.

"Thought so. Next time, aim for his nose. Asshole could do with some facial realignment." Connor snorted, and I glanced back at Adams, hardly surprised to see the puck bunny all over him.

There was something about men in pain that activated a woman's caregiver instincts. I'd probably done him a favor and sealed the deal between them. But she was welcome to him. Abel Adams was a disrespectful asshole, and quite frankly, he didn't deserve to wear a Lakers jersey. But he was an asset on the ice, even if most of us only tolerated him at best.

"Do I even want to know?" Austin asked.

"Let's just say we had a disagreement."

"Asshole probably deserved it," Leon muttered.

I flexed my hand, wincing at the tender spot across my knuckles. I wasn't a particularly violent guy off the ice. But the second the words were out of his mouth, I saw red.

"He better stay the fuck out of my way this season," I mumbled, grabbing a menu to distract myself.

Because all I could think about was ducking out of the bar and going back to the house.

To find Aurora.

CHAPTER 13

AURORA

TURNED out Noah wasn't only a boob guy—he was an ass guy too.

After the yoga pants incident, I managed to avoid him for the rest of the weekend. He'd kissed me, and then he'd realized it was a mistake.

Story of my life.

I let out a small, defeated sigh. Noah Holden didn't like me—he liked the idea of me.

Number one: I was Austin's sister, which made me off-limits, and guys loved that. The thrill of the chase, especially something forbidden. Two: I was clearly out of my depth in their college-hockey world, which kicked in his protective instincts because, despite his reputation, Noah was a good guy. And three: I wasn't knocked on my ass by his charm and good looks.

Well, mostly.

The truth was Noah did affect me. More than I cared to

admit. But it was a moot point. We'd agreed to be friends. Now that the semester had started, and with it hockey season, I expected our fledgling friendship would fizzle out soon enough.

It was probably a good thing though. I wasn't cut out to be a Lakers girl—or anyone's girl, for that matter. No, I came to Lakeshore U for a fresh start. Getting tangled up with a guy—a hockey player, no less—was a bad idea.

The worst.

Thankfully, I had classes to keep me occupied now. The English program at Lakeshore U wasn't as renowned as the program at Fitton U, but I was still looking forward to spending my days immersed in literature and creative writing.

"Austin, I'm ready," I said as I hurried down the stairs.

"You look... nice." A frown crinkled his eyes.

"This just so happens to be my lucky sweater," I lied, aware that the oversized sweater hung off my frame like a burlap sack. But I didn't want to spend my first day of classes obsessing over my appearance. So after showering, I reached for my favorite sweater. It swamped me, but there was something comforting about that.

"You're okay, right?"

"I'm fine." I smiled. "Ready?"

"As I'll ever be," he grumbled, slinging his backpack over his shoulder. "My class schedule is on another level this year. I hope I can hold it all together."

"I have every faith in you, Brother."

"Thanks. Come on." He held the door open for me, and I slipped past him.

"I can't believe you still have the Camry."

"She's my baby." He tapped the hood, dented and

dinged from years of reckless driving, before climbing inside. I followed, slipping into the passenger seat and buckling up.

It had been years since we did this. When I was in seventh grade, Austin had gotten his driver's permit and drove me to school sometimes. But it hadn't lasted long when he realized having a ride was a total chick magnet. I was quickly shoved aside in favor of his girl of the moment —and there were many.

"It brings back memories," I mused.

"Yeah, listen, Rory—"

"Let's not do this," I said with a weak smile. "I know there are things we still need to talk about, but it's my first day of college. I'm nervous enough as it is."

His gentle laughter hit me right in the chest. "You don't need to be nervous, Sis. You've been an English buff since you were old enough to read."

I poked my tongue out at him.

"You always were the brain box," he said.

"And you always were the athlete."

Silence settled over us. We'd always been different. Austin was the epitome of popular. People gravitated toward him, his good looks and laid-back personality. Of course, it helped that he played hockey and was good at it.

Really damn good.

Having a comprehension level beyond my age didn't really have the same effect on people. But books were my friends. I grew up on Austen and Brontë, Tolkien and Martin. Reading was my escape.

My sanctuary.

Nothing could hurt me between the pages of a book. So

more and more, I turned to my fictional friends, living out a literary fantasy instead of dealing with real life.

Austin didn't get it. And our mother certainly didn't get it. But kids were cruel.

People were cruel.

"Did you get a hold of student housing yet?" Austin asked.

"No. I'm going to go into the office today."

"I meant what I said, Rory. You can stay with us for as long as you need to."

"Thanks." I glanced out of the window, watching the scenery roll by. From the tree-lined streets to the little boutique stores downtown with their colorful canopies, and cloud-streaked blue skies, Lakeshore really was beautiful. Now that I was here, I could see why Austin had traded life back home for his life here.

Unease churned in my stomach.

"Austin, can I ask you something?"

I didn't want to broach the subject, not now, when we were so close to campus, but I couldn't stop myself.

Part of me—the girl abandoned by her brother—needed to know.

"Sure, you can ask me anything, Sis."

"Are you annoyed I came here?"

"What?" He balked. "Where the fuck did that come from?"

"You left Syracuse behind and built a life for yourself here. Me showing up could be a reminder of all the things you came here to forget."

"Aurora, fuck," he breathed, gripping the steering wheel tightly. "It isn't like that. Shit, wait a minute."

Austin pulled over, the car idling on the sidewalk.

"Look, I won't deny I was a little shocked when you told me you were transferring to LU, but I never, not for one second, resented you for it. You're my sister. My family. If anything, I'm fucking relieved that you're here, and I can keep an eye on you."

"You mean that?" Emotion clogged my throat, and I realized how much I needed to hear it.

"Of course I do. Come here." He reached for me, pulling me into a fierce hug. "I'm sorry, Rory. I'm sorry for all the shit we went through. I'm sorry for leaving you there to clean up her mess. But I had to get out. I had to—"

"I know you did. I know."

We held on to one another tightly, the pain from our past filling the cracks between us.

"I know we still haven't talked much"—Austin pushed me away gently to look at me—"but I'm here whenever you're ready. I'm here."

I nodded, not trusting myself to speak. Because although his apology was what I needed at that moment, it didn't erase years of pain and anger.

"You're better, right?" he asked. "I mean, you seem better now."

"Yeah, Austin. I'm better."

He bought the lie, flashing me a bright smile before pulling me back in for another hug. "It's really good to have you here, Rory. I've missed you."

"Yeah," I murmured, wishing I could believe his words.

Wishing more than anything, that they were true.

I was in Heaven.

Literary Heaven.

Professor MacMillan was an imposing woman. Tall and heavyset, she commanded the stage with her presence and obvious love of literature.

"In this class, you will be required to read and critically analyze a number of texts from the nineteenth century."

A frisson of excitement went through me. I'd already read at least three of the four required on the reading list. But George Eliot would be new to me.

"Psst," the girl next to me mouthed. "Do you have a spare pen I can borrow? Mine's out of ink already."

"Sure." I dug one out of my beloved Jane Austen book spine print pencil case and handed it over.

"Thanks, I love your case," she whispered. "Let me guess, team Darcy?"

"Actually, I'm team Bertram."

"Touché. I'm a total sucker for Mr. Darcy. Cliché, I know. But once I saw Colin Firth's performance, I knew there would never be another Austen man for me." She smirked. "I'm Harper."

"Aurora."

"What do you make of MacMillan so far? I heard she ran a tight ship, but this is some next-level shit." Harper grinned, and oddly, I found myself grinning back.

She was the opposite of me—ash-blonde hair, slim, with bright blue eyes that sparkled when she smiled. I couldn't help but think she would be exactly Noah's type.

Dammit.

I wasn't supposed to be thinking about Noah. I was supposed to be focused on class. But he had a way of worming himself into my thoughts.

I needed to pay the student housing office a visit sooner rather than later.

"Hey, want to get coffee after this?" she asked. "Compare notes."

"I... sure." I smiled.

"Great, we can walk out together."

Trepidation trickled through me, but it was laced with hope.

Hope that I'd made the right choice coming to Lakeshore U.

Hope that maybe, just maybe, I could make a friend or two that didn't want to ruin my life and steal my boyfriend.

The lights dimmed, and Professor MacMillan introduced each slide, giving us time to take notes. A bunch of students had iPads and laptops, but I preferred the old-fashioned method. Something about handwriting the notes made the information stick a little more. It seemed Harper had the same idea as she scribbled notes next to me. But she glanced up when my purse vibrated.

"Is that you?"

"Crap," I fumbled down by my feet, trying to locate the damn thing.

Harper chuckled at my panic. "Relax, she can't hear it. She's too busy listening to the sound of her own voice."

Thankfully, I managed to set it to silent before it vibrated again. Then, I glanced at the incoming messages. "Unbelievable," I muttered under my breath.

"Problem?" Harper whispered.

"Just a stupid group chat I'm in with my brother and his idiotic friends."

"Are they hot?"

I frowned. "I'm not really sure how to answer that."

"Do they go here?"

"Yes, my brother is a senior."

"Interesting."

Was it?

I didn't respond, refocusing back on MacMillan's dissection of the common themes of English Literature post-1800s.

"We will read and critically analyze Austen"—Harper let out a soft whoop of approval and smiled—"Brontë, Hardy, and Eliot. The reading list is mandatory, not optional, so I suggest if you haven't already read the course texts, you start pronto."

Harper scoffed. "Come on, who hasn't read Pride and Prejudice at least once," she whispered, and I smothered a chuckle.

When the lights finally came back on, I was eager to get started on the first assignment.

"She's... intense," Harper said as we packed away our things.

"Yeah, but I like that. That she seems passionate about the course material."

We filed out of the room and fell into step beside each other.

"So, are you local?" Harper asked.

"I'm from Syracuse."

"Cool. I hail from Cleveland. So I'm pretty local. But I'm staying in the dorms. Have you checked out Roast 'n' Go yet? They make the best chai tea I've ever tasted. I swear that stuff is like a drop of heaven in a mug."

"No, I haven't been yet."

"Well, you're in for a treat. The gluten-free muffins are to die for too."

"Gluten-free?"

"Oh yeah," she said. "I'm celiac."

"That must be tough."

Harper shrugged. "I mean, you get used to it. But sometimes I just crave a large pizza or big bowl of pasta, you know."

"Can you eat gluten at all?"

"I can, but the side effects are nasty, so I try to cut it out completely. Shark week is a killer, though, because I crave carbs so badly. I found this great online bakery that specializes in gluten-free brownies, and oh my God, they are delicious. But honestly," a sigh of longing escaped her lips, "nothing beats the real thing."

We exited the building and cut across the lawn, heading toward the Student Union building.

"Aurora," someone yelled, and Harper's mouth dropped open as she noticed Austin jogging toward us.

"Hmm, Aurora, why is Austin Hart heading in this direction?"

"He's my brother."

"Your brother, right. You didn't think to mention that before?"

"Why would—"

"Hey." He reached us, running a hand through his dark tousled hair. "How did your morning go?"

"Good," I said. "Actually, I made a friend. Austin meet Harper—"

"Dixon. Harper Dixon. I'm a huge fan."

Austin grinned, that cocky smirk of his sliding into place. Oh, Jesus. He was going to hit on her, and Harper was going to fall for it.

Screw that. She was my friend first, and I wasn't about

to let her slip through my fingers for a tangle in the sheets with my brother.

"Knock it off, Austin," I said. "Harper is off-limits. She's my friend. I'm pulling the sister card."

"Aurora," Harper's face turned fire-truck red.

"I'm doing you a favor," I said. "He'll sleep with you and toss you aside like you're nothing. Any girl who reads Austen knows she's worth more than that."

"What the fuck is happening right now?" Austin frowned. "Because you lost me at Austin."

"Aus-ten," I emphasized. "As in Jane Austen."

"The actress?"

Harper snickered. "Close, but no, she's a novelist. The incredible mind behind characters such as Mr. Darcy—"

"Mr. Darcy? Who the fuck is—"

"Did you want something, Austin, or can this wait until later? We were just on our way to the coffee shop."

"Fine, I can take a hint." He hooked his arm around my neck and pulled me close. The way he had when we were kids. When life was simpler. "I'll check in with you later."

"Okay."

"Harper, nice to meet you." He gave her a salute but didn't lay on the charm too thick.

Thank God.

I wasn't sure I would survive losing my first friend to my brother's sexual proclivities.

"Sorry about that," I said.

"Sorry?" Harper gawked at me. "You're Austin Hart's sister, and you're apologizing to me? Girl, you just made my entire semester. This is so freaking cool."

It hit me then, an icy chill going through me.

"You're a hockey fan, aren't you?"

"Hells yeah." She beamed. "My dad played for the Lakers back in the day. I've followed them ever since I was old enough to attend games with him."

"That's... nice."

It wasn't.

It was my worst freaking nightmare.

"Why do you look like I just kicked your puppy? Austin Hart is your brother. I find it hard to believe you're related to a Laker and don't like hockey." I grimaced, and she frowned. "Oh. Wow, this suddenly got all kinds of awkward. I mean, I wouldn't say I'm obsessed or anything. I just enjoy a game now and again."

"Harper, it's fine. I knew what I was signing up for when I came to LU. It's a hockey college. I know that. Just promise me you won't go all dreamy-eyed every time my brother shows up out of nowhere."

"I'll try my best." She grinned. "Does this mean you're friends with the entire team?"

"I... I live with Connor Morgan and Noah Holden."

"Holy shit. Now there's an introduction I wouldn't mind."

"Connor?" I asked, hopeful.

"No way, he's got a serious girlfriend. I'm talking about Noah. He looks like he'd be down for a good time."

"You mean, you haven't heard the stories?"

"Of course I have." Her eyes lit up with interest. "I subscribe to The Daily Puck. He's always in the gossip column."

"I bet he is," I murmured.

"Sorry, what?"

"Nothing." I forced a smile.

I don't know why her words hurt so damn much. I knew

Noah was a self-professed manwhore. I also knew he was popular with the ladies.

I also knew he was kind and funny and didn't take himself too seriously.

But I didn't *know* him.

At least not in the way I wanted to.

And I never would.

CHAPTER 14

NOAH

"JESSICA RABBIT, TWO O'CLOCK," Leon said, and our heads all turned to find a stunning redhead making her way across the café.

"Now there's a woman I'd like to get acquainted with," Austin whistled through his teeth.

But I felt a streak of guilt.

"Maybe we should quit it with the stupid bunny scale," I suggested, and all eyes locked on me.

"The fuck? Did you bang your head on the ice this morning?" he said. "The bunny scale is almost as old and sacred as the team."

"Case in point," I argued.

"It's only a bit of harmless fun, Holden."

I found Adams across the room, and anger flared inside me. It was only a bit of harmless fun until somebody got their feelings hurt.

I guess I'd never cared before when engaging in locker

room talk with the guys because it didn't affect me. Most girls knew what they were signing up for when they batted their eyelashes or whispered sweet nothings in a player's ear. Scoring a Laker was like hitting the jackpot on campus. Even if they secretly hoped to be the one to break the mold.

But when things were personal, it was a different story.

Except, things aren't personal because Aurora isn't your girl.

"Shit, she's coming over here."

I glanced up right as she arrived at our table. "What can we do for you, beautiful?" Leon drawled.

"Actually, I was hoping to talk to Noah."

"I'm sorry," I said, "do I know you?"

"Not yet." A suggestive smirk played on her lips.

The guys snickered around me, probably anticipating whatever bullshit was about to come out of my mouth. But they were going to be sorely disappointed.

"Sorry, but I'm kind of busy."

She stepped between my legs and gazed down at me, licking her lips seductively. "I think I can make it worth your while."

"Maybe another time."

Confusion flashed over her expression, quickly morphing into disappointment. "Sure. Another time." She slipped her hand into a pocket and pulled out a slip of paper. "Call me. Anytime."

I nodded, taking the number from her because what else was there to do when a total knockout offered you her number?

"Have you lost your fucking mind?" Leon stared at me. "When Jessica Rabbit offers herself up on a platter, you take it."

"I've got class."

"In an hour," Mase said, watching me with a strange look in his eye.

"I'm not feeling it." I shrugged.

"Then I'll take that." Leon leaned over and snatched the number off me. "When I tell her you're not interested, I'll be right there to comfort her."

"Have at it, man."

"Are you sure you're feeling okay?" Austin said. "Because that's twice now you've—"

I dragged my finger across my throat, cutting him with an icy stare.

"What's this, Holden? You a little off your game?" Ward grinned, and I flipped him off. I might have taken him under my wing since he arrived on campus earlier in the summer. But he was still a rookie—he still had to earn his skates.

"The only game that matters is on the ice."

"Amen, bro. A-fucking-men." Austin lifted his can of soda and tilted it in my direction. "We're going all the way this season, assholes. I can feel it in my bones."

"I can feel something in my bone-er. Larissa Cummings." Leon waggled his brows as he read out her number. "Fuck, even her name is hot."

"There is something very wrong with you," I said.

"Takes one to know one, Holden."

"What—fuck." I ran a hand over my face, trying to figure out an escape route.

Sam was headed in my direction, and she looked needy. But there was no way out, and from the glint in her eye, she knew it.

"Hi guys, mind if I sit? It's been a shitty morning."

"What's up?" I asked, shifting up a little to give her plenty of space.

"I barely slept. I thought I heard something at my window."

"Sam, you live on the third floor."

"I know that, Noah." She tsked. "But I heard what I heard, and then I totally freaked myself out. So I was wondering... stay with me tonight?"

"Sam... we've been over this." I lowered my voice. "I can't."

"Why? Are you seeing somebody?"

"No, that's not... no." I glanced around, grateful that everyone had found something more interesting to focus on than our conversation. "I just don't think it's healthy for you to depend on me when we're not together."

"But we're friends. And it never bothered you before."

It hadn't. I liked hanging out with her. It was different to constantly being around the guys. And yeah, it came with the added bonus of no-strings orgasms.

At least, it had until she started to get clingy.

"It's different now," I said. "You—"

"Jeez, Noah. You're acting like I proposed. I know the deal. I just thought... forget it. I'm sure Ward will come over and keep me company."

"It won't work, you know."

"What won't?"

"Trying to make me jealous."

Sam stared at me as if she was searching for something. Whatever it was, I doubted she would find it. I couldn't change the way I felt, and it wasn't fair to lead her on.

"Then there shouldn't be any problem then." She got

up and walked off, and I let out a weary sigh, dragging a hand over my jaw.

"She's really laying it on thick," Mase said.

"You're telling me," I mumbled.

"You did the right thing. Set and enforce clear boundaries. She'll get the hint eventually."

"Yeah. I'm going to hit the gym."

"Again? Don't you have a one o'clock class?"

"Yeah, but I can squeeze in a quick workout."

I needed to burn some energy and try to take my mind off things.

"You're a machine, Holden." He chuckled.

Not really.

I just needed the distraction.

More than ever since Aurora arrived.

"Noah, son, take a seat." Coach Tucker motioned for me to sit, and I dropped down, feeling the walls close in around me.

I both loved and hated it in here.

It wasn't that his office wasn't a nice space. It was. Light, airy, a trophy cabinet full of all his silverware. But being hauled in here usually meant one of two things. Bad news or bad fucking news.

"What's up, Coach?" I asked, tapping my knee rhythmically.

"Tell me you've got a plan to lift your GPA, son. Because I'm looking at your transcripts, and I'm concerned."

"It's all in hand, Coach. I struggled with some of my

classes last semester. But my credits are a breeze this year. You don't need to worry."

"Except I am." He threw the envelope onto the desk. "I'll level with you, Noah. Here at LU, we pride ourselves on being the best. But that means the best versions of ourselves off the ice as well as on it. If your GPA slips any lower—"

"It won't, sir. I promise. I'll turn things around."

Because I didn't have any choice.

"Glad to hear it, son. We have a big season ahead of us. No one wants a repeat of last year."

"I've got this," I said, unsure who I was trying to convince more—him or myself.

"Good. Now get out of here."

"Thanks, Coach." I got up and made my way to the door, but his voice gave me pause.

"And, Noah?"

"Yeah, Coach?"

"Freshman year is done. Over. The hard work starts now."

I nodded, fighting the urge to flinch at his words.

The hard work starts now.

How many times had my old man said that to me growing up? How many times had it been followed by a barrage of insults and disappointment? I wasn't smart enough. I didn't have his genes. I wasn't his kid.

Of course, I was his fucking kid; I was his carbon copy —same dark unruly hair, defined jawline, and dark brown eyes. Except, he never smiled. So I'd made it my mission in life to smile as much as I could, even when it was fake, even when it was the last thing I wanted to do.

Because *not* turning out like him became the only thing that kept me going.

"What did Coach want?" Aiden caught me outside his office.

"Just wanted to touch base."

"Everything good?"

"Everything's fine. You ready to take us all the way this season?"

"Born ready." Aiden smirked.

"Glad to hear it." We exited the hockey facility together.

LU was lucky to have such a state-of-the-art facility, but when your team was four-time Frozen Four winners with one of the highest percentages of players to get drafted from the NCAA to the pros, money and sponsorships poured in.

"Seeing Dayna tonight?"

"No, she's got a deadline."

"At least she'll be here soon, permanently."

"Not soon enough." A faint grin traced his mouth. "We're going to look at some apartments next weekend."

"Nice. I know I gave you shit about her over the summer, but I'm happy for you."

"Watch it, Holden, or I'll start to think you're having a change of heart where relationships are concerned."

"Un-fucking-likely." Laughter bubbled out of me, but it sounded all wrong. He didn't seem to notice, though.

"You know, I thought you and Sam were going to fall into something."

"Nah, she's not my type."

"Tall, blonde, and beautiful, she's exactly your type. And she isn't a bunny; that's always a bonus."

"We're just friends. At least, we were. Before she started to get weird."

"Honestly, I never dreamed I'd settle down. It was the last thing on my radar. My first love has always been hockey. But then I met Dayna, and I realized it doesn't have to be a choice. You can have hockey *and* the girl."

"Nah, Cap." I clapped him on the shoulder. "That's your dream, not mine."

"You're only a sophomore, Holden. Give it another year, and you might feel differently."

"I'm not relationship material."

"Listen, this thing between you and Adams, do I need to be worried?"

"Nope."

Aiden's brow lifted with suspicion. "You sure about that? The wicked bruise he's sporting would suggest otherwise."

"His mouth got the better of him, and I shut him up." I shrugged. "Way I see it, as long as he doesn't run his mouth again, we won't have a problem."

"Just... come to me next time. I'm captain now. It's my job to make sure my players aren't beating the crap out of each other off the ice."

"He's an asshole."

"I don't disagree, but he's our asshole. We're a team, Holden. I can't have anything jeopardizing that. So whatever's going on between the two of you, bury it before official practice starts."

"Don't worry, Cap. I won't do anything to jeopardize the season."

But as I said the words, Aurora's face popped into my head. Her plump ass in those ridiculously tight yoga pants

Fuck.

I was in trouble.

A whole heap of trouble if anyone ever found out about my little infatuation with Austin's sister.

But I was Noah Holden. I knew the art of distraction just like I knew how to paint over the cracks and pretend everything was fine.

Aurora was my best friend's sister. Ergo, she was my friend.

That was acceptable.

That was safe.

That was all she could ever be.

Laughter greeted me when I finally got home.

After my little chat with Coach Tucker and then Aiden, I headed to the library to get a head start on my reading for this semester.

I'd picked Sports Business Management because I thought it would be a breeze. Turns out learning about economics, accounting, and marketing was harder than I thought.

"Holden, bro, get in here. We're teaching Rory how to play Puck Wars."

I dumped my bag at the bottom of the stairs, grabbed a bottle of water from the refrigerator, and headed into the living room. "Hey," I said.

"You're late. Get accosted by a bunny on your way home?" Connor smirked, and I flipped him off.

"Actually, I was at the library."

"How very studious of you."

"We can't all be fucking geniuses like you, Morgan."

"What can I say, man? I've got the brains and the good looks. Isn't that right, kitten?" He leaned up, and Ella smacked a kiss on his lips.

"Mmm, you taste good," she murmured, scraping his jaw with her fingernails.

"Okay, you two, let's keep it PG-13, please," Austin grumbled, jabbing his thumbs on the controller. "You need to block me, Rory, or I'm going to—GOAL," he fist-punched the air, and she threw her controller down.

"I'm done. Connor, you're up."

"Nooo, Sis, don't be like that. You were kind of getting the hang of it."

"I've never been any good at computer games." She stretched her arms above her head, making her t-shirt ride up her body. My gaze followed, my dick twitching behind my sweats.

It was another literary-inspired shirt, this one reading *book boyfriends do it better*.

Fuck, I'd like to test that theory.

As if she heard my thoughts, her eyes snapped to mine, narrowing with suspicion. I winked before joining Austin on the couch.

"How was Marketing?" he asked me.

"Okay, I guess. The professor is a relic. Made it crystal clear he doesn't go easy on athletes."

"Sounds like a hoot," Connor said.

"Yep. Hence, why I spent the afternoon in the library trying to get a head start on the reading."

"I feel your pain." Austin gave me a sympathetic glance. "This semester is going to be a killer."

"I don't know. I'm kind of excited," Connor said. "Time to think about the future, bro. The draft is calling."

"Fuck yeah." Austin leaned over to high-five Connor, the two of them grinning. "You going to follow your boy when he gets called up to the pros, El?"

"What kind of question is that, asshole? Of course, she is."

"Con..." she sighed.

"Uh-oh, do I detect trouble in paradise?"

"Just got to talk her into putting down roots with me." Connor said with utter conviction.

"That's just it, though, babe. When you go pro, you won't have roots."

"No, but I'll have money. Lots and lots of money."

"He's not wrong, El."

"Oh, trust me, she knows."

"Only because you don't shut up about it." She rolled her eyes. "You haven't even graduated yet, and you've already spent your signing-on bonus."

Austin and I raised a brow at Connor, and he spluttered. "In my head. I've spent it in my head. Relax, kitten, my mom taught me well."

Connor was signed with the Flyers. His future was golden. But it was good odds that Austin would go pro too. Same with Aiden, who was already in talks with the Detroit Red Wings.

I'd almost signed on with the New York Rangers in my senior year of high school, but my old man had other ideas, and he ruined everything. It was a complete shit show that had put the final nail in our complicated relationship. We barely spoke after that, and the second graduation rolled around, I was out of there.

I haven't looked back since.

Timothy Holden was no one to me.

No one.

But no matter how much I told myself that, how much I tried to move on from my past, I couldn't.

Not until I proved to him and the rest of his family that I was worth something.

That Noah Holden could make it on his own.

CHAPTER 15

AURORA

"So I was thinking..." Harper said over her steaming mug of chai tea. "Maybe you can introduce me to Noah."

"Seriously? You'd go there after half the female population has already experienced Noah Holden's... stick?"

"What?" She shrugged. "So long as he's safe and doesn't treat me like shit. It's just sex, Rory."

Just sex.

People kept saying that. As if I knew what they were talking about. I mean, I knew. I wasn't completely naïve. But I'd never had *just sex*.

I'd had sex with my boyfriend—my ex-boyfriend—and then I'd found out he was also having sex with my best friend. My much slimmer, prettier, popular, and sexually experienced best friend.

Talk about self-esteem killer.

And I didn't have much of that to begin with.

But maybe Harper, Dayna, and Ella were onto something. Maybe I needed to embark on a journey of self-discovery and casual sex. No strings. No promises.

No heartbreak.

Just me and some guy and a bucket load of vodka, probably.

Who was I kidding?

I wasn't confident enough to do the casual sex thing.

It's why Ben's betrayal had cut so deep. He knew what a big deal it was for me to trust him with my body—my heart—and he'd thrown it back in my face with zero regrets.

Why would I ever put myself through that again?

"So..." She watched me expectantly. "Will you do it?"

"I... Yeah, sure."

What the hell was I supposed to say?

Sorry, I can't because I'm harboring a secret crush on Noah that I know will never amount to anything, but I'd prefer it if you didn't have hot, sweaty sex with him because it'll ruin my fantasy. Thanks.

"Great, maybe I can come over later to study." She waggled her brows, a wicked glint in her eye. "I've heard he has a thing for blondes."

"Apparently so." I sipped my coffee, watching students come and go. I definitely preferred Roast 'n' Go over Joe's. It had absolutely nothing to do with the lack of hockey players at all.

"Don't look now," Harper whispered. "But there's a cute guy sitting along the back, and he's totally checking you out."

"I very much doubt—"

"He is." She nodded with enthusiasm. "He hasn't taken his eyes off you since we sat down."

"Maybe he's looking at you," I said.

"Trust me. He isn't. Anyway, he's really cute. You should go over there and give him your number."

"Why the hell would I do that?" Panic rose inside me, making my palms sweat.

"Because..." She chuckled. "It's college. Freshman year. Don't you want to live a little and soak up all the new experiences?"

"Harper, I'm sitting here in a t-shirt that says *I read books for fun*." Not to mention the messy bun I was sporting, the shapewear leggings, and well-worn Chucks.

"I'm not following."

Of course, she wasn't. Why would she?

"Forget it," I mumbled. "I'm not going over there."

"You don't need to because coffee hottie is headed this way."

"He's—" I glanced over, and sure enough, a cute guy in a sweater two shades darker than my eyes was walking toward us. "Totally coming over here. Oh, God."

"Breathe, Rory. It's just a guy." Her laughter did little to ease the churning in my stomach.

"Hey." He arrived at our table, giving me a nervous smile. "I'm Ryan. I wondered if you had room for another one?"

"Oh, actually, I'm—"

"Perfect timing, Ryan." Harper shot up out of her seat. "I was just leaving. You can take my seat."

"Harper," I hissed under my breath, but the meddlesome hussy flashed me an encouraging smile, mouthing, 'He's cute. Enjoy.' She winked and excused herself before I could protest.

"Do you mind?" He sat down. "Sorry, I didn't get your name."

Because I didn't give it to you. I swallowed the words.

"I'm Aurora."

"Ah, the goddess of dawn." Amusement twinkled in his eyes.

"Sorry, what?"

"Your name. It means 'goddess of dawn.' The Aurora Borealis is a spectacular natural light phenomenon in the arctic. I've always wanted to go."

"Oh, okay." My brows knitted. "I'm not sure that was my mom's inspiration."

"Still, it's a beautiful name for a beautiful girl."

"I... thanks." My cheeks flamed. Despite his genuine smile, I couldn't believe his words. Because I didn't *feel* them.

"I like your t-shirt." Ryan nodded toward my chest. "Avid reader?"

"You could say that."

"Favorite author?"

"I like the classics. Austen, Brontë, Hardy..."

"You're a romantic."

"I wouldn't call Hardy a romantic."

"Granted, Hardy leaned more toward realism and a critique on societal norms at the time, but his works still contain a lot of romantic elements."

"You're an English major?"

"Third year."

"And who is your favorite author?"

"It's a toss-up between Tolkien and Martin."

"Do you prefer books or the adaptations?"

"Is that even a question? The books. Every single time." He grinned, and I found myself grinning back. "Would you like another coffee?" He motioned to my empty mug. "I don't have a class for another forty minutes."

"I..."

What had Harper said about embracing freshman year and living a little?

But could I do it? Set myself up for what would only be an inevitable disappointment?

I took a deep breath and smiled. "Okay."

"Great, what are you having?"

"A vanilla skinny latte, please."

He got up and smiled down at me. "One vanilla skinny latte coming up."

"So..." Ryan hovered as we stood outside the coffee shop.

We had chatted for the last thirty minutes. He'd given me the lowdown on the first-year classes, and I'd listened attentively.

"Thanks for the coffee," I said.

"Can I maybe get your number? No pressure"—he held up his hands—"but I had fun and would like to do it again sometime. Who knows, maybe I can help you out with MacMillan's class."

"Sure, why not?" I grabbed my cell phone and handed it to him. Right as it bleeped with an incoming text.

And another.

And another.

"Uh, Austin and Connor want to know if you're going to be home for dinner. Apparently, it's Hot Dog Tuesday." His brows furrowed as he handed me back my phone.

"Oh my God," I breathed, suppressing my mortification. "It's not what you think. Austin is my brother, and Connor is his friend. I'm staying with them temporarily."

"For a second, I thought I had some serious competition."

"I... don't really know what to say to that." Nervous laughter bubbled out of me. "I need to get to class, but I'll see you around, Ryan."

"Yeah, see you, Aurora." His gaze lingered as I took off down the path toward the Department of English building.

And I realized I hadn't gotten his number.

So much for my attempt at living in the moment.

"So?" Harper leapt out from around the corner. "How did it go?"

"Were you waiting for me all this time?"

"No, silly. I got talking to some guy. I think we're going out on the weekend." She shrugged as if it was just business as usual. "Did you get Ryan's number?"

"Almost."

"What the hell does that mean?"

"We got distracted, and then I kind of ran off."

"Okay." She laced her arm through mine. "Tell me everything."

"There's not much to tell. He's an English Lit junior. Lives with his best friend downtown and picks up some shifts at a bookstore downtown during the weekend."

"Are you seeing him again?"

"I don't know. I didn't plan on seeing him today until you ambushed me," I pointed out.

"I was doing you a favor. He was cute and looked like your type."

"My type?"

"Yeah, you know, studious, cute in a geeky kind of way."

"Oh."

"Don't look so offended. It's not a bad thing. I just have this excellent sixth sense when it comes to these kinds of things. I'm like a real-life Cupid."

"Right." I barely kept the amusement out of my voice. "So if my type is a studious geek. What's your type?"

"Hockey hottie, of course." She grinned. "Although I'm not choosy. I'll take any brand of athlete."

"Of course." My lips thinned.

"Don't look at me like that, Miss Judgy Pants. I'm not looking for anything serious, and so long as everyone consents and is safe, I don't see the problem." She shrugged.

"No, you're right. It's your life, your body."

I'd had a similar conversation with Noah. Maybe he was right. Maybe I was too judgmental. Or maybe part of me was jealous, and it came off as hostile.

But that was on me.

It was my issue.

My cell phone started vibrating like crazy again.

"Someone's popular," Harper said.

"Ugh, don't. It's my brother and his friends. They added me to a stupid group chat." I opened the chat and skimmed the messages. "Apparently, it's Hot Dog Tuesday. They want to know if I'm going to be around."

"Tell them, yes, but you're bringing a plus one."

"I'm not asking Ryan to—"

"Not Ryan, silly." She grinned. "Me."

No.

Such a simple word. So why was it so freaking difficult to say?

No, I don't want to come to Hot Dog Tuesday.

No, you can't come to the house with me.

No, I don't want to hang out with you and my brother and his friends.

But my mind was always the enemy, overriding my desire *not* to spend the evening with Harper and Austin and the guys.

"Cute place," she said, letting her pretty gaze fall over the house.

"It's only temporary," I reminded her.

My visit to the housing office yesterday was a total bust. The water damage was worse than they initially thought, and it was going to take longer to fix it. They said they'd have an update by the end of next week.

"I like my own space. But if I had a choice, I'd pick living with three gorgeous hockey players any day."

"Are you sure you're not a bunny?" I asked.

"Please," she huffed. "I don't subscribe to the whole groupie thing. I just happen to have a thing for athletes. Especially ones who know how to handle their sticks, if you know what I'm saying."

"Oh my God," I breathed, practically choking on the air caught in my lungs.

Harper was something else.

Funny. Bold. One hundred percent unapologetic. She

was beautiful enough to be a puck bunny, but there was something different about her.

At least, that's what I told myself as I let us into the house and called out, "Hey, I'm home."

"We're in the yard," Connor yelled, the back door slamming.

"I guess we're going to the yard."

"Lead the way." Harper looked ready to explode right out of her skin.

"Can you at least try to act cool?"

"Please. I am quite capable of containing myself." She smoothed her shoulder-length blonde hair out of her face and swiped her tongue over her teeth. "I look okay, right?"

My brow lifted. "Seriously?"

"What? I want to make a good impression."

"Whatever," I murmured. "Let's get this over with."

We made our way through the house. I discarded my bag on one of the chairs before grabbing us both a drink. Harper opted for a beer, but I stuck with water. Although, maybe a drink would distract me enough to get through the next hour or so. I didn't want to have dinner with the guys, let alone watch Harper have dinner with them.

Just as I expected, the second we reached them, she stole the spotlight. Austin was on her in a second, introducing her to Connor and Noah.

Because, of course, Noah was here. So were Mason and Leon, who I'd learned was one of the team's rookies. But they seemed less interested in my new friend and more interested in the ruck of sausages sizzling away on the grill.

"How was your day, little Hart?" Connor joined me as I hovered on the periphery, watching Harper, Noah, and my brother debate the Lakers' chances of making it to the Frozen Four again.

She was one of them, I realized. Just a female version. They laughed and chatted like old friends. But Harper didn't look at Noah like they were friends. She looked at him like he was a prize to be won. A challenge to be conquered.

Jealousy snaked through me. Did he like her? Blonde, slim, and drop-dead gorgeous, Harper was exactly his type. Not to mention the fact she was a hockey fan and had a direct link to the team.

She'd walked into a yard full of Lakers and acted like she belonged there.

I could never do that.

"Rory, get over here," Austin called, one-handedly manning the grill while hanging on Harper's every word.

"What's up?" I asked.

"How was your day?"

"It was fine."

"Don't be shy, Rory," Harper smirked. "Tell him about your big news."

"W-what?"

Everyone stared at me, and I wanted the ground to open up and swallow me whole.

"Yeah, shortcake, why don't you tell us all your big news," Noah's eyes twinkled with interest.

"It was nothing."

"Oh, come on," he teased, "don't be shy."

"Aurora has a date. Well, she will when we track the coffee shop cutie down and tell him she would love to go out with him." Harper clapped her hands like a proud parent, and my insides withered.

God, she was embarrassing.

"Harper," I hissed, turning red all over. "It's not... it wasn't..."

I peeked over at Noah, but his expression remained indifferent. But then, why would he care if I went on a date? He was still hooking up with girls.

"Big whoop," Mase mumbled. "Can we eat now?"

"You don't have to be so rude," Harper snapped at him.

"Sorry, who the fuck are you again?"

"I'm Aurora's friend, and you're an asshole, Mason Steele."

"Friend, sure. Because we all want a friend who sells us out to our brother and his friends. Way to go, blondie." He turned his attention to Austin. "Hit me up with one of those dogs. I'm starving."

Harper looked at me, her expression a little crestfallen. "Aurora, I didn't—I have a habit of getting over-invested. I'm sorry if I made you feel uncomfortable."

"Relax, Rory's fine, right?" Austin slung his arm around her shoulder and held my stare. "You are okay, right?"

"I'm fine," I said, wanting to disappear.

"Good." He gave me a small nod, turning his attention back on Harper. "You hungry?"

"Always." But she wasn't looking at my brother...

She was looking at Noah.

"I think I'm going to grab a sweater," I said. "Will you be okay?"

"Of course, she will." Austin guided her toward the table. "We'll look out for her."

"Right." I headed toward the house, but not before glancing back at them. Harper was the center of attention, completely at home with a group of guys she barely knew.

She said something, and Noah exploded with laughter, the two of them leaning in close, continuing whatever joke they were sharing.

My stomach tumbled, and I ducked into the house, my mind running a mile a minute.

For as much as I wanted Lakeshore to be my fresh start, it felt an awful lot like high school all over again.

Even when I'd been with Ben, it didn't stop the intense feelings of worthlessness I felt every time we were around his friends. I knew everyone thought he could do better than me because *I* thought it. But thinking it about yourself and having other people constantly point it out was like a tiny hammer chipping away at your soul. Over and over until there was nothing left but a gaping hole inside you.

He'd told me to ignore them, that they were only jealous, but some of the worst moments in my life were overhearing cruel comments about our relationship.

Why is he with her?

He could do so much better.

She's definitely punching above her weight.

She must be paying him to date her.

Even when people thought they were being complimentary—talking about my big boobs or shapely ass—it hurt. Because being reduced to nothing more than skin and bones and flesh was dehumanizing.

I hurried to the downstairs bathroom and locked myself inside.

I needed a minute.

It wasn't like I could even go out there and eat my feelings away. Because if I started...

No.

It wasn't an option.

Knowing my luck, if I relaxed my diet a little, I wouldn't only gain the freshman fifteen, I'd gain the freshman twenty-one, and then there would be no hope of ever getting it off.

Five minutes passed. Then ten. But nobody came after me.

Why would they?

Harper had their full attention, and once again, I was left to wilt in the shadows.

CHAPTER 16

NOAH

"Aurora's been gone a while," Harper said.

"I'm sure she's fine." Austin drained his beer and slammed it down a little too enthusiastically. "She's probably upstairs reading."

"Still, I should probably—"

"Stay. Drink. Eat."

Jesus, he was so fucking obvious.

I got it. Harper was hot, and she knew hockey. Her old man had played for the Lakers back in the day, and that little tidbit of information had us all hanging on her every word.

James Dixon was a legend, a whispered myth in the locker room. He'd won two Frozen Four championships with the Lakers before crashing out of the NHL during his rookie year thanks to a brutal MCL injury. So to have his flesh and blood sitting right there was pretty fucking awesome.

At least, it would have been if I could stop thinking about what Harper had said earlier.

Aurora had a date.

Date.

Date.

Date.

The word rattled around my head like a sack of bricks.

It was probably a good thing. She could go on her date, and I could get past my weird little infatuation with her.

Only, every time I thought about another guy taking her out, I wanted to murder something with my bare hands.

"I'll go check on her. I want to get another drink anyway," I offered.

"I'll have another," Austin said, not taking his eyes off of Harper for a second.

She didn't seem interested, though. She was too busy eye-fucking me at every opportunity. I didn't have the heart to tell her she'd earned her way to the top of my *never going to happen* list the second she'd walked into the yard with Aurora.

I was a dog, but I wasn't an asshole.

Mase and Connor both watched me as I headed toward the house, but I didn't acknowledge them. It wasn't like I was going to do anything stupid.

I just wanted to get a drink and check on Aurora. My friend's sister. My housemate. My friend.

Keep telling yourself that, asshole.

She wasn't downstairs, though, so I headed up to her room, knocking gently.

"I'll be right out," she called, but I heard the slight wobble in her voice.

"I'm coming in, shortcake." I pushed the door open, and our eyes locked.

"What are you doing up here?"

"We missed you. It's not Hot Dog Tuesday without you."

She rolled her eyes at that. "I just needed a minute."

"What's the matter?" Stepping into her room, I closed the door behind me.

"Nothing, I'm fine."

"Shortcake..."

"I'm just having a crisis of confidence. I'll be fine in a minute."

"Harper." I guessed.

"I thought she was like me. But she isn't. Quite the opposite, actually." She stared off toward the window as if she could see her new friend down there, laughing and joking with the guys as if she belonged there.

"She's hot and knows hockey." I shrugged. "We guys are easily pleased."

The second the words left my mouth, I regretted them. Her expression dropped, hurt flashing in her eyes.

"Shit, Aurora, I didn't mean—"

"Yeah, you did. But I get it." She gave me a small, resigned smile that made my chest tighten. "Harper is beautiful, and she's practically Lakers royalty. What's not to like?"

"Where is all this coming from?" I asked, annoyed as fuck to hear Aurora talking about herself like this.

But she refused to look at me.

Going to her, I slid my fingers under her jaw, coaxing her face to mine. "Shortcake..."

"We should probably go back down there before

someone comes looking. In case you haven't worked it out already, Harper is hoping the two of you will—"

"No."

"No?" Her nose crinkled. "But—"

"She's your friend. I wouldn't do that to you."

"Oh."

"You look surprised, shortcake. I know I have a bit of a reputation, but I'm not a bad guy."

"No, you're not." Her eyes searched mine, and I wanted to give her the answers she was seeking.

But I couldn't.

Because things had already gone too far when I'd kissed her.

"Noah, I—"

"So, who is this guy Harper mentioned?"

"Ryan?" She frowned as if she couldn't believe I asked.

I couldn't believe it either.

"I'm not sure I'm going to go out with him," she said, leaving the rest of her sentence unspoken.

"You should."

"You think I should... right, got it."

"I'm just saying it might be good for you to get out there, have some fun. Harper said he's an English major, so you'll have a lot in common."

"Yeah, you're right." The smile didn't reach her eyes, hurt gleaming there, cementing the guilt in my chest. "Maybe I will."

"Good."

"Good."

The air crackled between us as we stared at each other. I didn't want her to date some English major. I didn't want her to date anyone. But it wasn't about me; it was about

Aurora—her self-esteem and self-worth. If going on a few dates with a guy who wasn't me helped give her some confidence, then it was a good idea.

No matter how much I hated the idea.

Until she said, "Maybe you should take Harper out, and we can double date."

Because... Fuck. That.

I wanted her to feel better about herself. I didn't want to feel shitty about myself, watching her with some guy who wasn't me.

I couldn't be that guy, though.

Even if she wasn't Austin's sister, I didn't have time for a relationship. And I would never ask Aurora to be in a friends-with-benefits situation.

No matter how much I wanted her.

And I did.

I'd had a little taste, and now I wanted to devour her. Preferably with my teeth and tongue.

"Noah?" Her eyes twinkled with uncertainty as she gazed up at me. But I saw the flicker of hope there. The willingness to tug gently on the thread that seemed to stretch and tighten between us every time we were close.

I wondered if she knew that she was throwing off all the right signals.

Something told me she didn't.

Aurora was too blinded by her skewed perception of herself to believe that I could ever reciprocate whatever was bubbling between us.

"I don't date, shortcake." I sealed our fate. "You know that."

"You won't make an exception this one time? For me?"

Such a loaded fucking question.

She meant Harper, but there was another question in there somewhere.

"No exceptions to the rule."

Disappointment glittered in her emerald eyes. "I see. She's going to be disappointed."

"I'm sure she'll find someone else. We should head back downstairs."

Because I needed to get out of this room, out of her space. Before I broke my own fucking rules... again.

I turned and walked to the door, but Aurora called after me.

"Noah?"

"Yeah, shortcake?" I glanced back at her.

"Why did you kiss me?" Defiance shone in her eyes, and I realized she wasn't going to let this go.

And part of me was proud of her for standing up to me. For calling me out on my bullshit and demanding an explanation. But I couldn't walk this path with her.

I wouldn't.

So I said the only thing I could think of to draw an impenetrable line between us.

"It was a mistake."

"What are you two doing over there?" Austin called over to the girls.

After we'd come back downstairs, Aurora kept her distance, choosing to sit as far away from me as possible.

I didn't blame her.

I'd been a total asshole.

Much to Austin's disappointment, Harper had joined her, and the two of them spent the last thirty minutes laughing and giggling at whatever they were looking at on Harper's phone.

Aurora was putting on a brave front, though. Connor and Austin might not have noticed, but I did.

I was noticing too much about her lately.

"You know, it's rude to share private jokes when you're not in private," Connor said, sipping his beer.

"If you must know, we're looking at Austen memes."

"Don't look at me," Austin groaned. "It's Aus-ten, not Aus-tin."

"The author who wrote that Darcy dude chicks go ga-ga over?"

"Yep. We're both huge fans." Harper nudged her shoulder, and Aurora flushed.

"I'm not obsessed or anything."

"I don't get it." Austin sat back in his chair and ran a hand through his hair. "What's so special about him?"

"Rich, handsome, and an avid lover of the written word. What's not to love?" Harper shrugged.

"It's more than that," Aurora said, surprising the shit out of me.

She'd been quiet since we came downstairs. Laughing and joking with Harper, sure, but she'd avoided any of our wider group discussions.

"Enlighten us, little Hart. Maybe these assholes will learn a thing or two." Connor winked at me, and I flipped him off discreetly.

"Mr. Darcy is the epitome of a gentleman," she said quietly. "He didn't try to change Elizabeth or mold her into what he thought she should be. He treated people, even those outside his own social standing, with dignity and respect, but above all, he was open and honest, and he loved Elizabeth not for what she was, but who she was."

"Sounds like a snooze fest, if you ask me," Mason said.

"You would say that." Harper sneered, and the two of them shared a hostile look.

"What the fuck is that supposed to mean?"

An icy chill went through the air.

"Come on," she scoffed, "you all walk around campus like God's gift to women."

"So you haven't been batting your eyelashes at Holden for the last hour, throwing out major 'I want to ride your stick' vibes?" His brow cocked with contempt.

"I... that is not the point." Harper stuttered, turning beet red, and Aurora paled.

Fuck.

"My stick is always available," Austin said through a shit-eating smirk.

"That was gross and unnecessary." Aurora grimaced. "You ready to go?"

"Go? You can't go, little Hart, it's Hot Dog—"

"Sorry, Con. But Harper has to get back for her shift at Millers."

"Millers' Bar and Grill?" Connor asked, and she nodded.

"That's the one. I pick up some late shifts. I'm a night owl, and the extra money helps."

"Nice, but it doesn't mean you can't stay, Rory, baby." He pouted, laying it on thick.

"Another time. Come on," she said to Harper, who followed her up.

"Thanks for the hot dog." Harper smiled at him before turning her gaze in my direction. "Noah."

Fuck.

She had the look, only confirming what Mase had said a minute earlier. But she didn't seem to care one bit as she openly checked me out, eyes glittering with approval.

"Hopefully, I'll see you around."

"Uh, sure," I murmured, not wanting to offend Aurora's new friend.

The girls disappeared into the house, and Austin whistled under his breath, "Jesus, she's hot."

"She's fucking annoying," Mase said.

"You're just pissed she only had eyes for Holden," Connor said.

"Fuck that. She's not my type. I like girls who are less... whatever the fuck that was."

"You mean you like girls who can't think for themselves." Amusement laced Leon's words.

"What's up with Rory?" Connor asked Austin. "She seemed... off."

"I guess she isn't used to this." He shrugged, finding the label of his Heineken bottle hella interesting.

"Used to what?"

"I dunno, she's always been a bit socially awkward. It's like her thing or something."

"She's not usually so quiet around us," Connor added. "She seemed kind of... sad."

"I don't know what to tell you, she had some shit going on when she was younger, but that was a long time ago. I'm sure it's nothing."

"Didn't seem like nothing," I said, instantly regretting it.

"Jesus, what are you two?" he grumbled. "Her therapists? Aurora has always been withdrawn. It's just how she is. I need to take a piss." He got up and stormed toward the house.

"Was it something I said?" I let out a strangled laugh.

"Anyone gets the impression we're missing something?" Connor said.

Yes, yes, I did.

But the question was, what?

The next day, I sat in class, still pondering how to fix things with Aurora, when a familiar face entered my periphery.

"Sam, what are you—"

"Surprise." She sat down beside me and started getting out her things.

"Wait, you're taking this class?"

"Well, yeah. I wouldn't be here otherwise. I thought it would be a nice surprise."

Oh, it was a surprise, alright.

"I had to switch a couple of my classes due to a clash, and this one came up, and I've always wanted to take an accounting class. So now we can be study buddies, yay."

My brows furrowed as I fought the urge to ask her what the hell she was doing. But it wasn't like she'd switched to one of the sports electives.

I couldn't dictate what classes she did or didn't take. But it threw a serious kink in my plan to put some space between us.

"I aced math in high school," she whispered while the professor made his way onto the stage.

"You did?"

"Yep. I'm not just a pretty face, you know."

My lips quirked. When she wasn't coming on too strong, Sam was fun to be around. She didn't take herself too seriously and never cared too much about what she looked like. It's one of the things I'd like about her. Her easy, laid-back, approachable personality.

But I still wasn't sure we could go back to how things were before we fell into bed together.

Or if I even wanted to now that—

I stopped *that* train of thought. Aurora wasn't mine. I didn't owe her anything. I'd told her to go on the date with the English major, for fuck's sake.

My fist clenched on the desk, and Sam leaned in. "What's wrong?"

"Nothing. He's about to start," I tipped my head in the direction of the professor, who thankfully chose that second to introduce himself.

The minute he started talking about accrual and consistency principles, I realized I'd made a mistake taking this class. I fucking hated numbers. But it was too late now.

After ten minutes of listening to him drone on, I'd all but zoned out.

"Noah," Sam nudged me in the ribs, and my head snapped to hers. "Are you asleep?"

"Nope. Just resting my eyes."

"Seriously, if you want to keep your GPA up, you need to—"

"Okay, *Mom*," I said through gritted teeth.

She rolled her eyes, and I regretted ever confiding in her that I hadn't passed all my credits freshman year and that this year I was going to have to work my ass off if I wanted to stay eligible for my scholarship.

Thanks to Sam's nagging, I managed to stay alert for the rest of the class. But I didn't feel any better about things when we filed out of the room.

Dragging a hand down my face, I let out a frustrated sigh.

Sam chuckled. "Feeling the pressure?"

"Something like that."

"Don't worry, babe." She laced her arm through mine and tucked herself into my side as if she belonged there. Unease trickled through me. "Stick with me, and I'll make sure you ace this class."

"I…"

She had a point. I needed all the help I could get. But letting her help me meant spending more time with her. The very thing I wanted to avoid.

I couldn't afford to screw up this semester, though.

"Yeah, sounds good," I said, gently nudging her away.

Sam's whole face lit up. "Perfect. We can plan a study schedule and get to work right away."

"Perhaps we should meet at the library or Joe's."

Her expression dropped, but she quickly recovered, painting a smile on her face. "Don't be silly, Noah," she said. "We can study at my place. We'll have no distractions there. It's the perfect solution."

Fuck. My. Life.

CHAPTER 17

AURORA

RYAN WAVED when he spotted me.

"Hi," I said, shucking out of my jacket. "Sorry, I'm late. I got held up."

I didn't tell him that Connor had staged a date-rvention after I'd told him that Harper had tracked Ryan down and given him my number. The whole thing had been bizarre, to say the least, culminating in Connor giving me his three golden rules of dating.

Number one: Limit myself to two drinks max—no one liked a white-girl wasted date; Number two: Let the guy order—guys liked to feel important. And number three: Don't put out on the first date—guys, despite what they said, enjoyed the chase.

Then he'd wished me luck and told me that if I needed bailing out at any point, he could provide an escape plan, no questions asked. I'd almost asked why he was giving me all the dating advice and not my brother—who was nowhere to be seen—but I didn't. Austin was... Austin. He'd missed me. He wanted to fix things. But he hadn't really changed.

Noah wasn't around when Connor waved me off, but I was hardly surprised. He'd made it perfectly clear where we stood the other night.

For the rest of the week, I'd replayed the conversation over and over, trying to dissect it. To read between the lines. But there was no hidden meaning, no secret message. He couldn't have made it any clearer.

"Noah?"

"Yeah, shortcake?" He looked back at me.

"Why did you kiss me?" I asked with a defiant tilt of my chin.

His expression guttered, and then he said four little words that crushed me.

"It was a mistake."

"Oh, that's okay," Ryan said, pulling me from my thoughts. "I was running late too. Can I get you something to drink?"

"Sure, I'll have a skinny vanilla latte, please."

Ryan headed for the line, and I dug my phone out of my purse. I already had three messages.

> Harper: I want to know EVERYTHING. Call me as soon as you get home.

I rolled my eyes, not deigning a reply. The other two were from the group chat.

Connor: Remember: two drinks max, let him order, and do not under any circumstance put out on a first date.

Austin: Jesus, Morgan. That's MY SISTER you're talking about!!!

Quickly, I texted them back.

Aurora: I'm muting this chat now.

Connor: Go get 'em, tiger.

Austin: I swear to God, asshole. Quit with that shit.

Ignoring the little pang of disappointment I felt that Noah had nothing to say, I silenced my notifications and slipped my phone back into my purse. Right as Ryan appeared with my drink.

"One skinny vanilla latte." He slid the mug toward me. "I also got us a double chocolate muffin each. Enjoy."

My stomach dropped.

"Oh, I'm not hungry, thanks."

He glowered, clearly offended. "It's only a little muffin, babe. It won't hurt."

"I…"

This is exactly why I'd declined his offer to go for dinner. I didn't want to feel obligated to eat in front of him. To have him scrutinize my meal habits. To become fixated on every little thing. What would I order? How many calories would it have? How long would I have to workout to burn it off? Would he comment if I chose something light?

"You're not one of those girls, are you?" Disapproval creased his features.

"Sorry, what?"

"Like all obsessed with what you eat? Because, you know, it's really a simple case of cause and effect. So long as you burn more than you put in, you'll be fine."

I pressed my lips together, giving him an awkward smile. *If only it were that easy.*

"You won't find a better chocolate muffin in all of Lakeshore. Just try it." He pushed the plate toward me with an encouraging smile, all while the walls closed in around me.

"I ate before I left, sorry."

He let out a little huff of disapproval. "Fine. Let it go to waste then."

Shame filled my chest. It was just a muffin. One little muffin. If I limited what I ate for the rest of the day, it would be fine. But I couldn't do it. I couldn't eat it.

I sipped my coffee, hoping Ryan would fill the awkward silence. He seemed pissed, though, leaving his muffin untouched too.

The plates taunted me, making me wish that I could just be normal and eat the damn muffin. But I couldn't do it, not with him watching me. Not with the nausea building inside me, making me feel like I was riding the Tilt-a-Whirl at the fairground.

"So..." I said, attempting to smooth over the rocky start. "How are your classes going so far?"

"Oh, everything is—" His cell bleeped, and he held up a finger. "Sorry, I need to check this."

"Oh, okay."

It went on like that for fifteen minutes. Every time the conversation got going, his cell would vibrate, and he'd snicker at something, fingers flying over the screen as he texted back.

I didn't know who this asshole was sitting opposite me, but it wasn't the pleasant, cute guy who had approached me the other day.

"Excuse me," I said, tired of his dismissive attitude. "I need to use the restroom."

I got up and hurried across the room, a sinking feeling going through me. Ryan wasn't at all what I'd expected, and there was absolutely no spark between us. If anything, he seemed completely disinterested in me, which was weird, considering he had pushed for my number.

It wasn't like I'd agreed to meet him with the expectation of starting anything romantic, but it would have been nice to make a new friend.

Washing my hands, I checked my reflection, tucking a stray hair behind my ear. I was glad I hadn't dressed up; the vibe here was laid-back. And Ryan hadn't looked twice at me anyway, so any effort on my part would have been wasted.

When I returned to the table, Ryan had his phone pressed to his ear. I didn't mean to eavesdrop, but it wasn't like I had much choice, given I needed to return to our table.

As I drew closer, there was something about the way he laughed that sent a chill down my spine.

"I don't know. I think she's got some weird food hang-up. I bought her a muffin, and she freaked out. I mean, she's not a whale or anything." He laughed again, making my heart drop. "Hell yeah, her porn star tits are every guy's wet dream, but she gets zero points for effort. She looks like a thrift store reject in this godawful—" He looked up, and the blood drained from his face. "Shit, I gotta go. Aurora, it's not—"

I turned around and made a beeline for the door, abandoning my jacket and the stupid muffin. The second I hit the sidewalk, the tears unleashed, running down my cheeks in rivers.

Ryan was supposed to be nice.

A good, nice, safe guy.

I should never have come tonight. But I'd let Harper believe I could do it—that I could go on a casual date with someone. Maybe part of me had also wanted to get back at Noah for encouraging me to say yes.

And look how it backfired.

Pulling out my cell phone, I managed to text Connor.

Aurora: Can you pick me up?

Connor: What happened?

Aurora: Turns out English majors are assholes too.

Connor: Shit, send me your location. I'll be there ASAP.

Aurora: Thank you. And Connor...

Connor: Yeah, little Hart?

Aurora: Don't tell Austin please.

Connor: Consider it done.

"Thank God," I breathed as Connor's truck came into view.

Except, it wasn't Connor who hopped out.

"Noah?" I gawked at him as he strode toward me.

"What happened?"

"N-nothing, I... nothing."

"Aurora." His voice was a low gravelly warning that made my stomach twist and tighten. "I swear to God if he hurt you—"

"He didn't, not in the way you're thinking."

Noah's brow crossed as he stared down at me, anger radiating from every solid inch of him.

"Where's Connor?"

I could have sworn hurt flashed in his eyes, but I had to be seeing things because Noah had made it clear where he stood.

Where *we* stood.

He'd pushed me into Ryan's arms. So why the hell was he standing here, looking ready to defend my honor with nothing more than his fists and anger?

"Ella called upset. Something about her gran. He headed over there, and I headed here."

Oh. That killed any seed of hope I'd felt that his white-knight routine might be anything more than friendly concern.

"Is she okay?"

"You're standing on the street corner with mascara running down your face, shortcake, and you're asking if Ella's okay? I will never understand women." He smiled, but it didn't reach his eyes.

"Take me home, Noah."

It wasn't supposed to sound so suggestive, but the words were out now, hanging between us like an undetonated bomb.

"Are you sure I don't need to hunt him down and kick his ass because I will, you know?"

Why? The word teetered on the tip of my tongue, but I refused to ask. I couldn't put myself out there only to be knocked down again.

Noah didn't want me.

Or at least, he didn't want me enough.

And I got it. I wasn't the type of girl people expected him to hook up with. I didn't fit the mold.

"Can we just go, please?"

"Shit, yeah, come on." Noah wrapped his arm around me and led me to Connor's truck.

The air was stifling as we both climbed in, the silence almost too much to bear. Noah gripped the steering wheel and stared out the windshield.

"Noah?"

"Just... give me a minute."

A beat passed, and another.

I didn't know what to say. I hadn't expected him to show up.

He exhaled a long breath and fired up the engine, the truck rumbling to life beneath us.

"He made you cry." His hands tightened, the blood draining from his knuckles.

"It's not as bad as it seems. I... I reacted badly to some stuff he said."

"What stuff? And don't try to pacify me with some vague bullshit, shortcake." Noah's gaze flicked to mine. "I want to know *exactly* what he said."

"Well, tough shit because I don't want to talk about it."

"Aurora..."

"Noah..."

"God, you're infuriating, woman."

"Me? *Me*?" I snapped.

"I just want to help," his voice softened. "But you're so fucking stubborn."

"Ha," I scoffed, disbelief plunking in my chest. "It was your *help* that landed me in this situation in the first place."

"My help... what the fuck are you talking about?"

"Forget it." I backtracked because getting worked up over something I couldn't change was pointless.

We were responsible for our own actions. Noah might have told me to go on the date with Ryan, but I was the one who said yes. All because I was butt hurt that he was pushing me into the arms of a guy who wasn't him.

I stared out the window for the rest of the journey, refusing to engage with Noah. It was bad enough he'd been the one to come and get me. Now he knew that I'd gotten upset. His white-knight routine wouldn't let him stand down without some kind of answer, but I wasn't sure I could give him any.

What Ryan said, the way his words affected me, was a deeply personal thing.

It was so easy for people to dismiss or invalidate other people's feelings or extreme reactions to things that seemed so trivial. But until you'd walked in someone else's shoes, you couldn't truly know what it felt like to experience life through their lens.

I wasn't the ten-year-old girl I'd once been. The girl who had stood in front of more than one photographer only to be told she was too big for their vision and to come back in a few months when I had dropped a few pounds. But I wasn't healed either.

Because those kinds of scars ran deep. So deep that they became a part of you. A stain on your soul. And every negative interaction after that pivotal moment only served to deepen the cracks.

By the time we pulled up to the house, the air inside the truck was so thin I could hardly breathe. Shouldering the door open, I leapt out and hurried toward the house.

"Shit, shortcake, would you just wait a—"

But I was already gone, flying through the house and upstairs toward my room. I didn't want to talk about it. I didn't want to have some big heart-to-heart with Noah only for him to reject me again. I just wanted to be alone. And maybe eat my body weight in ice cream and then hate myself for it. Because adding a little bit of self-loathing to the mix sounded about right.

I didn't make it to my room though.

I didn't even make it to the second-floor stairs.

"Not so fast." Noah snagged me around the waist and

pulled me into his strong, muscular body. "Talk to me, shortcake."

"And say what?" I shrieked. "That it was a bad idea going out with Ryan tonight? That he's just like every other guy out there? Or do you want to know how it felt to hear him telling his friend that I had porn star tits but looked like a thrift store reject? That I should be thankful I'm not a whale but should really try and work on my appearance so that assholes like him will find me more visually pleasing? Tell me, Noah, what exactly would you like me to say?" I stared up at him, tears clinging to my lashes, my chest rising and falling between us.

Noah's expression darkened, the muscle in his jaw working overtime as he stared back at me. "He said that?"

"I... I don't want to talk about it."

"Tough shit, shortcake. Because I do, I want to know every single word that came out of that asshole's mouth. And then I want to hear it again, so I can make sure I've got it right for when I beat the shit out of him for making you cry."

"I don't need you going around campus fighting my battles, Noah."

"Maybe I want to."

"This white-knight routine you've got going is cute and all, but I don't need your help." I yanked out of his hold and marched up the stairs to my room.

This time, he didn't follow.

Why would he?

This wasn't some fluffy romance novel where the hero had a sudden epiphany that he wanted the heroine despite two hundred pages of them bickering and arguing at every turn.

Inside my room, I made a beeline straight for the bathroom, slamming the door behind me. My clothes came off in a whirlwind of anger and shame. The stupid *godawful* shapeless t-shirt I'd worn. The shapewear leggings that did a bad job of disguising my thunder thighs and round ass. And my jacket... shit, I'd left my jacket behind.

Tears stung my eyes as I stood in front of the mirror in only my underwear, my gaze snagging on every flaw. Every single imperfection.

She's not a whale.

But I sure felt like one. I slid my hands down my waist, the flare of my hip, my fingers snagging on the faded silvery pink streaks covering my hips and stomach.

I could vividly remember discovering them on my body when I was twelve. The shame I felt when my mom caught me checking them out in the mirror. She'd given me every skin product she could get her hands on to undo their appearance: bio oil, cocoa butter, retinol cream.

But nothing worked.

Nothing *fixed* them.

Because I was broken. Tainted. And my body had failed me.

"It's fine," she muttered with disappointment. *"A good editor will airbrush those right out."*

I was so upset I binge-ate an entire box of Reese's peanut butter cups and spent the night vomiting. Austin had briefly checked in on me, but he had an important game to prepare for, and I didn't want to ruin his mindset, so I'd lied and told him I ate some bad chicken.

I always did that—protected him from the truth. It was bad enough that Mom hated him because he looked so much like our father. A permanent reminder of the man she'd loved and lost.

They couldn't stand to be around each other, and I was caught in the middle. Except, Austin didn't realize that she made my life hell too.

He thought she was just hard on me. Overcritical.

Because you never told him.

But how could I? How could I look him in the eye and tell him that Mom—the woman who was supposed to love me unconditionally—had broken me?

Grabbing the nearest thing, I hauled it at the mirror and flinched as it cracked, a few pieces clattering onto the vanity. Oddly, I felt better because it was broken now.

Just like me.

CHAPTER 18

NOAH

I HEARD something smash inside Aurora's room, and before I could stop myself, I shouldered the door open and barged inside.

Right as Aurora appeared out of the bathroom.

"What was that?" I asked, casting a gaze over her, relief sinking into me that she seemed to be in one piece.

"Nothing."

"Shortcake, what—"

Fuck.

It hit me then; she was half-naked. Her delicious curves were on full display as she stood in nothing but her plain black cotton bra and panties. There wasn't an ounce of lace or silk in sight, and yet, she was quite possibly the most beautiful thing I'd ever seen.

"Oh my God, Noah," she shrieked, "turn around, please."

"Why? You're beautiful, Aurora."

"Stop." Her expression didn't just fall; it shattered. "Please, don't say that. It isn't fair."

She hurried over to her desk chair and snatched a t-shirt off the back of it, yanking it over her head. It swamped her, but she still stretched it down over her legs as if she couldn't bear me looking at her.

Disappointment curled in my stomach as I asked, "Fair?"

"You know what I mean. This, us, you've made it pretty clear that kissing me was a mistake. I don't need you rubbing salt in the wound."

"Let me be real fucking clear, shortcake." I strode toward her until we were almost chest-to-chest. Her breath caught at my proximity, a shudder rolling through her as I reached for her cheek, cupping her face.

"It was a mistake when I kissed you."

"Noah, please just—"

"Because all I've thought about since is doing it again. But you're Austin's sister, Aurora, and the team has strict rules about that kind of thing."

"And you. You have your own rules." There was that flicker of defiance in her eyes again. "You don't date."

"No," I swallowed over the lump in my throat, my heart doing little flips in my chest. "I don't." I moved closer, dipping my head, forcing her to crane her neck a little.

"Noah, what are you—"

"I'm glad Ryan turned out to be an asshole because now I won't feel bad about doing this."

Gliding my hand along the side of her neck, I kissed her. Slicking my tongue into her mouth and taking what I'd wanted ever since tasting her last weekend. Aurora went tense, and for a second, I thought she might fight me. But she melted against me, sliding her hands up my chest and kissing me back.

Fuck, she felt good, pressed up against me, her tongue soft and eager. Sliding one hand down her spine, I grabbed a handful of her plump ass and pulled her onto my waiting boner.

"If you need any reassurance that you get me hot, shortcake, here it is."

"Noah," she choked on my name, and an image of her on her knees, choking on my favorite body part, filled my mind.

Shit, Holden. Slow down. Don't scare her away.

Aurora was fragile, that much was obvious, and I knew I needed to handle her with care. I had absolutely no problem with that though. I could take my time with her. Teach her. Guide her.

But like a bucket of ice water, she rasped, "Austin, Connor—"

"Not sure I like hearing you moan another man's name when my lips are on your skin, shortcake."

She fisted my t-shirt and shoved me gently. "What if they come home?"

"Then you'd better be quiet when I make you come all over my fingers." I slid my hand around her front and cupped her pussy through her panties.

Aurora's knees buckled, but I was there to catch her.

"Oh my God, you can't say that." She blushed, and I had the strongest urge to strip her bare to see if she turned the same shade of pink everywhere.

"Just did, shortcake. And there's plenty more where that came from." I dropped a kiss on the end of her nose, but she'd gone tense again.

"What are we doing, Noah?" Her eyelashes fluttered. The pink streaks along her cheeks darkening.

"You want the truth, shortcake?" She nodded, and my chest grew tight. "This is a terrible idea." I touched my head to hers, breathing her in. "You're my best friend's sister. I'm a hockey player. I don't date. And you don't date hockey players anymore."

"You're right"—a faint smile traced her mouth—"it is a terrible idea."

"A really, really bad idea." I lowered my mouth over hers, a whisper of a kiss. "We should probably stop."

"We should definitely stop." Aurora went up on her tiptoes and curled her arms around my shoulders, holding on as if she might never let go.

We stayed like that, staring at each other, breathing each other's air, kissing, but not kissing.

Until something snapped.

I don't know who moved first, but we crashed together in a kiss as hard and unrelenting as my dick straining behind my sweats. My hands were everywhere, in her hair, mapping her curves, tracing the lines of her body.

"Fuck, you're sexy," I drawled, smirking at her as she tried to steal another kiss.

"Don't tease me, Noah."

"That's half the fun, shortcake." My hand slipped under Aurora's t-shirt, stroking her warm skin. But it wasn't enough. I wanted to see her again—to memorize every inch of her body.

Curling my fingers around the hem of her t-shirt, I started to work it up her stomach, but she grabbed my hands. "Don't..."

"Shortcake," I whispered the word onto her lips, "let's

get one thing straight. I love your body. I love your curves. I love your ass and your tits. God, I love your tits."

"Oh my God," she let out a quiet, nervous chuckle. "You're crazy."

"About you. I'm crazy about you, Aurora. I know shit is complicated. I know there's a bunch of stuff that we should probably figure out before we go any further, but don't you ever just want to say to hell with it all and just live in the moment?"

"If that's your pickup line, I can see why you have so much sex."

"Shit, Aurora." I pulled away, a sinking feeling spreading through me. "I don't—"

"Sorry, I'm sorry." She grabbed my hand and tugged gently. "I'm just nervous. You make me nervous. The way girls fall over their feet for a shot with you. Beautiful girls, Noah. Girls who—"

"I'm going to stop you right there." I pressed a finger to her lips, trapping whatever self-deprecating bullshit was about to come out of her mouth. "There isn't a single thing wrong with you or your body."

"Noah—"

"No, Aurora. Let me show you. Let me show you how much I want you."

Because if I didn't get to touch her in the next five seconds, there was a good chance I might combust and blow in my sweats. Every muscle in my body was wound tight, pure lust vibrating through me.

I'd told myself to do the right thing. Over and over, I'd told myself not to touch Aurora again. But I'd never been very good at following the rules. And she was one I wanted to break again and again.

It was more than that though. I wanted her to see what I saw every time I looked at her. I wanted her to feel sexy and feminine and wanted.

She deserved that.

I didn't know much about what had gone down with her mom or Austin or her ex, but I had a good suspicion it had shaped her. Molded and defined her.

Hurt her.

I knew a little something about that. About how hard it was to silence the ghosts of your past.

"Okay. One night. You get me for one night."

I frowned. "One night, shortcake? I'm not sure that's going to cut it for—"

She pressed a finger to my lips, offering me a sad smile. "One night. We both know that's all it can be."

One night, my ass.

But I didn't argue. Something told me Aurora would double down and put a stop to this if I pushed. So I conceded, giving her a small nod. Letting her think she'd won the war when really, she'd only won this battle.

"Now, come here." I grabbed the hem of her t-shirt again, twisting it around my fist to pull her closer.

"Lights off," she breathed, a hint of vulnerability in her voice. "I want the lights—"

"Not happening, babe. I want to see your eyes the first time you come for me. Now stop talking and get naked."

A tremble went through her. "You first."

"It would be my pleasure." I quirked a brow, smirking.

I made a show of stripping out of my t-shirt, flexing my biceps a little. Feeling ten feet fucking tall when her eyes turned molten emerald.

"Like what you see, shortcake?" I asked, pushing my sweats over my hips.

"Oh my God, Noah! A little warning next ti—" She stopped herself.

"Sorry, what was that?"

She gave me a pointed look. "Okay, I got a close look at the goods. You can go now." Backing away from me, a hint of amusement played in her expression.

I liked this version of her—flirty and playful. Not taking herself too seriously. And I fucking loved that it only seemed to come out around me—at least, I hoped it did.

Licking my palm, I fisted my dick, pumping it slowly.

"Oh. My. God." Aurora's eyes grew as big as saucers, her chest harshly rising and falling as she watched me jerk myself. "That is... wow." She choked on the words.

"Take it your ex didn't ever let you watch?"

"Ex-talk is off the table. Period."

"Good, because I like imagining that you've never been touched."

"Virgin fantasy, how original." She rolled her eyes, her gaze locking back on my junk.

"Your turn, shortcake. Show me the goods." I smirked, smothering a groan as I tortured myself with slow strokes.

"I-I can't..."

"Yes, you can. I already got a peek at you just now, and I liked, no scrap that, I fucking loved every inch of what I saw."

I stalked forward, and she inched back, but she had nowhere to go, falling onto her bed with a little huff.

"Arms up, shortcake." I dropped to my knees before Aurora, pride welling in my chest when she obeyed. I could see the hesitation in her eyes, the urge to get up and run from me.

But she didn't.

Instead, she shocked the shit out of me and said, "If you want me naked, hotshot, then show me."

My fucking pleasure.

I grabbed the hem of her t-shirt and slipped it over her head, throwing it somewhere behind me. Then I kissed her jaw, teasing my lips down her neck and along her collarbone while I unclasped her bra.

"Noah." She sucked in a sharp breath, trying to wrap her arms around her midriff.

I covered her hands with my own and gently pried them away. "Let me see you, shortcake. All of you."

Her tits were heavy and full in my hands and so fucking perfect. I flicked my tongue across the peak, closing my mouth around her nipple and sucking.

"Noah..." She whimpered, shoving her fingers into my hair as I continued lapping at her skin, teasing her. Switching from breast to breast.

So fucking turned on, I palmed my cock again, jerking myself faster this time.

"One day, I'm going to fuck you right here." I trailed my fingers between the deep valley of her cleavage, smirking at the way a shiver ran through her.

Aurora was shy and, if I had to guess, fairly inexperienced, but she liked hearing me talk dirty to her. It was in every breathy moan and little sigh she made.

"Kiss me," she said. "I need you to kiss me."

Our mouths fused together as my hands explored her body. Aurora tensed a couple of times when I ran my hands across her stomach, but I kissed her into submission, coaxing her to let me take control.

To trust me.

"Time for these to come off, shortcake," I rasped, letting my fingers dance along the edge of her panties.

"I'm not—"

"Lie back on your elbows. I want you to watch me worship your pussy."

"Jesus, Noah..."

"Not Jesus, babe, but I am going to make you sing my praises."

Aurora dropped back onto her elbows, her eyes burning with lust, her skin flushed pink.

I pushed her thighs apart, giving her a second to get with the program. When she gave me a small nod, it was game on.

Sliding my fingers into the elastic of her panties, I slowly peeled them down her body. "Beautiful," I pressed a kiss to her inner thigh, tracing my tongue over the faded silvery lines.

I didn't give a fuck if she had a stretch mark or two. Her body was incredible, and the fact that she trusted me enough to see her like this did things to me.

Things that scared the shit out of me.

Aurora fought me, trying to press her thighs together, but I slid my hands under her knees and pushed them open, wedging my shoulders between her legs, pinning her there.

"Noah, what are you—oh God." The words got stuck on a moan as I licked her pink, glistening pussy.

Her eyes shuttered, her head dropping back.

"Eyes on me, shortcake," I demanded.

I needed her to see me, to know exactly *who* was doing this to her.

I needed her right here with me.

Spreading her open with one hand, I flattened my tongue against her clit, toying with it before sucking gently.

"Sweet baby Jesus," she cried, fisting my hair. "That is... *God*." Her body bowed off the bed as I speared my tongue inside her, licking with fervor.

"You taste like my new favorite meal, shortcake." I blew a streak of warm air over her pussy before easing two fingers into her and curling them deeply.

She was tight, clamping down around me as her legs began to tremble.

"Noah, I'm close... I'm... *ah*."

I tongued her clit again, working her with both my fingers and my mouth until she was a breathless, boneless mess beneath me.

"Yes... yes..." She came hard, whimpering into her fist as I licked her through the ebbing waves.

"Mmm." I crawled over her and nudged my nose up against hers. "Hi."

"Hi." Aurora gave me a shy smile.

"Still doubting my attraction to you?"

"I... stop looking at me like that."

"Like what?" My brow arched.

"Like you want to devour me."

"Newsflash, shortcake, I think I just did." I kissed her, sliding my tongue into her mouth and letting her taste herself.

"Noah," she sighed, anchoring her arms around my neck.

"We can stop," I said. "If you don't—"

"I want." She scraped her nails across my jaw. "I really want."

"Thank fuck. Get comfortable, and I'll grab a condom."

Aurora nodded, shifting up the bed as I went to my wallet and grabbed a foil packet.

Things were moving fast, really damn fast. But if she was serious about only giving me one night—no matter how much I planned on fighting her on that little issue—I was going to take it.

When I turned around, she was laid out in the middle of the bed like a fucking vision. Dark hair sprawled out around her, the sheet draped over her luscious curves like some Greek goddess immortalized in an oil painting.

"Look at you." I rubbed my thumb over my jaw as I stalked toward her.

Leaning over, I grabbed the corner of the sheet and tugged gently.

"Noah!"

"No hiding from me, remember?"

Ripping the packet open, I rolled on the condom and crawled over her body.

"I'm nervous." A violent tremor went through her. "It's been a while."

"I'll go slow." I rolled my hips, nudging up against her warm, wet heat.

"Don't." Her eyes flared. "I want you to make me forget, Noah. I want—"

"Honey, we're home—" Rang out through the house.

"Oh God, Connor," Aurora shoved me off, grabbing the sheet.

"And we brought pizza," Austin yelled.

"Fuck. *Fuck*." I jumped up and raked a hand through my hair.

"What do we do? I can't... they can't—"

"Breathe. Just breathe, shortcake." I discarded the condom and started pulling on my clothes, my dick seriously protesting at being shoved back into my sweats. "I'll handle them, okay? I'll go down there and distract them, and you can catch your breath."

"O-okay." Still clutching the sheet, Aurora slid off the bed and stood.

"Everything will be fine," I said. "We'll figure this out."

She nodded, but I saw the doubt in her eyes, the wild panic.

I was losing her when we hadn't even gotten started yet.

Well, fuck that.

Closing the distance between us, I cupped her face and lowered my head. "This isn't over, shortcake. Not by a long shot."

CHAPTER 19

AURORA

I'D ALMOST HAD sex with Noah Holden.

Practically begged him to make me forget.

Oh my God.

Warring emotions coursed through me. On the one hand, I felt a bottomless pit of guilt. He was Austin's friend —his teammate. He was the guy my new friend wanted to ride like a bucking bronco.

He was Noah freaking Holden.

But it was that very knowledge that had a small part of me cheering for my inner hussy. I hadn't flinched or recoiled from his touch. I hadn't freaked out—*too much*— when he insisted that we keep the light on. I hadn't refused to take off my t-shirt.

I'd been buckass naked in front of one of the most gorgeous men I'd ever encountered, and the world hadn't ended. I hadn't combusted or gotten sick or died of shame and embarrassment.

I'd survived.

Better than survived, I'd been to orgasm-heaven at the mercy of his skilled tongue and fingers.

Noah Holden ate my pussy, and I'd loved every single glorious second of it.

Because he knew. He knew how to coax me out of my head, how to make me ignore my overcritical, self-deprecating inner critic. He knew exactly what to say, how to touch me, how to make me feel like the most beautiful girl he'd ever laid eyes on.

For those few minutes, I wasn't Aurora the whale or Aurora with the porn star tits or Aurora with the thunder thighs. I was just Aurora.

And she was fucking beautiful.

But beauty was fleeting, and the voice of shame was a cruel, spiteful thing. It chipped away at old insecurities until they were impossible to ignore. Until everything good I'd felt earlier slipped between the cracks of my tattered heart.

He'd said we weren't done.

But how could we not be?

We might have shared a connection behind closed doors, out of the public eye, but in the harsh light of day, the truth was Noah was out of my league in every way that mattered.

My cell vibrated, and I snatched it up, pain squeezing my chest at the sight of his name.

Noah: All clear.

Aurora: Thanks.

Noah: I'm going to hang out with them for a bit but once they crash, I could sneak up to your room and finish what we started...

Aurora: I don't think that's a good idea.

Noah: Soon, then?

Aurora: Noah, we said one night.

It was going to hurt enough tomorrow when we had to go back to ignoring each other. When I had to watch his flock of puck bunnies throw themselves at his feet all over campus.

Noah: And I didn't get one night. I barely got part of one.

Aurora: Noah, come on. You know we can't.

Noah: Fuck that. We can. I want you, shortcake and I know you want me. You were drenched for me.

Squeezing my thighs together, I tried to suppress the memories of his long skilled fingers, and his expert tongue as he tasted me over and over.

Jesus. It was one thing to want a guy like Noah from a distance. Distance was safe. You couldn't lose what you'd never had. You couldn't miss it. But knowing what it was like to be in his orbit for a moment in time, knowing it was only temporary. Finite. That was a bitter pill to swallow.

Noah: I want you, Aurora. Anyway I can get you.

Aurora: I won't survive you, Noah... we're not the same.

Noah: Give me a chance, please.

God, he wasn't making things easy. But if I'd learned anything about Noah, it was that he was as stubborn as he was determined.

Noah: One date... if you hate it, we can go back to being just friends.

Just friends.

Like we could ever be *just friends* after tonight.

But a date?

He wanted to take me out on a date. That wasn't casual sex. That wasn't casual at all.

> Aurora: You don't date, remember?

> Noah: And you don't get involved with hockey players. If you ask me, we're a match made in heaven, shortcake.

My mouth twitched, and I quickly texted back before I changed my mind.

> Aurora: One date. But no one can know, Noah.

> Noah: It'll be our little secret.

Secrets were a slippery slope. I knew that firsthand. I'd lived it. And yet, I wanted a date with Noah.

Because he made me feel beautiful, Noah had made me feel worth something.

And despite the little voice in my head telling me that it was a *really* bad idea, it was a feeling I wanted to hold onto for as long as possible.

"What an asshole," Harper said as we wandered across the lawn toward the student center.

"Yep. That's why I don't date."

"But I don't get it," she frowned, "he approached you. I was so sure he was one of the decent ones."

I shrugged. "I don't know what to tell you. He was more interested in my *porn star tits* than me."

She tsked in disgust.

I hadn't told her the entire story—the part where he'd laughed to his friend about my appearance. I also hadn't told her about Noah coming to my rescue, something that had made the last two hours awkward, to say the least.

"So, do you think he likes me?" she asked.

"Sorry, what?"

"Noah, silly. Do you think—"

"Harper, you can do so much better than Noah Holden."

I was going to hell.

There was a spot reserved just for me with the placard *worst friend in the history of friends*.

"Yeah, but like I said, I don't want to marry the guy. He's just so freaking hot."

"What about Mason? Or my brother?"

"Hold up," she grabbed my arm, stopping me, "I distinctly remember you telling him I was off-limits."

"My bad." I flushed. "I don't know why I said that."

"Rory"—her gaze narrowed—"is there something going on between you and Noah?"

"What? No. He would never want someone like me."

"What the hell does that mean?"

"You said it yourself, Harper. Ryan is more my type."

"Aurora, I didn't—shit. Me and my big mouth. Babe, you're gorgeous. You have those big, beautiful eyes and that ass. And don't forget your porn star tits." She grinned. "I know we hate Ryan-the-asshole, but he does have a point. You do have great boobs."

"I..."

"Oh, come on. I would kill to have your curves. I'm lucky if I can fill a B cup with padding."

"Harper, you're stunning."

"This is true." Her smile grew. "But it doesn't mean I don't have body hang-ups. I hate my knees and the way my collarbone juts out. I won't wear strapless tops because it totally freaks me out.

"So you've got hips, boobs, and an ass. Guys dig that. They like a little something to hold onto." She winked.

"I wish I had your confidence," I whispered.

"You know there's this motivational quote I love that goes, 'Confidence is silent, insecurities are loud.' You can't always take what you see at face value."

She was right, part of me knew that. But when you'd spent your entire life being cast aside for prettier, slimmer girls, it was hard to empathize.

"Anyway, back to my original question," she said. "Are you lusting after a certain Laker right-winger?"

"No." She raised a brow, and I shook my head emphatically. "Absolutely not."

"Fine. If you say so, but aside from the fact that he's your brother's best friend *and* his teammate, it would be totally okay if you did have a thing for him, you know."

I didn't like the way she looked at me, as if she knew the truth.

This was bad.

Very bad.

"Well, I don't, so it's a moot point."

"Then you won't mind if I ask him out."

Crap.

"I... sure. Go for it. But just for the record, I think it's a bad idea."

"Don't you know, Rory?" Harper flashed me a confident smile that made my stomach tumble. "Sometimes bad ideas are the best kind."

I'd left Harper at Roast 'n' Go to head to the library. There were a couple of books I needed to check out for one of my classes, and I couldn't find them online, so I was hoping the library had some copies.

"Aurora," Ella greeted me at the desk. "I didn't expect to see you here."

"It is the library, no?"

"Of course," she chuckled. "I just meant... oh, ignore me. It's been a strange morning."

"Everything okay?"

"Yeah." She hesitated. "I mean, I think so. Connor has been acting a little weird."

"Weird, how?"

"I feel silly even saying this, but he's being kind of secretive about things."

"Secretive... Connor?" The guy couldn't hold his shit for

anything.

"I know, it's weird, right? He's usually an open book, but I get the feeling he's keeping me at arm's length, and it's freaking me out."

"I'm sure it's just the pressure of senior year. The guys talk about it non-stop, and I know the team wants to go all the way this season."

"Yeah, you're right." The smile she gave me didn't reach her eyes. "I'm probably overreacting. It doesn't help that it's shark week. My hormones go haywire this time of the month. Anyway, what can I help you with?"

"I'm looking for these three books." I handed her the slip of paper I'd scribbled down the titles on. "I tried online but got nothing."

"Let me see what I can do. I'll be right back."

"Thanks."

Ella disappeared into the back, and I waited, startled at the vibration of my cell phone.

My stomach fluttered at the sight of Noah's name.

> Noah: Shortcake, I need your opinion on something… can you meet me ASAP?

My brows furrowed.

> Aurora: I can't right now. In the library hunting down some books.

Noah: What time is your next class?

Aurora: Less than an hour. What do you need my opinion on, maybe I can help over text?

Noah: It's more of a visual thing.

"Got them," Ella appeared, and I quickly pocketed my phone, ignoring the vibration.

"Do you need to get that?" she asked, and I shook my head.

"No. It's just Austin being his usual annoying self."

"Want to follow me, and I'll show you where they're located?"

"Great, thanks." I followed Ella as she headed toward the back of the library. "How is that going, by the way? I hope the guys aren't giving you too many headaches?"

"It's okay. Now that the semester has started, we all come and go a lot."

"Wait until the season officially starts, then you'll barely see them."

"It's that bad, huh?"

"You think hockey rules their lives now? Wait until October, when it can get intense. Thirty-four games over five months, more if they qualify for the post-season tournament."

"It's sound exhausting just thinking about it."

"It is. But hockey is in their blood."

"Do you worry about what will happen when Connor

turns pro?" I asked, thinking back to their conversation the other night.

"I'd be lying if I said no." She gave me a weak smile. "He says we'll make it. But I've read the stories. NHL wives following their husbands across the country, putting their dreams on hold while he gets to live his."

"It sounds like you have a lot to talk about."

"That's just it. There isn't a choice for me, Rory. Connor's the love of my life, and I'm in. I'm all in. But I'm scared too."

"I think that's understandable. Connor's life is going to change in so many ways. But he's going to get to live his dream. Not many people can say that. And he gets to share it with the girl he loves."

Ella inhaled a sharp breath, rubbing her eyes. "Whew, I'm sorry. I didn't mean to offload all that on you."

"It's fine. I hope I helped."

"You did." She touched my arm. "I can see why Connor likes you so much. Here we are. I don't know exactly where they're shelved, but they should be in this section."

"Perfect, thank you so much."

"I'd stay and help, but I need to get back to the desk."

"You've been a lifesaver, thanks."

"We still need to arrange drinks. I'll see when it's good for Dayna. Maybe we can invite Mila and Harper too."

"I'd like that."

"I'll set it up. If you need anything else, just holler."

I gave her a little nod before meticulously working my way through the stacks. There was something about the smell of musty old books that comforted me.

The first two titles were easy to locate, but the third wasn't where I expected it to be, so I moved deeper into the stacks, losing track of time as I searched and searched.

Finally, I spotted it on the highest shelf, taunting me. Because, of course, it had to be all the way up there. Glancing around, I spotted a step. It would give me some extra height, but I still wasn't sure I'd be tall enough.

Determined not to be defeated, I retrieved the step and positioned it on the ground in front of me, testing its strength with one foot first. With a deep breath, I stepped onto it and got my footing before reaching up. My fingers grazed the spine, but I couldn't quite reach still.

"Dammit," I hissed, going up on my tiptoes as I tried to stretch my hand further. "Almost there, just a—"

"Need a little help, shortcake?" Noah's deep silky voice startled me, and I started to topple. "Oh, shit." He rushed over to me, catching me as I almost went flying.

"You," I half-smiled, half-groaned, righting myself.

"Me." He grinned, stepping back to give me space.

"I'd ask what you are doing here, but something tells me I don't want to know."

"You reminded me I needed to pick up a book too."

"What book?"

"A book... with words."

"Sounds interesting. And what words would be in this book?"

"Stuff."

"Words about stuff." I narrowed my eyes, fighting a smile. "You, Noah Holden, are a terrible liar."

His eyes dropped to my mouth, hunger simmering in his gaze. "I had to see you."

"So you followed me to the library? You know stalker tendencies aren't exactly a turn-on."

"No, like I said, I needed to pick up a book." His mouth twitched.

"Noah..." I sighed, not entirely comfortable with playing these games with him here, in the library. With Ella somewhere in the vicinity.

"Shortcake..." He prowled toward me, crowding me against the stacks. His hand came to rest above my head, effectively trapping me there, his intense brown eyes searching mine.

"You wanted my opinion on something?" I blurted, needing a second to catch my breath.

When he looked at me like that, I couldn't think straight. And I needed to think straight because we were in public.

"I did." It sounded more like a question than a statement.

"Another ruse?" I asked, and his mouth twitched again.

"Busted. But in my defense, I haven't stopped thinking about last night." Noah brought his hand to my face and brushed the flyaway hairs out of my eyes. "Want to fool around in the stacks?"

Before I could stop him, he nuzzled my neck and started kissing and nipping the skin there. Shivers ran through me, making my stomach clench. God, his mouth felt good.

My fingers found their way into his hair, and my head dropped back, a small needy whimper building in my throat. "Noah," I breathed. "We shouldn't."

"You're saying one thing, shortcake"—he lifted his face, his eyes burning with lust—"but your body is saying another."

"We can't..." I pulled him closer, leaning up to brush my mouth over his.

We stayed like that, suspended in time. Until we both snapped, our mouths coming together in a clash of teeth and tongue.

"Did you dream of me, shortcake?" he murmured between sweet, sweet kisses. "Because I sure as fuck dreamed of you."

CHAPTER 20

NOAH

Fuck.

I couldn't get enough of her.

Aurora—her delicious curves and sweet kisses—were turning out to be my new favorite obsession.

"Noah," she breathed, gently shoving at my chest. "What are we doing?"

"If you have to ask, shortcake, I must be doing it all wrong." I dipped my head to steal another kiss, but she dodged my advance.

"Noah, I'm serious," she whisper-hissed, glancing down the aisle.

"Relax, no one is coming down here."

"Ella works here, Noah. If someone sees us—"

She had a point. But I wasn't ready to lose her just yet.

"Go out with me. Tonight."

"Tonight? Noah..."

"You know you want to, shortcake. There's something between us—"

She raised a single dark brow and smirked, dropping her gaze to the less-than-obvious bulge in my jeans.

"Not that. Although, I wouldn't say no if you wanted to give him some attention."

Aurora's cheeks turned two shades darker. "You are so bad."

"You have no idea," I whispered, leaning in to brush my mouth over the corner of hers. "Say, yes, shortcake. Just say yes."

A beat passed, the air around us crackling with tension. She wanted to say yes. It was right there in her bewitching eyes.

Cupping Aurora's face, I touched my head to hers and peppered little kisses over her lips. "Say—"

"Yes, okay," she answered on a little sigh. "Yes, I'll go out with you. But don't make me regret it, Noah."

She looked like she wanted to say more, but the words never came.

"Tonight?"

"I can't. Not tonight. I promised Harper we'd hang out."

"Fine. Tomorrow, be ready by seven-thirty. I know just the place to take you."

I was infatuated with her, so desperate to kiss her again that I didn't hear the footsteps.

But Aurora did.

"Someone's coming." She scrambled out from between me and the stacks, smoothing down her hair and the cute as fuck sweater swamping her frame.

"Sorry, I didn't mean—Noah."

Fuck.

"Hey, El," I said, lifting my hand in a small wave.

"What are you doing here?"

"Picking up a book." I grabbed the first book I could put my hands on and waved it toward her.

"You're reading Anna Karenina?"

"Yep. I'm a big fan of"—I checked the spine—"Tolstoy."

"You do know that's an eight-hundred-page love affair about Russian high society, politics, and religion, right?"

Double fuck.

Aurora smothered a laugh as she peeked over at me.

"I swear you get weirder," Ella murmured. "Did you find everything you needed, Rory?"

"Yeah. Good thing Noah appeared. I almost fell trying to get the last one down from up there."

"That is lucky." Suspicion danced in her eyes as her gaze flicked between us. "Well, I just need to grab a couple of books and get back to the desk. I'll see you both soon."

Ella reached around me and grabbed two books, then took off down the aisle.

"Do you think she suspected anything?" Aurora gnawed the end of her thumb, her eyes bouncing between me and the direction Ella went.

"Nope, I think we're good," I lied. Because Ella definitely suspected something.

The last thing I wanted was Aurora to worry because I fucked up. But it was like a switch had flipped, and I couldn't stop thinking about her.

I had never been as turned on as I was last night, jerking myself while she watched me through big, inexperienced eyes.

Fuck, the things I wanted to do to her—to teach her.

But pursuing this thing with Aurora meant going

behind Austin's back, and that didn't sit right with me. In fact, it made me feel like a giant fucking asshole.

Not enough to walk away from her, though.

We could keep this thing a secret, and nobody had to get hurt.

"I should go." Aurora grabbed her stack of books, dropping her gaze to the book still in my hands. "Enjoy your book."

"Not so fast, shortcake." I hooked my arm around her waist and tugged her back to me.

"Noah, what—"

I kissed her, drowning out her protests as my tongue slicked against hers. Aurora melted into me, a sexy as fuck whimper vibrating deep in her throat as I slid my hand into her hair, tilting her face so I could deepen the kiss.

Never, *never* had I enjoyed kissing a girl so much.

And I'd kissed a lot of girls in my short lifetime.

She was so pliant in my hands. Soft and willing. As if she was handing me all her trust to show her the way.

"I can't wait to get you naked again."

"That wasn't the deal," she reminded me.

"Deal, smeal." I kissed her forehead, staring into her eyes, feeling the thread between us coil tighter and tighter. "You owe me a date, shortcake."

"Goodbye, Noah." She wrenched out of my hold.

And this time, I let her go. Because tomorrow night...

Tomorrow, Aurora Hart was mine.

Oomph.

The air left my lungs as Connor slammed me into the boards.

"You're looking sloppy, Holden." He grinned, slapping me on the back as I tried to right myself.

"Five goals in the net would say otherwise." I smirked.

"Hey, assholes. Quit flirting," Aiden yelled. "Run it again."

"Jesus, he's like Coach Tucker on crack," I murmured.

We'd been at it an hour already. My legs burned the only way they could from skating up and down the ice for sixty minutes. But the twitch and tingle in my glutes and calves was a feeling I'd learned to love over the years.

"You heard the man. Let's run it again." Connor smirked, cutting in front of me to take up his position on the ice.

"Your speed is good, Holden. But you've got to be ready to receive the pass from Banks."

"It's different," I said.

Last year, Linc and I had worked on this play over and over to the point where I could pull it off with my eyes closed. But Leon was new; he was still learning the ropes. We were still learning to read each other.

"We'll get there," I said, shooting Leon a reassuring look, tamping down the lick of frustration I felt.

Hockey was a team sport. There was no place for egos or one-man shows. But sometimes, I struggled to put my performance in the hands of others.

Because you couldn't count on anyone but yourself.

Not true, I reminded myself.

This team was my brothers. My family. The only family I had now, given I'd completely cut off my old man and my family back in Buffalo.

But it didn't always come easy letting them in.

We ran the play again, Leon's pass finding my stick with precision. Cradling the puck, I switched hands, hurtling toward the net. Austin grinned, making himself larger than life in an attempt to distract me.

But I had this.

I motherfucking had—

"Eat that, asshole." I cut right, skating around the goal while Austin was left to retrieve the puck from inside his net.

"Better," Aiden yelled. "Much fucking better."

I skated over to Leon and held up my hand. He slapped his glove against mine, grinning like the cat who got the canary.

"Nice work, rookie."

"Thanks, man."

Aiden called us in, and we all joined the huddle. "We're looking better. Keep it up, and we might stand a shot at the Frozen Four yet. Official practice starts Monday, but I think Coach Tucker will be impressed with where we're at. Good work, everyone."

"We heading straight to TPB?" Connor asked me as I pulled off my helmet.

"I can't tonight."

"What, why not?"

"I have a thing." I shrugged, trying to play it cool.

"A thing"—Mase stuck his head between us—"You mean a booty call."

"Nope."

"A date then?" He cocked his brow, concern shining in his eyes.

"Come on, Mase, you know me better than that."

"Mase is right, Holden. You're being awfully evasive."

"If you must know, I'm meeting Sam to study, happy?"

"Study, is that what we're calling it now?"

"It's true. She turned up in my accounting class and offered to help me ace the semester. Fuck knows I'm going to need all the help I can get," I muttered as we headed off the ice and down the walkway into the locker room.

"Study buddies," Connor tsked. "That's the oldest trick in the book. First, you'll be reciting the accounting principles, and then, you'll be banging her over the desk."

"Not going to happen," I said over my shoulder.

"Famous last words, Holden. Famous. Last. Words."

They didn't know that Sam was just a cover. That I'd be out with Aurora, hopefully kissing the fuck out of her.

A flash of heat went through me. I'd never chased a girl before. They usually fell in my lap or turned up at my door half-naked. But I liked it.

I liked working for it, knowing that the reward would be oh-so-sweet.

"What's going on?" Austin asked, barreling past me and dropping onto his bench.

"Holden has a study date with Sam."

"It's not a study date, asshole. It's a study meeting."

"Seriously, you're going to blow off Happy Hour at TPB for studying?

"Official practice starts Monday. You need to quit Happy Hour," Aiden barked across the room.

"Relax, I'll only have a couple." Austin waved him off, stripping out of his gear. "He's worse than Kellan."

Debatable. Kellan—our old captain—had been nicknamed Grandpa for a reason. The guy was deadly on the ice but a total fun sponge off it. At least Aiden hadn't issued us with a bunch of unrealistic rules.

Yet.

"I'm going to hit the showers and call it a night."

I had a date to get ready for.

One my teammates could never know about.

But first, I had to lay my cover plan.

I convinced Sam to meet at Joe's. It was public, and had lots of witnesses should my friends feel the need to snoop any more than they already had.

Sam had picked a table in the back, but she saw me the second I entered the shop.

'Hi,' she mouthed with a small wave.

I made my way over, running a hand through my still-damp hair. I'd come here straight from practice, wanting to give Aurora enough time to get ready for our date.

"Hey, am I late, or are you early?" I chuckled. "I thought we said five-thirty?"

"We did, but I wanted to get a head start and make sure I've covered all the bases." She spread out her notes.

"Wow, okay," I said, feeling way out of my depth. I thought we'd discuss the course outline and go over some theories. "This is... wow."

"It's like you don't know me at all." She smiled.

"Can I get you another drink before we get started?"

"Sure, I'll have a latte, please."

"Want a cookie or anything?"

"I wouldn't say no to an oatmeal with raisin."

"Got it."

I joined the line and placed my order. The barista flashed me a coy smile when she took my payment.

"Can I get you anything else?" she asked.

"I think I'm all set, thanks."

"See you around, Noah." My name was a dirty whisper on her lips.

Jesus.

I suddenly saw things through a whole new lens. What had once been a bolster to my ego was now a little annoying. But I only had myself to blame. I'd flirted and fucked my way through freshman year. If people didn't know me, they knew of me.

Aurora was right, my reputation did precede me, and it had never bothered me before. Not for a second.

Until now.

After collecting my order, I headed back to Sam. "One latte and oatmeal cookie."

"Yum, thanks. So where do you want to start?"

"With the basics, I guess. I mean, I know the principles, but I don't *know* them."

"Sure, we can work through those. Hey, after this, do you want to grab some dinner? Or we could get takeout and go back to my place—"

"Sam..."

"Relax, Noah. I'm not inviting you back for sex, although I wouldn't say no." She smirked, laughing it off when I didn't take the bait. "But it would be nice to hang out. I don't like being in the apartment by myself after what happened."

Shit.

"I... umm, I can't tonight."

"Oh, okay." Her expression dropped. "Another time maybe?"

"Yeah, of course."

That appeased her but made me feel like an asshole. I didn't want to cross any lines with Sam, not again. But I also didn't want her to become a problem if she sensed I was involved with someone else.

"Let me know when you're free then, and we can arrange something."

I went with a half-hearted, non-committal, "Mm-hmm."

"Great, ready to get started?" She licked the crumbs off her fingers, keeping her eyes locked on me as she sucked them clean.

In a past life—a pre-Aurora life—it was a move I would have found sexy, if not mildly amusing. But it did nothing for me now because the only girl I could think about was her.

Aurora Hart.

Her smile and curves, her unassuming wit and banter. She had no idea how funny or gorgeous she was, and in a campus full of puck bunnies and an endless supply of casual hookups, that floored me.

"Noah." Sam snapped her fingers, jolting me out of my thoughts.

"Huh?"

"I said do you want to borrow my notebook?"

"Oh, yeah, thanks."

"Are you okay? You seem distracted."

"Who, me? I'm fine."

"Okay, well, make a start on those three questions so I can get a feel for where you're at. Then I can tailor our sessions to your weaknesses."

Fuck, that word.

It splintered through me like ice.

My old man fucking *loved* that word, wielding it like a weapon. Cutting me down time and time again until he only had to open his mouth and I flinched.

"Noah."

"Yep, on it." I read the first question and started writing down some thoughts.

"So, how's it going with your new housemate?"

"What?" My head shot up.

"Aurelie, was it?"

"Aurora, and it's fine. She's no trouble." I kept my answer vague.

"Yeah, but it can't be ideal having your teammate's little sister living with you."

"It's really no bother." I kept my head down, trying to figure out which definition went with which principle.

"She seemed so different compared to Austin. I mean, he's so... hot and charismatic, and she's so drab, and I don't want to sound like a bitch, but it didn't exactly look like she takes good care of herself."

"Newsflash, Sam," I snapped, that protective streak of anger I felt whenever someone talked shit about Aurora zipping down my spine. "You do sound like a bitch."

"What? I'm just saying she's—"

"Enough already. I thought we came here to study, not talk shit about Austin's sister."

"Geez, pissy much? I was only making conversation." She gave a little huff, going back to the textbook in her lap.

The silence was awkward as fuck, but I'd take it any day over listening to her talk shit about Aurora.

CHAPTER 21

AURORA

> Noah: The coast is clear, shortcake.

I gnawed at the end of my thumb, pacing my room.

A date.

I was going on a date with Noah Holden.

What the hell was I thinking when I'd agreed to this?

Except, I hadn't been thinking because he'd kissed me into submission with his treacherous lips and dirty whispers.

Damn him.

The chime of my phone startled me, and I snatched it off my desk.

Noah: If you're not down here in five
minutes, I'm coming up. And fair warning,
if I come up there, we may never make it to
our destination.

Aurora: Noah!!!

Noah: Come on, shortcake. Put a guy out
of his misery and get your cute ass down
here.

God, how did he do that? How did he make me feel all giddy inside? I still had insecurities—they were always there, hovering under the surface, waiting to strike—but Noah had a way of making me forget them.

He made me feel special.

Beautiful even.

And part of me didn't know what to do with that because that part could only see this ending one way.

With me getting my heart broken.

Again.

But I craved his attention. His sweet kisses and eager touch. I craved to feel like one of the popular, pretty girls. I craved to know what it was like to be in his orbit, even if it was only for a little while.

With a deep, steadying breath, I checked my reflection one more time and headed out.

Aurora: Are you sure this is safe?

Noah: Big brother and Connor are holed up
at TPB for at least another couple of hours.
We're all good.

Noah: I've got you, shortcake.

Something softened inside me. Noah, despite his playboy image, was a good guy. And he had a way of making me believe in myself.

Don't get too carried away, Aurora. You don't even know what this is yet.

I grabbed my keys off the sideboard and made my way outside. Noah's face lit up when he saw me, his eyes tracking my movements with predatory focus.

Grabbing the door handle, I yanked it open and hopped up into Connor's truck. "This isn't weird at all," I said.

"It was either this or Austin's Camry. Figured you would prefer the lesser of two evils." He winked, easing the knot in my stomach. "Shortcake, you look... fuck. Your tits look incredible."

"Noah!"

I flushed all the way to the tips of my toes, desperately wanting to tug at the scoop neckline on my sweater dress. But I knew Noah liked my boobs, so I didn't want to hide under a baggy outfit.

Not tonight.

His heated smile reassured me I'd made the right decision.

"You love it."

Yeah, maybe I did—just a little bit.

I also loved the maroon t-shirt hugging his biceps, giving me a peek of the tattoo on his arm. He looked like sex on a stick with his slightly disheveled hair, curled at the ends, and his intense brown eyes.

Jesus, I was in so much trouble.

"So where are we going?" I rushed out, trying to distract myself from how hot I'd suddenly gotten.

"It's a surprise."

"I hate surprises."

"Pretty sure you'll like this one." He shifted the truck into reverse and backed out of the driveway.

"How come you don't have a car?" I asked.

"Because college is fucking expensive."

"You're on a scholarship, right?" I'd heard the guys talking about it the other day.

"I am. Full ride. It covers tuition, accommodation, and maintenance, but it didn't include new wheels, unfortunately."

"You couldn't ask your parents for help?"

"Nice try, shortcake. But I'm sure Austin's already told you I don't talk about my family."

"Sorry, I didn't mean to pry."

"It's no biggie. I haven't spoken to my old man since I left Buffalo, and I'd like to keep it that way."

His voice was laced with so much bitterness, but I also heard a tinge of sadness. I had to fight the urge to ask what had happened between them. Noah was entitled to his privacy, the way we all were.

I noticed he took the road heading out of Lakeshore and said, "We're leaving town?"

"Figured it was for the best." He shot me a playful smile. "Besides, this way, I get you all to myself."

"I like the sound of that," I whispered, wondering who this girl was. Because I didn't date or put myself out there. But Noah made me want things.

Scary things I hadn't allowed myself to want since Ben broke my heart into a thousand pieces.

"What's your cover story? For tonight, I mean? Actually, don't answer that. I don't want to know," I chuckled, but it came out strangled.

"You don't need to worry, I promise." Noah reached over and grabbed my hand, pulling it on his knee.

It felt awfully intimate. But then, everything did with Noah. Every time he smiled at me, the rest of the world melted away, leaving just the two of us.

Only that was the fantasy. The reality was much different.

"What's going on in that head of yours?" he asked, threading his fingers between mine.

I went with the truth.

"I'm still not sure what I'm doing here, Noah."

"You owe me one night, remember?"

He grinned. I nodded.

One night.

Was that all he—

"Don't look so worried. I like you, shortcake. And I'm pretty sure you like me. So we're just two people who like each other spending time together. Does it need to be anything more than that?"

Insecure Aurora wanted to tell him it did. But I wasn't that girl tonight.

I wasn't.

So I pasted on a smile and said, "No, it doesn't."

Even though my heart silently roared *liar*.

"What is this place?" I asked Noah as he pulled into a parking lot behind a small, old building.

"The Regal Movie Theater."

"We're watching a movie?" I don't know why, but it wasn't exactly what I'd imagined when Noah asked me out.

"We are. Don't sound so disappointed," he chuckled.

"Disappointed, no. Confused, a little," I admitted.

"It'll make more sense once we get inside. Come on."

He climbed and came around to open my door, helping me out. My feet had barely touched the ground when he'd pulled me into his arms, gazing down at me with a softness that stole my breath. "Hi," he said.

"Hi."

"I've been waiting to do this ever since you came out of the house." His hand glided along the side of my neck, holding me while his mouth sealed over mine, and he kissed me, slow and soft and oh-so-perfect.

"Mmm," I murmured, overwhelmed by the feel of his lips on mine, kissing me. The woodsy scent of his cologne.

Noah was perfect in a way I couldn't quite comprehend. And he was here.

With me.

He touched his head to mine, inhaling a sharp breath. "We should head inside before we're late."

Grabbing my hand, he tugged me around the front of

the building and inside the double doors. It wasn't your high street movie theater like AMC or Cinemark. Stepping inside was like stepping into the 1920s, the geometric wallpaper and green and gold carpets, a nod to the art deco designs of that era.

"It's beautiful," I said.

"I'm glad you like it." With a hand on the small of my back, Noah steered me toward the ticket booth.

"What film are we—" My eyes snagged on a familiar poster, emotion rising inside me like a tidal wave. "This is... I can't believe you did this."

"I pay attention, shortcake. I figured you'd enjoy it." Noah rubbed the back of his neck, looking all kinds of nervous.

It was such a nice thing to do.

"We don't have to watch this," I said. "I can't imagine it's your kind of thing."

He grabbed my hand and marched me to the booth. "Two tickets for Pride and Prejudice, please."

The man handed Noah two old-style cinema ticket stubs.

"What are you feeling?" He nodded toward the concession stand. "Popcorn, nachos, or candy? Or we can get a mixture."

"Oh, I'll just have a bottle of water, thanks."

"No chance, shortcake. If I'm going to sit through this film for you, the least you can do is share some snacks with me."

"I... you choose."

His brows furrowed. "That's like giving a kid in a candy shop free reign."

I smiled, but it was forced.

Did he notice?

Did he notice that I never dipped my hand in the chip bowl at the house when we were all hanging out? Or that I kept it to one hot dog sans bun and a plateful of salad at Hot Dog Tuesday?

"Last chance before I let loose." He grinned.

"Go for it."

Noah came back armed with snacks.

"You really went all out," I said, a pit of dread spreading in my stomach.

"Better to be prepared. Come on. The film is about to start."

We walked down the small hall, and Noah led me over to one of the ornate gold doors. "So, full disclosure," he said with a glint in his eye. "This isn't like a regular movie theater."

"Oh?"

"You'll see. Come on." He opened the door and let me go on ahead. The lights had already dipped, but a romantic glow cast around the room from the lamps on each table next to the chaise love seats.

"What is this?" I whispered.

"It's all part of the Regal experience."

It was my turn to frown as I noted the other couples snuggled into the seats, which really resembled small fancy couches.

"I—" The words died in my throat. This was intimate and romantic and totally not what I expected.

Noah moved behind me, dropping his mouth to my ear. "Move your cute ass, shortcake, or we're going to miss the movie."

His voice rolled through me, making a shiver run down my spine. He hadn't said anything suggestive or sexual, and yet, my body stirred to life.

"We're over there in the back," he said, pointing to the other side of the room.

It was only a small screening, with about ten love seats littered throughout, all positioned to give people privacy. I spotted a couple in the front making out, and Noah chuckled.

"Kissing is allowed at the movies, you know, shortcake. Maybe if you're lucky, you'll get to find out."

Jesus.

Sometimes, when he was like that—playful with a hint of teasing—it sent my heart into a stuttering mess.

Because he was Noah freaking Holden, and I was just a girl from Syracuse. A girl with more hang-ups than she cared to admit and self-esteem issues to boot.

And I still couldn't believe I was here on a date with him.

Albeit a secret date that no one could ever know about.

That killed my good mood a little.

We found our seats, and Noah offloaded his copious number of snacks onto the table. I sat down, hyper-aware of how close we were going to be.

And sure enough, the second Noah sat beside me; our thighs brushed as he got comfortable. But then, he slid his arm along the back of the love seat, and his fingers started toying with the ends of my hair.

This was going to be torture.

He leaned in close, his warm, mint breath fanning my cheeks. "So what's this movie about?"

"Noah!" My breath caught as he gazed down at me.

It was on the tip of my tongue to ask what we were doing. But he slipped his hand into my hair and angled my face to allow him to slide his mouth over mine. His tongue peeked out, tasting me, and I whimpered.

"Fuck, I love those little sounds you make."

Somewhere in the back of my lust-addled mind, I heard the film's opening credits. The birds chirping as the sun rose behind Kiera Knightly reading.

"Noah, the film," I said, breaking the kiss and sliding two fingers over his lips.

"Yeah, I know." And he looked regretful about the whole thing. "Maybe I didn't think this through," he whispered, kissing the tips of my fingers before tucking me into his side and getting us comfortable.

"Thank you." I gazed up at him. "I love it."

It's the nicest thing anyone's ever done for me.

"I'm going to preface this by saying I am straight. One hundred percent hetero," Noah whispered to me as we watched the film. "But even I can appreciate Darcy for what he is."

"Oh yeah?" I chuckled softly.

"The guy is a total snack."

"A snack?" My brow quirked up.

"Total. Snack. I can see why you love him."

"Actually, my favorite Austen hero is a guy called Edmund Bertram, but Mr. Darcy has been winning hearts for years."

"I can't believe I'm saying this, but I get it."

"Glad I could enlighten you. Noah," I added. "Your pocket is vibrating."

"Shit. Let me get that." We broke apart, and he dug the phone out of his jeans, scanning the screen.

"What is it?" I asked, noticing how still his expression had become.

"I need to take this. I'll be right back, okay?" He kissed the end of my nose and ducked out of the theater.

When he came back a minute later, something was off.

"Is everything okay?" I whispered as he sat down.

"Yep. Come back over here." He reached for me with a smile, but I saw the shadows in his eyes.

Noah felt distant after that. He smiled in all the right places and laughed along with me to Matthew MacFayden trying to win Kiera Knightley's heart, but whoever had called him had stolen all of his attention.

By the time the end credits rolled, I had a sinking feeling in my stomach. But I pasted on a smile because I didn't know what else to do.

"Thank you," I said as the light came up. "I really enjoyed that."

"It wasn't as bad as I expected it to be," he said a little dismissively. "We should probably figure out how to get you home without anyone suspecting anything."

"Oh, okay." My old friend dejection crept in like ice spreading through my veins.

Something had changed. I assumed it was the phone call, but maybe it wasn't. Maybe Noah wasn't feeling our date anymore.

We walked back to Connor's truck in awkward silence.

He didn't hold my hand or wrap his arm around my waist like he had done earlier.

He didn't even look at me. And I'd never felt like more of a fraud.

When he opened the passenger door for me and helped me inside, I gave him a small, hopeful smile, but he didn't return it.

I waited until he got into the driver's side and turned to him. "Noah," I said, and he lowered his gaze to mine. There was a coolness there that hadn't been there before, and the churning inside me only worsened. "Have I done something wrong?"

Regret flashed in his eyes for a second, but it was gone in another. "No, you've been great. We had fun, right?"

Fun.

The word rattled around in my head, but I refused to think the worst because it was Noah. He cared about me.

"We could... go somewhere," I barely managed to get the words out. "It's not that late and—"

"I can't tonight." He fired up the engine, the temperature between us falling subzero.

What little bit of hope I had left, withered and died.

Had I done something wrong?

I racked my brain, replaying the night over in my head. We'd both been having fun. He seemed into me. We'd kissed again, and it had been magical.

At least, I'd thought it had.

With every passing minute, my inner critic grew louder and louder. It wasn't my own voice; it never was. It was the voices of every person in my life who had ever made me feel worthless.

My mom.

The photographers.

Kids at school.

Ben.

The guy at the costume party.

Ryan.

Their flippant words and cruel taunts spun around my head until the truck felt too crowded, and my skin felt too tight until I was itching to get out into the fresh air.

I couldn't breathe.

I couldn't—

"You should probably get out here," Noah's voice pierced my thoughts, "so no one sees the truck. I'll be back later."

"W-what?" I stared at him, confused. Then I realized the truck was idling on the street.

Surely, he wasn't going to abandon me on the side of the road.

"The house is only a two-minute walk in that direction." He pointed up the street.

"I know where the house is, Noah. I just... I don't understand what's happening." *I don't understand why you're doing this.*

"I need to handle some things," he clipped out, barely looking at me. "But I'll see you tomorrow, okay?"

His eyes flicked past me to the door, and without another word, I stumbled out, completely dumbfounded.

I'd barely gotten the door shut before the truck took off down the street, my fragile heart cracking in my chest.

Noah had been so persistent. He'd pushed and pushed for this.

One date.

One more night.

I stupidly thought—*hoped*—the night would end with us together, picking up where we left off last night. So, what the hell had just happened?

I didn't know what to think.

But I couldn't shake the feeling that maybe Noah had left me for a better offer.

CHAPTER 22

NOAH

I STUMBLED out of the Uber and up the driveway.

It was a miracle I could even stand after the copious amounts of vodka coursing through my bloodstream. But the second I'd dropped Aurora back at the house, I'd dumped Connor's truck outside Lakers House and walked to the nearest bar.

Thankfully, it wasn't a popular haunt with LU students, and I'd managed to get a table in the back to drink my sorrows away in private.

Timothy fucking Holden.

The bane of my existence.

The man I hated more than anything else on the planet.

His call had hit me out of left field. Timothy never called me. Not unless it was bad news.

I hadn't called back.

I couldn't.

I didn't want to hear his voice. To give him an opportunity to remind me what an utter disappointment I was to him and the family.

Fuck him.

But I'd made the fatal error of listening to his voicemail. Just hearing his arrogant aloof voice demanding I call him sent my mood tumbling into the depths of hell that not even vodka on tap could cure.

The house was steeped in darkness when I reached the door. Digging my keys out of my pocket, I fumbled with the lock. "Stupid fucking thing."

I contemplated hammering on the door to get someone's attention, but it was late. Everyone would be sleeping now. If Connor and Austin had even made it back. Connor was most likely at El's, while Austin was probably balls deep inside some puck bunny somewhere on campus. And Aurora—

I couldn't even think about Aurora without wanting to slap myself in the face.

I'd treated her like absolute shit, bailing on our date and kicking her out of the truck onto the street like she was nothing more than dirt on my shoe.

Not my finest moment.

But the call had thrown me for a loop. And hearing *his* voice again had dredged up some serious bad fucking memories.

I didn't want her to see me like that—angry and bitter. Not when I'd worked so fucking hard to bury that guy.

One voicemail from him, though, and the veneer shattered.

Fuck.

I finally got the door open and staggered inside, kicking off my sneakers and locking up behind me. I needed to soak up some of the liquor stat. But I didn't trust my stomach could handle food, so I opted to chug two glasses of water instead to try and flush out the toxins.

Giving myself a few minutes to try and sober up, I headed upstairs. But the second my feet hit the first floor, my eyes went to the stairs leading to Aurora's room.

I needed to apologize, to explain that running out earlier had nothing to do with her and everything to do with me and my fucked-up past.

Sober Noah knew it was a bad idea going up there. I was so fucking drunk, and she was probably sleeping. But I couldn't go to bed without seeing her.

I couldn't.

Grabbing the rail, I hauled myself up the second staircase. I sounded like a baby fucking elephant, but the room was spinning again, making it really difficult to see.

"What's going on—Noah."

She stood there like a vision. Hair scraped off her face in a messy bun, an oversized t-shirt hiding her sexy-as-fuck curves, and not an ounce of makeup on her face.

She looked like she'd just rolled out of bed, and she'd never looked more beautiful.

"Really?" Her brow arched with irritation.

"What?"

"You just said I looked beautiful."

"I did?"

Huh.

"Are you drunk?"

"I'm not sober, shortcakes." She smothered a chuckle, and I grinned. "You think I'm funny."

"I think you need to go back to your own room, Noah."

Her exasperated gaze drilled holes into my face. "It's late, and I don't have the energy to deal with you right now."

I took a step toward her and another, swaying towards her as if some invisible line was reeling me in.

"Just how much did you drink?"

"Not enough," I murmured.

"Noah... did something happen after you left me?"

"I—shit." Acid rushed up my throat, flooding my mouth. "I'm going to—" I barged past her, running for the bathroom. Dropping to my knees, I clutched the bowl as I purged two hours' worth of vodka.

"Noah?"

"Don't come in here," I murmured, heaving some more.

Fuck.

It burned.

"I'm going to get you some water and your toothbrush."

I murmured some nonsensical reply. Everything hurt. My stomach. My head. My muscles.

My cold fucking heart.

All because that piece of shit I got to call my father still had a hold on me.

Because I couldn't let him go.

"Hey." A dark-haired angel appeared in my blurry vision. "Come on, let's get you cleaned up."

Aurora helped me to my feet and stripped me out of my puke-splattered t-shirt. "Clean tee," she said, handing me the t-shirt. "Toothbrush and water is right there on the vanity. Think you can manage or do you need me to help?"

"I can manage."

Because it was already shameful enough that she had to witness this.

Way to go, Holden. You're a fucking idiot.

She gave me a small nod and went to leave, but I snagged her wrist. "Aurora—"

"Not now." She yanked her arm free and left me alone.

I cleaned up the best I could, brushing my teeth twice and giving my face a wash. I didn't bother with the t-shirt; I never slept in pajamas.

When I went back into her room, Aurora was perched on the edge of her bed, the bedside lamp casting a soft glow around the room.

"How are you feeling?" She stood.

"Like something crawled inside me and died, and I still can't see straight." I ran a hand through my hair and down the back of my neck.

"You can sleep in here tonight. I'll take the floor."

"Shortcake..." I closed the distance between us, getting so close she had to crane her neck to look up at me.

"Don't do this, Noah. Not tonight, not while—"

"Shh." I pressed a finger against her lips, heat licking my insides.

I was drunk, but I wasn't fucking blind.

"I'm sorry. I really fucked up tonight."

"Go to bed, Noah." She moved around me, but my arm shot out, pulling her down on the bed with me.

"Noah!"

We landed in a tangle of limbs, and she started to scramble away from me.

"Stay, please. What if I get sick again and choke on my own vomit?"

"That is disgusting."

"Or what if I fall into a liquor-induced coma, huh? You should probably keep an eye on me."

Her eyes narrowed with indignation. But maybe,

maybe, there was a flicker of amusement there too. "You, Noah Holden, are incorrigible."

"Say what now, shortcake?"

"It means..." I grinned, and she rolled her eyes. "Oh, hush. Stay on your own side, and no touching." My mouth twitched, and she added, "I mean it."

"Pinky promise?" I held up my pinky, and she gawked at me.

"Go. To. Sleep."

I shucked my jeans off, and we both shifted around until we pulled up the comforter over us. Aurora rolled onto her side away from me, giving me her shoulder, and turned out the light.

"Hey, shortcake?" I whispered.

"Noah!" she hissed.

Reaching for her, I brushed the curve of her shoulder. "Do you hate me?"

"I don't particularly like you right now." She shoved my hand away.

Shit.

My stomach dropped, and not in an I'm-about-to-puke-because-of-all-the-vodka way.

"Aurora, shortcake, I'm sorry." I shuffled closer, sliding my arm over her waist. She didn't fight me this time, but she did go deathly still. "Is this okay?"

Testing the waters, I pressed closer until her ass was nestled against my crotch.

"Noah..." She breathed, but some of the ice in her voice had thawed.

"This is nice," I whispered into the crook of her neck, breathing her in. Trying really fucking hard not to let myself get carried away. Because she smelled incredible, and she felt even better.

"I never do this," I murmured.

"What?"

"Snuggle."

"I find that hard to believe," she scoffed.

"It's true. No sleepovers. It's my number one rule."

Until you came along, and my rules went up in flames.

"I'd hardly call this a sleepover, Noah. It's more like nurse duty."

"Po-tay-to, po-tah-to."

"Go to sleep," she sighed.

My hand slipped along her thigh and found the hem of her t-shirt, but Aurora covered my hand with hers, stopping me in my tracks. "Don't."

"Shit, yeah, okay."

I went to pull back, but she held my hand tighter. "You really hurt me tonight, Noah."

"I know, shortcake. Fuck, I know." Shame slithered through me, coiling in my chest. "The last thing I ever wanted to do is hurt you, but things are complicated."

She didn't reply, her silence deafening.

"I'll make it up to you," I added. "If you'll let me, I'll —Aurora?"

Her breathing had evened out. She'd fallen asleep in my arms.

I pressed a kiss to her shoulder and closed my eyes. Aurora didn't want to acknowledge it, but she was taking one of my firsts tonight.

I didn't do sleepovers. Even with Sam, I'd made a point of never waking up at her place. It felt too intimate, too heavy.

But there was something about being here with Aurora that scared the shit out of me.

Because it felt real.

It felt...

Permanent.

I woke to a phone vibrating.

My phone.

"What the—" I snatched it off the floor and silenced the ringtone.

Aurora stirred beside me, and before I could panic about what the fuck I was doing half-naked in her bed, memories of the night before came flooding back.

Her standing in the hall while I tried to stay upright. Me puking in her bathroom like the pathetic piece of shit I was. Pulling her down on the bed and wrapping myself around her like a fucking koala.

Jesus.

Gently, I eased myself out of bed. Aurora looked so peaceful, I didn't want to disturb her. I didn't particularly want to leave without saying goodbye either, but it was early, and I needed to go.

If Austin weren't already home, he would be soon. And who knew when Connor might show.

Leaning over her, I brushed the hair from Aurora's face and whispered, "See you later, shortcake," before slipping from her room.

Connor wasn't home. His bedroom door was ajar, and there was no sign of him. But Austin was. I could hear the fucker snoring like a grizzly bear. I prayed to God he hadn't checked in on Aurora before he went to sleep, but he didn't strike me as that kind of brother.

Connor seemed more interested in her life than Austin did.

Tiptoeing down the hall to my room, I ducked inside and threw my shit on the bed. I'd spent the night with Aurora after abandoning her on our date, getting shitfaced at some bar, and puking in her bathroom. I couldn't even remember getting home, for fuck's sake.

Not my finest moment.

Most of the anger I'd felt bubbling inside me last night had subsided. But I wasn't surprised. Aurora had that effect on me.

I dumped my puke-stained t-shirt in the laundry hamper and grabbed a towel. A tepid shower would blast the majority of my hangover away, and the rest would be cured with eggs and bacon.

At least, I hoped like fuck it would, or the day was going to be a long, painful slog.

By the time I was showered and dressed, my stomach rumbled, and I felt semi-human.

Austin followed me down, rubbing his eyes. "Morning," he said, helping himself to coffee.

"Late night?" I asked, and he smirked.

"You could say that."

"Shit, man, were you with a tiger?"

"What—"

I pointed to the wall mirror and then to his neck. "She scratched you up good."

"She was a feisty little thing." He chuckled, gently prodding the red angry scratch marks along his collarbone. "Have you seen Rory?"

"No, why?" I rushed out a little too hastily. "Have you?"

"Uh, no. That's why I asked you." His brows knitted. "She must still be sleeping."

"I'm making eggs and bacon, you want?"

"Does a bear shit in the woods? So how was last night?" I gawked at him, and he added, "With Sam. Are you feeling okay? You're acting weird."

"Just tired. It was a late night."

"Oh, it's like that, huh. I knew you wouldn't be able to resist. She makes it too easy for you. Did you act out a little student/teacher role-play?"

"Like I'd ever tell you," I laughed, hoping like hell he wouldn't catch on to the tightness in my voice.

"Come on, man. It's not like I haven't heard it all before. You used to enjoy a little story trade over breakfast."

"We were studying."

"You're really going to stick to that story? I know we give you shit about her, but none of us care if you're fucking Sam. You don't need to be all weird about it."

"I'm not—"

"'Morning," Aurora padded into the kitchen with a yawn.

"Hey, Rory, answer something for me," Austin said, and I wondered where the fuck he was going with this.

"Sure." She helped herself to coffee, avoiding looking in my direction.

"Do you think a guy and a girl can ever be just friends?"

"Why do you ask?"

"Because lover boy over here reckons he studied with Sam last night, but I call bullshit."

"I don't know." She worried her lip with her thumb. "Was this study session somewhere public, like the library or a coffee shop? Or was it at her place? Was there alcohol involved? Or—"

"How the fuck should I know?" Austin barked, frowning at his sister. "Ask Noah."

Fuck.

Her gaze lifted to mine, betrayal and hurt shining there.

It hit me, then.

Aurora had heard everything.

CHAPTER 23

AURORA

I GRIPPED my coffee mug and calmly headed for the door. "I have to get to campus early. I'll see you later."

"Uh, sure," Austin frowned. The second I was out of the room, I heard him say, "Was it something I said?"

Sam.

He'd been with Sam.

God, I felt sick.

Had he left me to go and fuck her? Get drunk with her? Only to come home and torture me some more.

I was such an idiot.

Noah wanted me. I didn't doubt that. But he didn't want me enough to avoid sticking his dick in some puck bunny.

I hurried upstairs to my room and slammed the door behind me right as my cell vibrated. It wasn't any surprise to see Noah's name.

Noah: It's not what you think. I swear to
God, shortcake. Just... let me explain.

It never was.

The first time I asked Ben if there was something going on with Tierney, he'd looked me in the eye and told me I was being ridiculous. He'd gaslit me into thinking I was overreacting. Tierney Jenson was my best friend, she was an integral part of our friend group, so it only made sense that sometimes the two of them hung out. He'd even had the audacity to say that if I couldn't trust him, maybe we shouldn't be together.

He'd played on every insecurity I had and manipulated me into a docile, acquiescent girlfriend which made his betrayal that much harder to bear.

Because I'd allowed it to happen.

I'd ignored my gut, convincing myself that he loved me. That he would never hurt me. Even though, deep down, I knew something was off.

Emotion welled inside me, but I refused to cry. Not over Ben and certainly not over Noah Holden.

Maybe I wasn't the kind of girl who got the guy, but I had enough dignity to know when to walk away.

Another text came through, but I didn't read it. Instead, I turned off my cell phone, dragged my weary butt into the shower, and washed away all memories of Noah Holden's treacherous kisses.

The day dragged. I kept my cell phone off, avoiding any public places I might run into the hockey team and, more specifically, Noah.

Harper had grilled me in our class together, but I lied and told her I wasn't feeling so good. It had been enough to placate her.

But as I was heading toward the library, the last person I expected to see heading toward me appeared in my peripheral vision.

"Austin's sister Aurelie, right?" Sam said.

"Aurora," I replied. "You're Noah's friend."

"Oh, sweetie, I'm far more than that." She gave me a saccharine smile.

I knew girls like Sam. The kind of girl who had claws and wasn't afraid to use them.

"If you say so." I went to move around her, but she stepped in my way.

"We should hang out sometime. Get to know each other."

My brows knitted because surely she wasn't being serious.

"Come on," she surprised the crap out of me by lacing her arm through mine and dragging me along with her. "It'll be fun. Noah said you don't have many girlfriends."

"He said that?" My stomach twisted.

"Yeah, last night when he came over to study."

"Oh."

"I'm in his accounting class. I'm going to help him ace the semester."

"Great."

"Yep. It's all part of my service. If you catch my drift."

"Sam, I'm not sure why you're telling me all this. Noah and I are—"

"Friends."

"Yeah, I guess you could say that."

"Which makes us friends."

Over my dead body.

"Sorry, but I need to get to my next class," I said, untangling myself from her grip.

"Oh, of course. Well, we'll have to plan something soon. Maybe coffee or drinks at The Penalty Box. Or we could catch a film at The Regal. It's this cutest little place Noah—"

My heart dropped as I blurted, "I really am late."

"Okay then, bye, Aurelie." I flinched at her blatant dig. "See you around."

She gave me a finger wave and took off down the path, leaving me gawking after her.

Sam knew. She knew about the movie theater because Noah had taken her there.

God, I felt sick.

But despite the weird vibes I got from Sam—the obvious warning in her passive-aggressive words—I couldn't help but see why Noah would want somebody like her.

Long wavy blonde hair. Slim, curvy body. Understated but super cute outfit. Sam looked effortlessly gorgeous. The kind of girl who people expected Noah to date. The kind of girl who looked good beside him. The kind of girl who would attract all the right attention.

The kind of girl his friends would high-five him for being with, not laugh behind his back at.

I backtracked, taking a different route to my next class to avoid bumping into her again. But I walked right into another familiar face.

"Aurora?" Ella smiled.

"Hey."

"What's wrong?"

"Nothing. I'm just heading to class."

"English Department?"

"Yep."

"Great, I'm heading there too." She fell into step beside me. "So how're things?"

"Fine, thanks," I lied. "What about you? Did you get a chance to talk to Connor?"

"Not really. But he came back to my place last night and... well, let's just say he reassured me that things are good."

A stab of jealousy went through me, but I managed to choke out, "That's great."

"What about you? Connor told me about that asshole, Ryan. I'm sorry. I was in a study group with him sophomore year, and I can't remember him being such a dick back then."

"It is what it is." I shrugged.

"You know, feel free to tell me to mind my own business, but I could have sworn I walked into something between you and Noah the other day at the library."

"He was just helping me."

"Right." She gave me a small, unconvinced smile. "You know, if he wasn't... just be careful, Aurora. Noah is—"

"Out of my league," I finished for her. "Don't worry. I'm well aware of that."

"Whoa, babe." She grabbed my hand and moved in front of me. "That's not what I meant at all. But Noah gets around—a lot. And in the whole time I've known him, he's never been with the same girl twice. Except for Sam, but that's different."

Just what I didn't want to hear.

"You don't have to worry about me, Ella." I forced a smile. "Noah is a friend, nothing more."

Her expression turned sympathetic. And I hated it.

I hated that she felt sorry for me.

Because, of course, Noah wouldn't change for a girl like me.

"All I'm saying is be careful. I know how charming these hockey players can be. Did Connor tell you our story?"

"Austin mentioned something, but he didn't go into detail."

"Freshman year, I slept with Connor. He'd been chasing me for a while, and I finally agreed to go on a date with him, and well, one thing led to another, and we slept together. But what I thought was the start of something was just one night to him."

"That's—"

"Not the worst of it." She grimaced. "I was a virgin. I gave Connor my virginity, and he ghosted me."

"Wow. I don't even know what to say to that."

"Right? I was so embarrassed and hurt. I swore off hockey players and managed to avoid Connor for two whole years."

"Well, he must have made it up to you?"

"Not really," she chuckled. "I'd had a string of bad dates,

was feeling down on myself, and my friend Mila—the girl you met at the party—she talked me into going to a party at Lakers House. Connor cornered me, and the rest, as they say, is history."

"My ex-boyfriend was sleeping with my best friend behind my back for months before I walked in on them," I blurted out.

"Oh my God, babe, that's horrible."

"Yep. He was the captain of our high school hockey team. I thought we had our future all planned out while he was busy hooking up with Tierney every time my back was turned, laughing at me. *Pitying* me."

"I don't know what's worse. His betrayal or hers. You never break girl code for a boy."

I nodded. "It made me reevaluate our friendship for sure. But it also made me realize that she was only friends with me because she pitied me."

"Pitied you?"

"When you look like this"—I brushed a hand down my body—"kids can be cruel."

"Aurora, that's not—"

"Please don't insult me by telling me it's not true. I've lived it for years, Ella. If they weren't whispering dirty slurs about my boobs, they were calling me wide load or thunder thighs."

"Sorry, you're right. I didn't mean to invalidate your feelings. You're beautiful, Aurora. I hope you know that. At least you've put them in your rearview mirror now."

"Yeah." I gave her a tight-lipped smile.

"People suck."

"They really, really do."

We reached the building, and Ella held open the door

for me. "We should definitely go out for that drink," she said. "I have a friend, Jordan, I think the two of you would really hit it off."

"Oh, I'm not looking to be set up on any more dates."

"Relax, Jordan is a she, and whilst you are exactly her type"—Ella grinned—"she is completely smitten with her girlfriend, Noelle."

"I'm in, so long as we can go somewhere the guys won't be."

A mischievous glint flashed in her eyes. "I know just the place."

I avoided the house for as long as possible, but eventually, I had to go back. Of course, I chose the exact moment everyone had decided to gather in the kitchen.

"Rory, baby, that you?" Connor called.

"It's me."

"Get your cute butt in here. We've got takeout."

Resisting the urge to bolt upstairs, I held my head high, gave myself a silent pep talk, and headed for the kitchen.

"Hey."

"Where the hell have you been all day?" Austin said.

"It's this thing called class. You should try it sometime."

"Funny. I mean, our messages. You haven't been answering."

"Oh, I forgot to charge my phone last night, and it died pretty much the moment I got on campus."

"They have those FuelRod kiosks all over campus. You could have—"

"It's good to switch off for a few hours," I cut him off. "With all your hockey group chats, you should try it once and a while."

"Noodles, little Hart?" Connor slung his arm over my shoulder. "Or there's sesame chicken or crispy shredded beef."

"I'm good, thanks. I already ate."

"What did you have?" Austin studied me.

"Excuse me?" I didn't like the insinuation in his voice.

"To eat? What did you have?"

"Not that it's any of your business," I snapped. "But I had a roasted vegetable and pesto salad from Roast 'n' Go."

"Rory, baby, you're killing me here," Connor groaned. "Where's the meat? The carbs? The tasty goodness."

"It wasn't that bad." An awkward chuckle spilled out of me.

"Maybe not. But we've got enough to feed an army here. Sit, eat, hang."

"Con is right, Sis. Eat with us. It's one takeout. It won't hurt." His heavy stare was too invasive. As if he saw the truth in my eyes.

That even if I wanted to eat with them, I couldn't bring myself to do it.

"Yeah, come on, little Hart. We can—"

"Something smells good." Noah wandered into the room, freshly showered and annoyingly gorgeous. His eyes flashed to mine, apology shining there. But I glanced away as if his gaze burned.

"I have a bunch of reading to get through." I grabbed a bottle of water from the refrigerator and an apple from the fruit bowl. "But enjoy all your carbs."

"Aurora—"

I waved them off, heading out of the kitchen.

I had no plans to study. Not tonight. Tonight, I had a date with my favorite book-boyfriend.

Mr. Edmund Bertram.

It had been at least a few months since I'd slipped between the pages of Mansfield Park. But every time was like coming home.

Inside my room, I powered up my cell phone while changing into my fluffy lounge pants and hoodie, grabbed my tattered copy of the book, and got comfortable on the window seat.

It was easy to open the book and fall back into the bookmarked scene because I knew the story. Lovers of Austen's works rarely loved Fanny Price the way they loved Elizabeth Bennet or Elinor Dashwood. She was self-righteous to a fault, uptight, and awfully judgmental. But I'd always related to the quiet parts of her.

I knew her struggles, her inner turmoil, and her low self-esteem. I knew what it felt like to be invisible and deeply, deeply misunderstood.

If only I could find her ability to speak up when it counted.

I'd tried over the years—I was still trying. But finding my voice after a childhood of being silenced and ignored, it wasn't easy.

My cell phone vibrated, but I ignored it. And the second message. And third.

But there was no ignoring the knock on my door five minutes later.

"Shortcake?" Noah called. "I know you're in there."

"Go away, Noah."

"I'm coming in."

I leapt up. "Don't you—Noah! You can't just barge in here."

"We need to talk."

"No, we really don't."

"Yeah, we do. Please." His expression softened that smile of his casting its usual spell over me.

But I wasn't going to fall for it. Not this time.

"Don't look at me like that," I snapped, and his mouth twitched as if he knew exactly what he was doing.

"Like what?"

"Fine. If you won't leave, I will." I marched past him, indignation burning through every inch of me.

"Shortcake, Aurora, come on... Connor and Austin just left. So we have privacy. Just hear me out. Please—"

"Why? Why do you keep doing this?"

"What?" He jerked back as if I'd slapped him. "I came to apologize and explain. I already texted you, but since you turned off your phone and you're ignoring me, I'm assuming you didn't read them."

"Just go, Noah. I'm not doing this anymore. I was stupid to think you'd give up your old habits just because we've been... whatever the hell it is we've been doing."

"Don't you think you're overreacting a little? It was a study session. Nothing happened."

I snorted. "You couldn't fool my brother with that bullshit excuse, and you're definitely not fooling me."

"I don't need to fool anyone." Hurt flashed in his expression. "Because it's the truth."

"So you're trying to tell me that you abandoned our date—literally abandoned me on the side of the road—for a study session? I might be a fool, Noah, but I'm not an idiot."

"The fuck are you talking about, woman? The study session with Sam was my cover for taking you out. I didn't see her after I dropped you off."

"You didn't?" I frowned.

"No. And you would have known that if you gave me a chance to explain."

"Sam made it sound like—"

"Sam?" He gritted out, his expression turning thunderous. "When the hell did you talk to Sam?"

"She ambushed me on campus. I got the impression she was staking her claim."

"Sam is a friend."

"That you slept with," I pointed out.

He ran a hand over his jaw, grimacing. "Made the mistake of sleeping with, yes. But I haven't touched her in weeks."

"You haven't?"

"No, I swear, I haven't been with anyone since—" He stopped himself, but I couldn't stop myself from asking, "Since when?"

"Since you got here."

"Well, that's a lie."

His brows pinched. "So now you're keeping tabs on my sex life?"

"You brought Fallon back to the house. The first weekend I was here. I heard you two going at it."

"I don't know what you think you heard, but I swear on my life, I have never brought Fallon back to the house. Or any girl, for that matter."

I chose to shelve that little tidbit of information for another time. Choosing to double down on my accusation instead. Because he was lying—he had to be.

"I heard you."

"Shortcake." He took a step toward me. "I'm telling you, it wasn't me."

"Well, it wasn't Connor. And Austin wouldn't—"

"That sneaky fucker," Noah breathed.

"What?" It was my turn to frown.

"Austin's been seeing someone. Acting all cagey about it. It's Fallon. I'd bet money on it."

"We don't know that."

"Well, I know I wasn't in the house banging her that night. So unless we had an intruder or Connor is cheating on Ella, then I hate to break it to you, shortcake, but it was big brother."

"That is... Oh my God, I think I'm going to puke. I heard my big brother having sex." I clapped a hand over my mouth, bile churning in my stomach.

Amusement danced in Noah's eyes, but it did little to ease the knot in my stomach. Just because he didn't drop me for Sam last night didn't change anything.

If anything, the whole debacle only reaffirmed that I was out of my league.

When I'd calmed down, Noah took another step closer. "I didn't sleep with Fallon. And I certainly didn't fuck Sam last night or any other girl, for that matter. I had some family stuff to deal with."

"Family stuff?"

"Yeah. And no, I don't want to talk about it." I went to speak but he added, "That's not me trying to give you more ammunition to go off on me. I just don't talk about him. I can't."

"I believe you." I did because I knew all about difficult families. But the rest? I didn't know what to think, but my gut said Noah was telling the truth. Which meant I'd gone full Fanny Price on him.

Crap.

"I'm sorry I jumped to conclusions," I said. "But I'm way out of my league here, Noah. I tried to tell myself I could do it, that I could put aside all my insecurities and fears and just enjoy this. But I realize now I can't do it. You're Noah Holden, and I'm not the kind of girl who dates hockey players."

Not anymore.

"What are you saying, shortcake?" The muscle in his jaw ticked, his eyes locked on mine. Pleading with me not to say whatever was on the tip of my tongue.

I inhaled a sharp breath, hesitating. I needed to do this.

I needed to protect myself.

My heart.

"I'm saying," I forced the words out. "I can't do this."

CHAPTER 24

NOAH

SHE DIDN'T WAVER as she said the words.

Not even a little.

Regret cut me right through the chest because I'd done this.

I'd made her doubt me—my intentions—to the point where she wholeheartedly believed she wasn't good enough for me.

Well, fuck that.

Aurora Hart was the sun that I gravitated to. Ever since she'd arrived in Lakeshore, I'd barely looked twice at another girl.

Because all I saw was her.

Call it fate or kismet or the universe's strange way of telling me it was time to grow the fuck up. It didn't matter. There were only two time periods in my life now.

Before Aurora.

And after her.

I wasn't about to add a third.

"No," I said.

"N-no? Seriously?" She recoiled. "It's not your decision to make, Noah."

"Sure it is. Fifty percent of it, at least."

"What part of you left me on the side of the road after blowing so hot and cold that I got ice burn, don't you understand?"

And there it was.

The elephant in the room.

The one thing I never wanted to admit to her or anyone else.

But if she was going to trust me, if she was going to give me a chance to make this right, I had to give her something.

"My old man is an asshole." A shuddering breath rolled through me. "The worst kind. He called me last night when we were at the movies. Timothy Holden never calls me. It threw me for a loop and dredged up some stuff I try hard to keep buried. I didn't want you around the fallout, so I bailed."

Her brows furrowed as she looked at me. I wondered if she knew that no one had ever looked at me the way she did.

Girls looked sure, but they didn't *look*. They only saw Noah Holden, the hockey star. The fuckboy. The guy who didn't date or get too close or take life too seriously.

They never looked past all that surface-level shit because they didn't care.

But Aurora looked, and I was so fucking desperate to know what she saw.

"Say something," I said, my voice raw with vulnerability.

I'd never put myself out there, not for anyone.

Only her.

Fuck.

I was in too deep. It was too quick. Too fucking complicated. But I didn't care because the second she said she couldn't do this anymore, I knew, without a shadow of a doubt, that I wanted a shot at something real with her.

"Tell me about your dad."

"I... fuck, Aurora. I can't. Ask me anything but that. Please." My voice cracked, the shaky foundations of my life in Lakeshore threatening to fracture open.

"Fine," she conceded. "Where did you go after you left me?"

I breathed a sigh of relief. "To a bar. Ordered a vodka on the rocks and told the guy to keep them coming."

"You were pretty wasted."

"Shortcake, I was toasted. But you looked after me."

"Only because you gave me no choice." A faint smile traced her lips, some of the tension between us ebbing away.

"For what it's worth, I am so fucking sorry. You deserved more than that. But he's my kryptonite, always has been. It's why I moved to Lakeshore and never looked back."

"What do you mean, you moved here?"

"I left Buffalo the second I graduated and haven't been back since."

"I'm sorry."

"It is what it is." I shrugged. "I work hard every day to be better than he is. And every day, I think I'm moving past my shitty childhood but..."

"You never forget."

"No, shortcake. You don't." I closed the distance between us, stopping just short of her. "I know I fucked up, but it was about me, not you."

"You have to realize I'm not like the girls you're used to being with, Noah. I don't put myself out there. And when I do…" She trailed off, struggling to maintain eye contact.

"What really happened with your ex?"

"I told my brother we mutually ended things, but we didn't. He… he decided he didn't want me anymore, so I declined my place at Fitton U and transferred here. Austin and I aren't close, but I thought having a familiar face around would make things easier."

"That's not the whole story, is it?" I asked.

"No. So I guess that makes us even."

"You know, shortcake. If we're going to do this thing, then we should probably be more open with each other."

"Who said I've forgiven you?"

I inched closer, reaching for her. My arm went around her waist, crushing her to me.

"Noah!"

"I'm not ready to say goodbye to this yet."

"I don't trust myself around you, Noah. You draw me in, and I can't afford to lose myself again. To get swept up in this fantasy and—"

"Shh." I pressed a finger to her lips, unwilling to hear the doubt in her voice. "Give me another chance."

"Noah…" she murmured.

I was wearing her down. Slowly breaking down her walls. And I wouldn't stop until she gave me a chance.

"We're not done; you know we're not. There's something here, shortcake. Something real."

"And when something better comes along? What then, huh?"

"Fuck, Aurora."

Anger welled inside me, and I hated—fucking *hated*—that she believed in herself so little.

"Nothing better will come along, so get that thought out of your head. I know you probably don't want to hear this. But I slept with a lot of girls last year. Too many. But I didn't have a sleepover with a single one. You own that first. You, shortcake."

Her breath caught.

"I've also never taken a girl on a date since starting at Lakeshore U. Another first."

"So you've never taken Sam to The Regal?"

"What the fuck?" I balked. "Did she say that? Because it's a fucking lie, shortcake. I have never taken anyone else there, I swear."

"Why would she say that?"

Why indeed. I shoved down the anger bubbling inside me and focused on Aurora.

"I'll deal with Sam." She nodded, and I moved on. "We've never had a girl in our group chat before."

"That is not a thing." Aurora fought a smile.

"Sure it is."

"I'm not giving you that one. Austin only added me to the group chat to coerce me into the costume party."

"Okay, then, what about this one." I leaned down, brushing my mouth over hers. Once. Twice. Aurora's eyelashes fluttered, the softest whimper escaping her lips as I pulled away. "I have never felt this way before, short-cake," I whispered. "You do something to me, and I'm not ready to give that up yet."

"You're making it really hard for me to say no to you."

"So don't." I touched my head to hers.

"You're going to break my heart," she said—a definitive, bold statement. As if there was no doubt in her mind that this ended any other way.

It didn't sit well with me that she was so convinced I would hurt her.

But then, I hadn't exactly proved otherwise.

Brushing my knuckles down her cheek, I pressed a kiss to her brow. "Just think about it," I said before pulling away.

"Where are you going?" she asked, eyes cloudy with confusion as I walked backward toward the door.

"Giving you some space."

"What if I don't want space?"

"I'm not going to let you use me for my irresistible body, shortcake." I winked. "If you want me, you have to be prepared to accept me. All of me."

"I—"

"Don't make a decision now. Sleep on it."

"Sleep? You think I'm going to get even a wink of sleep after this conversation."

The corner of my mouth lifted in a faint smirk as I forced myself to grab the handle.

"Welcome to my world, shortcake."

I lay in bed, cell phone in hand, one arm tucked under my head as I stared up at the ceiling, debating on whether or not enough time had passed before I texted her.

I didn't want to look needy or too keen.

Oh, who the fuck was I kidding?

After making her doubt herself—and me, for that matter—I wanted to make sure Aurora knew exactly where my head was at regarding her and our relationship.

Relationship, fuck.

I was getting ahead of myself.

I'd be lucky if she would even agree to another date, let alone anything more... serious.

I wasn't even sure I was ready for that. All I knew was I wanted to make Aurora smile. To show her every day how beautiful and funny she was. I wanted to make sure she never doubted herself again.

Fuck it.

My fingers flew over the screen, a smirk tugging at my mouth as I typed.

> Noah: Sleeping yet, shortcake?

> Aurora: You're supposed to be giving me space...

> Noah: I am. You're in your bedroom. And I'm in mine. That's a whole lot of space if you ask me.

Too much space for my liking. But this wasn't about me and my needs—it was about her.

Aurora: You have a strange perception of things, Noah.

> Noah: Just so we're clear. Is thirty-five minutes an acceptable amount of time for giving of said space?

Aurora: You told me to sleep on it, that would require actual sleeping, Noah.

> Noah: I'm an idiot. You should never listen to anything that comes out of my mouth.

Aurora: That's a shame because you said some pretty sweet things to me earlier.

Shit. She'd got me there.

The urge to get up and go to her was so strong that I had to plaster myself to the bed. It wouldn't help my cause. Not tonight.

No good decisions were ever made when tensions were running high.

I knew that better than anyone.

> Noah: Get some sleep, babe. You're going to need it for Operation Darcy.

I don't know where the fuck that came from, but I decided to roll with it.

Aurora: I already told you, I'm more of a
Bertram fan.

Noah: Humor me, shortcake.

Because I didn't know the first thing about Austen and her
top-tier fictional male characters.

Aurora: Fine. What exactly does Operation
Darcy entail?

Noah: You'll see. Sweet dreams babe. I'll
see you tomorrow.

She didn't reply right away, and for a second, I thought I'd
lost her again. But when my phone chimed, and her
response lit up my screen, my heart did a funny little flip in
my chest.

Aurora: Good night, Noah. Dream of me.

"Morning, sunshine," Connor said when I entered the kitchen. "How are you feeling?"

"Huh?"

"Last night, after all the takeout? You said—"

"Oh, yeah. My stomach," I said, catching on. "I feel better, thanks."

"You must have delicate insides, Holden. Because I ate my body weight in food, and I've been fine."

"Must be," I mused. "Austin and Aurora still sleeping?"

"Austin didn't make it home, and Aurora already left."

"She did?" My brows furrowed. "But it's still early."

"Said something about an early study group."

"I bet she did," I murmured under my breath.

"What was that?" Connor asked.

"Nothing. Coffee?"

"No, I'm good. You know, Ella told me some interesting gossip the other day."

I stilled, ice flooding my veins. "Did she?"

"Yep. Said you and little Hart were looking all kinds of cozy in the stacks at the library."

"It was nothing."

He sat back in his chair, a smug expression on his face. "Or it was something, and you're just in denial."

"Morgan..." I let out a heavy sigh.

"Look, Holden. I love you like a brother; you know that. But Rory is... she isn't like you. Anyone can see the girl has issues."

My fist clenched against my thigh as I tried to tamp down the anger rising inside me.

"That right there"—he motioned to my fist—"that is going to land you in all kinds of trouble. She's a good girl, Holden. She talks a good talk and hides her pain well, but she isn't fooling anyone. Whatever happened with the ex, with their parents... it wasn't good."

"Yeah."

"Just tread carefully."

"You're not warning me off?" I asked, my brow arching with surprise.

"You're a big boy. You can make your own decisions." He stood and approached me, laying a hand on my shoulder. "I just hope that, for everyone's sake, you make the right one."

He gave me a short, sharp squeeze before taking off.

Fuck, he was right.

Aurora had secrets.

The kind that haunted you.

I knew because I had them too.

In so many ways, we were the same. Maybe that's why I was so fucking drawn to her.

Pulling my cell phone out of my pocket, I pulled up our chat.

> Noah: Running away from me, shortcake?

Her reply was instant.

> Aurora: Never. I had an early study group.

> Noah: I was hoping we could have breakfast together.

Aurora: With Connor and my brother? How
romantic and totally not awkward...

Noah: Austin stayed out all night and
Connor would have made himself scarce.

Aurora: They can't know about us, Noah.

Noah: For now...

Aurora: What are you saying?

Shit, what was I saying?

Austin would kick my ass six ways from Sunday if he
knew I'd been fooling around with his sister. It wouldn't
matter what my intentions were or what Aurora had to say
about it because he thought we were the same.

That I was like him.

And I guess I was.

At least, I used to be.

Besides, hadn't Connor literally just told me to make
the right decision? Pretty sure he wasn't giving me the green
light to pursue Aurora.

My cell chimed again.

Aurora: Noah?

Fuck. I couldn't do it. I couldn't make good choices where she was concerned because Aurora Hart was under my skin. And I didn't want to dig her out.

> Noah: I'll see you later, shortcake.

She couldn't hide from me all day.

I drained the rest of my coffee and stood, formulating a plan of action. I wanted to give Aurora space, but patience had never been my strong suit.

If I gave her too much space, I risked losing her. And if I crowded her, I risked driving her away. But I had no experience in this field. I didn't date, and my last girlfriend had been back in tenth grade, right around the time I discovered sex.

My cell phone vibrated again, and I chuckled at her eagerness. But my good mood plummeted into the fucking gutter when I saw the message.

> Dad: We need to talk. Call me.

Yeah, like that was ever going to happen. I had nothing to say to him.

Not a damn word.

I only kept his number stored in my contacts so he

couldn't catch me unaware. Whatever Timothy Holden wanted, he could rot in hell for all I cared.

> Noah: Not interested. Don't call me again.

I hit send and did what I should have done a long time ago —blocked his number.

He was my past.

I refused to let him jeopardize my future.

CHAPTER 25

AURORA

"Guess who has a date Friday night with a football player?" Harper slid into the seat beside me and started emptying her bag out onto the desk.

I eyed the growing pile of things, and she chuckled. "I'm looking for his number. He gave it to me at the end of my shift last night, and I stuffed it in here and didn't have time this morning to—found it. Mathieu. He's from Quebec and has this sexy-as-hell French accent."

"And where is Mathieu taking you?"

"We haven't decided yet, but I'm thinking drinks and dancing. Oh hey, you should totally come. I can see if he's got a friend—"

"I'm good, thanks. But I hope you have fun."

"Oh, I'm sure we will."

It was on the tip of my tongue to ask what changed her mind about asking Noah out, but I didn't. I already felt guilty enough.

I was trying—*failing*—not to think about him every two seconds, but it was impossible after last night.

I'd told him I was done, and he'd refused to accept it. More than that, he'd given me a piece of himself and trusted me with his secrets.

He'd used the one weapon in his arsenal that I couldn't defend myself from.

The truth.

Noah didn't talk about his family—the way Austin and I didn't talk about ours. But last night, we'd begun to share pieces of ourselves. And although I was supposed to be keeping my wits about me where he was concerned, it felt like we'd begun to lay foundations between us.

I was trying so hard not to read too much into it, but it felt significant, and I'd barely slept replaying our conversation over and over.

"Rory, earth to Aurora." Harper snapped her fingers in my face, and I jolted out of my thoughts.

"Sorry, I was distracted."

"I can see that. Everything okay?"

"Fine."

"So I was thinking... the Lakers have their first game next weekend. It's only an exhibition game, but I was hoping you might want to come with me."

"Harper, I'm not sure—"

"Yeah, of course." Her expression dropped, and guilt churned in my stomach. "It was a crapshoot. I'll have to go stag or something. Don't worry about it."

"Isn't there anyone from your dorm you can ask?"

"Yeah, maybe." She suddenly found something on her desk more interesting.

I frowned. "Harper? Is everything okay?"

"Yeah." Her smile didn't reach her eyes. "It's all good."

Thinking about it, Harper didn't talk a lot about dorm life. She didn't really talk much about anything outside of class, her job at the bar, and hockey.

"I'll go with you."

"You will? But I thought—"

"You'd do it for me."

"I would." She grinned.

"Then consider me in. Go Lakers." I fist-pumped the air.

It was a terrible idea. But the people pleaser in me wanted to make her smile.

"Yay." She clapped quietly. "You won't regret it, I promise. Besides, you'll get to see big bro and his friends play."

I gave her a half-hearted smile. "So long as you don't embarrass us."

"Hey, I'm not *that* bad."

"I bet Ella is going. We could all get tickets."

"Sure."

"Where is Professor Mac—and out of thin air, she appears."

"Sorry I'm late," she announced, dropping her bag on the lectern. "Today, we're going to look at gender roles and the emergence of strong female characters as a catalyst for challenging gender stereotypes and ideologies at the time. Before we—"

My cell vibrated, and I slid it out of my pocket, smiling at Noah's name. Glancing up to find Harper focused on Professor MacMillan, I opened the message.

Noah: Being hot or being cold?

Aurora: I'm sorry, what?

Noah: Do you prefer being hot or being cold?

Aurora: Is that even a thing? I like being... comfortably warm.

My lips twisted with amusement.

Noah: You're supposed to pick one.

Aurora: Fine. Cold. I like being able to layer up and snuggle under a blanket.

Noah: You know, I've heard that I make an excellent blanket.

Aurora: I'm sure your adoring fans all love you for your snuggling capabilities.

Noah: I'm not going to take the bait, shortcake. I might have history around campus but I'm a changed man.

Another text came through while I debated on how to reply. Only this one was an image. An image of a really badly hand drawn pin reading 'CSA.'

Aurora: I'm scared to even ask...

Noah: Casual Sex Anonymous. I've been
sex-sober now for almost a month.

I smothered a laugh of disbelief. Harper glanced over,
raising a brow, and I mouthed, 'house group chat.'

Aurora: A changed man indeed. You're
really pulling out the big guns.

Noah: Desperate times and all that.

Aurora: I have to go, I'm in class.

Noah: Meet me at lunch.

Aurora: I can't, I'm having lunch with
Harper.

We hadn't planned anything yet, but he didn't need to know
that. I still hadn't figured out how I felt about everything—
specifically, giving Noah another chance.

Something told me he was going to make it impossible
for me to say no to him. But I didn't want to rush into
anything. Besides, watching him work for it was an endless
source of entertainment.

He sent me another image, this time, it was a selfie, and

he was pouting at the camera, wearing a disappointed frown.

I barely choked down the laugh stuck in my throat. He was such a goofball. But there was something very endearing about that.

The fact, he didn't take himself too seriously.

"Who's making you smile?" Harper whispered.

"Connor," I blurted, almost choking on the lie. "He's such a goof."

"The funny ones always have the dirtiest mouths. Ella is a lucky woman."

I couldn't work Harper out. She was bold and brash and clearly owned her sexuality. But sometimes, when she looked at me, I saw a shadow lingering in her eyes.

"What?" she asked, sensing me watching her.

"I'm glad we met, Harper," I said with a smile, even though guilt streaked through me, making me feel a hundred times worse.

But I couldn't tell her the truth.

She'd hate me.

Besides, there wasn't anything to tell yet. Not really.

At least, that's what I kept telling myself.

"Me too, Rory." She smiled back. "Me too."

It turned out Harper couldn't do lunch. She had a study group. But I didn't tell Noah that.

I still had a lot to think about.

Like the fact my brother and the rest of the team seemed to be everywhere I turned on campus. I managed to avoid Noah for the time being, but my brother was another matter entirely.

"Rory, wait up," Austin called, waving at me from across the student center.

He said something to the pretty blonde he was with, and the two of them shared a tense word before he left her standing there. She looked suspiciously like Fallon, but she stormed off before I could get a good look at her.

"Girl trouble?" I asked, and he grimaced, dragging a hand down his face.

"Don't ask."

"So it's true, you and Fallon are—"

Surprise crossed his expression. "We are not talking about this."

"But it's okay that you brought her home and had loud, dirty sex?"

"You heard us?" The blood drained from his face.

"You weren't exactly quiet. I thought it was Noah because I assumed my brother would never do something like that to me."

"Shit, Sis, I'm sorry. I was really fucking drunk, and she was—"

"Yeah, okay." I lifted my hand, cutting him off. "I don't need to know the details."

"Do the guys know?"

"Noah figured it out."

"Fuck, is he pissed?"

"You're asking this now *after* you had loud, dirty sex with her?"

"Please stop saying that." He paled some more. "It's weird."

"And listening to your sex noises was completely normal." I rolled my eyes.

"I'm sorry, okay? No one said anything, so I figured we'd gotten away with it."

"Are you two, like a thing?"

"We're... It's complicated," he sighed. "Has Mom called you? She keeps leaving me voicemails."

"No, I haven't spoken to her since I got here."

"Can you call her? Try and get her off my back."

"Austin..."

"I know, I know. But I have a lot riding on this season. I don't need her sticking her nose in. And now you're here—"

"You're pinning this on me?" Disbelief coated my words. "Has it ever occurred to you that maybe she just misses her son?"

He let out a bitter laugh. "We both know that is not true. She's never had time for me or my dreams."

"It's one phone call, Austin. Would it really hurt you to appease her?"

God knows, I'd spent half my childhood doing it.

"She'll listen to you," he said.

"Seriously? That's your comeback. Unbelievable." Irritation skittered down my spine.

"What?"

"You really have no idea, do you? What it was like for me growing up with her?"

"I know, Rory." His jaw clenched. "I was right there."

"That's just it. You weren't there, Austin. You were always at practice or hanging out with your friends or off at hockey camp."

"That's not—"

"Yeah, Austin." Sadness clung my words. "It is."

"I couldn't be at home, around her."

"I know, but I was there too. And I needed you. I needed —" *My brother.*

"Aurora?"

"It doesn't matter," I said, shoving down all the hurt, the pain and betrayal. "I need to get to class."

"Come on, Sis. We need to talk about this. I know it isn't good timing, but we could go and get a coffee and—"

"I can't."

"Aurora..."

"I'll see you later." I gave him a weak smile and took off across the lawn, trying to swallow down the ball of emotion lodged in my throat.

CHAPTER 26

NOAH

> Noah: Favorite animal?

I glanced up at the professor, checking that the coast was clear, and hit send. Her reply was almost instant.

> Aurora: Dog. They're so loyal and intelligent and cuddly. You?

> Noah: I'm not really an animal guy but if I had to pick, I'd say dog. They're so loyal and intelligent and cuddly.

> Aurora: Are you mocking me?

> Noah: I would never! Favorite snack?

Aurora: It's a toss-up between sushi and zucchini fries.

> Noah: Firstly, zucchini fries is not a snack, it's a vegetable parading as a tasty snack and secondly, sushi is a crime against humanity.

Aurora: It's delicious. You should try it sometime.

> Noah: What will you give me in return?

Aurora: That's not the game, Noah. You're supposed to want to try the sushi for your own personal growth. Not because I'm giving you something as a reward.

My mouth twitched. Fuck, I liked her like this. Sassy and sarcastic.

> Noah: But rewards are so much fun.

Aurora: Go away, Holden. I'm in class and you're distracting me.

It felt good to know I was distracting her—the way she always distracted me. But it no longer felt like a bad thing. After a few texts back and forth, Aurora had managed to erase my bad mood. I craved her replies, the next snarky thing she might say.

I was so fucking gone for this girl, and there was every chance she wouldn't let me back in.

No. I refused to believe that. Because we had something. I didn't know what it was or how it was going to play out, but I sure as fuck wanted to find out.

"Hey," Sam slid into the booth I'd managed to grab at the coffee shop. "What's up?"

Irritation rippled through me, but I kept my cool. "Did you talk to Aurora yesterday?"

"She told you." Her expression fell flat.

"In not so many words, yeah."

"I don't know what the big deal is. I suggested we hang out. If she's going to be around—"

"What are you doing?"

"Excuse me?"

I inhaled a thin breath, dragging a hand down my face. This could go one of two ways, and maybe the easiest option was to leave it. But I needed to show Aurora that I was on her side.

That I could change.

"What are you doing, Sam? The break-in, turning up at my class, offering to tutor me. I want to believe you're just being a good friend, but I can't shake the feeling this is all leading somewhere."

"I... God, okay." She inhaled a deep breath, fidgeting in her seat. "I didn't want to say anything yet because I know things have been weird between us... but I love you, Noah. I'm in love with you."

What. The. Fuck.

"You don't love me, Sam." Strangled laughter bubbled

in my chest because she'd lost her goddamn mind. "You love the idea of me."

"W-what do you mean?" Tears welled in her eyes.

"If you really loved me, you wouldn't have gone home with Ward the other week." My brow arched, and she visibly paled.

"I just wanted to make you jealous. I wanted—"

"Fucking my teammate doesn't exactly scream 'I love you,'" I deadpanned.

"I thought..." Her expression hardened, a stone mask falling over her. "You really don't care, do you?"

"You know I care about you... but as a friend. The second I realized you were reading too much into things, I backed off. I tried to let you down gently. But I don't know how else to make you understand that I don't want more with you. I'm sorry, but—"

She shot up out of the booth and glowered at me. "Is there someone else?"

"Sam, this isn't about someone else." An exasperated sigh slipped out. "It's about us. You. You're a good friend, but that's all it will ever be for me. I'm sorry."

Inhaling a shuddering breath, she composed herself. "You're a selfish asshole, Noah. You don't care about the girls you sleep with or their feelings. I've been there for you. I've stood by your side, waiting for you to realize that what we have is different. But I see it now. It was all just a game to you. A way to pass the time."

"Sam, come on. That's not—"

"Fair?" she sneered, bitter laughter spilling off her lips. "Nothing about life is. I think we should have some space from each other. Please don't text me or come around to the apartment. I need... time."

My brows pinched. Was she for real? She was putting *me* in time-out?

What the fuck was happening?

"Sam, I'm not sure—"

"I can't do this right now." She sniffled, dabbing her eyes with the ends of her scarf—a scarf that looked vaguely familiar.

"The only thing missing is my favorite scarf. You know the one you got me for my birthday? The black one with the daisies on it."

Unease washed over me. Fuck. I was right. All along, I was right.

"Sam is that—"

"Goodbye, Noah."

She all but ran out of the coffee shop while I stared after her, utterly confused. And there was only one person I wanted to talk to about it.

I grabbed my cell phone off the table and opened the chat with Aurora.

> **Noah:** Do you have a free period this afternoon?

> **Aurora:** I have an hour free after this class ends. Why?

> **Noah:** Long story… I'd rather tell you in person.

> **Aurora:** This isn't another trick question, is it? You're not going to turn up outside my class and accost me in the hall?

Noah: I spoke to Sam. Things got... weird.
I really need my shortcake. Please.

My shortcake?

Shit.

Aurora wasn't mine—but I wanted her to be.

I did.

Aurora: Fine. But we're on campus. It
doesn't leave a lot of places to be discreet.

Noah: I know a place.

Aurora: ???

Noah: The arena.

I checked my phone again, waiting for Aurora's text. We'd
arranged to meet at the arena, but she couldn't access it
without a keycard. And I figured the rear exit was the best
shot at being discreet.

My cell finally vibrated.

Aurora: I'm here.

I got up and jogged to the exit, opening the door. The second Aurora appeared, some of the tension coiled inside me unraveled.

She gnawed on her thumb, watching me through big, surprised eyes. "Are we allowed to be in here?"

"Kind of comes with the territory, shortcake." I tugged my Lakers jersey with a grin.

"Noah..." She sighed in that exasperated way of hers as if I was exhausting. But I kind of liked how much I affected her.

"Have you ever been here?" I asked, grabbing her hand and tugging her down the hall.

"Austin gave me the tour last year when I visited. But it wasn't exactly a behind-the-scenes look around."

"What's up with that? One minute, he's protective big brother, the next, he seems—"

"Like a disinterested asshole?"

"You said it, shortcake." I smiled, but something inside me twisted.

"Mine and Austin's relationship is complicated."

"I'd like to know. I mean, if you want to tell me."

Aurora frowned, a hint of distrust in her expression.

It stung, but I didn't blame her.

"I'm sure you didn't bring me here to talk about Austin and me. What happened with Sam?"

I couldn't work out if she were deflecting for her or my sake, but I let it slide.

She was here—she'd turned up for me. And that was more than I deserved.

"Come here." I shouldered the door leading to the rink

and inhaled a deep breath. There was something invigo-
rating about being out here. The sharpness of the subzero
temperature making my lungs contract and expand.

"It's cold," Aurora said.

"It's home," I replied.

"You really love it, don't you? Hockey?" She peered up at
me, a thousand questions in her emerald eyes. None I had
answers for yet.

But I could answer this.

"Hockey has always been my first love."

"My brother used to say that, and I always wondered
why he chose to love something that would never love him
back."

"Maybe that's why," I said, knowing exactly what Austin
meant.

Hockey couldn't disappoint you. It couldn't hurt or
abandon you. The ice was always solid beneath your skates.
Even if you fell down, it would hold your weight, let you get
back up, and try again.

"Is that how you feel about it?" she asked as we climbed
the steps to the back row of seats and sat down.

"Short answer, yes," I said. "The long answer is much
more complicated."

"I have time." Aurora smiled, and fuck if it wasn't like a
direct shot to the chest.

"I didn't grow up in a happy home, shortcake. My mom
and dad were constantly fighting. He was a mean son of a
bitch with a sharp tongue and high expectations. And eventually, it drove her away."

"Noah..." Aurora laid her hand on my arm. But it wasn't
enough. I pulled it down to my thigh and threaded our
fingers together.

"She left when I was seven. The only glimmer of light in that hell hole, and she just left me there."

Fuck.

Talking about it made all those emotions rush to the surface.

Fear.

Confusion.

Hurt.

Heartbreak.

"When I realized she was gone and wasn't coming back, I cried for a week straight. Timothy Holden didn't like tears."

I could still hear him now. *Crying makes you weak, Son.*

"You talk about him in the past tense," Aurora said.

"Because he's dead to me."

"Noah..." She sucked in a sharp breath, sympathy gleaming in her eyes.

"Don't feel sorry for me, shortcake. Getting the scholarship to LU was the best thing that ever happened to me. And when I turn pro, I'll put Buffalo in my rearview mirror for good."

"Our dad never stuck around either," Aurora said quietly. "My mom is... difficult, to say the least. You know she was a model in her heyday." I nodded, and she went on, "Well, she still picks up the odd job, but as you can imagine, the aging process is against her in an industry built on beauty and youth."

"I didn't know... about your dad, I mean."

"I'm not surprised Austin doesn't talk about it. Things between him and Mom have always been strained, ever since Dad left."

"And you and your mom?" I asked, already sensing I knew the answer.

"I have and always will be Susannah Hart's biggest disappointment."

Pain shattered the air. It was so palpable that I wanted to hunt down Mrs. Hart and give her a piece of mind.

Aurora was beautiful inside and out, and to think her own mother had ever made her feel anything less made me want to roar at the world.

"I... fuck, shortcake. I don't know what to say."

"There is nothing to say. I spent years, *years* trying to be the daughter she so desperately wanted. But I eventually realized it would never be good enough for her.

"That *I* would never be good enough."

"I know a thing or two about being an eternal disappointment," I said.

"Look at us"—she flashed me a weak, sad smile that made my heart ache—"bonding over our shitty parents."

Sliding my hand along her neck, I buried my fingers in the silky strands of her hair and lowered my head to hers. "You're beautiful, Aurora Hart. Inside and out. I need you to know that."

Her breath caught, a shy smile tugging at her lips. "I wish I could believe you." I reared back, frowning, but she went on. "I have spent my entire life being told there is something wrong with me, Noah. Even if I wanted to believe you, those scars are too deep to let me." She gave me a little shrug.

"That's fucked up." I sat back, running a hand through my hair.

"I was eight the first time a photographer told me my thighs were too big. Eight."

Pure anger coursed through me, but I didn't interrupt or argue because this was her story to tell, her truth to confront.

"It was a swimwear shoot, and all the other girls had these cute one-pieces on. I remember walking onto the shoot, and every single one of them looked at me like they didn't understand. Like I didn't belong there. Just because I didn't have a thigh gap." Brittle laughter spilled out of her.

"I hid in the bathroom for twenty minutes, hoping they would do the shoot without me. But my mom"—she made a harsh tsking sound in her throat—"my mom couldn't let it go. She convinced the producer to let me be in the shoot still, but I had to go in the back, hiding myself under a beach towel while all the other girls ran around in their pretty swimming costumes."

"That is..." I didn't even have words.

"Only one story of many, sadly. Mom refused to listen to their feedback. Over and over, she made me go to shoots, begged casting agents and photographers to cast me. She had a lot of sway back then. But that never stopped their brutal honesty."

"You don't model now?" I asked.

"God, no. I would rather eat glass than ever step in front of the camera again. When I was twelve, I had a pretty awful experience with a photoshoot coordinator, and that was that."

I sensed it wasn't quite that cut and dry, but I didn't push. Aurora had shared something deeply personal with me, and I didn't want to overstep.

"Thank you for telling me. For trusting me. I'll never repeat a single word of it. You have my word."

She nodded. "Talking about it is never easy, and I'd

prefer to pretend that it's someone else's childhood. But you deserve to know why I reacted so badly before... when I thought..." Her gaze dropped, shame leaking into the air around us.

"Hey, look at me." I slid my fingers under Aurora's jaw, coaxing her back to me. "You never have to shy away from me, shortcake. I look at you and..." Fuck, she was so beautiful, and she really had no idea. "You take my breath away."

"Noah..."

"It's true. I love your quirky t-shirts. The way you wear your hair all messy and effortless. I love your smile and the way you verbally spar with me. There isn't a single thing I'd change about you."

"I just don't understand." Her smile slipped. "You could literally have any girl on campus. Fallon... Harper... Sam."

"Firstly, Fallon is screwing your brother. I will *never* go there again. Secondly, Harper ruined her chances with me the minute she became your friend." I winked at her, and she chuckled softly, the sound like music to my ears.

Fuck, I loved her laugh.

"And lastly, I told Sam exactly where I stand with her."

"I take it, it didn't go well?"

"It was the strangest thing. She told me she was in love with me. When I told her I didn't feel the same, she told me I was a selfish asshole, accused me of playing games with her, then told me she needed time from me."

"Wow, that's... I don't even know what to say to that. She loves you."

"She isn't in love with me, shortcake, she's in love with the idea of me. Part of me gets it. She caught feelings, and I didn't. But I swear to you, I never made her think—"

"I know," she said.

"You do?"

"If there's one thing I've learned about you, Noah, it's that despite the rumors and gossip, you're a good guy. If you say you didn't lead her on, I believe you."

"That's not the weirdest thing," I admitted.

"It's not?"

"Remember she said her apartment was broken into? Well, I always thought something was a little off about it. Pretty sure she was wearing the scarf she told me went missing that night."

"You think she made it up?"

"I think love makes you do crazy things."

"Maybe you should tell somebody. That's pretty wild, Noah."

"Nah, Sam is harmless. A little certifiable, maybe, but harmless all the same. Why? Worried about me, shortcake?"

"Maybe, just a little." She smiled.

"Does this mean you're ready to give me another chance?" Hope was a living, breathing thing in my chest.

"Honestly, I don't know."

"Well, shit. I thought we were making progress."

"I like you, Noah. I like you a lot. But that terrifies me."

"I like you too, shortcake." I brushed the hairs from her face, dropping my gaze to her lips. Wondering how hard she would kick me in the balls if I kissed her right now.

"But we're so different," she added.

"You're wrong, you know. We're more alike than you think. I mean, you grew up with shitty parents; I grew up with shitty parents. Your favorite animal is a dog; my favorite animal is a dog. You like Mr. Darcy; I like Mr. Darcy... it's practically a match made in heaven."

"You're crazy," she laughed. A real honest-to-God laugh that filled the arena and made my heart fucking soar.

It was a sound I wanted to bottle. To record and play before every game. Because knowing I was the one who made it happen made me feel ten feet fucking tall.

"Can I ask you something?" I asked.

"Sure."

"Does Austin know about how bad things were with your mom?"

Her expression dropped, and just as I suspected, I had my answer.

CHAPTER 27

AURORA

"I..." I inhaled a sharp breath.

"Hey, it's okay." Noah took my hand, squeezing it gently. "I shouldn't have—"

"No, it's fine. Austin was always distant growing up. Mom hated that he reminded her of Dad, and the two of them bickered over everything. I was in the middle a lot because despite how difficult she was, she was still my mom, you know?" I shrugged, hating that I needed to justify our complicated relationship.

"He knew she pushed me to do the modeling thing, but he was three-and-a-half years older than me and was already in deep with hockey. All he wanted was to get a scholarship and get out of Syracuse, so I got really good at hiding the truth."

"You protected him, you mean." Noah's jaw clenched, anger rolling off him in dark angry waves. "He should know—"

"He knows. Some of it, anyway. I... uh... in seventh grade, I was in a bad place. My body developed a lot quicker than other girls in my class, and I couldn't handle it. I hated myself. I couldn't look at myself in the mirror. I started restricting what I ate, my mood plummeted, and leaving the house gave me this intense feeling of dread."

It was a bad time. I was withdrawn, fixated on my changing body, and stuck in a vicious cycle of crash dieting and binge eating when I didn't see the results I wanted.

And I never saw the results because my body was supposed to be curvy. Despite Mom's better judgment, I was supposed to have boobs and hips and a plump ass. A fact that had taken me a long time to accept.

"Austin tried to talk to me. He tried to figure out what was going on. But I lied. I always lied. I ended up in therapy, but I never told him the real reason."

"Did it help? The therapy, I mean?"

"Somewhat. I was diagnosed with anxiety and something called OSFED. Other Specified Feeding or Eating Disorder."

I watched Noah's reaction, wondering if I had gone too far. But it was like a floodgate had opened, and everything began spilling out.

"We don't have to talk about this," I said, suddenly feeling stripped bare to this gorgeous, popular, funny guy who could do so much better than me and all my emotional baggage.

"I want to know, shortcake. I want to know every—"

A loud whirring noise started up, and Noah touched his head to mine, letting out a long breath.

"What is that?"

"That is the Zamboni," he said, pointing to the far end

of the rink. A man in a Lakers cap opened the gates, and the machine appeared.

"We should probably get out of here," I said.

"Yeah." Noah hesitated. "But this conversation isn't over."

"Okay." I nodded.

We slipped out of the rink and walked hand in hand down the hall, back toward the rear exit. When we reached the end, I tugged my hand free and looked up at him. God, he made my heart race. I'd only had this feeling twice in my life, and how Ben made me feel was nothing compared to how I felt when Noah looked at me.

It terrified me.

Made the scared young girl inside me panic. Because she knew what it was like to be ridiculed and hurt by people that were supposed to care about her.

People who were supposed to *love* her.

Ben had been so convincing when we first started dating. He'd been kind and supportive and patient. He'd been exactly what I'd needed. And I'd fallen for it.

I'd lowered my guard, and, in the end, he'd crushed me.

"What?" Noah asked as I gazed up at him.

"My heart is telling me to give you a chance. But my head knows better."

Noah didn't date. He didn't do girlfriends or sleepovers or romantic gestures.

Except, he had... with me. And I wanted to believe it meant something, that I was different. But how could I be?

His expression darkened as he crowded me against the wall. A small gasp escaped my lips as he caged me there, his hand going above my head. The air crackled between us as he stared at me, his eyes drinking me in, the invisible thread tugging deep in my stomach.

Noah had the power to destroy me. Wreck and ruin me. But I'd promised myself when I came to Lakeshore that I wouldn't let life pass me by. How I felt about myself and my body would always be a work in progress. There would be setbacks and bumps along the way, but I could survive them.

I could.

Because my appearance—my body shape or weight— didn't define me. It didn't make me more or less deserving than anyone else. It was a part of me, but it wasn't my entirety. I knew that.

Deep down, I knew that.

But sometimes, it got buried so far under the daily struggles, the constant little voice in my head telling me that I needed to hide my body, my imperfections, to make myself less, that it was impossible to *feel* it.

"Want to know a secret, shortcake?" he whispered. I nodded, inhaling a sharp breath as his lips ghosted over mine. "I can see the fear in your eyes. You're scared of me... of what this thing might become between us. But you're not the only one, Aurora. Be scared with me, shortcake. Be—"

I kissed him. Grabbing his jersey, I pulled Noah into me and kissed him with everything that I had.

Deep laughter rumbled in his chest as he curved an arm around my back and pressed me closer until our bodies were aligned in perfect symmetry. He was tall and strong, and he made me feel safe.

He made me feel special and beautiful and desired.

Our tongues tangled slowly and teasingly. It was sensation overload, my heart crashing violently in my chest at his admission and the way he kissed me like I was his air.

It was such a heady feeling, one I tumbled into, *falling... falling... falling* until I felt weightless. And nothing else mattered except that he kept kissing me. Touching me.

Wanting me.

"Fuck," Noah breathed. "You get me so fucking hot. But we should slow down. Before I do something we might both regret."

But I didn't want to slow down. I wanted to speed up.

I wanted to live.

For once, I wanted to be reckless and wild. To be so caught up in the moment that there was no space to think about all the what-ifs and maybes.

I tried to kiss him again, but Noah held back.

"Aurora, babe. We should—"

"No."

"No?" He frowned, pure desire simmering in his eyes.

"You're seriously ruining the mood right now, Holden."

"The mood—shortcake?"

"Is there somewhere here we can go that doesn't have cameras?"

His brows furrowed before realization dawned on his face, and he exhaled a steady breath. "You're going to be the death of me, woman."

Noah snatched my hand and pulled me across the hall to a door marked *storage*. We stumbled inside, and he wasted no time crowding me against the wall again. Blood pounded in my ears, my heart beating wildly in my chest as he watched me, a playful glint in his eye. His hungry gaze dropped to my boobs, and he grinned.

"I am such a sucker for these t-shirts." He reached out,

tracing the lettering. This one read *I should infinitely prefer a book*. "Exactly how many literary quote t-shirts do you own?"

"One for every day of the week plus a couple of extras." I blushed.

"Adorable."

"You sure you don't mean geeky." I arched a brow, and Noah locked eyes with me, regret bracketing his mouth.

"You know, I think I knew, even then."

"Knew what?"

"That I wanted you. But it was the yoga pants that sealed the deal."

"So that's it then? You only want me for my ass?"

"I want you, Aurora Vivienne Hart because you are funny and kind, and you see me."

"I..."

"Shh"—he traced his thumb across my lips—"we don't need to do this now. I like you, and you like me. That's enough, isn't it?"

"Y-yeah."

It was.

Because anything else was too much to process.

"Then let me show you, shortcake." He kissed the corner of my mouth, dragging his mouth down my jaw and neck, taking his time to caress my skin while his hands roamed over my curves as if he couldn't get enough of them.

"Noah, wait." I fisted his jersey in my hand.

"What's the matter?"

"I... I want this to be about you."

"Me?" I nodded, and he rasped, "Fuck."

I pulled him closer, turning us so that his back hit the wall.

"Shortcake, you don't have to—"

"I want to."

I leaned in, kissing him. Peppering kisses over his mouth and down his throat. One of his hands slid into my hair, but he didn't try to take control. He let me do my thing.

"Can you take this off?" My voice quivered, matching the slight tremble of my fingers as I reached for the bottom of his jersey.

Noah intervened, yanking it off his body. My mouth turned dry at the sight of him. It wasn't anything I hadn't already seen, but he was so freaking beautiful, his body honed and crafted to utter perfection.

"Like what you see, shortcake?"

"I really, really like this." I trailed a finger down his abs, tracing every dip and ridge, the deep V disappearing into the waistband of his sweats. "And I really like this." Palming him through the soft material, Noah groaned.

"He really, really likes you too."

I chuckled, some of the nervous anticipation ebbing away.

Being with Noah like this was a rush. A high I never wanted to end.

"Don't tease me, shortcake. Touch me." He gave me an encouraging tilt of his head, and I slipped my hand into his sweats, finding him commando.

"Really?"

He smirked. "I don't like to feel restricted. I have enough of that on the ice."

"Poor baby." I wrapped my hand around his thick length, slowly pumping.

It was so erotic, watching his head fall back against the wall, his eyes blown with lust as I touched him.

"Does it feel good?"

"So fucking good... anything you do to me will feel good, shortcake." Noah reached for me, brushing his thumb over my lips again, letting it linger there.

I opened my mouth, letting him slide it past my lips, twirling my tongue around the tip.

"Fuck," he breathed.

Without overthinking it, I dropped to my knees and tugged his sweats down.

"Aurora—"

"I want to." I gazed up at him, my skin vibrating with anticipation. "I want to taste you."

"Shit, yeah... okay. But if you don't want—"

"Noah?"

"Yeah, shortcake?"

"Stop talking now." I closed my fist around him again and flattened my tongue, running it along the underside of his shaft.

"Holy shit," he rasped, sliding his hands into my hair, tugging gently, sending bolts of desire shooting through.

"Tell me how you like it."

"Like that." He inhaled sharply as I licked him again. "Use your tongue and your mouth. Worship my cock, babe."

"Noah!" I shrieked, my cheeks burning.

He chuckled. "You love it."

Yeah. A little part of me did.

Noah didn't treat me like glass. He was respectful and

patient, but he didn't pander to me. And I appreciated that. I liked that he pushed me out of my comfort zone.

Taking him into my mouth, I hollowed my cheeks and sucked him down, testing my gag reflex. I couldn't fit him all the way, but I did my best, using my hand to compensate.

"Yes, fuck... *yes*," he choked out as I choked on his dick. But there was something powerful about having a guy like Noah Holden at your mercy.

I pulled off him, and his salty taste flooded my mouth, but I didn't let that deter me. Swirling my tongue around the tip, I jerked him with my hand before taking him into my mouth again, letting the tip of his dick hit the back of my throat before I came up for air.

"I'm so close, baby." Noah's fingers tightened in my hair, his hips bucking a little as I drove him wild. "Jesus, short-cake," he praised as I worked him faster, following the signs of his body, his moans of pleasure.

"Gonna come... fuck, I'm gonna—"

He tried to pull away, but I grabbed his thigh, anchoring us together as I swallowed him down.

"Fuck... *fuck*."

I smiled up at him, feeling strangely proud of myself.

"Up you go, shortcake," he said, yanking me to my feet. Noah pulled me into his chest, his mouth capturing mine in a bruising kiss. He didn't care that he could taste himself. In fact, it only seemed to turn him on more.

"That." *Kiss*. "Was." *Kiss*. "Amazing."

"I owed you," I said.

It was a joke, but his expression dropped.

"Owe me?" He cupped my cheek. "Let me make one thing clear, shortcake. This isn't transactional. You never owe me anything for making you feel good. I need you to understand that."

"I..."

"This thing between us is not a business arrangement. Got it?"

"Got it." My heart soared in my chest because it was easy to run away with myself when he spoke like that.

To believe that maybe this time would be different.

He's Noah Holden—his first love is and always will be hockey.

I silenced the little voice of doubt, refusing to let anything ruin the moment.

"That being said, I'd really, really like to get you off now."

I pressed my lips together, giving him a shy nod.

"Tongue or fingers?" The heat in his eyes burned into me, searing me from the inside out. I hesitated and he added, "Use your words, Aurora."

"Fingers," I said, voice a little shaky. "I want you to kiss me while you touch me."

"Good girl." He spun us, trapping me between the wall and his body, and wasted no time shoving his hand inside my pants.

"Noah," I gasped as he worked me open and pressed two fingers slowly inside me, his thumb applying just the right amount of pressure on my clit.

"Look at you, shortcake." He leaned in, ghosting his mouth over mine. "So wet for me."

My hips began rocking, searching for more... more... *more*.

"That's it, baby. Ride my hand. Take what you need."

"God, Noah..." I panted, barely able to catch my breath

because it felt so damn good, like a warm wave rolling through me again and again. Rising higher and higher. "More, I need—"

Noah kissed me, his tongue licking into my mouth, mirroring the way his fingers curled inside me. It was sensation overload, my body trembling with pleasure so intense I didn't know whether to beg him to stop or beg him to *never* stop.

"I can feel your pussy fluttering around my fingers," he murmured the dirty words against my mouth. "I think she likes me."

"Noah!"

He pulled back slightly to look at me, mischief twinkling in his eyes. "I think she especially likes it when I do... this." He rubbed a place deep inside me, and his name fell from my lips in whispered prayer as I splintered apart.

Noah.

Noah.

Noah.

I came down to him grinning—no, smirking—at me.

"Yeah, she fucking loved that."

"Oh my God... stop," I breathed.

"That was fun."

"It was."

"You know what this means, shortcake." I arched a brow, and he chuckled. "I'm going to have a really hard time keeping my hands off you."

CHAPTER 28

NOAH

SNEAKING AROUND with Aurora was my new favorite thing.

It was three days since we'd shared parts of ourselves at the rink, and I found any and every excuse to be around her.

"Noah, the guys could be home at any second," she panted, bucking her hips against my hand as I curled two fingers deep inside her.

"You'd better be quiet then, shortcake. We wouldn't want big brother to hear you crying my name."

"Oh, God." Her head fell back, her skin flushed, and her eyes hooded as I stood over her.

"You are so fucking beautiful." I brushed my thumb over her clit, watching her body contract and quiver.

Aurora was so fucking responsive. I loved it.

"Lift your t-shirt for me," I said.

"*Noah!*"

"Come on, shortcake. Show me the goods." A smirk

played on my lips as she gazed up at me with big willing eyes. "I want to see you play with your tits while I get you off."

She hesitated for a second but then slipped her hand to the bottom of her t-shirt, shoving the material up and over her stomach.

"All the way. Good girl," I rasped as she pulled it over her head and discarded it on the floor. "Unclasp your bra."

"Noah..."

My fingers stilled, and her eyes narrowed. "You stopped."

"And I won't start again until I get what I want."

"If this is all part of Operation Darcy, you're doing a poor job of living up to his expectations."

Curling my fingers deeper, I rubbed that spot inside her that made her cry out, her fingers twisting in the bedsheets. "Did Darcy touch Elizabeth like this, though?"

"God, more..." Aurora sank back on her elbows, her body rippling with pleasure. "More..."

"Unclasp your bra, shortcake."

Her fingers fumbled with the front clasp, but then the material fell apart, and her big, heavy tits spilled out.

"Fuck, yeah."

She looked sensational like this. Wanton and flushed, writhing beneath me. I wanted to fuck her. To spread her legs open and slide inside her. Just. Like. This. But technically, she still hadn't agreed to give me another chance, and between classes, dodging her brother and Connor, and stealing time together, we'd barely come up for air.

Next week, things would change, though. Official practice started Monday, and the season two weeks after that.

If Aurora thought things were intense now, things

would become a whole other level of intensity then. But I didn't want to think about that right now. Not while her pussy fluttered around my fingers, greedily begging for me.

"Play with your tits, shortcake. Show me how you like it."

"Noah, I..." Her eyes closed. "I can't."

"Aurora, look at me." They snapped open again, and my chest swelled with pride at how responsive she was to my gentle command. "It's just me and you, shortcake. You have nothing to be embarrassed about." *Not a damn thing.* "Touch yourself for me."

Testing the waters, she ran her fingers along the swell of her stomach, sucking in a sharp breath as she swirled the tip around her navel.

"That's it," I praised.

Sliding her hand higher, Aurora toyed with her nipples, and I almost fucking came at the sight.

It was such a different experience with her. Sex was usually a transaction. One I enjoyed and made sure the girl went away with a smile too. But there was no connection, no bone-deep desire to discover all the ways I could make her fall apart, crying my name.

With Aurora, I wanted that. I wanted to teach her and guide her. I wanted to explore sex, together. I wanted so many fucking things. I had to remind myself to take it slow with her.

Loosening the string on my sweats, I pulled out my dick and wrapped a fist around myself, and started pumping. I hadn't planned to get off, but she got me too fucking hard.

Aurora's eyes grew big again, molten with desire as she realized what I was doing. "That is so hot," she whispered, playing with herself.

"Can I come on your tits?" The words were out before I could stop them.

"Y-you want to…"

"Yeah"—the corner of my mouth tipped—"I really fucking do, shortcake."

"Okay." She nodded, her eyes fixated on my dick.

"See what you do to me, Aurora. How hard you get me."

Fuck, I wasn't going to last. I circled her clit, applying more pressure to get her there before I exploded. She began moaning, whimpering my name over and over.

"I'm coming, Noah," she cried. "I'm co—"

"Fuck." I jerked myself faster, that familiar tingle in my spine building. "Holy fuck."

Release barreled through me, and I came hard, painting her pretty tits with my cum. Reaching down, I dragged my finger through the mess and spelled out Noah.

"Did you just… write your name?" Her green eyes were heavy-lidded and full of surprise.

"Yep. Just in case there was any doubt about who you belong to." I winked, tucking myself back into my sweats. Then I fell down on the bed beside Aurora. "That was fun."

"It was." Something flashed in her eyes.

"What are you thinking?"

"Harper asked me to go to the exhibition game. I said yes."

"Going to cheer me on from the stands, shortcake?"

Damn, I liked the idea of that. Her behind the glass, wearing my jersey.

She blushed. "You don't mind that I'm coming?"

"Mind? Why the fuck would I mind? Of course, I want you there."

"I didn't know—"

"Aurora, let me get one thing straight. You might not have agreed to give me another chance yet. But I'm taking it anyway, okay?" I threaded my fingers into her hair and kissed her.

"Yes."

"What?" I drew back, staring at her. Certain I must have misheard her.

"Yes, I'll give you another chance."

"Seriously?"

She nodded. "But I don't want to tell anyone, not yet."

"Shortcake—"

"No, Noah. I'm not ready to put myself out there like that. You're... you. And I'm—"

"Mine." I grinned, but her expression sobered.

"Don't make me regret this, Noah."

"I won't." I kissed her again, hoping she could feel the promise in every slide of my mouth over hers. "I swear."

"Favorite place?" I asked her as we sat on the couch, watching a movie.

Connor and Austin hadn't made it home—too preoccupied with the women in their lives—so we snuggled up on the couch, keeping a respectable distance, and turned on a movie.

Aurora glanced up at me, her green eyes glittering in the dark. "Will you think I'm a complete loser if I say the library?"

"Never." I dropped a kiss on the end of her nose. "But you're going to need to explain that one to me, shortcake."

"Growing up, I read a lot." She shrugged. "Too much, probably. But I had no one, Noah. My mom was too obsessed with her career and her endless disappointment with me. Austin was focused on hockey. On being as far away from Mom as possible. I struggled to make friends... so I turned to books."

Fuck, I hated hearing her talk like this. But I didn't interrupt because the fact she was gifting me these pieces of her past was a fucking honor.

"Books became my sanctuary, and the characters inside the pages became my friends. It's sad, I know."

"Not at all, shortcake. I just wish I could go back in time and knock some sense into your brother and the kids at school."

Things between Aurora and Austin were strained, but I hadn't pushed her to talk about it, hoping that she would open up to me when she was ready.

"At the time, I couldn't get out of my head, but now I can look back and see what a vicious cycle it was, how my feelings and emotions became so intrinsically tied to my eating habits and self-esteem. It's like a web, the threads getting so entangled you can't pull them apart."

"What about your ex?" I broached the subject that had been gnawing away at me. "How did he factor into everything?"

She peered up at me with big, uncertain eyes. "When I started high school, I thought things would be easier. Austin was a senior. I thought he would look out for me. And other girls had started to develop, so I wouldn't stand out so much. But it was no different than junior high.

"Austin barely acknowledged me, and I spent my days

trying to avoid my classmates as much as possible. Wearing baggy shirts, hiding in the girls' bathroom."

"Fuck, shortcake."

Her pain was palpable, swirling around us like the air after a storm. Thick and heavy.

"Anyway, enough of that," she said. "What about you, where is your favorite place?"

"Is it cliché if I say the rink?"

"Only as cliché as me saying the library." She smiled, and my chest swelled.

"You're so fucking beautiful," I whispered, leaning in to brush my nose over hers.

"When you look at me like that, I almost believe it."

"Good." I pulled my cell phone out of my pocket and switched it to camera mode.

"Noah, what are you—"

I kissed her again, snapping a selfie of us. And another as I buried my face in her neck, licking and nipping her soft skin as her laughter filled the house.

"If anyone sees these—"

"They won't." I grinned. "They're for my eyes only, shortcake. Although I wouldn't mind some nudes. You know, for my own personal collection."

"Absolutely not." She gave me a pointed look. "It's taking everything inside me not to steal your phone and delete the ones you just took."

"We'll see."

Because now I'd said the words, I could imagine her spread out on my bed, naked, skin flushed, and eyes heavy. Yeah, I needed a permanent reminder of that.

One I could keep and use when I was on the road with the team.

"This is nice," I said, pulling Aurora closer to my side.

"Yeah," she murmured. "How are you feeling about the season?"

"I'm ready. Freshman year was a chance to prove myself, but in some ways, the pressure is really on now. Especially if you're in the crowd."

"I'm sure you'll have a number of adoring fans screaming your name," she chuckled, but it was lost on me.

"Don't do that, shortcake. Don't try and downplay this."

"Noah—"

"No. Quit acting like I make a habit of doing this with other girls because I don't. You're the exception to the rule, Aurora. The only girl I want cheering me on."

"I… sometimes you really are the sweetest." She laid her hand against my cheek, dusting a kiss over my lips. But it wasn't enough. I needed more.

I needed so much more.

"Okay, movie time is over," I announced, crowding her back onto the couch and climbing over her.

"Noah, we can't—"

"Sure, we can, shortcake. They won't be home for—"

The door lock rattled, and I stilled above her. "You have got to be fucking kidding me."

"Bad luck, Romeo," she pressed her hands against my chest, giving a little sigh as she shoved me away.

"This isn't over."

"Famous last words, hotshot."

Connor and Austin's voices filled the hall, their heavy footsteps growing nearer.

"Honey, we're home," Connor called.

I moved to one end of the sofa, and Aurora kicked her feet up, putting a physical barrier between us. She smoothed her hair and pulled a cushion on her lap, cuddling it.

Jealousy streaked through me, and I realized at that point that I'd lost my fucking mind.

Jealous of a cushion, really, Holden?

"Hey," she said as they entered the room.

"We were just watching a movie."

"Romantic," Connor chuckled, and I glowered at him.

"You have a strange perception of romance, Con, if you think watching Noah eat his body weight in popcorn is romance. Poor Ella." She slid her gaze to mine, silent laughter shining in her eyes.

"Quit talking about Rory like she's stupid enough to fall for this asshole's lack of game," Austin grumbled, throwing himself down in the chair.

"What's up with you?" I asked.

"Women are fucking crazy."

"Fallon?"

"Yeah."

"I was wondering when you were going to fess up."

A sheepish look slid over him. "No hard feelings?"

It was on the tip of my tongue to tell him he was the one who probably needed to feel bad going after my sloppy seconds. But I figured Aurora wouldn't appreciate that, so I swallowed the words.

"It's your funeral," I said. "Those Beta Pi chicks are intense."

"You're telling me. She freaked out on me mid-sex because—"

"And that's my exit cue." Aurora got up. "I'm going to call it a night."

"Rory, baby, don't go. I feel like I've barely seen you this week," Connor pouted. "If I didn't know better, I'd say you've been distracted." The corner of his mouth tipped with amusement.

Fucker.

He knew.

Connor knew we were... doing whatever this was.

"What can I say, Con? It's exhausting living with you three. A girl needs her space."

"Any word from housing?" Austin asked, and Aurora tensed.

"They said it could be a little while longer."

He gave her a small nod.

I didn't want to think about her moving out, not being here every day. I liked having her around. So did Connor. But Austin was too damn stubborn to pull his head out of his ass and fix things with her.

"Don't worry. I won't overstay my welcome," she said, barely meeting her brother's gaze. "If it looks like it won't be ready anytime soon, I'll start looking for something else."

"Rory, baby, you don't have to do that. The season starts soon, and we'll hardly be here," Connor said.

"Con's right, shortcake. We like having you around." I glanced at Austin, waiting for him to agree.

But he didn't.

"It's not a bad idea," Austin said like the fucking coward he was. "Rory probably wants her own space now."

"Yep." She smiled, but it didn't reach her eyes. Eyes that glistened with hurt. "Night, guys."

Aurora hurried from the room, taking the air with her.

Connor blew out a low whistle. "Was that really necessary?" he turned his attention to Austin.

"What?"

"You offered to let her stay here, practically begged us, and now you want her gone?"

"I just think some space will do us good. She's—"

"You're an asshole." I shot up.

"Holden," Connor warned.

"What the fuck? You're acting like her best friend. I asked you to look out for her, not become best buddies."

"She's clearly hurting," Connor interjected. "You asked us to let her stay here, to look out for her, and we have. You can't be mad at us for caring about her. She's your sister, bro. Family."

"I know. Fuck, I know, okay." He jammed his fingers into his hair, violently tugging the ends. "It's just having her here dredges up some stuff I haven't dealt with."

"Well, deal with it. Because she's one of us now," Connor said. "And if she needs a place to stay, she has one."

I was grateful that he was standing up for her, but it should have been me.

I should have been the one to set Austin straight.

It was a line I couldn't cross, not until Aurora was ready.

I could try and make her believe in herself, show her how beautiful she was, try my hardest to make her believe it, but I couldn't push her, not about this.

Not when the fallout could be detrimental for us both.

CHAPTER 29

AURORA

"Aurora, meet Jordan. Jordan, this is the girl I've been telling you about."

"Oh my God, you are gorgeous," Ella's friend smirked, her heavy-lined eyes sweeping down my body in a slow perusal.

"See, I told you," Ella winked at me.

"Oh yeah, you would have been so my type if I wasn't already madly in love with this one." She grabbed another girl's hand and tugged her into our small circle.

"Aurora, this is my girlfriend, Noelle."

"Hi, Aurora, it's nice to meet you."

"Hi." I lifted my hand in a small wave. "I love your dress. It's so unique."

"I make most of my own clothes." Pride glittered in her eyes as she ran a hand down her *Alice in Wonderland* print skirt. "Fashion and design major."

"Wow, that's so cool."

"Ella tells us you're an English major," Jordan said.

"Yep. Fellow bookworm."

"I hate to say it, but I'm less of a bookworm and more of an is-there-a-movie-adaptation-I-can-watch person."

"Hi." Dayna appeared breathless and flushed. "Sorry, I'm late. Aiden and I were—"

"Not sure we need to hear any more Dayna and Aiden sex stories," Jordan chuckled.

"Oh no, we weren't having sex. We went to view some apartments."

"I can't believe you're going to move in with *Aiden Dumfries*. It's almost as bad as this one planning her white picket fence future with Morgan." Jordan smirked at Ella, and Ella stuck her tongue out in return. "Don't tell me you're hoping to snag a hockey player, too, Aurora. Because I'm not sure my anti-Lakers brain can handle it."

"Oh hush, babe." Noelle nuzzled her girlfriend's neck. "We all know you're a closet Lakers fan."

"Never," she protested. "And that is a hill I will happily die on."

The girls all laughed, and I smiled along, not really following. Too busy scanning the bar. A quirky place on the edge of town, Ella had reassured me it wouldn't be full of hockey players or the puck bunnies who followed them around.

It was different compared to The Penalty Box. There, everyone was out to prove something—at least, the girls were all looking to land themselves a hockey hottie. But here, the vibe was more laid-back and casual. I didn't feel as out of place in my leggings, and oversized sweater dress with the word *bibliophile* stamped across the front.

"Shall we get a table?" Dayna suggested. "I'm starving."

Oh, God. A sinking feeling went through me. Ella hadn't said anything about eating, or I seriously would have reconsidered coming.

"Sounds good." Noelle drifted toward an empty booth, Dayna hot on her heels.

"What's wrong?" Ella asked as I hesitated.

"N-nothing." A pit churned in my stomach. "I didn't realize we were getting food. I already ate."

"Oh shoot. Do you mind if the rest of us eat?"

"I…" What could I possibly say without making things awkward? So I went with a simple, "Of course not."

Jordan watched me, something like understanding in her gaze. But she didn't say anything, and I didn't ask her what she was thinking.

I was too busy freaking out about surviving a meal with them. Maybe a drink or two would help. Something to distract me.

Something to take the edge off.

"Are you sure you don't want anything?" Dayna pushed her half-eaten bowl of loaded fries toward me. "I'm so full I can't eat another thing."

"Honestly, I'm fine." I gave her a tight smile, sipping on my cocktail, trying to focus on the sweet sugary taste and not the plates of half-eaten food all over the table.

"Actually, I'm going to use the restroom. Excuse me." I hurried out of the booth and made my way across the bar toward the neon sign for the restrooms.

The last hour had been pure torture. Not because I was

hungry or even wanted to eat. But because of what me *not* eating with them represented.

Eating was a social thing, especially in college. But I'd manage to avoid it mostly or easily deflect the fact I wasn't eating.

It felt different tonight. It was an unpleasant reminder that despite my progress over the last couple of years, I still had a lot further to go. The knot in my stomach had only twisted and tightened as the night wore on, the heavy weight of shame crushing my chest.

Something so simple—so *vital*—as eating, and even now, I couldn't do it. The second Dayna mentioned getting something to eat, my stomach felt like it was in a vise, my throat turning dry, my palms sweating, and my heart trying to beat out of my damn chest.

It was frustrating, to say the least.

I rushed into a stall, dug my cell phone out of my purse, and contemplated texting Noah.

But I didn't.

I'd already revealed enough of my emotional baggage to send him running for the hills.

Instead, I grounded myself, breathing in slow and deep. Over and over until I finally felt like I could breathe again.

When I finally exited the restroom, I didn't expect to see Jordan outside, waiting for me.

"What is it?" she said.

"Excuse me?"

"I saw the way you paled when Dayna mentioned eating. And then again, just now, when she offered you her leftover fries. So, what is it?"

"I-I don't know what you're—"

"It's BED for me." I gawked at her, and she added,

"Binge eating disorder. I've been in and out of therapy since I was thirteen."

"Oh."

"Oh?" She chuckled, her brow arching with mild amusement. "I'm right, though, aren't I? There's something."

"Yeah," I whispered, feeling a stab of shame, "there's something."

"Well, when you're ready to talk about it, call me."

"Just like that?" I asked, dumbfounded. "You barely know me."

"I know Ella vouches for you. That's good enough for me."

"Why?"

"Because college can be a scary place. Especially for people like us."

People like us.

She made it sound so easy.

"Listen, I know we don't know each other very well, but take it from someone who knows a thing or two about what it's like to fight your own mind day in and day out. Whatever your something is, it doesn't define you, Aurora. It might be a real fucking pain in the ass sometimes, but it doesn't define you. Think about it." She smiled, turning to go back into the bar, but I called after her.

"Jordan, wait."

"Yeah?" She glanced back at me.

"Thank you."

"Anytime."

I watched her go, feeling oddly hopeful. Things with Austin were strained to say the least, and I still had Mom to deal with. But I'd made friends. I'd stepped out of my comfort zone and pushed myself to get out there and meet people.

Even if things with Noah fizzled out once the hockey season got underway, I was confident I could make life at Lakeshore U work. Because Jordan was right, my past—my problems—didn't define me.

I just had to believe it.

"And then this one had a total bi-awakening, and the rest, as they say, is history."

"I don't remember it quite happening that way. But I won't steal your thunder." Noelle grinned at Jordan, the two of them lost in their own little world. "What about you, Aurora?" She turned her attention to me.

"One ex, and no, I don't want to talk about him."

"That bad, huh?"

"It wasn't good." I reached for my glass, draining the contents.

We'd moved to a more relaxed seating area a while ago, and the drinks were flowing.

A little too easily.

I didn't make a habit of drinking a lot, but I felt surprisingly at ease in their company. It also helped that there wasn't a puck bunny in sight.

"I like it here," I said. "It has a nice vibe."

"Yeah, we come here when we want to avoid the regular crowd," Ella said, shooting Jordan a knowing glance.

"And be graced with my presence, you mean." Jordan smirked.

"Jordan doesn't frequent The Penalty Box anymore."

"Go on, El, tell her why."

Ella grimaced. "There may have been an unfortunate incident sophomore year with the hockey team."

"Not hockey team. Hockey player. And no, I don't want to talk about it," Jordan huffed. "I'm still not over the fact you ditched me for Morgan."

"You love Connor."

"Who loves Connor?" He appeared out of nowhere.

"Where the hell did you come from?"

"Nice to see you too," he murmured. "Funny story, I was walking past the bar and saw you all and figured I could stop by and say hey to my girl."

"Babe"—Ella let out an exasperated sigh—"you know Zest is a Lakers-free zone."

His smile wavered, guilt flashing in his eyes. "Good thing I didn't bring the guys then."

"Oh no, Morgan. What did you—" Jordan's eyes grew to saucers as she watched Aiden and Noah swagger toward us.

Noah found me immediately, the faintest smile tipping his mouth as he read my sweater, silent laughter dancing in his gaze.

"Guys, you're supposed to be at The Penalty Box," Dayna said, letting Aiden manhandle her into his lap.

"We fancied a change of scenery."

"Hi," Noah whispered as he sat down beside me.

"Hi. This is... unexpected."

"Don't look at me, shortcake. It was all Morgan's idea."

Thankfully, Connor and Jordan were still arguing about the three of them encroaching on her Lakers-free zone. But even she couldn't resist the Connor Morgan charm.

"Fine, you can stay," she conceded. "On one condition."

"Name your price."

"Drinks are on you for the rest of the night."

"You drive a hard bargain, Hannigan, but consider it done."

"Having fun?" Noah asked, careful not to get too close. But I was hyper-aware of him. Of his woodsy cologne, how his black t-shirt hugged his broad shoulders and thick biceps. The adorable way his hair fell into his eyes.

Eyes that hadn't stopped looking at me since he sat down.

"Noah, you're being too obvious," I scolded, twisting away from him a little.

A second later, my cell phone vibrated. I dug it out of my bag, hardly surprised to see Noah's name.

> Noah: You look sexy as fuck tonight, shortcake.

> Aurora: On a scale of one to ten, how drunk are you?

> Noah: Zero. I need to keep my wits about me. I'm trying to impress a girl.

> Aurora: Lucky girl.

> Noah: Pretty sure I'm the lucky one.

Our gazes collided, and he smirked.

Aurora: You are incorrigible.

Noah: I think you mean irresistible.

I smothered a laugh. He had more ego than I had literary quote t-shirts.

"Something funny, Rory, baby?" Connor called, and I met his knowing gaze with an indifferent smile.

"Not really."

"Huh." He grinned, and Ella elbowed him in the ribs, the two of them sharing a whispered word.

"Why do I feel like I'm missing something?" Jordan said.

"Probably because you are, babe," Noelle chuckled, getting up. "Dance with me." She held her hand out, and Jordan slid her own into it.

"Always."

"Dancing!" Dayna clapped, grabbing Aiden's hand. "Come on, babe."

"Freckles, come on. It's—"

"Please," she pouted, whispering something in his ear.

"Fine. Let's go." The two of them followed Jordan and Noelle out to the dancefloor.

"Do we need to stay and make sure you two make good choices?" Connor said, failing to hide his amusement.

"Connor," Ella said, shooting me an apologetic smile. "Just remember what we talked about," she added quietly.

The second she and Connor were gone, Noah turned to me. "And here, I always liked Ella."

"She's only looking out for me."

"Do I even want to know what she said?" Hurt flashed in his eyes.

"Nothing I haven't already told myself a hundred times already."

Silence hung between us.

"Dance with me." His hand inched closer to my thigh, brushing the curve of my knee, setting off a swarm of butterflies in my stomach.

"Noah, we can't—"

"Sure, we can, shortcake. No one here cares. It isn't a Lakers hangout."

"Aiden and Connor—"

"It's one little dance." His hand wrapped around mine as he got up, pulling me with him.

It was a bad idea, the worst. I didn't dance. Let alone dance with a guy like Noah. But I was powerless against him.

He pulled me into the sea of bodies, crowding in close as he swayed his hips. "Dance with me."

My eyes shuttered as I tried to calm my racing heart. But I was so nervous, the lights and noise and crowd making it difficult to breathe until I felt his mouth at my ear.

"I'm right here, Aurora. Nobody is watching you but me." His hand drifted down my waist, anchoring us together.

And then we were dancing, moving as one to the beat. I tried to search for my friends in the crowd, but I only saw Noah. His smile. His deep brown eyes that always seemed to see right past my defenses.

"What?" I asked, shrinking under the intensity of his gaze.

"You, shortcake. Only you."

My brows pinched. "Are you sure you're not drunk?"

"Is it so hard to believe I want you?" He moved his mouth to my ear again. "That I can't wait until the day I get to feel your pussy fluttering around my dick?"

"Noah," his name caught in my throat as a breathy moan. Because he was so outrageous but in the best kind of way.

"You know you love it, shortcake." His eyes found mine once more. "We both know she loves it."

"She?" His eyes dropped down my body, and I choked on another breath. "You are something else."

"Come home with me tonight."

"Yeah, duh, we live together."

"No, shortcake, I mean, come home with me." He gazed at me. "Connor is staying at Ella's, and I heard Fallon apologizing to your brother earlier. Pretty sure he'll be balls deep—and you don't want to know that information."

"Correct."

"So... will you?"

"Will I what?" My heart crashed violently in my chest as I played dumb.

Because this was crazy.

He was crazy.

He lowered his head, getting in my space, stealing my air. Noah wasn't just some guy. A Laker. A playboy. A good time. He was so much more than that.

I felt it every time he looked at me.

"Say yes, shortcake. Let me take you home."

"I..." I gave him a small, shy nod.

Maybe I would regret it tomorrow, but I also knew

without a shadow of a doubt that I would regret it if I said no.

"Yes," I breathed.

His eyes sparked with heat, making my insides quiver and shake as I moved my mouth to his ear and whispered, "Take me home, Noah."

CHAPTER 30

NOAH

> Connor: I hope to God you know what you're doing.

> Noah: No idea what you're talking about. Aurora wanted to leave, I offered to take her home.

> Connor: Tell me that again after Austin breaks your face.

Fuck.

My fist rubbed on my thigh as Aurora sat beside me quietly in the Uber.

"Everything okay?" she asked.

"Never better." I kissed the top of her head.

The temperature had cooled between us a little since

the bar. The dance. The proposition. But the heat—the tension—was still there, simmering under the surface, making itself known.

My phone chimed again, and I discreetly opened Connor's text.

> Connor: For what it's worth. I think you'd be good together. So I'm only going to ask this once… can you really give her what she needs?

I turned it off. I didn't need him breathing down my neck about this. I wanted Aurora—fuck, I wanted her so much—and she wanted me. We were adults. What we did was between us and no one else.

Sure, if it were up to me, I'd have laid it out for Austin before now. Talked to him man to man. Teammate to teammate. But Aurora wasn't ready for that. And I respected her too fucking much to go behind her back.

Austin was her brother; he wasn't her keeper.

"What's wrong?" She tugged my arm, and I lowered my head to hers.

"Nothing."

"Let me guess"—a resigned sigh slipped from her lips —"Connor—"

"How did you know?"

"Because Ella texted me too."

"They need to learn to butt out."

"They only care."

"They think I'll break your heart." *But no one is worried you'll break mine.*

"Noah, I—"

"Shh, shortcake. I don't want you to think about anything right now except all the dirty things I'm going to do to you the second I get you alone."

A shiver ran through her as I brought a hand to her neck, brushing my thumb over her jaw. "You do things to me, Aurora Vivienne Hart."

"Noah, I—"

Of course, the Uber driver chose that second to pull up outside the house. I climbed out first, helping Aurora out.

Anticipation zipped between us, the air snapping and crackling.

"You good?" I asked her, and she nodded. Those bewitching green eyes of hers searing me right down to my fucking soul.

We walked to the house side by side. We didn't touch or speak or even look at each other, but damn if it wasn't the best kind of foreplay. The air was charged between us, full of delicious anticipation. A band pulled so tightly that it was mere seconds from snapping.

But knowing she was the present I got to unwrap tonight was a rush like no other.

The second we were inside the house, I kicked the door shut and crowded Aurora against the wall. "Look at you," I drawled, letting my eyes run over every curve. "You drive me wild, shortcake. And you're mine."

All fucking mine.

Slowly, I lowered my face to hers, trailing my fingers along her collarbone and threading them into her hair to angle her face right where I wanted it. "Just so we're perfectly clear," I breathed the words into her lips. "This is—"

"Noah, don't." She silenced me with a finger to my lips. "I know what you're going to say. You can't promise me anything beyond tonight, and I'm not asking you to. I'm not. But I want you, Noah Holden, more than I have ever wanted anything in my life. And just this once, I'm going to allow myself to have it.

"Even though I feel like I'm going to wake up any second and realize this was all a dream, I still want to enjoy every second while it lasts."

Fuck.

Fuck.

My heart jackhammered in my chest as she gazed up at me.

Gently, I tugged her wrist away. "You're wrong, you know, shortcake. Something tells me one night with you will never be enough."

Alarm flashed in her eyes, quickly giving away to confusion. Even now, even after everything, Aurora still doubted us.

She still doubted *me.*

I'd obviously done a piss-poor job making her realize that this wasn't fleeting for me. It wasn't some casual sex arrangement.

I liked her.

I liked her a lot.

More than I'd ever liked another girl in my life.

And despite every warning bell in my head telling me not to go down this road with her, despite knowing that things could get really fucking messy, I couldn't stop myself.

Aurora was the breath of fresh air I didn't know I

needed. The light that burned away the darkness shrouding my past. And now I'd had a taste; I didn't ever want it to end.

"Noah, I—"

I kissed her. Curving my hand around the back of her neck to allow me to control the moment. But Aurora willingly handed me the reins, melting into me with a breathy whimper.

"Your room or mine, shortcake?"

"Mine."

"You want a drink? A snack? Any—"

"Noah?" A faint smile traced her lips.

"Yeah?"

"Take me upstairs."

"Come on." I took her hand and tugged her toward the stairs, but instead of leading, I pulled her around me and said, "Up you go."

Her brows crinkled. "Why—"

"I want to watch your ass sway for me, shortcake."

"Pervert."

"For you, always." I grinned, and she gave a little shake of her head as she took off up the stairs.

My dick strained behind my jeans, so fucking hard for her. Aurora didn't even need to touch me to get me going. Every look, her snark and sass, the fact she trusted me with her body, it was a huge fucking turn-on.

When we hit the second floor, I couldn't resist grabbing her ass and wrapping my other arm around her waist, lowering my mouth to her ear. "I can't wait to be inside you, shortcake."

"Noah..."

"Come on, before I fuck you right here out in the hall."

A shiver went through her, the way it did whenever I whispered dirty things to her.

By the time we made it to the third floor, my hands were all over her, and we stumbled into her room in a tangle of limbs and hot, wet kisses.

"Off, your clothes need to come off."

"Noah..." she breathed, her hands tracing a hesitant path down my chest.

I grabbed her hand and pushed it to my rock-hard dick, needing her to feel what she did to me.

"This is yours," I drawled, sucking on the skin beneath her ear.

"Oh, God."

"Feel how much I want you?" Easing back, I gazed down at her, dragging my thumb over her parted lips. She nodded, and my mouth curved. "Let's get you naked."

"No," she said. "I want to do it."

Hell yes.

"Sit on the edge of the bed."

I pulled off my polo shirt and threw it on the floor before unbuttoning my jeans and dropping my ass to the end of the bed. Aurora smiled down at me, her eyes swirling with desire and uncertainty.

"I..."

"Strip for me, shortcake. Let me see your gorgeous body."

Her eyelashes fluttered, her hands sliding down to the hem of her sweater dress. She sucked in a sharp breath before sliding it up her body and pulling it off, leaving her standing there in nothing but her leggings and bra.

"Look at you." I reached for her, spanning my hand around her waist to pull her between my legs.

Aurora pressed a hand to my shoulder, steadying herself as I leaned in and pressed my mouth to her stomach, trailing my lips over the swell of her hips.

"It feels so good," she moaned, her other hand going to my hair, fingers sinking into the unruly strands.

"You're still dressed," I looked up at her with a smirk.

Aurora slipped her hands into the waistband of her leggings and pushed them over her hips and down her legs. I helped her get them off and then let my eyes feast on her body. On every dip and hollow, the soft lines of her curves.

"When you look at me like that, I feel beautiful," she whispered, her voice cracking with a mix of lust and uncertainty. "Help me with my bra?"

"With pleasure." Skimming my hands up her waist, I reached around and unhooked the clasp. "Fuck, I love your tits." I squeezed one into my hand, massaging it. But it wasn't enough; I needed to taste her.

Lowering my mouth, I flicked my tongue over the dusky bud, reveling in the way she responded. "Feel good?" I asked.

"So good." Her hands went back to my hair, letting me worship her tits with my mouth. My teeth and tongue. I couldn't resist sliding my fingers between her cleavage, imagining what it would be like to put my dick there, letting me use her to get off.

My spare hand dropped to her panties, rubbing her through the thin material. "Are you wet for me, shortcake?"

"Why don't you find out," she sassed, her eyes shining with lust.

And I fucking loved it.

Hooking the material to one side, I slid two fingers

between her folds, pushing them inside her. Aurora cried out, gripping my hair and pulling me closer.

"So fucking ready for me," I crooned as I dragged my fingers out of her and plunged them back inside, my eyes fixated on the apex of her thighs.

"More," she panted. "I need—"

Adding my thumb to the party, I rolled it over her clit in slow, torturous circles. Letting the pleasure build inside of her like a wave rolling onto shore.

"Yes, God, yes."

Lifting my head, I smirked. This would never grow old, watching her fall apart at the mercy of my hands or mouth or tongue. Which was really fucking strange since I was a one-night-stand kind of guy.

But with Aurora, I wanted more.

I wanted all the nights she would give me.

Working her with my fingers, I let my mouth drift back to her tits, tonguing the dusky peaks until she was practically grinding on my hand, desperate for release.

"Noah... God, it's... ah," Her moans filled the room, and her legs trembled around me.

"Come for me, shortcake," I demanded. "Come all over my fingers."

Aurora grabbed my shoulder, her fingers digging into my skin as she shattered on a breathy cry. Pulling her down on my lap, I brought my fingers to her lips and said, "Taste yourself."

Her eyes grew big, darkening with lust as her lips parted, her tongue flicking out. The warm wet heat of her mouth almost undid me, a low groan keening in my chest.

Grabbing Aurora by the back of her neck, I kissed her

hard. Fucking devouring her as I gripped her hips, grinding against her.

"I want you." She touched her head against mine, inhaling a shuddering breath.

My heart crashed wildly in my chest, and I realized I was nervous. I never got nervous about sex. But it wasn't just sex with Aurora—it was so much more.

"Hold on," I rasped as I flipped us over so she was laid out on the bed.

Her hands immediately went to cover herself, but I tugged her wrists away, looking my fill. "So fucking perfect."

"Noah..." she half-moaned, half-begged.

"You never have to hide from me. Not for a second." I grabbed my wallet out of my jeans pocket and threw a foil packet down on the bed before shoving them down my hips and kicking them off.

Blood roared in my ears as I tore open the foil packet and rolled it over my aching dick.

I was so fucking hard for her.

Aurora's eyes flared as I covered her body, hooking my arm under her thigh to spread her open. "Okay?"

She nodded, eyes heavy with desire. Aurora wound her arms around my neck, holding on, and I pressed into her, inch by inch, until we both groaned.

"Fuck." I stilled for a second, trying to resist the urge to fuck into her like my life depended on it.

Because, holy shit, she felt good.

"Noah?" It was a quiet, hesitant question.

"Yeah, just... give me a second." Aurora squeezed her inner muscles, and I almost choked on a breath. "Keep that up, shortcake, and this is going to be over before we even get started."

She laughed. A soft, gentle sound that reverberated deep inside me.

"You think I'm joking? Your pussy has my dick in a vise."

"I... sorry." She blushed, burying her face into my shoulder.

"Don't apologize. Don't ever fucking apologize. You feel amazing." I nudged her backward, needing to see her eyes. Needing her to see me as I slowly pulled out, holding for a second before sinking back inside. Watching her eyelids flutter, her breath hitch as I filled her, so fucking deep.

She felt incredible.

"Noah," Aurora cried again, and my fingers dug into the soft flesh of her thigh.

"Wrap your legs around me," I demanded, sliding my hands under her ass to lift her onto my dick, thrusting harder, needing to be closer.

Needing more.

So much fucking more.

"Fuck, you feel like you were made for me." The words spilled out as I fucked into her. *Faster... deeper... harder.* Chasing the inevitable fall.

"Kiss me," she begged, scraping her nails against my jaw as we stared at one another.

I couldn't look away, couldn't take my eyes off of her as she slowly unraveled beneath me.

My hand drifted up Aurora's stomach until my fingers collared her throat gently. I held her there, ghosting my lips over hers. Flicking my tongue into her mouth, devouring her as I moved above her.

"Noah... Noah," she panted between kisses. "It's... ah..."

"Shh, baby. I got you. I got you."

"More, I need more."

"Tell me what you need, shortcake." I nudged my nose up against hers, kissing the corner of her mouth.

I'll give you anything.

Fuck. The thought hit me so out of left field that a little shock rocked deep inside my gut.

"Noah?" she blinked, staring at me with confusion.

"You want my fingers too?" I brushed off her concern— my momentary panic—slipping a hand between our bodies. The second I rubbed her clit, Aurora went off like Fourth of July fireworks, her pussy quivering around my dick as a violent orgasm slammed into her.

"Yes... God, yes," she cried.

Head thrown back, lips parted, and skin flushed. She looked so fucking beautiful.

And so fucking mine.

Because it hit me then that this wasn't just sex.

I wasn't going to get my fill and move on.

No amount of time would ever be enough with her.

"Fuck, Aurora..." I slammed into her again, over and over, feeling a lick of heat shoot down my spine. "Fuck." My release barreled into me, and I came hard, my entire body shuddering as I collapsed on top of her.

She ran her fingers along my spine, stroking my skin, touching me almost reverently.

"You good?" I asked, lifting my eyes to hers.

"Yeah." She smiled. "That was..."

"Yeah."

I swallowed, suddenly feeling out of my depth, suddenly feeling the weight of responsibility. Aurora wasn't like any other girl I'd ever been with. I couldn't thank her for the ride and get the hell out of there—I didn't want to. But she was my best friend's—my teammate's—sister.

"Noah, what is it?" she asked, the contentment in her eyes dulling a little.

"Nothing." I smiled, but it felt all wrong. "You were great."

Fuck. I winced as the words spilled out.

"Shit, I didn't mean... Look, Aurora—"

"It's okay." She gave me a sad smile. "I understand."

"You do?" I stared at her in confusion.

"It's just sex, Noah." The little half-shrug she gave me gutted me. "We don't have to make it weird or anything."

Just sex.

She thought—

Fuck that.

I flattened my palms on the mattress and leveraged myself above her, staring down at her. "Let me make one thing clear, shortcake." I inhaled a sharp breath because this would change things. It would change everything. But it felt right. "Nothing about this is just sex."

"I—"

"No, Aurora. I need you to understand that this means something to me—you mean something. It might be new, a little scary, and complicated, but don't insult me by trying to downplay what just happened between us."

"Noah, I didn't... I'm sorry. I guess I'm just scared. You're... you." Hesitation glittered in her eyes as she whispered, "And I'm..."

"Mine."

CHAPTER 31

AURORA

"Mine."

The word echoed through me, settling deep in my soul.

Noah stared at me, waiting. But I couldn't find the words to respond.

His.

Noah had claimed me as his.

He'd said things before—hinted that he felt whatever was developing between us. But I hadn't wanted to believe it. I couldn't.

This was different though.

We'd had sex. And sex changed things.

I didn't regret it. How could I? Being with Noah was one of the best moments of my life. But that pesky little voice inside my head—the one that liked to constantly remind me that guys like Noah didn't end up with girls like me—wouldn't silence.

It wouldn't quit.

"You're freaking out," he said.

"I..." My eyes shuttered. I needed a reprieve from the intensity of his gaze. The way he looked at me and saw straight into my damaged soul.

But when I opened them again, Noah was still staring at me.

"Okay, hotshot. Give me some space." I gently shoved him away, and he clambered off me.

With a quiet little huff caught somewhere between amusement and disbelief, Noah went to dispose of the condom, and I got into bed, pulling the sheet over my body.

When he came back into the room, he paused in the doorway, watching me.

"What?" I asked.

"Is this the part where you tell me that we had fun, but you want some space?"

"Isn't that your line?" My brow arched, and his expression darkened.

"Low blow, shortcake."

Tension stretched between us. Fraying at the edges. Making my stomach churn.

"Sorry"—a soft sigh escaped me—"that wasn't a nice thing to say."

"So why'd you say it?" Noah came around and sat on the edge of the bed, not caring one bit that he was buck-naked.

My eyes drank in the sight of him. The cut lines of his body, the smooth sun-kissed skin stretched over corded muscle—the tattoos decorating his skin like intricate armor.

"This isn't my life, Noah. I don't get the guy. The happy ending."

"What did he do to you, shortcake? Your ex?" His eyes searched mine as he reached for me, brushing the flyaway hairs from my face, silently begging me to let him in. To give him the truth.

"He hurt you, didn't he?" he added when I said nothing.

A bitter laugh bubbled in my throat.

"He didn't hurt me, Noah. He completely destroyed me," I whispered, pain lashing my insides.

"You can tell me, Aurora. You can trust me."

"I..." But I couldn't say the words.

How could I?

How could I tell him that my boyfriend and my so-called best friend had been sleeping together behind my back?

That when I found them together in his bed—the bed where I'd given him my virginity—that they'd looked at me with so much pity, a part of me had withered and died.

"Did you really think that we'd go the distance?" he'd said, gazing at Tierney in a way he'd never *looked at me.*

Not once.

Because that was my destiny, to be the girl on the side-lines. Always overlooked for the pretty, popular girl.

And one day, maybe not tomorrow or in a week or even next month, Noah would realize that.

He would realize he could do so much better than me.

"It's okay," he said, sensing my discomfort. "We don't have to talk about it now."

I nodded. Because what else could I do?

I wasn't sure I would ever be able to give him the truth. To tell him how, after Ben dumped me for my best friend, I'd binged so hard that I'd made myself physically sick. And then I'd smashed up every mirror in my bedroom because I saw exactly what he saw, a fat ugly girl unworthy of his love.

For weeks, I couldn't look at myself without doubling down on my self-hatred. I was so disgusted and angry for ever letting myself fall for the fantasy.

For ever believing him.

Every day at school, I had to relive the pain and heartache all over again. Seeing the two of them with our friends, their friends because, let's face it, they had only ever been friends with me because of Tierney and Ben in the first place. They were the perfect couple, and Tierney was the girl everyone expected Ben to be with.

Pretty, popular... *perfect*.

"I'd kick his ass if I could," Noah said, reaching for me. He cupped my face, brushing his finger along my jaw. "Austin mentioned he's at Fitton U." I nodded, and then he said, "You know the Falcons are in our conference."

"I know."

"So maybe I'll get my chance."

"Coach Tucker would kick your ass six ways from Sunday," I said, trying to ignore the way my heart ratcheted in my chest.

"It'd be worth it, though." He leaned in, ghosting his lips over mine. "Scooch up, shortcake."

I moved over, and Noah swung his legs up on the bed, sliding his arm around my shoulder and pulling me into his side.

"This is nice," he said, stroking his hands over my skin.

My curves.

"Yeah." I snuggled closer, closing my eyes and breathing him in.

It was nice.

Too nice.

Noah made me feel beautiful. He made me feel cherished and desired and worthy.

But it was a dangerous path to tread again. Because when he realized the truth—when he realized I wasn't enough—my heart wouldn't just break.

It would shatter.

And I knew there would be no coming back from that.

I woke to an empty bed, the tangled sheets beside me already cold. For a second, I wondered if it had all been a dream. But my body ached in the best kind of way, memories of Noah kissing me, touching me... *loving* me.

But it was the morning after, and he was gone.

A sinking feeling went through me as I reached over, fumbling on the nightstand to grab my cell phone. He wouldn't leave me. He wouldn't—

> Noah: Sorry I had to sneak out. Austin locked himself out, so I had to get up and let him in, and I didn't want to risk sneaking back into bed with you. Last night was... perfect. You were perfect, shortcake.

Perfect.

The word sank into me, soothing the tight knot in my stomach. But perfect was an illusion, wasn't it?

At least, for me.

A loud knock on my door startled me.

"Rory?"

"Yeah?" I called.

"We need to talk."

"Austin? I just woke—"

"Please," his voice cracked. "I'll make fresh coffee. Meet me downstairs."

Quickly, I texted Noah.

> Aurora: Do you think Austin knows?

Panic rose inside me, making my insides shake and quiver.

> Noah: About us? No. Although maybe it wouldn't be such a bad idea to broach the subject with him.

> Aurora: Not yet. It's too soon.

We hadn't even defined whatever it was we were doing.

Noah: And I want to respect your wishes, I do. But when will be the right time, shortcake?

I didn't reply fast enough, and Noah texted again.

Noah: Can we talk about this in person?

Aurora: Later. If I survive my 'talk' with Austin.

"Coffee's ready," my brother called, and I climbed out of bed with a little huff.

Everything had been so wonderful last night, but as I suspected, I'd come back down to earth with an almighty bang this morning.

Pulling on a Lakeshore U hoodie, I went to the bathroom and then headed down to find my brother.

"Morning," he said gruffly.

"Hey, what's up?"

"Sit. I'll get you coffee."

"Thanks. Is everything okay, Austin?"

"This arrived this morning." He pushed a small box toward me. "It was addressed to me, but it's for you."

"It is?" My hand hovered over the flap, trepidation bubbling inside me. "What is it?"

"You tell me."

"What—" I sucked in a thin breath as I opened the flaps and glanced inside. "She sent this."

It wasn't a question because the care package, if you could call it that, had Susannah Hart written all over it.

"What the fuck is all that?" Austin gritted out.

"Really?" I asked with barely contained sarcasm. Because while my brother had chosen to ignore my issues over the years, he wasn't a clueless idiot. So the fact he was acting like one pissed me the hell off.

"Why the fuck is she sending you diet pills and supplements? And brochures for local cosmetic surgeons?"

My stomach didn't just drop, it plummeted into my toes. "W-what?"

"See for yourself."

With trembling hands, I removed the bottles of pills from the box, and sure enough, there was a heap of literature about local clinics providing Cellulaze, Lyma, and various other cellulite-reduction therapies.

"I..." Bile clawed up my throat.

"Aurora, I swear to fucking God. If you don't tell me what's going on—"

"It's nothing," I said, swallowing hard, refusing to do this.

To give him an explanation now, after all this time, when all I'd ever wanted was for him to understand.

To be there for me.

Despite the embarrassment I felt, and the sheer mortification, I got up calmly to leave.

But Austin was too quick, darting in front of me. "No way. No fucking way. We are talking about this. We are—"

The coil inside me snapped.

"Talking about it?" I seethed, my body trembling with

frustration. "Where were you five years ago when I needed to talk about it? Or last year, when I—" I stopped, forcing myself to take a breath, to think rationally.

Austin slumped against the counter, staring at me like he didn't recognize me. Yet, somewhere in his gaze was a flicker of realization.

Of regret.

"I don't understand," he said quietly.

"Of course, you don't understand. You've never been around long enough to."

"Rory, come on, that isn't fair."

"Fair?" Strangled laughter bubbled inside me, erupting like a volcano. "You're either really fucking delusional, Austin, or you've actually convinced yourself that, somehow, I'm okay. That I'm not severely damaged from years of dealing with Mom.

"Do you know how many therapists I saw between the ages of eleven and fifteen? Do you have any idea how many times I crash dieted only to binge and undo all my hard work?"

Those words... God, I hated those fucking words.

I could hear her voice as plain as day. *Perfection doesn't come for free, Aurora. It takes a lot of hard work and commitment.*

"I—"

"Of course, you don't. Because you weren't there, Austin. You checked out on me just like you checked out on Mom. And I get it. I get it wasn't easy for you there. In that house. I know the two of you never saw eye to eye. But at least you had hockey. At least you had friends and girlfriends and somewhere to escape to. I had nothing.

"Nothing." The truth of the words sank into me. Ripping my insides apart and leaving me hollow.

"You had Ben. You had Tierney and your friends. You had—"

"I was almost fifteen by the time I made friends with Tierney." And then, it had only been out of pity.

"I spent years living under Mom's shadow. And even now, I can't escape her." I grabbed one of the pill bottles and thrust it toward him. "Welcome to my life, Austin."

"I... fuck." He jammed his hands into his hair. "Fuck." It was a quiet, pained sound. "Has she done this before?" He eyed the box.

I nodded, too choked up to reply, shame clinging to every inch of me.

Susannah Hart had made it her life's mission to try and *fix* me, and I'd broken myself over and over, gathering what scraps of dignity I had left to stand up to her.

"That's messed up, Rory. I knew it had been bad for a while. With the modeling stuff, but I didn't know..."

"Because you didn't want to know." I gave him a sad smile.

"You could have told me."

"Would it have changed anything? You were obsessed with hockey, with getting a scholarship and leaving Syracuse." *Leaving me,* I swallowed the words down. "All you ever talked about was getting out of there. Leaving and never looking back."

"I didn't mean you, Rory."

"It felt like it. You had friends and hockey, and this whole life I wasn't a part of. I had no one, and you had the world at your feet."

"You could have talked to me. You could've made me

understand how bad it really was. I know I've always been a bit of a selfish asshole, but you're my sister, Rory. Family."

It wasn't that simple, though.

Not when I'd learned a long time ago that the word family didn't mean anything, not really. Mom was my family. Dad too. And neither of them had provided us with a warm, loving, stable environment. Family wasn't loving and supporting someone because you had to; it was loving and supporting someone because you *chose* to.

"It doesn't matter now," I said. "I left." *I got out.* "She can't hurt me anymore."

The lie hung in the air between us.

"I'm going to call her. This shit ends now."

"No."

"No?" He recoiled. "What do you mean, no?"

"This isn't your battle to fight, Austin."

"Fuck, it's not. You're my—"

"Sister, yes. Just like I was your sister the first time she dragged me to a shoot. And when she put me on a juice diet for a week because the photographer said I needed to lose a few pounds. Or when the kids at school started calling me thunder thighs. Or wide load. Or melons."

His expression dropped, morphing from shame to disbelief to downright anger. But his sudden protective big brother act was too little, too late.

I needed him back then—I didn't need him now.

"I didn't tell you, and yes, that's on me. But you never asked, either. You never looked hard enough to realize what was really going on. And that's on you, Austin. Don't bother calling Mom. I'll deal with her. Just like I always have."

Just like I probably always would.

CHAPTER 32

NOAH

By the time I got back to the house, my hair was damp, and my skin was covered in a sheen of sweat. But after last night, I'd needed to burn off some steam. To try and get my thoughts straight.

Spending the night with Aurora had been the best fucking night of my life. But she was still holding back.

Part of me got it. She wanted to go slow, to give us a chance to see where things would go without having our relationship picked apart by our friends, her brother, the team, and all that came with it.

But I didn't want to keep things a secret. Not when I was ready to jump headfirst into this thing between us.

Yanking the back door open, I slipped into the house, not expecting to find Austin hunched over the table, brochures and bottles scattered all over the place.

"What's going on?" I walked over to him and eyed some

of the literature, snatching one of the brochures up. "What the fuck is this?"

"This is my mother's attempt at fixing Rory."

"The fuck?" My eyes ran over the advertisement for Cellulaze, whatever the fuck that was. "She... she sent Aurora this?" I eyed the pill bottles, dread sinking in my chest.

White, hot anger shot through me. Aurora had told me things were bad with her mom, but hearing it and seeing it were two very different things.

"Actually, she sent it to me." Austin let out a weary sigh, dragging a hand down his face. The guy looked fucking gutted. "But I'm guessing that's because she doesn't have Rory's address."

"That's fucked up, Austin."

"You're telling me." He met my gaze, shame bleeding into his expression. "She never told me. All these years, and she never told me how bad it was."

Fuck.

I didn't want to do this, not after last night. Not after the intense feelings I had for his sister. But he was one of my best friends, and for as much as I was pissed with him on behalf of Aurora, I could also see the pain in his eyes.

Sliding onto a chair, I said, "Want to talk about it?"

"Yes... no. Fuck, I don't know, Holden. It's not that easy."

"Try," I said, sensing he needed this.

"Dad left when I was like seven or eight." He gave me a small dismissive half-shrug. As if it didn't matter. As if he was supposed to be over it. But I knew better than most that it didn't work that way.

Time didn't heal things, it only patched over the gaping

holes. The cuts and bruises. Held them together with jagged edges and shaky stitches and fake smiles.

"He couldn't deal with Mom anymore. Her obsession with always looking perfect. The way she'd drop everything for a job opportunity. Aurora was just a little kid, and she didn't understand. But I did. We were nothing more than a burden. A responsibility she never wanted."

"What happened after he left?"

"I... shit, man." He dropped his head, running his hand back and forth over his hair. "I don't do this. I don't talk about this. Ever."

"Maybe it's time."

His eyes lifted to mine, hollow and empty. "Like you talk about your family?"

"This isn't about me right now."

"No, I guess it's not." Silence echoed between us. Then he ran a hand over his jaw, releasing a long steady breath, grounding himself. "So my Dad left, and for a while, it wasn't so bad. Mom managed to pull herself together. Aurora was barely four. She needed a lot of attention.

"But by the time she turned seven or eight, things started to change. Mom couldn't look at me without getting upset about Dad abandoning us. She'd get drunk and spew these cruel, hateful things at me. So I started making myself scarce. Hanging out with friends more or down at the rink."

"And Aurora?" It took everything in me to keep a level head. To not go off at him for checking out on her.

But she was right. I couldn't fight her battles.

Not this one, at least.

"Mom started taking her to shoots. I always knew Aurora didn't really want to do it, but she liked making

Mom happy. At least, I thought she did." His jaw clenched. "I didn't know... fuck."

"Did you know she had an eating disorder?"

"The fuck?" His eyes widened with disbelief. "How the hell do you know that?"

"It came up." I shrugged.

"I mean, I knew she got into these cycles of crash dieting and then binge eating. But I thought it was a girl thing. I didn't think... She really told you that?"

I nodded, guilt crushing my chest. But it was nothing compared to the guilt in Austin's eyes.

"I ignored all the signs. Told myself she was just shy and awkward and found it hard to make friends. I didn't think —" He stopped himself, slamming his fist down on the table. "I'm surprised she can even bear to be around me."

"You're her brother. Family. That means something."

"Did she... tell you anything else?"

"You should talk to her."

"Listen, I owe you, man," he said. "When I asked you to look out for her, I didn't expect you and Con to welcome her into the fold without question. Thank you."

"Any time." The words almost choked me.

"You know, I was worried there for a second," he chuckled, "that she might fall for it."

"It?" I frowned, waiting for the penny to drop.

"Yeah, that Noah Holden charm girls can't seem to resist. But thank God she didn't because that would have been all kinds of awkward, am I right?"

"Y-yeah."

"We're the same, you and I, Holden," Austin went on as if his words weren't slicing me open, picking apart every doubt and insecurity I had about pursuing Aurora. About being her person.

Because fuck, I wanted that.

I wanted her smiles and tears and *her* doubts and insecurities.

I wanted every single beautiful piece.

But he would never see me that way.

He would never see me as good enough for her.

"We know the score. We know that hockey is the only thing we can ever rely on. The only thing that matters."

"What about Fallon? I thought you two were—"

"I like her, sure. And it's fun while it lasts. But eventually, I'll go pro, and she'll want more than I can give her. You know, I'm glad Aurora broke it off with Ben. They wouldn't have gone the distance."

"No?" A trickle of unease went through me, and my palms started sweating.

"Aurora needs someone who can be there. One hundred percent. Someone who can give her what Mom and Dad and I never did. Stability. Reassurance... Love. She needs someone who will put her first. No matter what."

"She does," I said, his words echoing through me.

"Thanks for listening." Austin stood, shoving all the brochures and pill bottles back into the box. "I needed to get that off my chest."

"What are you going to do?" I asked, my gut churning violently.

"I'm going to give Aurora some time to cool off, and then I think you're right. We need to talk." He smiled, looking ten times lighter than he had when I'd first sat down. Which was fucking ironic considering how *crushed* I felt. "Thanks again, man. You're a pain in the ass some-times, Holden. But you're a good guy. One of the best."

I'd felt the best last night with Aurora wrapped in my arms; I'd felt on top of the fucking world. Like maybe I could have it all like Connor and Aiden—hockey *and* the girl.

But now I just felt numb.

Austin was right. After everything Aurora had been through, she deserved a guy who could give her the world. Who could put her first. Someone who could be there no matter what.

Once the season started, hockey—the team—would once again become my life. Between classes and games, there wouldn't be much time left for a relationship.

The kind of relationship Aurora needed.

We could try, yeah. But how the fuck was I supposed to leave her, knowing her doubts and insecurities would only grow louder and louder every second I was gone.

This was exactly why I'd always kept things casual. Because as soon as somebody caught feelings, shit got complicated. It got messy. It had literally turned Sam into a Single White Female 2.0.

I didn't want to hurt Aurora. I cared too much about her to put her through any unnecessary heartache.

Just then, my cell vibrated, and her name flashed across the screen like a fucking sign from the universe.

Aurora: Can you meet me?

Fuck.

> Noah: I can't right now, sorry. Team stuff.

The second I hit send, I wanted to take it all back. But I couldn't shake Austin's words—his indirect warning.

> Aurora: Oh. Later then?

> Noah: Yeah, later should work. I'll text you when I'm done here.

> Aurora: Okay.

Another text came straight through.

> Aurora: Noah... we're good, right?

> Noah: Of course, shortcake. Talk later.

"What the fuck is the matter with you?" Connor asked the second Ella's door swung open.

"Can I come in?"

"No," he said as Ella shouted, "Yes," from somewhere inside her apartment.

"Kitten, you promised me—"

"Don't mind Connor," she appeared, ducking under his arm. "What's up?"

"I fucked up."

"Well, in that case... come in, make yourself at home, don't mind my blue balls."

"Babe!" Ella elbowed him in the ribs.

"Thanks, I appreciate this." I made a beeline for her couch.

"So... You fucked up?" she asked, sitting in the chair opposite me.

"I slept with Aurora."

"Well, we didn't think you were taking her home last night out of the goodness of your chivalrous heart," Connor scoffed, and I flipped him off.

"Babe, be a doll and go get us all a drink. Something tells me we're going to need it."

"Did something happen? With the sex?" Ella blushed a little, and I arched a brow.

"Really, El. The word sex embarrasses you, and yet you have no problem with fucking your guy like a porn star in our *shared* house. The house with walls thinner than—"

"Watch it, Holden." Connor thrust a beer at me and went to sit beside Ella.

"This intervention is about your sex life, not mine," she scolded.

"The sex isn't the problem."

"That good, huh? Who knew little Hart would be a fire-cracker between—"

Ella slapped her hand over his mouth and shook her head. "You were saying, Noah?"

"In case you haven't noticed, Aurora has... issues."

"Don't we all, sweetie." Ella gave me a reassuring smile that did little to ease the giant fucking knot in my stomach. "But yes, I gathered there's some stuff going on with her. She confided in you about it?"

"Some of it."

"That's good that she feels she can talk to you about it. Although, I'm surprised she told you the truth about her ex."

"What about her ex?" I frowned, not liking the sheer panic in her eyes.

"She didn't tell you? Oh, shit. Me and my big mouth. It doesn't matter. It's nothing. Forget I ever said—"

"Ella..." I growled.

Connor shoved her hand away and glowered, jabbing his finger at me. "Growl at my girl again, Holden, and you and me are going to have a problem."

"What do you know?" I asked, forcing myself to calm the fuck down.

"Noah, it's not my story to tell."

"Kitten, you should tell him. She's as good as his girl. He has a right to know."

Ella scoffed, "Jesus, you're such a bunch of overbearing assholes. And I'll have you know, Connor Morgan, just because I'm yours doesn't ever mean you have the right to know things that are deeply personal to me."

"El, babe, I didn't—"

"Shh." She silenced him with a finger to his lips. "I will tell Noah, but only because he looks so sad and pathetic. And because I expect him to do the right thing with this information." She arched a brow at me, and I held up my hands.

"I promise."

"Good. Firstly, what did she tell you about the ex?"

"That he decided he didn't want to do the long-distance thing, so he ended things. She gave me the impression he really hurt her."

"I wish it was that simple." Ella's featured tightened with a mix of anger and sympathy. "He was sleeping with her best friend behind her back. Aurora found out when she walked in on them."

"She..." My body trembled with barely restrained anger.

"Yeah, it was bad." She looked to Connor for help, and he let out a heavy sigh.

"Motherfucker." I curled my fist against my thigh.

"Yep," Ella said. "I can't even imagine how that must have felt... and then to have to keep going to school with them. Seeing them every day. Knowing the whole time they were laughing behind your back."

"I'll kill him," I said. "I'll fucking kill him."

"You might just get your chance," Connor murmured, and my head shot up.

"What did you say?"

"Coach posted the schedule earlier. We play Fitton U the second weekend of the season."

"Connor! Don't encourage him."

"Babe, the guy sounds like a total douchebag. And it's Rory." He shrugged. "I love her like a sister."

Ella's expression softened. "Yeah, she is pretty great. She deserves—" She stopped herself, but it was too late.

Her unspoken words hit me like bullets, tearing through the ice around my heart.

"Deserves better than me?"

"Noah, that's not what I was going to say."

"No, but you've thought it."

"We're just worried, man." Connor squeezed Ella's hand, drawing a line between us.

"Aurora isn't like us. She doesn't know how to live in our world. If you two go public, she'll be picked to shreds by the puck bunnies on social media. She's not ready for that. Not to mention the fact Austin will break your face."

"She doesn't want to tell anyone yet."

"See, case in point. She doesn't want to tell anyone because she knows what will happen. And what are you going to do every time someone scrutinizes your relationship? You already gave Adams a black eye. You can't go around beating the crap out of every guy or girl on campus who says something that might upset her."

"I would never hit a girl," I scoffed, offended that he would even suggest it.

"And then you'll be a grenade on the ice, one second away from detonating every time someone upsets her. That kind of anger isn't good for you, and it isn't good for the team. Look at what happened to Dumfries, where he ended up because he let his temper get the better of him."

"That asshole who trash-talked his mom deserved it."

"Yeah, and he was lucky it was off-season. Or else he could have kissed his senior year goodbye." Connor rubbed his jaw. "Actions have consequences, Holden. You know that. It's what I tried telling you before you crossed the line with her."

"So that's it then? I just end things with her?"

"No, Noah. That's not what we're saying—"

"Uh, yeah, babe. It kind of is." Connor gave me a sympathetic smile. "It's for the best, Holden, you know that. Save her the heartache now rather than down the line when you're both in too deep."

"Yeah." I ran a hand down the back of my neck, exhaling a steady breath.

He was right.

They both were.

Aurora had said it herself. We were too different. I didn't date for a reason, and if the story about her ex was true, she had every reason to swear off guys for the rest of her life.

Especially hockey players.

If we let things go any further, the fallout will only become messier.

She'd known. She'd fucking known I would break her heart. But she didn't know I'd be breaking my own too.

"I'm sorry, man," Connor said.

"Yeah," I got up and headed for the door. "Me too."

CHAPTER 33

AURORA

"Hello, is this Aurora Hart?"

"It is."

"It's Melinda calling from student housing. I just wanted to let you know we have some good news. Your apartment should be ready midweek. You can come by and collect your keys Tuesday."

"Oh, I see."

"You don't sound too pleased?" she said.

"Oh no, I am. Thank you. I'll see you Tuesday."

The relief I'd expected to feel when I finally got the call that my apartment was ready never came. Because the truth was, I'd gotten used to living with the guys.

Liked it, even.

We weren't always in each other's pockets, and I still spent a lot of time in my room by myself, but it was nice to know that someone was usually there if I wanted to hang out or chat.

It was nice having people and being a part of something.

But I guess I had overstayed my welcome. Austin wanted me gone, and if things went sour with Noah, then having my own place wouldn't be such a bad idea.

I rechecked my phone to see if Noah had texted yet, but there was nothing. And for as much as I tried not to let my thoughts run away, I couldn't shake the feeling something was wrong. That maybe he was pissed at me.

Pulling up our chat thread, I texted him.

> Aurora: Hey, just seeing if you're done with the team stuff yet? I have some news... the housing office called. My apartment is almost ready.

> Noah: That's great. Not sure I'll be done anytime soon. Things got a little out of control and we're knee deep in a gaming tournament. Rain check?

My heart sank.

> Aurora: Oh. Okay, sure. I have a ton of studying anyway.

I waited for his reply and waited.

But it never came.

And the pit in my stomach only churned deeper.

By the time I returned home, my inner voice had taken me hostage, spewing cruel, hateful things at me. Maybe Noah was lying. Maybe he was with Sam or some other puck bunny. But the house was empty which made sense if the guys were really off doing team stuff.

I wasn't hungry, but I forced myself to eat a couple of sushi rolls chased down by a bottle of water. Then I headed up to my room and prepared to call Mom. I'd been putting it off since this morning. But I needed to speak to her before Austin made good on his word and called her.

Part of me hoped she wouldn't answer, but the other part—the part stricken with shame and hurt when Austin had presented her care package to me—was ready for a fight.

She answered on the third ring with an indignant huff. "Aurora, you are alive then."

"Don't be so dramatic, Mom. I told you last time we spoke I've been settling in."

She hummed with disapproval.

"I got your care package."

"Oh good, did you take a look at—"

"Why the hell would you send that to me?" I seethed. "Via Austin of all people?"

"Well, you didn't leave me your address. I had to get it to you somehow. I've been worried sick about you, sweetheart. I know how much of a toll freshman year can take on a young woman's body. I don't want you to fall back into old habits, Aurora. You need to make sure you're eating properly and—"

"Mom, stop."

"Excuse me?"

"I said stop. I didn't ask for your advice or help, and I certainly didn't ask you to send me a bunch of diet pills and brochures for—"

"Now, who's being dramatic, Aurora? I didn't send them to upset you. I sent them to make you—"

"STOP," I shrieked, tears of frustration rolling down my cheeks. "Just. Stop."

"Aurora?"

"This has to end, Mom. I'm not you. I'm never going to be you. And I'm certainly not going to pump myself full of drugs or start having cosmetic surgery to try and be you."

"But you could be so beautiful, sweetheart. If you just—"

"Just what, Mom?" My voice cracked. Frustration bleeding into heartache. The type of soul-deep pain only someone who is supposed to love you could inflict. "Become somebody else? By dieting to the point of starving myself? Just to lose a few pounds? I have boobs Mom; I have hips and an ass and do you know what? Those things don't make me a bad person. They don't make me any less deserving or beautiful than anyone else."

"But—"

"No, Mom. *No*." God, it felt good to say that word.

No.

"I am done with your unhealthy obsession to fix me."

I didn't need to be fixed like a doll with broken parts. I was a person with feelings and thoughts and imperfections, just like the rest of the world.

"Aurora Vivienne Hart, you will not speak to me with such—"

"Goodbye, Mom." I cut her off. "Please don't call me again unless you want to apologize."

I hung up, something akin to relief unfurling in my stomach as the tethers between us frayed and snapped.

And drifted away like ashes in the wind.

Something inside me changed after the call with Mom. I realized that I could spend my entire life living in the shadows, scared of what might happen, or I could step into the light and *live*.

What other people thought about me didn't define me, but how I felt about myself did. And since arriving in Lakeshore and meeting Connor and Noah and Ella and Dayna and Harper, I'd slowly begun to learn to love myself again.

But no one made me feel more beautiful than Noah. And I didn't want to hide that away. I wanted to celebrate it, which was why I decided to come clean to Austin.

I figured I had to be the one to do it—he was my brother, after all. So, I'd baked up a storm, rustling up batches of the cookies they all loved so much while I waited for them to get home.

I was fully prepared for him to be pissed and probably a little confused. But the bottom line was I cared about Noah, and I wanted everyone to know because he deserved someone to choose him too. Not Noah the hockey star or Noah the charmer or Noah the playboy, but Noah Holden, the boy from Buffalo, New York. The boy who had never come first to his parents.

By the time the front door opened, their heavy footsteps filling the house, I was a trembling mess. But I could do this.

I needed to do it.

"Hey," I called. "I'm in the kitchen."

"Rory? What are you still doing up?" Austin asked, eyeing the clock on the wall.

Crap.

I hadn't even realized how late it was. Probably because I'd spent a couple of hours cleaning the kitchen within an inch of its life.

"Did you... clean?" He frowned, scanning the spotless kitchen.

"And baked." I pointed to the plates of cookies.

"Shit, little Hart," Connor said. "You didn't need to do this."

"I wanted to. There's something I want to talk to you about. Where's Noah?" I craned my neck over their big, imposing frames, expecting to see him in the hall.

Connor paused mid-bite, glancing at my brother and back again.

"What's wrong?" My stomach tumbled at the panicked expression in his eyes.

"Uh, he and a bunch of the guys headed to a bar—"

"Holden was on fucking fire tonight," my brother chuckled, completely oblivious to the fact he was driving the knife deeper and deeper into my heart. "I haven't seen him like that since he was a freshman. Twenty-bucks says he has a bunny hop tonight. The guy needs a good session after his recent dry spell."

Oh, God.

I turned away from them, clapping a hand over my

mouth and forcing myself to take a deep breath, trying to keep the contents of my stomach on the inside.

"What did you want to talk to us about anyway?" Austin asked, and I inhaled another deep breath, clutching the edge of the counter.

"Oh, I... my apartment is ready." I turned slowly, swallowing down the acidic lump in my throat, blinking back the tears that were threatening to fall. "I can pick up the keys Tuesday. Yay."

Connor winced, apology glittering in his eyes.

Because he knew.

He fucking knew what was happening.

He knew, and he didn't give me any warning.

"Oh shit, Rory." Guilt coasted over Austin's expression. "You don't need to go. The guys and I talked, and you're welcome to stay." He smiled. "I know things have been all messed up between us. But I like having you around. In fact, I was hoping we could talk."

"It's late. I have early classes." I rushed out, my heart bleeding out in my chest. "But, tomorrow? I can do it tomorrow," I managed to add.

"Yeah, tomorrow sounds good."

"Well, enjoy the cookies."

"Rory," Connor called, but I hurried out of there, barely holding myself together.

I ran up the first set of stairs, forcing one foot in front of the other. Just a little further, and then I could break.

Behind closed doors where no one else would see—

"Aurora, wait..." Connor called after me, and I glanced back over my shoulder, unable to stop the tears from streaking down my face. "It's for the best," he said with a sad smile.

"Yeah," I sniffled. "You're probably right."

He looked like he wanted to say more, but he didn't, and I took off.

The second I was inside my room, I closed the door and sank to the floor. Tears ran down my cheeks in rivers as I wrapped my arms around my knees and tried to hold myself together.

I'd always known Noah Holden had the power to ruin me.

I just didn't think he'd actually do it.

I didn't see Noah again before I moved out. But then, cowards had a habit of hiding.

He'd sent me one text. One lame-assed apology I deleted before I'd even finished reading it. If he couldn't look me in the eyes and give me the truth, I didn't want his excuses.

His lies.

Connor and Austin were there, though. Ella and Harper too. It only took the five of us less than two hours to pack up and move my meager possessions to the other side of campus to my freshly painted apartment.

"It's nice," Austin said from the doorway.

"Yeah, I think I'll be happy here."

"Listen, I know we talked yesterday, but I still can't shake the feeling I'm missing something. You know, if something happened with Mom—"

"I told you I set things straight with her. If she wants to

apologize and try and have a normal relationship with me, she knows where to find me."

"I'm proud of you, Sis." He came closer, hesitating. "And the therapy stuff? You're going to find someone local?"

I nodded. "Ella's friend Jordan has a couple of recommendations I can check out. See if we're a good fit."

He nodded, rubbing the back of his neck. "Rory, I'm so fucking sorry—"

"Hey, no more apologies, remember?"

I don't know how I'd managed to drag myself out of bed yesterday morning and meet Austin for coffee, but I had.

I guess I'd gotten too good at plastering over the cracks and pretending everything was okay. It hadn't been easy sharing the parts of myself with him that I'd always kept a secret. But after telling him the truth—about Mom, about Tierney and Ben, about my eating disorder, about all of it—I'd felt lighter somehow.

We still had a lot of work to do, but it was a start. Austin was my brother, and I wanted him in my life. Even if he was a selfish, clueless asshole at times.

But there was one secret I'd kept from him.

One secret I would never tell.

Noah.

There didn't seem any point in rocking the boat between them, not when the season had officially started. I'd spent my entire childhood protecting him—I could do it for a little while longer.

Besides, Noah had made his choice, and it wasn't me. Austin knowing the truth wouldn't change that.

"I'm going to miss having you around, Sis," he said, pulling me into his arms.

"I'll miss you too. But we'll still see each other."

"Damn right, we will. It's Hot Dog Tuesday, I expect—"

"I can't tonight."

"Hot date?" he grinned, and I let out a strangled laugh.

"I wish. But no, I told Harper I'd stop by the bar and hang out during her break."

"I'm sorry I tried to hit on her," he said, looking all kinds of awkward.

"You're forgiven."

"Hey," Ella poked her head inside. "We're all done here. Connor's hungry, so we were thinking of heading across the street to the pizza place if you want to come?"

"Sounds good to me, but tell him no fucking pineapple," Austin grumbled. "Unless you want me to stay—"

"No, go," I said. "I'm fine. I want to finish unpacking and try out the bathtub."

"We'll hang out soon."

I nodded, and he strode out of the room.

"How are you holding up?" Ella asked once Austin was gone.

"I'm okay."

"You know, Noah did—"

"Please, El, don't. When I say I'm okay, I mean I can just about hold it together so long as nobody mentions his name." I gave her a tight smile.

She knew the truth about Noah, and it only made the pain worse.

"Of course, I'm sorry. This place is nice."

"Yeah, it is."

"Anytime you want company, you only have to ask. And you have Harper. I'm sure she'll be over all the time."

"Ella, I'll be fine. I always planned on moving into my own place anyway. It isn't a big deal."

"I know. I'm just... Oh, come here." She pulled me into her arms, squeezing the crap out of me. "You're beautiful, Aurora. Inside and out. I hope you know that. And one day, the right guy will come along and sweep you off your feet."

I was pretty sure he already had, but I didn't tell her that.

"I was going to tell him, you know," I said as she headed for the door.

"Tell who?"

"Austin. I was going to tell him about Noah and me. Crazy, right? I was going to risk my heart all for a guy who never wanted it in the first place."

"Listen, maybe you should—"

"It's fine." I waved her off. "I'm fine. Go eat before Connor hulks out. I'll see you tomorrow."

She hesitated, a strange expression on her face. But then she gave me a small nod and slipped into the hall, leaving me alone.

But I wasn't alone, not really.

Not anymore.

Things might not have worked out with Noah, but I was determined to make life in Lakeshore work.

More than ever.

CHAPTER 34

NOAH

"What the hell was that, Holden?" Coach Tucker boomed across the ice, earning me a snicker from Adams.

"Feeling a little off your game, Holden," he drawled. "Maybe you should—"

I shoulder-checked him into the boards, feeling a lick of satisfaction at his grunt of pain.

"Asshole," he yelled after me, and I flipped him off over my shoulder as I skated away.

"Tell it to someone who cares, fucker."

"You need to get it together," Connor chased me down the ice.

"I'm fine."

"You look fine." He rolled his eyes.

"Leave it, Morgan. I'm just burning off some steam."

"Tell that to me when Coach replaces you with one of the rookies." He blocked off my route, and I drew to an abrupt stop. "We agreed this was the right thing."

"We did."

So why did it feel like my heart had been yanked out of my fucking chest?

Three days.

Aurora had been gone three days, and I'd only seen her once around campus—briefly across the cafeteria before she noticed me and hurried the fuck out of there like she couldn't stand the sight of me.

Not that I blamed her.

I'd taken the coward's way out, texting her when I should have been man enough to look her in the eye and explain everything.

I couldn't do it, though. I couldn't bear the thought of seeing the disappointment in her eyes—the heartbreak.

The anger.

Aurora deserved someone who could put her first, who wouldn't make her life any harder than it already was.

I wasn't that guy.

Behind closed doors, we were fucking perfect together, but Connor was right; out in public, we'd create a storm. One I wasn't sure Aurora could weather.

He slammed his glove against my shoulder. "So pull your head out of your ass and get in the game, okay?"

I nodded. Because what else could I do?

"Okay, bring it in," Assistant Coach Walsh yelled, whispering something in Coach Tucker's ear as we all glided toward the huddle.

"Mase, Aiden, Connor, looking good out there. Noah, son, I don't know what the fuck that was, but I hope to God you fix it before the exhibition game tonight. Everyone else, good effort. Hit the showers."

I went to skate off, but a hand landed on my shoulder.

"Not you, kid," Coach Walsh smirked. "You and I are going to run a little one-on-one."

"Practice is done."

"Practice is done when I say it is," Coach Tucker shot me a withering look. "He's all yours, Carson."

"Let's go, hotshot." Coach Walsh grabbed his stick and skated out to the center rink.

"Whatever you think you're doing, it won't work," I said, facing off against him.

"No? Because you looked tense out there just now. Like you were holding back, and it was making you sloppy."

"I... I'm fine," I gritted out.

"Then you'll have no problem beating my ass in a little one-on-one." He grinned, baiting me.

"It's your funeral."

"That's a whole lot of trash talk you got there for someone who failed to score a single goal in practice."

Fuck.

He had me there.

"Three. Two. One—" He dropped the puck between us, and we scuffled to gain control. He was quick, but I was faster, swiping the puck ahead of me and taking off, hot on its tail.

I heard Coach Walsh close in behind me, but I didn't take my eye off the puck, hooking the toe of the blade around it and controlling it with the stick as I skated toward the goal.

Like lightning, Coach Walsh whizzed past me and dropped back to defend the net. "Take your best shot," he taunted through a cocky smirk, making himself big and imposing.

I pushed every thought out of my head. Every memory

of Aurora. Every stolen kiss. Every touch. Every smile and laugh.

Every regret.

As I approached the goal, I didn't allow a single thing to penetrate my laser-sharp focus.

Pulling the puck toward my body, I transferred my weight onto my outside leg. The second it hit my midline, I pushed my top hand away and snapped down on the puck, sending it flying toward Coach Walsh.

The buzzer rang out, a smug grin tugging at my lips as I sailed past him, doing a victory lap, flipping my stick to my side and pulling it down sharply as if holstering it.

"That, that right there, is why you're here, Holden. Why, one day, you'll turn pro. Just don't let your personal shit off the ice interfere with business on the ice. I know where that path leads, kid, and it isn't pretty."

"That's why you quit, right? Because you couldn't play without Dalton?"

He cut me a hard look, but his expression faltered when he cast his eyes over to the memorial seat placed in honor of Dalton Benson.

"Hockey was our dream. It didn't feel right to go after that without him."

"He'd have wanted you to play."

"Yeah, well, I couldn't do it. But I like to think he's proud of my work with the team."

"I'm sure he is, Coach."

"Now, want to tell me what's on your mind?"

"Not really."

"Fair enough. But you come to the game tonight ready to win, okay?"

I nodded. Because he was right, I couldn't let life off the ice interfere with my performance on the ice.

"Okay, hit the showers. And Noah?"

"Yeah, Coach?"

"The Lakers isn't just a team; it's a family. You need to talk? We're here."

"Thanks, Coach." I swallowed over the giant fucking lump in my throat as I skated off the ice and headed for the locker room.

Wishing it was that simple.

"That's what I'm talking about," Connor jumped on my back, almost sending me crashing to the ice. But Mason and Austin were there to catch me, the four of us, high-fiving and whooping so hard it was impossible not to grin.

It was only an exhibition game, but nobody wanted to lose the first game of any season. Even one that didn't count toward conference rankings.

"You were on fire," Austin slapped me on the back. "Play like that for the rest of the season, and the championship is ours."

Connor caught my eye and gave me a small nod of understanding.

He'd seen Aurora in the crowd. We all had. But no one else understood what it meant to me. Well, maybe Aiden and Mason suspected, but neither of them had explicitly asked about it, and I'd offered no explanation.

She'd come to support us, and the second I found her sitting between Ella and Harper in one of her oversized sweaters wearing a deer-caught-in-the-headlights expression, it was enough to light a fire under my ass and play some of the best damn hockey I'd ever played.

"Gather in," Coach Tucker called. "That is how you do it, gentleman." A cheer went up around him. "But the hard work starts next week. Everyone knows opening weekend sets the tone for the season. So I want you to work hard in practice and focus on each game as it comes, okay?"

"You got it, Coach," Aiden said, taking his role as captain and spokesperson for the team very seriously.

A couple of us smirked at him, and he discreetly flipped us off.

"Okay. Get out of here and go celebrate. But not too much. The season is upon us, and I expect you all to be on your best behavior from here on out."

Everyone grumbled their agreement as we headed off the ice to the locker rooms. But I couldn't resist the urge to look back to the glass one last time.

Only Aurora was gone.

And with it, my short-lived good mood.

"Is it always like this?" Ward asked as we sat in our usual booth at The Penalty Box, watching a group of puck bunnies put on quite the show as they danced to the heavy beat.

"Welcome to game nights at TPB," Austin clapped him on the back. "It's the perfect trifecta: First win of the season. Happy Hour. And bunnies on—"

"Babe, you made it." Connor pulled Ella onto his lap, nuzzling her neck.

"Harper and Aurora are around here somewhere too."

"She came?" Austin glanced around.

"Yeah, Harper wanted to introduce her to some people."

"What people?"

"Down, *Deputy Dad*," Ella chuckled. "I'm sure she's fine." Her gaze snagged on mine, but I dropped my head, finding the label on my beer suddenly more interesting than their conversation.

"I think the blonde has got her eye on you." Mase nudged my shoulder.

"Not feeling it," I said with a dismissive shrug.

"What about the brunette?"

My eyes snapped up and found Aurora across the bar. I half-expected her to look away, but she didn't, holding my gaze. It was the look I'd wanted to avoid. So much disappointment and anger swirling in her sparkling, green depths that even from across the room, it was still like a punch to the stomach.

I looked away first, guilt slamming into me like a sledgehammer.

"You want to talk about it?" Mase whispered, and I shook my head.

"Hey, you good?" Connor asked.

"Yeah." I drained my beer and slammed it on the table. "I need to take a leak."

Sliding out of the booth, I made my way across the bar to the restrooms. A couple of people clapped me on the back, calling out congratulations and well wishes for the season ahead. The girl waiting on her friends outside the women's restroom batted her eyelashes as I passed, giving me a long lingering look. One I knew meant I could drag her into a stall with me, and she'd love every second.

But I gave her a polite smile and slipped past her, going in alone.

If I couldn't have Aurora, I didn't want anyone.

I made quick work of taking a piss and washing my hands. When I exited the bathroom, I half-expected to find the girl waiting for me. Instead, I found a teary-eyed Sam.

"You shouldn't be here," I said, ducking around her.

"Noah, wait, please. I just want to talk. To explain..."

"Not interested, Sam. If you don't want to cause a scene, I suggest—"

"Please." Her voice cracked, and something inside me faltered.

"Sam," I let out a heavy sigh, running a hand through my hair. "This isn't a good idea. I don't—"

"I know. God, I know I messed things up, okay? But I just wanted to explain. To try and fix things. You owe me that much."

It was on the tip of my tongue to tell her I didn't owe her a damn thing, but she looked so fucking sad. About as sad as I felt. And maybe that little part inside of me hurting took pity on her because I said, "Fine. Five minutes. Come on."

I led her toward the back door that led to the small outside area. It was mostly smokers out here, so there wasn't anyone from the team around.

I found us a corner seat in the back, out of earshot of everyone, and sat down.

"God, Noah. I don't even know where to begin."

"Maybe with the fact you lied about the break-in."

"I did." A fresh wave of tears filled her eyes. "When I felt you start to pull away, I panicked. You were the closest thing I had to a best friend, Noah. I loved hanging out with you. And when we had sex, I told myself it meant something. That you felt the same."

"Sam, I was always upfront with you." I ran a hand down my face.

"I know that. But I let it get all twisted up in my head."

"So you pretended your apartment was broken into? That's messed up."

"I am so sorry. It started as a harmless, little white lie. I thought it would bring us closer together."

"Sam... you realize how weird this all sounds, right? It's not normal behavior to manipulate people like that."

"I know. I have a lot of stuff I haven't dealt with from my past. It's not an excuse, and I know that. I just needed you to know that I'm sorry. I shouldn't have done any of it. Lying about the break-in. Turning up in your class. Ambushing Aurora." My brow arched, and she added, "I knew the second I heard you talk about her. You got this look in your eye."

"I did not—"

"Yeah, Noah. You did." She gave me a sad, resigned smile. "It's why I followed you that night after we studied at Joe's. Because it was the same look I get whenever I talk about you."

"You followed me..."

"I didn't mean to. It just happened... I'm so sorry."

"I don't know what you want me to say."

I didn't deny it because she was right. Aurora had knocked me on my ass the second she'd called me out at the bar that first night we all went out.

"Nothing. I'm not asking you to forgive me. I just want

to explain and say I'm sorry. You're a good guy, Noah. And you deserve to be happy." She got up, drying her eyes with the heel of her palms. "Maybe one day we can be friends again."

I stood, feeling all kinds of awkward.

"Can I... have a hug? For old time's sake?"

"Sure." Not wanting to make her feel any worse than she already did, I wrapped her into my arms.

I'd known Sam had issues which was why we'd bonded in the first place. But I'd underestimated how deep her trauma ran.

"I hope you find what you're looking for, Sam," I said, hugging her tight.

She clung to me a second longer, gentle sobs racking her body. When she stepped back, she drew in a sharp breath and composed herself. "Thanks for hearing me out." She reached for me, squeezing my hand. "Bye, Noah."

I gave her a sharp nod, watching as she walked away. Right past—

"Aurora." Her name slipped off my lips in a harsh breath.

She stared at me—betrayal shining in her eyes.

I rushed over to her, holding up my hands. "It's... fuck, it's not what you think."

"I'm not sure you can even begin to imagine what I'm thinking right now."

"I guess I deserve that."

"You deserve a hell of a lot more than that," she seethed, that fire I loved so much simmering in her eyes.

"How have you been? How's the new place? The guys said it's nice and that you're all settled. Maybe I can come over and—"

"No."

"Y-yeah. That's probably a bad idea." I raked a hand through my hair, my stomach dropping into my fucking sneakers.

"So, you and Sam—"

"No. *No!* That wasn't what it looked like."

"It never is." She gave me a sad smile. "I should probably go. Harper is hanging around here somewhere, waiting for me."

"Yeah, okay. It was good to see you, shortcake."

Her breath caught, her eyes shuttering as pain washed over her features.

"Aurora, I'm sorry, I'm so fucking—"

"There you are." Austin appeared, hooking his arm around her neck. "What's going on?"

"Nothing." She flashed him a bright smile. "I was looking for Harper and ran into Noah. I was just congratulating him on a good game."

"Hell yeah. First of many, am I right?"

"Yeah." My eyes flicked to Aurora, and she pursed her lips.

"Anyway, I have to go find Harper before she sends out a search party. See you two later."

She kissed Austin's cheek, and jealousy flared inside me. Because that's who I was now—a guy getting jealous over one of his best friends getting kissed by his sister.

Fuck my life.

Austin watched her go and then glanced back at me. "Did she seem okay to you?"

"Yeah, why?"

"I don't know, something's different about her, but I can't put my finger on it."

"I'm sure she's just finding her feet now she's in her own place."

"Yeah. Just keep an eye out for her for me. I worry now she's not under our roof."

"I hate to break it to you, man"—I nudged his shoulder as we made our way back into the bar—"but Aurora's all grown up."

"Yeah." He gave me a grim smile. "That's what worries me."

His eyes bored into mine, and I wondered if he knew. I wondered if he could sense the lies woven into my words.

The betrayal.

But most of all, I wondered if he knew that I was pretty certain I was head over skates in love with his sister.

CHAPTER 35

AURORA

"THIS PLACE IS REALLY NICE, RORY." Harper sat down on the couch and smiled at me. "It's a shame it isn't a two-bed. I could have moved in."

"You don't like living in the dorms?"

"I don't hate it, and it beats living at home with my dad, but I don't know. It's not everything I thought it would be."

"Well, you're always welcome to hang out here."

"Don't say that, or you'll never get rid of me."

That shadow passed over her expression again, but I didn't push. If Harper wanted to open up to me, she would.

"How is it being on your own? Missing the guys yet?"

"It's different," I said.

"Good different? You seem a little quieter since you moved out."

"Actually, Harper, I need to tell you something." I inhaled a deep breath, shoving my trembling hands under my thighs.

"Okay."

"So you know how you asked me if there was anything going on with Noah and me, and I said no?"

A knowing smile tugged at her lips. "I was wondering when you were going to fess up."

"You knew?" My eyes widened.

"I didn't *know*, but I suspected. There was a change in you. Subtle, but it was there. Not to mention you were always texting and you'd get this look."

"I did not get a look," I said.

"Did too." She grinned, easing some of the guilt I felt.

"I'm so sorry I lied, Harper. But it was Noah, you know? He's... and I'm..."

"You, Aurora Hart, need a serious dose of self-love. You're smart and gorgeous, and you bagged yourself Noah freaking Holden."

"Actually, he ended things. With a text." I winced.

"He... *what*?"

"Yep." I swallowed down the jagged ball of emotion, forcing myself not to get swept up in the pain and betrayal I felt every time I thought about how he'd left things. "We... uh, we had an amazing night together, and then he just... ended it."

"Wow, what a jerk."

"The funny thing is, I get it."

She gawked at me like I'd lost my mind. "What do you mean, you get it?"

"He panicked. I have a lot of baggage, Harper. Stuff I haven't really dealt with. Stuff I'm still dealing with. And he's... a hockey star. I mean, he's slept with half the female population at LU. I can't compete with that.

"Things between us were real, and that freaked him out.

To be honest, it kind of freaked me out. I'm not built to be in the spotlight and being Noah's girlfriend..."

"Is a one-way ticket to campus infamy."

"Gee, thanks."

"Oh, hush," she said. "I didn't mean it like that. But any girl who bags herself a Laker becomes puck bunny enemy number one. Those girls don't mess around online."

"Yeah."

Of course, I knew what being with Noah would open myself up to. It's one of the reasons I'd kept holding back.

I'd been the girl at the brunt of jokes for years. It hadn't gotten better when I dated Ben. It had just become more passive-aggressive, more under the radar. Because while people had no problem hurting my feelings, they didn't want to offend the popular hockey player.

God, people sucked.

"So you haven't talked to him about it at all?"

"No. I've basically been avoiding him."

"Aurora, you need to talk to him. He owes you that much."

"I hate saying this because I know how weak it makes me look. But maybe it's for the best, Harper. I was kidding myself for ever thinking it could work."

"No, I don't accept that. I don't accept it at all. Love doesn't color inside the lines, Rory. It's not a one-size-fits-all. It's wild and messy, and it breaks boundaries."

"Noah doesn't love me," I scoffed because the idea was preposterous. "We were just fooling around."

"Right. Just fooling around with the hockey playboy who's never slept with the same girl twice."

"Actually, he slept with Sam more than once."

"Not the point here." She scowled. "He cares about you.

And maybe he walked away because he thinks it's the only way he can protect your heart."

"My heart was always going to get broken, Harper. Girls like—"

"I swear to God, Rory, if you say 'girls like me don't get the guy' one more time... I will scream. For someone who claims to be an Austen fan, you really need to work on your self-confidence."

"Uh, overcritical mother with an obsession with physical perfection." I raised my hand.

"Father, who wishes I had a dick instead of a vagina." She pointed at herself, cocking a brow.

"What are you—"

"Story for another time," she said, brushing me off. "The point is, we all have shit going on, babe. We're all a little bit broken and messed up. But it's college. Our time to shine. Our time to say fuck it to the haters and go out there and grab life by the balls and *live*.

"We get one shot at life, Rory. Do you really want to spend it scared? Watching opportunities like being Noah freaking Holden's girl pass you by?"

"No?"

"Oh my God." She grabbed a cushion and threw it at me. "You need to go over there and demand an explanation. Because what if Noah made the biggest mistake of his life, and he's just too stupid to see it?"

"He is kind of stupid." My mouth twitched.

"Damn right he is."

"I'm scared, Harper."

Because I'd been here before. Putting myself out there, trusting my heart, and the boy promising to keep it safe.

"In the words of Charlotte Lucas, 'We are all fools in love.'"

My brows furrowed. "That doesn't even make sense in this context."

"No, but it sounded good, didn't it?" She chuckled. "Look, I get it. You're scared you'll put yourself out there again, and Noah will reject you." I nodded, and her expression softened. "But what if he doesn't, Rory? What if he just needs you to make the first gesture? What if he's just as scared as you are?"

"I..."

"Doesn't sound so silly now, does it?" A flicker of amusement passed over her. "How about this? If it all goes horribly wrong, I'll be right here with copious amounts of sushi rolls and zucchini fries to make it all better."

"How did you—"

"I notice things." She shrugged, giving me a small, knowing smile. "And when you're ready to talk about that, I'll be here to listen."

"You're a good friend, Harper."

"I know." She pulled out her phone and opened the notepad app. "Now let's figure out exactly what you're going to say to Noah to make sure he knows he gave up the best thing that ever happened to him."

I couldn't do it.

All week, I tried—*and failed*—to text Noah to ask him to meet me. It might have had something to do with the fact that every time I saw him around campus, there was always a puck bunny, or three, hot on his tail.

Beyond a polite hello or smile, he never engaged them, but they were a permanent reminder of what life with Noah Holden would be like.

I'd been that girl before. Did I really want to subject myself to the scrutiny and judgment again?

But Harper was right. I didn't want to stand in the shadows while life passed me by, either.

God, I was a mess.

So I did what I did best. I threw myself into my studies and lost myself between the pages of Austen and Brontë, Hardy and Eliot. I fell in love with Edmund Bertram all over again.

But something was missing.

Noah's cocky charm, his teasing, and his humor had left a hole that no fictional character could replace. Because I realized now Noah had done something no one else ever had, not even Ben.

He'd made me laugh.

And for the stolen moments we'd shared, he'd made me love myself. He'd unlocked a part of me that I thought I'd lost forever.

And I was determined to hold on to her. To let her flourish and grow and *live*.

"Rory, wait up."

I turned to find Ella hurrying toward me. "Oh hey, how are you?"

"I'm good, thanks. You?"

"I'm okay."

"Jordan said the two of you hung out last night."

"We did. We're going to meet again soon."

We'd met at Zest and talked about everything and nothing. It felt good to talk to someone who knew what it was like to live with an eating disorder. Who knew what it was like to constantly battle your own mind.

"Good, that's... good. Are you coming to the game Friday?"

"Austin got Harper and me tickets, but I'm not sure yet."

"You should be there."

I gave her a small nod. "How is he?"

"Miserable. But it's the first game of the season, so he's focused on that."

"Of course."

"Listen, Aurora, I know I was always against the idea of the two of you—"

"You don't need to do this, El."

"Yeah, I think I do." Guilt shone in her eyes, making my stomach dip. "He came to see us."

"Noah?"

She nodded. "The day after the two of you... you know, spent the night together."

"Oh."

"He was freaking out. Austin opened up to him about some things, and I think it scared him. Anyway, Connor and I... well, we may have insinuated that he should probably end things before you both got in too deep."

"I see."

"I am so sorry."

"You only did what you thought was best."

"You're not angry?"

"I'm not thrilled that people who I considered my friends, interfered in my relationship. But I trust your heart was in the right place."

"You're right. We had no business getting involved, and I've just felt awful about it. I've wanted to come clean all week, but I just didn't know how to tell you."

"So what changed?"

"I saw Noah earlier, and he looks... God, Rory, he looks broken. I mean, he's putting on a brave face for the team. But he's hurting, babe. If I didn't know better, I'd say he's heartbroken."

"I..." I pressed my lips together. Because she was wrong, she had to be.

Wasn't she?

"Being with a hockey player isn't easy. The intense game schedule, the prospect of spending a life on the road, chasing his dreams. But it's worth it. The way Connor loves me, it's worth all the self-doubt and lonely nights, and confidence crises.

"If there's even a part of you that thinks you could love Noah one day." She reached for my hand, squeezing gently. "Then don't give up on him."

Don't give up on him.

Except, I hadn't given up on him.

He'd given up on me—on us. He'd decided what I could or couldn't handle and ended things before they even got started.

But was it all just to protect me?

Or was it to protect himself?

He'd been abandoned by his mom, turned his back on his father, and as far as I was aware, he had no other family.

But hockey was his life. The team was his family. And me?

I was the one thing that threatened all that.

"Aurora?" Ella said.

I gave her a small, hopeful smile and said, "I think I need your help."

If I thought things were crazy the night of the exhibition game, it was nothing compared to the opening game of the season.

Ellet Arena was a sellout. Over five-and-a-half-thousand fans adorned in cyan and indigo crammed into the seats, ready to cheer their team on.

"Rory, Harper, over here." Ella and Dayna waved at us from the row behind the glass.

"Holy shit, these are good seats," Harper bounced on her feet, her excitement infectious.

"You made it." Ella pulled me down beside her. "How are you feeling?"

"Surprisingly okay." A small smile played on my lips.

"I can't wait to see his face."

"What are you two whispering about?" Dayna asked.

"Nothing." Ella flashed her a bright smile. "How was Aiden before the game?"

"Focused. In the zone."

"And you? Are you nervous?"

"I can't stop shaking," Dayna confessed.

"Do you guys have, like, a pre-game ritual?" Harper leaned around me. "If you know what I'm saying."

Dayna flushed firetruck red, and Harper shrieked, "Oh my God, you do, don't you?"

"We... ah, you guys. Stop."

"Don't look at us," I said. "It's Harper and her lack of filter."

"What?" She shrugged. "We're all friends. Oh my God, here they come." Harper grabbed my arm, barely containing her excitement.

The referee conferred with Coach Tucker and the coach from the opposing team. Then players spilled over the boards, taking up their positions on the ice.

"LET'S GO, LAKERS," Ella screamed at the top of her lungs, scaring the crap out of us. Dayna gawked over at her, and she blushed. "Sorry, I get a little carried away."

"A little?" We all laughed. "I think you burst my eardrum."

"I'm just so excited and nervous for them."

A ripple of anticipation went through the arena as Aiden and the opposing center faced off against each other. But I wasn't watching the Lakers captain. I only had eyes for the right-winger.

Number 11.

A sharp breath punched my lungs as I watched Noah out there. He looked so focused, so freaking hot in his pads and jersey, my heart raced.

The referee dropped the puck, and Aiden was straight in with his stick, sending the arena into a frenzy.

"Hell, yeah," Harper whooped as he sent the puck flying back to Connor, and the Lakers' offense broke away, flying toward the attacking zone.

"Oh my God." I clutched Harper's arm, fixated on the way Noah glided across the ice, closing in on the goal. Connor passed the puck to Mason, who sent it soaring right into the blade of Noah's stick. He pulled back, took the shot, and scored.

Everyone was on their feet. Me included.

"GO LAKERS," Harper yelled at the top of her lungs, making me vibrate with laughter.

Noah celebrated with his teammates, and pride welled inside me. But it was nothing compared to the shock I felt when he searched the crowd, his eyes landing right on me.

Something passed between us, visceral and intense and *real*. A single moment that made me feel so much.

Then he was gone, swept up into the game.

And I realized Harper was right.

Love had no guarantees. It had no safety net or rulebook. And more often than not, it could go wrong.

So very wrong.

But it could also go right. It could be beautiful and exhilarating and wonderful. If only you were brave enough to take the leap of faith and trust your heart.

CHAPTER 36

NOAH

"WHAT THE FUCK is wrong with you?" Austin nudged my shoulder.

"I'm fine." I watched the rest of the team as they celebrated.

"You were on fire tonight, Aus," Mase said, tipping his beer toward him. "A shutout. Fucking A."

"I'm not going to lie." Austin grinned around the rim of his Heineken. "It feels good. First game in the bag, only another thirty-three to go."

"Bring it on."

I mumbled some inaudible response as I nursed my beer. My calves and glutes ached, and my lungs burned. God, my lungs fucking burned. But I loved the bone-deep exhaustion, the lingering trickle of adrenaline in my bloodstream.

The team was high on the win, and the atmosphere in

The Penalty Box was electric. Everyone was here to celebrate our first win of the season.

But my heart wasn't in it.

Because she'd been there.

Aurora.

My shortcake.

I'd spotted her behind the glass the second I got out on the ice. But, like the exhibition game, her presence only pushed me to play some of the best damn hockey of my life.

Hockey had always been about proving my old man wrong, about showing him that I could make something of myself, that I didn't need him or his money.

The only person I'd wanted to impress tonight, though, was Aurora. Which was fucking stupid since I'd been the one to walk away from her.

Jesus, I was a fucking idiot.

The only person who had ever wanted me regardless of my name or my skills on the ice, and I'd given her up.

Because I was a fucking coward.

"Hey, you good?" Connor asked, looking at me with a strange expression.

"Yeah, why?"

"Because I hate to tell you, man, but little Hart just walked in here. And she looks—"

"Fuck." My eyes found her across the bar, knocking the air clean from my lungs.

She was in tight black jeans that showcased her plump ass, her glossy dark hair spilling over her shoulders like a waterfall, drawing my eye straight to the sweater straining across her incredible tits.

"You are so fucking screwed." Connor clapped me on the shoulder.

"What are you—"

But he was already gone, stalking toward Ella like a caveman.

"I'm going to the bar," I said to the rest of the guys.

I needed a second to catch my breath. To figure out how the fuck I was going to be around Aurora without falling to my knees and begging for her forgiveness. Because as the days wore on, my confidence in the fact I'd made the right decision wavered more and more.

"Holden." Stu, the bartender, waved me down. "Good game, my man. You want another beer?"

"Thanks." I scanned the room but couldn't find Aurora anywhere.

I did, however, see Aiden striding toward me.

"Where the fuck did you get to?" I asked as he leaned against the bar beside me. He'd stayed behind when we all piled out of the arena to head to The Penalty Box.

"I needed a minute."

"I bet you did." I smirked, glancing over to where Dayna had joined the other girls.

He was so fucking obvious.

"Beer?"

"Thanks." He accepted the bottle of Heineken Stu pushed toward him, taking a long pull. "My old man got arrested tonight," he murmured.

"Shit, man. I'm sorry." We all knew that Aiden's old man, Dawson Dumfries, liked to play on the wrong side of the law, but he rarely talked about him. I got it. I knew a thing or two about shitty fathers, after all.

"Don't be," Aiden said. "It's the least he deserves. You played a good game tonight."

"Thanks." I worked out a kink in my neck. "It felt good to be back out there."

"No feeling like it."

"Damn right."

We clinked our bottles together, watching the rest of the team celebrate our first win of the season. But a flash of blonde over by their booth caught my eye, and then she appeared again.

Aurora.

Fuck, seeing her laugh at something Harper said was like a knife to my fucking stomach.

She looked happy.

She looked fine without me. When I was barely functioning.

Aiden drilled holes into the side of my head as he said, "Want to talk about it?"

"Nope." I drained my beer and slammed it on the bar. "I'm going to head out."

"You should stay. Celebrate."

"I can't be here. But have another drink or three for me." Clapping him on the shoulder, I took one last look at Aurora before melting into the crowd and heading for the exit.

But I hadn't even made it down the sidewalk when a voice stopped me in my tracks.

"Noah."

"Go back inside, shortcake," I said, turning slowly, wincing at the way her nickname rolled off my tongue.

As easy as breathing.

"Not until you talk to me." Defiance shone in her green

eyes like flecks of lightning. "You owe me that much, at least."

A beat passed, her accusation heavy in the air.

Except, it wasn't an accusation. It was the cold hard truth—I did owe her an explanation.

"You didn't come and find me," she whispered, the fire in her eyes guttering out.

"What?"

"After the exhibition game, I thought you might..."

"Shit, Aurora. I wanted to. So many times I wanted to, but—"

"So, what stopped you?"

"You're really going to make me say it?"

She nodded, those green eyes of hers pulling me in, dragging me under until I was fucking drowning in her.

"I'm scared, okay?" I admitted. "I'm fucking terrified that being with me will be too much for you, and in the end, I'll lose you anyway. That the thing I love more than anything in the world will drive away the girl I've fallen hopelessly in love with."

"W-what did you just say?" Her eyes grew big with surprise. But surely, she knew.

She had to know.

Didn't she?

"I love you, shortcake." I stepped forward, reaching for her cheek and brushing the stray hairs from her face. "I'm in love with you."

"You... you love me?" Aurora's eyelashes fluttered.

"Yeah, I do."

"Well, that changes things."

"It does?"

"Yeah, it—"

"Noah."

A chill went through me at the sound of that voice.

His voice.

Slowly, I turned, coming face to face with the man I hated.

The man I *never* wanted to see again.

"Hello, Son."

Aurora sucked in a sharp breath, finding my hand and threading our fingers together. A silent sign she was right here with me. No matter what.

"What the fuck are you doing here?" An icy chill went through the air. Because he couldn't be here.

He couldn't fucking be here.

"You wouldn't answer my calls."

"Because I have nothing to say to you. Not a damn thing."

"Son, please, I need to talk to you. It's important."

"No. No way." I stepped forward, jabbing my finger at him. "You don't get to just waltz into my life and start making demands, you piece of shit."

"Noah..." Aurora tugged my hand, but all I saw was Timothy Holden looming over a small, helpless boy. His cruel, hateful words landing like bullets. Tearing through muscle and bone to rip holes in my soul. Until his words no longer hurt, and he had to find new ways to keep me down. Broken. Bruised.

"You need to leave." My body trembled, a violent storm raging inside me.

"Son, I can't—"

"Fine." I yanked my hand out of Aurora's, needing to be as far away as possible from the man I would never let touch me again.

"Then I will."

"Noah," they both called after me, but I was gone. Blowing down the sidewalk like a tornado.

I couldn't be near him a second longer, breathing his air, staring at his eyes. Eyes that had haunted my entire childhood.

My legs ate up the sidewalk. I had no destination in mind except getting the fuck out of there.

"Noah, wait. Please, just wait..."

The desperation in Aurora's voice penetrated the angry vortex swirling around me, and I turned back just in time to catch her.

"I'm sorry," she breathed, hugging me tightly. "I'm so sorry."

"H-he..."

"I know, baby. I know." She pulled me closer.

"He's here, shortcake," my voice cracked, my carefully constructed walls crumbling down around me. "He's not supposed to be here."

"I know, I know."

I buried my face in the crook of her shoulder, breathing her in, letting her presence soothe me, letting her love fill every crack in my soul.

"You love me." I lifted my head to look at her.

"Yeah, hotshot. I do. So don't you ever do that again. If you freak out or get scared or panic, you need to talk to me." She laid her hands on my cheeks. "Promise me that you'll talk to me."

"I promise." I leaned in, brushing my nose along hers. "Can I kiss you now?"

Because I really fucking needed to kiss her.

"I thought you'd never ask."

I buried my fingers in her hair, anchoring us together as my lips came down on hers—soft and searching and full of apology.

"Noah," she breathed, clutching my hoodie as my tongue licked into her mouth.

"I got you, shortcake. I got you."

And I never planned on letting her go again.

When we broke away, her skin was flushed, and her eyes were full of love.

"Say it. I want to hear you say it."

"I love you, Noah Holden. I'm in love with you. And although it terrifies me, I don't want to lose you because I'm too scared to see where this takes us."

"You want me, shortcake?"

She nodded, a faint smile tracing her lips.

"I fucked up. I'll probably fuck up again. But I swear to God, Aurora, I'll never shut you out again."

"Okay."

"Okay?" I reared back. "Just like that? I feel like there's a catch somewhere."

"There isn't." Her smile grew. "Everyone deserves a second chance, Noah. This is yours. Just don't screw it up."

I wrapped my arms around her waist and ghosted my mouth over hers again. "I'm going to Darcy you so fucking hard that you won't know which way is up."

"That is not a thing." Her soft laughter filled the air, calming the storm still raging inside me.

"It is now. Just you wait." I nuzzled her neck, kissing the soft skin there.

"Noah?"

I lifted my eyes to hers, feeling winded all over again.

She was here.

And she was mine.

And even though I wasn't sure I deserved another chance, I was going to do everything in my power not to fuck it up.

"Yeah, shortcake?"

She smiled again and then said the three little words I needed more than anything.

"Take me home."

"This is nice," I said, walking around Aurora's living room.

"Yeah, it's better than a lot of places near campus."

"I'm sorry I wasn't around to help you move."

She shrugged, pouring us both a drink. "You didn't want to celebrate with the team tonight?"

"Honest answer?"

"Always."

"I couldn't be there. Watching you laugh and enjoy yourself with Harper and the girls. You looked... you looked like you'd moved on."

"Noah..." It was a choked whisper.

"I know, I know. I sound like a complete pussy."

"That's not what I was going to say." She came around to me, resting her hands on my hips. "I didn't tell you the whole truth about my ex—"

"Confession, I already know."

"Y-you do?"

"Ella told me."

"Oh. Well, when I found him in bed with my best friend, it broke something inside me, Noah. I was a mess. I didn't eat. And when I did, I ate myself sick. It wasn't a good time for me, and the worst part was I blamed myself. I told myself if only I'd been thinner, prettier, and more confident, he wouldn't have fallen into bed with my best friend.

"But I was going to fight for you."

"You were?"

She nodded, tears clinging to her lashes. "Sunday night, I was going to tell Austin about us. I baked cookies and everything."

"Shit, Aurora, I—"

"I think deep down, I felt you pulling away, and instead of letting fear overtake me, every insecurity I have forcing me into hiding, I decided to go after what I wanted. I decided to live instead of let life pass me by."

"Fuck."

She chose me.

Aurora chose me, and I... fuck.

"I could have let it break me, Noah. But I didn't. I dusted myself off and got on with it. Because of the way you make me feel about myself, the spark you ignited inside me, that was real. It wasn't a joke or some cruel prank. It was real, and that was enough."

"I'm such a fucking idiot."

"I won't argue with that." She gave me a coy smile. "But you're my idiot."

"Damn straight." I dropped a kiss on her head, holding her tightly.

Silently vowing never to let go.

Until she said, "Do you want to talk about your dad?" Aurora peeked up at me, understanding glittering in her eyes.

"The first time he hit me, I was eight."

"Noah, I—"

"No, let me get this out, please." She nodded, and I inhaled a shuddering breath. "I was a disappointment from the minute I picked up a hockey stick. Dad comes from a family of investors. Men good with numbers. I suck at numbers, shortcake. He was trying to teach me about the stock market and hedge funds, and I was more interested in shooting pucks into an overturned trash can in the yard."

"You were just a kid."

"It didn't matter. He wanted a carbon copy of himself, his father, and a long line of Holden men before them. And I wasn't it. Mom tried to shelter me from his disapproval, but they constantly argued over me, and then one day, she left.

"That's when his disappointment became anger. The first time he lost it, I came home with an F in math. He grabbed me by the arm so hard that he dislocated my shoulder."

"Noah," she gasped.

"It didn't happen often, and by the time I grew up, he'd pretty much washed his hands of me until hockey started going really well for me.

"In eleventh grade, pro teams started taking note of my performance on the ice. I was so fucking relieved. Anything to get out of that house and away from him. The New York Rangers offered me a contract, but he sabotaged it. They pulled the offer, and I was so fucking angry something inside me just snapped. It's the only time I ever hit him back."

Shame snaked through me. Timothy Holden was a real piece of work, but the fact I'd stooped to his level didn't sit well with me. I could still remember what it felt like when my fist, my knuckles collided with his jaw. The sickening crack. The blast of pain that streaked through my hand. The sheer anger and surprise in his eyes.

I didn't want to be that kind of man—a man who used his fists to solve his problems.

"We barely spoke after that." I let out a steady breath. "I already knew he wouldn't give me a dime for college. Not if I was dead set on pursuing hockey. So my high school coach helped me get the full ride to LU, and as soon as graduation came around, I left and promised myself I would never go back.

"He's tried a couple of times since I've been here to reach out. But I left my life in Buffalo behind the day I got on the Greyhound to come to Lakeshore."

"God, Noah. That's... horrible."

I shrugged. "We all have shit, shortcake. But whatever he wants, I'm not interested. I meant what I said before. As far as I'm concerned, Timothy Holden is dead to me."

"Oh, Noah." She looked at me with unshed tears, and my brows furrowed, dread churning in my gut.

"What is it? I asked.

Then she said the last words I ever expected to hear.

"He's sick, Noah. Your dad is sick."

CHAPTER 37

AURORA

Noah stared at me like he couldn't comprehend what I was saying.

"He's lying."

"I don't think he is. He seemed genuine."

"You talked to him."

"I didn't mean to." My expression softened. "But you ran off, and he begged me to listen. He has cancer, Noah."

"Cancer."

I nodded, hating that Mr. Holden had managed to ruin our moment.

He loved me.

Noah loved me.

It didn't seem possible, and yet, I felt it. I felt it all the way down to my soul.

It should have been one of the best moments of my life, and here I was, telling him that his dad—a man who deserved nothing but disdain and distance from Noah—had a terminal illness.

"Noah?" I reached for his hand, and he flinched, looking at me with empty eyes. "What do you need?"

For a second, I thought he might run. But instead, he pulled me into his arms, holding on like he thought I might disappear.

"I'm sorry," I whispered, rubbing my hands up and down his back.

"I hate him, shortcake. I fucking hate him. I've wished him dead so many times, and now..." His voice cracked, pain and frustration and sheer hopelessness bleeding into the space between us.

"It's okay, baby. It's okay."

I didn't know what else to say. I hated my mom. Resented her for every day of my life that I'd felt worthless and ridiculed. But she was still my mom. I couldn't ever imagine finding out she was dying.

"Fuck." Noah pulled away, pacing back and forth. "Fuck." He kicked the stool, sending it toppling over. "Shit, Aurora, I didn't—"

"It's okay," I said, picking it up and moving it aside. "You're angry."

"I'm... I don't know what the fuck I am." He shoved his fingers into his hair, tugging the ends.

"It's okay to feel angry and hurt and scared, Noah. There's no rulebook for this kind of thing. Do you... do you want to talk to him?"

"No," he snapped. "That is the last thing I want."

"Okay, okay. You don't have to do anything you don't want."

"God, I hate him. I fucking hate him for coming here

and ruining tonight." He stalked toward me, pulling me into my arms again. "I had all these big plans, shortcake."

"Plans can wait. I'm not going anywhere." I gazed up at him, wishing I could take away all his pain.

"You mean that?"

"I do."

Relief washed over him. "Lie down with me?"

"Come on." I took his hand, leading him into my bedroom.

I kicked off my boots and started pulling off my sweater, but Noah grabbed my wrist. "Let me."

I gave him a small nod.

Noah took his time undressing me, running his fingers over the dips and curves of my body, swirling the tip in my navel before gliding it up between the valley of my breasts. The intense heat I was used to between us didn't ignite as he explored my body. Instead, it was a slow burn that simmered, making me shiver and tremble.

"You are so fucking beautiful," he murmured, curving his hand around the back of my neck and kissing me. A soft, tentative kiss that made the hairs stand on end all over my body.

"Get on the bed, shortcake," he rasped,

I got under the sheets, watching as he stripped out of his own clothes, right down to his tight black briefs.

The whorls of ink around his bicep and down his forearm shifted and shimmered as he stalked over, climbing in bed beside me. "Come here you." His arm snaked out, drawing me into his body. "Is this okay?"

"More than okay." I nestled closer, relishing the feel of his skin against mine.

"Rain check on Operation Darcy?"

"We have time."

We had all the time in the world.

"I just... I don't know what I'm supposed to do with this information, shortcake."

"You don't need to make any decisions tonight." I brushed my fingers through his hair, and his eyes shuttered.

"Mmm, that feels so good."

"I'm right here, Noah. You can sleep, and I'll be right here."

"I don't think I can sleep. I'm too wired."

"Then we'll just lie here." I continued stroking his hair, and before long, his breathing evened out. "I love you, Noah Holden," I whispered against his lips before closing my eyes.

And falling asleep in his arms.

My eyes fluttered open.

"Good morning," Noah's gravelly voice vibrated inside me, making my stomach curl.

"Hi." I smiled, stretching like a cat.

He pushed the hair from my eyes and kissed me. "I like waking up next to you."

"I like waking up next to you too. How are you feeling?"

"Better, I think. I'm sorry I crashed on you."

"Don't be. It was a lot to process."

"I don't want to see him. I'm glad I know. And maybe one day, I'll reach out to him. But today is not that day."

"And that's okay. It has to be your decision, Noah."

He swallowed thickly. "You love me." The shadows in his eyes melted away, replaced with burning adoration.

"Yeah, I kind of do."

"I've never been in love before."

"Another first. I'm honored."

"Are you mocking me, shortcake?"

"Never." I grinned.

God, this was so easy.

So right.

"What?" Noah asked.

"I just—"

A loud bang pierced the air, and Noah groaned, "Expecting visitors?" He cocked his brow.

"At this time? No."

"I swear to God, if it's Austin or Connor, I will—"

"Austin?" I balked. "It had better not be Austin, or you're going to have to hide."

"Yeah, not happening, shortcake. So get that idea out of your pretty little head."

The knocking got louder, setting my teeth on edge. "Just... stay here." I climbed out of bed with a little huff and pulled on my nightshirt.

Slipping out of my bedroom, I closed the door behind me and crossed the living room.

"Rory, open up. I brought breakfast."

"Oh, shit," I whisper-shrieked.

It *was* Austin.

What the hell was he doing here at this time? It was nine-thirty on a Saturday morning, for Pete's sake.

"Just a minute," I called, panic rising inside me.

"Come on, Sis. It's going cold."

"I—"

Noah appeared, wearing nothing but his boxer briefs.

"What the hell are you doing?" I hissed.

"Time to pull off the Band-Aid, shortcake," he said, making a beeline for the door.

"Noah, I swear to God, don't you da—"

"Hey, man. What's up?"

"Holden?" My brother's mouth fell open as he took in Noah standing there at my door in all his half-naked glory. "What are you... no." He looked to me, then Noah, and back again. "No fucking way."

"Hey, Austin," I gave him a small wave.

"You two... together."

"Sorry, you had to find out like this, bro. But last night was kind of a shit show, and I really want to crawl back into bed with my girl. So unless we're doing this—"

"Your girl? As in, my little sister?"

"Surprise," I choked out.

"Oh, no. Hell, no. You're letting this asshole use you—"

"Whoa, back the fuck up. I'm not using anyone. I fucking love her."

"L-love her?" He exploded with laughter, the kind that scraped my insides raw.

I glared at Noah as we watched my brother barely hold together his amusement and utter disbelief.

"That's a good one, Holden. You almost had me there. Did you put him up to this, Rory? To get back at me for being an asshole? Because good one, seriously, you guys got me good."

"It's true, Austin." I stepped forward, slipping into Noah's side. "It wasn't supposed to happen. But it did."

"Hold up." Austin rubbed his temples. "You're saying... this isn't a joke?"

"Nope. I love her, and she loves me."

"Would you stop saying that? It's weird."

"Fine." Noah shrugged, smothering a grin. "But it doesn't change the fact it's true."

"Aurora wouldn't fall for your bullshit. She knows better than that." He looked at me, really looked at me, and I gave him a small smile.

"I don't know what to say, Aus. It's true. We're…"

"Together. We're together." Noah stood taller. "And I know you're probably going to want to break my face, but can you do it later because I'm barely awake, and I need—"

"Hold up. You're serious? The two of you are…"

"Yes," we both said in unison.

"Jesus. I need a drink. Here." He thrust the brown paper bag at us. "I'm outta here."

We watched Austin walk to the end of the hall and disappear around the corner.

"Do you think he's okay?" I said.

"I mean, he didn't try and murder me with his bare hands, so that's something, right?" Noah closed the door and locked it. "Just in case he comes back."

"Not funny."

"Let's go back to bed." He gave me a crooked grin, the one that made my stomach dance. "I wasn't done with you yet."

"Noah, we can't have sex after… that."

Whatever that was.

I glanced at the door again, half-expecting Austin to burst in at any moment.

"Who said anything about sex, shortcake? I want to snuggle."

"You want to… *snuggle*?"

"Yep, so get your cute ass in bed, and I'll grab us a drink."

"Hmm, a girl could get used to this," I said, and Noah kissed me.

"Good, because I plan on being around a lot."

Just then, both of our cell phones chimed.

"That doesn't sound good," I grumbled.

"Ignore him. He'll get over it eventually."

But I couldn't resist plucking my cell off the nightstand the second I wandered into the bedroom and read Austin's text.

"What does it say?" Noah asked, coming up behind me, armed with bottles of water and a packet of Oreos.

"Do you want the censored version or uncensored?"

"Hit me with the hard stuff. I'm a big boy. I can handle it."

"It says, and I quote, 'I hope you don't like Holden's pretty face too much because the next time I see him, it's my brotherly duty and prerogative to beat the living shit out of him. P.S. I'm pissed you didn't tell me. P.P.S. I swear to God, Rory, if he breaks your heart, I'll break his fucking legs."

Noah flopped down beside me and kissed my shoulder. "That could have been worse."

"Worse?" I shrieked. "He threatened to break your face *and* your legs. How could that possibly get worse?"

"He could have told me to end it. He didn't. It's basically his seal of approval."

"Your mind works in very mysterious ways."

"Trust me. He'll come around."

"How can you be so sure?" I asked.

"Because all he wants is for you to be happy, shortcake. And I intend on making you very, very happy."

"Is that so?" My heart soared at his sweet words.

"Starting right"—he leaned in, ghosting his lips over mine—"now."

"I don't like it, Rory. I don't like it at all." Austin folded his arms over his chest, pouting like a petulant child.

"You don't have to like it, Austin." I leaned up and kissed him on the cheek. "You just have to accept it. He makes me happy. Really happy. And people change. Heck, look at Aiden and Connor."

He made a disapproving sound in his throat but didn't voice any more reasons why Noah and I were destined for heartache.

The truth was, I didn't need his approval or blessing. I'd spent my entire life seeking the validation of others. I was over it.

That's not to say I wasn't feeling a little nervous about the dress the girls had insisted I wear for my date with Noah. But it accentuated all his favorite parts of my body, so I knew he'd love it.

Even if no one else did.

"Holy shit, little Hart, you look—"

"Yeah, yeah, Morgan. Leave it. I really don't need to hear how hot my sister looks for her date with my ex-best friend and teammate."

"You'll get over it, Aus. Rory, baby, could do a lot worse than Noah."

"What's that?"

Noah appeared in the doorway, and my heart stalled in my chest. He looked... God, he looked gorgeous. The plaid shirt fitted his broad chest to perfection, and he'd rolled his sleeves up to the elbows, revealing his sexy forearms.

I didn't even know forearms could be sexy until this moment.

"Sorry the plans had to change," he said. "The study group ran over, and I couldn't get away."

"It's fine. You need to ace that class."

"Damn right, he does," Connor said.

Noah had confessed that since he no longer wanted to study with Sam, he needed extra support with a couple of his classes. I admired him for seeking help. It wasn't always an easy thing to do especially when you were a star athlete destined for great things.

"You look beautiful, shortcake." He pressed a chaste kiss to my cheek. But it wasn't enough to appease my brother.

"Keep your hands to yourself, asshole."

"Austin," I sighed.

"Come on. Big brother will get over himself. Don't wait up, kids." Noah grabbed my hand and tugged me out of their house.

I missed living with them. Being in their space. But having my own place would be a blessing now that Noah and I were official.

"Are you going to tell me where we're going yet?" I asked as we headed toward Connor's truck.

"Nope. It's a surprise." Noah opened the door and helped me up.

"I hate surprises."

"Pretty sure you'll like this one." He slammed the door and went around the driver's side.

I smiled. We'd had this exact conversation before on our first and only date. But this time, things would have a different ending.

"I figured you wouldn't want to eat," he said. "But we can stop for sushi on the way or some of those zucchini fries you like so much?"

"I thought sushi was a crime against humanity?"

"Oh, it is, but for you, I'd suffer it."

"My hero." I flashed him a playful smile. "I actually already ate before I left. So I'm all set. But thank you."

The second we headed out of town, I had a sneaky suspicion about where we were going.

"The Regal," I said as he pulled the truck into the familiar parking lot.

"This is our do-over."

"I like the sound of that."

Noah parked and got out, coming around to open my door. We walked around to the front of the building hand in hand. My heart was so full of love there wasn't room to worry about what anyone thought of us together.

"There's one more surprise." Noah pulled open the door of the movie theater and ushered me inside. "I managed to pull some strings and get them to air an exclusive screening of Mansfield Park just for us."

"You did not."

"Did too. Just so happens the owner's son is a huge Lakers fan."

"Oh my God. I can't believe you did this."

"Believe it, shortcake. I figured it's time I meet this Bertram character you love so much."

"I... you, Noah Holden, are the best boyfriend ever." I threw my arms around his neck and kissed him.

"I do have one tiny request, though." A faint smirk traced his mouth as he pulled away.

"What?"

Noah leaned back in, brushing his lips along the shell of my ear, sparking a shiver down my spine. "I get to eat my favorite meal during the film."

"Noah!"

"I've missed her, shortcake. And I'm pretty certain she's missed me too."

"You cannot keep referring to my..." I swallowed hard, my cheeks burning.

"Pussy?"

"Yes, that, as 'she.'"

"Watch me." He winked, dropping a kiss on my head before he shoved his hands in his pockets and strolled up to the counter as if he hadn't just proposed going down on me in the theater.

Noah was something else.

Cocky. Charming. Unapologetic.

He was the guy who had stolen my heart and helped me learn to love myself again.

And he was completely and utterly mine.

EPILOGUE

NOAH

"Seriously, do you have to keep looking at me like that?" I asked Austin as he glowered across the locker room at me.

"It's my prerogative to want to break your face every time I see you macking on my sister. My fucking sister, Holden." He let out a pained groan, dropping his head back against the locker cages. "I'm never going to get over this shit. You've ruined senior year. My final season."

"Quit being a baby, Hart." Aiden came over and sat beside me. "You got outvoted. Deal with it."

"Outvoted?" Austin's head shot up. "The fuck?"

"Shit, you had to mention that?" I played along, and Aiden smirked.

"Wait a second, did you all vote?"

"Nobody voted," I said. "He's joking. It's a joke."

"Morgan, get over here." Connor padded over to Austin and loomed over him. "What's up?"

"Did you vote for Noah and Aurora to... you know."

"Go public?"

"Yeah."

"I didn't unvote it."

"Mase?" Austin called, and Mason grimaced.

"Sorry, man. But he was a miserable fucker without her."

"What about you two?" He pinned Ward and Leon with scathing looks. "Don't tell me you two agreed—"

"Nothing to do with us, man." Ward held up his hands like a pussy.

"You all suck big hairy balls. It's the golden rule of bro code. No sisters. If your mom was still around, I'd go bang her just to get even."

The second the words were out his mouth I saw the regret wash over him.

"Shit, Noah, I didn't mean—"

"Yeah, you did, asshole. But I'll let it slide this once because you're hurting, and I get it. I do.

"But I love your sister, and nothing you say or do is ever going to change that."

Some of the guys started cheering, and Aiden clapped me on the back. "Welcome to the dark side, Holden. It's fucking awesome."

Yeah, it was. It really, really was.

"If I were you, Aus," Connor started. "I'd just be grateful that Rory doesn't still live with us. At least you won't have to hear Holden banging the fuck out—Ow, fuck. You almost took my eye out." He swatted Austin's stick away. "You're an asshole."

"Perhaps dial down the sister-banging talk," Aiden suggested.

"That's something we can agree on," I said, pulling on

my skates. "Besides, you're aiming your anger in the wrong place."

"Oh yeah, and where should I be aiming it?" Austin arched a brow.

"At her ex."

A couple of the guys let out low whistles.

"Don't either of you go doing anything stupid," Aiden warned, and I gave him a butter-wouldn't-melt smile. "I mean it, Holden. Sudeikis is off-limits tonight."

"Yeah, yeah, keep your hair on. I'm not going to do anything rash."

Unless he so much as looked in Aurora's direction, then all bets were off. I had a fuckton of tension to burn. Things with Aurora were great. We were great. But I'd finally made a decision about my old man. A decision Aurora didn't wholly agree with.

I didn't want to see him.

Not now.

Not ever.

Maybe one day, I'd regret it. But he didn't deserve my sympathy or my fucking tears. Family was supposed to love you. To protect and support you. It wasn't supposed to use you as a goddamn punching bag.

The only thing I owed Timothy Holden was my hatred. And that's all he was getting from me. I had everything I needed. I had my girl. I had hockey. And I had the best damn friends a guy could ever need. *That* was family. The people who chose to love you because they wanted to, not because the blood flowing in their veins demanded it.

When—*if*—the day came I ever wanted to open that door again, I knew they'd have my back.

But today was not that day.

Speaking of my shortcake. I dug my cell out of my bag and quickly texted her.

Noah: You'd better be wearing my jersey, shortcake. I want everyone to know who you belong to.

Aurora: Is this how it's always going to be now?

Noah: What's that?

Aurora: You bossing me around and getting all growly and possessive.

Noah: I thought you liked me all growly and possessive.

Aurora: I don't hate it.

Noah: Jesus, shortcake. I'm not sure I can wait until after the game to see you. Sneak back here now and give me a good luck kiss?

Aurora: Behave. Good luck, hotshot. Kick some Falcon ass.

Noah: It would be my pleasure.

"Holden, son, that had better not be a cell phone I can see," Coach Tucker pinned me with a hard look.

"No, sir."

"Mm-hmm. I want you all out on the ice in less than five minutes. Holden, a word." He beckoned me over, and I grabbed my helmet before heading toward him.

"Yes, Coach?"

"I heard a rumor you might have a personal issue with one of Fitton's players?"

"Not me, sir."

"Good. Keep it that way. I'm pleased you and Miss Hart worked out your differences, but I won't tolerate personal issues bleeding onto the ice. You hear me?"

"Loud and clear, Coach."

"Good, now get out there and show them what you're made of, son."

With a sharp nod, I followed my teammates out, praying to God that I could keep my promise to everyone.

AURORA

"How are you feeling?" Harper asked as we watched the team gather around Coach Tucker and Assistant Coach Walsh for their last-minute pep-talk.

"Nervous. Really freaking nervous."

"Can you see him?"

I knew she didn't mean Noah. I'd had eyes on him since he appeared rink side.

She meant Ben. The one guy I *never* wanted to see again for as long as I lived.

But I needed to be here for this. For Noah and my brother.

And myself.

Because what Ben and Tierney did to me last year

wasn't a reflection on me, it was a reflection on the shitty people they were. And while I'd love nothing more than to kick him in the balls and tell him what a sack of shit he was, I'd settle for the Lakers wiping the ice with his team.

"I still can't believe Noah freaking Holden is your BAE," Harper laced her arm through mine and did an excited little shuffle.

"BAE?"

"Yeah, you know. Your babe. Boyfriend. Before anyone else."

"Right," I chuckled, certain she spoke a different language half the time.

"Oh my God, look, he's skating over here."

Sure enough, Noah was headed straight for the plexiglass separating us from the rink. He winked as he whizzed past, and Harper pressed the back of her hand to her forehead, pretending to pass out.

"Now, you're officially Noah's, and Fallon basically has your brother locked down. I need to set my sights on someone else."

"What about Mason?" I asked with a smirk.

"Mason? As in Mason Steele? As in the most arrogant, rude, egotistical asshole in the history of assholes? I'd rather stuff a cactus up my va—"

"Okay." I slapped my hand over her mouth, shooting our neighbors an apologetic smile. Dayna and Ella burst out laughing, and I rolled my eyes.

"Please, don't encourage her."

"She's not wrong about Mason though. He's like Grumpy Dwarf on crack. He might have that brooding bad boy image working for him and a monster dick if the rumors are to be believed."

"Hold up, monster dick?" Harper leaned around me to get to Dayna.

"Mm-hmm, so I've heard." She nodded.

"Interesting."

"What happened to 'you'd rather stick a cactus up your—"

Harper had the gall to press her hand against my mouth. "Maybe I spoke too soon."

"I'm not sure you and Mason are compatible," Ella added. "He usually picks the quiet, docile ones."

"You mean weak." Harper frowned.

"I wouldn't say weak, but he definitely has a type. Oh look, they're almost ready."

A ripple of anticipation went around Ellet Arena as Aiden and the Falcons captain faced off against each other.

Noah hung off to the right, waiting, his eyes fixed on the ice. My gaze fixed on him.

It was hard to believe that we'd almost let this pass us by. That we were both too scared of what the future might look like instead of focusing on all the wonderful things it could be.

My gaze roamed to Ben on the left wing. I couldn't help it. He'd been such a big part of my life. My savior and villain all rolled into one. But now I looked at him, and I felt nothing but pity. Because he had to live with the kind of person he was, and that was punishment enough.

It had to—

"Oh no," someone said, and I realized that all hell had broken loose on the ice, and the puck hadn't even dropped yet.

"Shit, it's Noah," Harper said as I struggled to focus on the blur of cyan and indigo jerseys squaring up to the

Falcons' players. Ben was right there in the thick of it, talking shit to Noah, who started pulling his gloves off. But then another one of our players skated right into the chaos, shielding Noah as he threw a punch straight into Ben's stomach. Helmets came off then and sticks were thrown down as the two of them started duking it out.

"Go, Austin," Harper whooped, and my mouth fell open.

"That's—" I realized now it was our goalie.

It was my brother.

The referees managed to restore order, and Austin was marched off toward the sin bin.

Noah caught my eye and mouthed 'Sorry,' at me, and my heart soared.

'I love you,' I mouthed back, blinking away the tears clinging to my lashes.

Because despite Coach Tucker yelling furiously at his team, demanding order, I couldn't deny the burst of pride I felt that Noah and my brother had stood up for me against what I could only assume was some trash talk from Ben and his teammates.

"Will they be in trouble?" I asked Harper.

"Coach looks ready to blow a gasket, and Austin will have to miss the next game, but it was worth it." She grinned at me, and I grinned back.

"So worth it."

"Now all we need is our guys to wipe the ice with them."

NOAH

The atmosphere in the locker room was solemn as Coach pinned each one of us with a scathing look.

"It's a good fucking thing you won out there. Holden, son. Care to explain what the fuck you were doing inciting a brawl?"

"Coach, I wasn't—"

"One of their players baited him, sir. Heard it with my own ears," Ward gave me a subtle nod.

"Baited... what are you? A bunch of twelve-year-olds pumped full of hormones? You're grown men. I expect you to act like it. And you, Austin. Don't even get me started on that little stunt you pulled."

"Couldn't let Holden have all the fun, Coach." Austin shot me a shit-eating grin. One I couldn't help but return.

"Is this a joke to you?"

"No, sir," he said. "But I think you should know that the asshole deserved it, Coach."

Even Coach Walsh's mouth twitched at that.

"Unbelievable," Coach Tucker murmured, stroking his jaw. "Whether he deserved it or not, I can't have half my team throwing down before the puck has even hit the ice."

"It won't happen again, sir," Austin said.

"You're damn right, it won't. Now get showered and get the fuck out of my sight while I decide what to do with you all." He marched off to his office, slamming the door behind him.

"On a scale of one to ten, how pissed do you think—"

"Not the time, Morgan." Coach Walsh shook his head. "Just tell me one thing, did he deserve it?"

I looked to Austin and understanding passed between us. "More than deserved it."

"Then, in that case, we draw a line. It's done. Next time we meet the Falcons on the ice, you take the high road."

"Yes, Coach."

"I'll go smooth things over with Coach Tucker." His eyes found mine. "Good game tonight."

After things had cooled down and the game had gotten going, I'd scored five goals.

There was no better feeling than watching Sudeikis' shoulders slowly droop as the minutes ticked by, and our score kept rising.

I'd half-stripped out of my uniform when Austin approached me.

"You good?" he said, and I nodded.

"You?" I dropped my eyes to his tender knuckles.

"It was worth it."

"Yeah. But why'd you do it?"

I'd been ready to beat the crap out of Sudeikis when Austin had glided in like a white knight on freshly sharpened skates.

"It was the least I could do. For both of you."

"Appreciated."

"Just... take care of her heart, Holden. That's all I ask."

"I will. I promise."

Austin held out his hand, and I shook it, letting him pull me into a one-armed hug. "I guess that makes us as good as family," he said.

"Hey, now, don't jump the gun. We're taking things slow."

"Slow my ass," Connor yelled. "I give it six months, and you'll be begging her to move in with you."

"No way, Morgan. I love living with you guys. Besides, if anyone's moving out soon, it's you."

"Well, I guess the race is on then." He winked. "May the best man win."

"You need to shut the fuck up before you're both home-less." Austin grimaced, running a hand over his head.

"Or I have an even better idea," Connor grinned. "Why not just ask Aurora to move back in?"

"Oh, hell no. Quit it with this shit too." Austin stomped off toward the showers, and Connor dropped down on the bench beside me.

"Things with Austin, okay?"

"Yeah, I think so."

"Good. Because I really didn't want to spend the rest of the year playing referee to the two of you. You and Rory coming to TPB to celebrate, or do you have celebration plans of your own?"

"We're going to stop by the bar for a little bit."

But not too long because I had plans.

Plans that didn't involve spending the night with our family and friends.

AURORA

"There she is." Noah banded his arm around me and pulled me back against his chest, nuzzling my neck. "I missed you."

Turning in his arms, I gazed up at him, my heart flut-tering wildly the way it did whenever Noah was close by. "You promised."

"I know, I know. But the asshole deserved it."

"It was kind of satisfying seeing Austin beat the crap out of him." I glanced over to my brother, and he lifted his beer in the air.

"God, I love you," Noah grinned, lowering his mouth to mine and kissing me.

My hands slid to his chest, ready to push him away because he was kissing me in public, in the middle of a bar, surrounded by our friends and family. But my fingers curled into his jersey, tugging him closer.

"Good girl," he whispered against my lips. "I want every single person here to know you're mine, shortcake."

"Even the puck bunnies?"

"Definitely the puck bunnies."

"Okay, Holden. Let my sister up for air," Austin grumbled, and I buried my face in Noah's shoulder, chuckling.

"He's a pain in the ass."

"He only cares," I said with a smile.

Things between me and Austin were still a little strained, but I guess being in love with his best friend wasn't something he could just get over. And that was okay, I didn't need his approval. I only needed his understanding and love.

That's all I'd ever wanted.

As for Mom, she'd been awfully quiet since our argument. I guess it was going to take some time for her to figure out if she could be in my life without trying to fix me, and if she couldn't... well, that was her loss.

I had all I needed right here.

"I guess," Noah said. "It must suck knowing that your best friend is going to do very dirty things to your sister the second he gets her out of here."

"Noah!" I swatted his chest, heat streaking through me.

"You love it."

Yeah, I kind of did.

"What's that all about?" Noah flicked his head over to Mason and Harper in a tense conversation. "What the fuck is she doing?"

"Oh, my God. She isn't…"

"Why do I feel like I'm missing something?" Noah searched my eyes, and I smothered a laugh.

"Trust me. You don't want to know."

"He'll never take the bait."

"He's a guy, and she's gorgeous. Of course, he'll take the bait."

"Not Mason. He's different."

"Different, how?"

"For starters, she wanted my stick first." Noah waggled his brows, and I rolled my eyes.

"That's because your stick has magical powers."

"My stick is pretty magical." His eyes lit up with amusement, but it simmered into something else. Something intense that stole my breath and made my knees weak. "Shortcake." Noah touched his head to mine. "Knowing you were in the crowd tonight, wearing my jersey… it was the best fucking feeling. I thought I didn't need anyone. But I need you, Aurora. I need you so fucking much."

"You have me, Noah. All of me."

NOAH

"Yeah, just like that. Fuck, babe… *fuck*." I choked out as Aurora ground down on top of me, riding me slow and steady. Savoring every fucking second.

My hands were everywhere, tracing her curves, the soft lines of her body. I couldn't get enough.

Every time I got her naked, I found new ways to make her shatter. It was my favorite pastime. Watching her confidence grow. Watching my girl come to life under my mouth and teeth and tongue.

"You feel so good." She threw her head back, circling her hips in a way that made my eyes cross.

"Look at me, shortcake." I cupped her jaw, forcing her to give me her eyes. Those green eyes I loved to drown in so much.

Her eyelashes fluttered as I thrust up into her, filling her so completely I didn't know where the fuck she ended, and I began. "It's deep," she whimpered.

My hand tightened around her hip as I drawled, "You can take it."

One of her hands slid up her stomach, massaging her heavy tits, and a bolt of pure lust shot through me.

"Jesus, I love your tits."

I still hadn't fucked them yet. But it was going to happen soon. I daydreamed about it. Spent half my life rock-hard just thinking about it.

But we were moving at Aurora's pace. Letting her get comfortable with her body. With letting *me* explore *her* body.

"And I fucking love that you have your own place now, and I don't have to worry about doing this." I lowered my head and wrapped my tongue around one of her dusky buds, drawing it into my mouth as my fingers slipped between our bodies and found her clit.

Aurora grabbed my shoulder, steadying herself as she cried out. "God, Noah... a little warning," she panted, her pussy fluttering around my dick as she raced toward the edge.

"That's it, baby. Give it to me... Come all over my dick."

"Yes, yes... God, Noah, more. More."

I fucked into her, grabbing her hips to get better lever-age. I loved hockey. I loved being on the ice and feeling the air whip around me as I glided up and down the rink. But this... being buried deep inside Aurora's perfect pussy, watching as she slowly came apart for me, there was no other feeling in the world.

"Fuck, I'm gonna come," I groaned, feeling my legs lock up.

"Together," Aurora pressed her head to mine, her green eyes glittering with ecstasy. "I want to go together."

I pinched her clit right as I thrusted hard and deep and groaned, "Now."

She shattered around me, clamping down on my dick as I came hard.

Winding my hand beneath her hair, I curled my fingers around the back of her neck and kissed her. "I love you," I breathed the words onto her lips.

"I love you, too." Her words sank into me, making the moment so much sweeter.

I'd been so convinced that I only needed hockey that I'd almost missed out on this.

On her.

But I'd been wrong.

Because you could have hockey *and* the girl.

And when you found the right girl, you held on and never let go.

The End.

BONUS EPILOGUE

AURORA

"Look at yourself, shortcake."

Noah ran his nose up the side of my neck, feathering kisses over my jaw, his eyes locked on mine in the mirror.

We were in his room, positioned in front of his mirror. Me wearing nothing but his jersey, cradled in his thighs as he sat behind me, his long fingers teasing my pussy as he praised me, touched me, showed me just how much he loved every single inch of me.

"You're a fucking vision."

"Noah," I gasped as his thumb passed over my clit. A slow, sensual drag that made my body arch into his touch.

"I can't get enough of you, Aurora. You make me so fucking hard."

As if I needed any reminder with his impressive length digging into my back.

He pumped his fingers in and out of me, watching me the whole time. It was so deeply intimate but whenever I got all up in my feelings, my negative thoughts, Noah did something like this.

Because although I knew he loved me irrevocably, sometimes I didn't love myself. Sometimes the voices in my head became too loud and I fell back into the vicious cycle of doubt and self-hatred.

Therapy helped. Jordan, Harper, Ella, and the girls were all amazing. My brother too. But it was a process. A journey. One that hadn't ended simply because I was in love.

And I was. Deeply, truly in love.

But it wasn't only the way that he loved me, it was the way he made me love myself.

Noah was patient and kind and he made me laugh every single day. But he also pushed me to step out of my comfort zone. To face my fears head on. I didn't always get it right and, more often than not, I freaked out. But he was always right there to comfort me.

My biggest cheerleader.

My confidant.

My best friend.

"I love your curves," he went on, trailing his hand up my stomach, the soft material of his Lakers jersey brushing my skin and making me shiver. "I love your hips and your ass. God, I love your ass."

He did.

He watched me do yoga at least twice a week. It usually ended up with him pouncing on me and showing me exactly how much he loved my ass... and my boobs... and the rest of my curves.

"I love your smile and the way you cry my name when you come." He grinned, his hand moving higher. "And your tits. Fuck, I love these."

He massaged one breast then the other, making me whimper and pant as his fingers kept working me.

My eyelids fluttered, the sensations crashing over me too powerful.

But then Noah's hand curved around my throat. "Look at me, shortcake," he rasped. "I want to see your eyes when you come for me."

"Noah," I cried, parting my thighs a little so he could go deeper.

I couldn't take my eyes off the spot where his fingers disappeared inside me. It was so freaking erotic watching him touch me, and something I could never have imagined myself, even in my wildest dreams, doing before him.

"Come for me, Aurora." He pinched my clit, sending sparks through me. "Now."

He rubbed his fingers deep and I went off like a rocket, my body trembling as I cried his name over and over.

"Such a good girl," he kissed my shoulder, holding me as I rode the intense waves of pleasure cascading through me.

"My girl," he added.

"I love you," I breathed, everything going lax and sated inside me.

"I love you too, shortcake." He smiled, his eyes glittering with adoration. "Always."

NOAH

Life was good.

No, scratch that.

Life was fucking amazing.

The team was on fire, winning four out of our last five games. And it was almost the holidays.

I'd never really cared for shit like that before. Growing up, the holidays were just another reminder of how shitty my life was. But this year, I planned to holiday the fuck out of it with Aurora.

I had a whole list of things I wanted to do with her. Skating at the outside rink downtown. The Christmas market. A holiday film viewing at The Regal. Tree picking at the local tree farm, although Connor had insisted we had to do that with him and Ella. Which was fine by me. I fucking loved my family.

The family I'd chosen. The family who'd chosen me right back. Buffalo was firmly in my past. Aurora, the team, hockey... they were my future.

And I'd made my peace with that.

My old man was still alive. He'd tried to reach out again before Thanksgiving. But I was done. Cancer or no cancer, I refused to let him back into my life.

Aurora, Austin, and their mom were a different story. A work in progress, Aurora liked to call it. I'd only met Susannah Hart once and it was enough for me to know I wasn't in any rush to meet her again.

Thankfully, though, she hadn't sent Aurora anymore care packages or tried to expend any advice on her daughter. Because if she ever pulled that shit again, it wouldn't only be Austin she had to deal with.

I'd be first in line to set her straight.

"Yo, asshole, you ready?" Austin bellowed from downstairs.

"Coming." I shoved my wallet in my jeans pocket and grabbed my hoodie.

"What took so long?" he asked.

"It takes time to look this good, you know." I smirked and he rolled his eyes.

"I still don't know what she sees in you."

"You need to get over it, Aus. It's been almost three months. I'm not going anywhere. Besides, secretly I think you're pleased I'm dating Aurora."

"What the fuck would make you think that?"

"Because one day, we might be more than just friends."

"The fuck you talking about?" He gawked at me, and I chuckled.

"We might be brothers-in-law."

The blood drained from his face. "Take that back, Holden. I swear to God, take it back right fucking now. Connor," he yelled. "He's doing it again."

"You called?" Connor stuck his head around the door.

"He's talking about marrying her again." Austin grumbled.

"Could be worse." Connor shrugged. "Rory could be dating Adams or Cutler."

"Not helping."

"Seriously, man, you need to let this shit go. Noah is a changed man. Maybe if you hadn't screwed things up with Fallon, you would feel differently about—"

"I didn't screw things up. I ended it. There's a difference."

"Sure, keep telling yourself that. Know what I think? I think you caught feelings, got scared, and ran like a pussy."

"You don't know what the fuck you're talking about." Austin scoffed.

"He has a point," I added.

"Oh, fuck off, both of you. I happen to like being single. It's too much drama having a girlfriend."

"I thought she wasn't your girlfriend."

"She wasn't."

Me and Connor shared a knowing look. Austin was full of shit. The first sign of things getting serious with Fallon and he had bailed.

"Whatever," he murmured, grabbing his car keys. "We doing this or what?"

"Hells yeah," Connor grinned. "Let's go pick my girl a ring."

AURORA

"Did you and the guys have fun?" I asked Noah as I stirred the spaghetti.

I'd spent the afternoon with the girls at Zest while Noah and the guys enjoyed a rare Saturday off.

"Uh, yeah. It was fine."

Glancing over my shoulder, I frowned. "Fine? What does that mean?"

"It was just a few drinks, nothing exciting."

"So why are you being all cagey about it?"

"I'm not."

"Noah." I glared.

"Shortcake." He grinned back.

"You're hiding something."

He got up and stalked toward me, hooking his hand around my waist and turning me in his arms. "Would I ever lie to you?"

"You tell me." I narrowed my eyes, fighting a smile.

He was impossible to stay mad at.

Lowering his face, Noah went to kiss me but I slid my hands against his chest. "Not so fast, hotshot. You're trying to distract me."

"No, I'm trying to kiss my girlfriend."

My heart fluttered. I loved hearing him say those words.

My girlfriend.

His.

His lips brushed mine, once, twice, and I felt myself start to fall under his spell.

"Noah," I murmured. "You don't play fair."

The fork slipped from my fingers, clattering to the floor as I wrapped my arm around his shoulder, drawing him closer.

"You taste good."

"Dinner is almost ready."

"Can't we skip it and go straight to dessert?"

"No, I made spaghetti."

"We can reheat it." He trailed warm wet kisses over my jaw and down my throat, making a shiver run through me.

"Wait," I said, curling my fingers into his hoodie. "What's going on?"

"Shortcake," he groaned, burying his face in my shoulder.

"Is it Austin?" I asked. "Did he—"

"Not Austin." Noah lifted his eyes, hesitation swirling there. "If I tell you, you have to swear not to breathe another word to anyone. I mean it, shortcake."

"My lips are sealed."

"Connor bought a ring." His mouth twitched.

"Oh my God. He's going to do it? He's going to propose?"

A slow smile spread over his face. "Yeah. He's got this

whole elaborate Christmas morning thing planned. But you can't tell him I told you. He'll kill me."

A secretive smile played on my lips. "I would never."

"Shortcake…" Noah's brows pinched. "Why do you look so… unsurprised?"

"I don't know what you're talking about." I went to turn around but he caged me against the counter with his hands.

"Aurora…"

"Noah…"

"You knew, didn't you?" Realization dawned in his rich brown eyes.

"I may have known… something."

"He told you. That asshole told you."

"Actually he told me and Dayna. He wanted advice on the ring style."

"That sneaky fucker. He told us—"

"That nobody else knew." I looped my arms back around his neck and flashed him my best puppy dog eyes. "He didn't want you to feel left out."

"I can't believe he told you first."

"I think it's sweet."

"Mm-hmm," Noah mumbled.

"Is it beautiful? The ring?"

"As far as rings go, yeah, I guess."

I rolled my eyes. "That's quite the endorsement."

"He looked so fucking happy when the woman handed him the box."

"Well, yeah. It's a big deal," I said. Ella was going to freak when he popped the question but if anyone would go the distance after college, it was the two of them.

"It is." Noah gazed down at me, the air growing heavy with anticipation.

"Noah?" I breathed. Because it no longer felt like we were talking about our friend's big news.

"One day, shortcake," he whispered.

At least, I thought I heard the words before his mouth crashed down on mine and he stole every rational thought from my head.

Just like he'd stolen my heart.

PLAYLIST

Stone Cold – Demi Levato
All Goes Wrong – Chase & Status, Tom Grennan
That Way – Tate McRae
heartLESS – You Me at Six
On Your Side – The Veronicas
Who You Are – Jessie J
Cold – The Veronicas
Sleep Alone – Ella Boh, Max Styler
Over The Love – Florence + the Machine
All These Nights – Tom Grennan
Beautiful People – Ed Sheeran ft. Khalid
Scars to Your Beautiful – Oceans, Anna Murphy
Anti-Hero – Taylor Swift
Automatic – Fly By Midnight, Jake Miller
Men on the Moon – Chelsea Cutler
I Think I'm in Love – Kat Dahlia
Beautiful – Christina Aguilera

ACKNOWLEDGMENTS

Thank you so much for reading Noah and Aurora's story. I hope you enjoyed it as much as I enjoyed writing it. Next up is Mason's story and I can't wait to dive into his mind!

As always, it takes a whole team to publish a book. So a quick shoutout to mine.

My beta team (and resident hockey experts) Jen, Amanda, Carrie, and Jenn, thanks for being on hand to answer any questions and offer feedback! And a special thank you to Lily and Courtney for helping to ensure I captured Aurora's struggles as authentically as possible. Kate - my editor - thank you! Darlene and Athena, thank you for always working to my crazy schedules. To all my Promo and ARC Team members, thank you for championing this series. And a special shoutout to my audio producer Kim over at Audibly Addicted for bringing this series to life - I'm so excited to hear the final audio.

And lastly, (but by no means least) to every reader, blogger, bookstagrammer, and booktokker who has read, reviewed, shared, or shouted out about this series - your continued support means the world to me.

Until next time...

L A xo

ABOUT THE AUTHOR

Reckless Love. Wild Hearts

USA Today and *Wall Street Journal* bestselling author of over forty mature young adult and new adult novels, L. A. is happiest writing the kind of books she loves to read: addictive stories full of teenage angst, tension, twists, and turns.

Home is a small town in the middle of England where she currently juggles being a full-time writer with being a mother/referee to two little people. In her spare time (and when she's not camped out in front of the laptop), you'll most likely find L. A. immersed in a book, escaping the chaos that is life.

L. A. loves connecting with readers.
The best places to find her are:
www.lacotton.com